For Alan K and Dabby Flint,
the original Wicklow Boys

If he doesn't approach me, I'll leave him alone.

Pete had been watching the boy for an hour now. The kid was blond, slight, couldn't be more than twenty, couldn't be more out of place in this bar, with its leather-skinned career drinkers bundled up in work shirts and steel-capped boots. The boy had blown in out of the cold a while back – blue-lipped, shivering, hands cupped beneath his armpits, his jeans and pink denim jacket scant protection against the blizzard raging outside. But it hadn't taken long for the boy to regain his mojo. Shaking off the chill, he'd made for the bar, slid onto a stool like he owned the place. Unselfconscious, unconcerned at the glances – not all friendly – that were shot his way. Pete's neighbour, a racist asshole who'd been knocking back boilermakers, started droning on about the Million Man March. Pete nodded along, but his eye kept being drawn to the boy, a magnetic pull that he'd given up fighting. Something had woken up inside him. Something had uncoiled, flickered to life.

If he doesn't approach me, I'll leave him alone.

Every so often the boy slid off his bar stool and weaved over to one of the tables, where he tried to engage the patrons in conversation. All he'd gotten so far, apart from a cigarette and a good-natured grope from a female barfly, were shaken heads and rude gestures. It was unclear what he was saying to the folks he approached – the bartender was into Kenny Rogers and was blasting that shit out loud – but he couldn't be soliciting sex. This part of town would be the last place you'd come for that, unless you were blind or stupid. Could be that he was asking for a ride; could be he was asking for a handout.

'Fuckin' queer,' a guy pinballing his way to the men's room mouthed as he passed the kid, but it was a half-hearted jibe. It was late and everyone had reached the maudlin stage of the evening. There was no sense of suppressed violence here, and the boy had picked up on this. This time when the fellow he'd been hassling waved him away, the boy flipped him the bird, then sauntered back to the bar.

The tables nearest the door emptied one by one, and the bartender started upending chairs, nodding along to 'Just Dropped In'. Time was running out. The boy made for the payphone. He dug out a clutch of coins, dropped them in, dialled. He was gripping the handset too tightly. He hung up, rested his forehead against the wall, shrugged, and then returned to his seat. The kid may be in trouble, but he still had that *thing*, that inner self-assurance that no amount of hardship could fully extinguish. That thing *she'd* had. It was in every fluid movement. Pete's neighbour belched, slapped a dirty dollar onto the counter, then stumbled out.

The boy looked over, downed his drink. Caught Pete's eye. Smirked. Hesitated.

If he doesn't approach me, I'll leave him alone.

The boy approached.

PART ONE:

MISSING

Wicklowboy22

Shaun learned the bizarre truth about his uncle in a cemetery on a damp October evening. Later, when he was back in the safety of his room, he'd think – with a certain amount of grim irony – that of all the places to hear that a relative had come back from the dead, a graveyard had to be the most apposite.

Up till then, the day had dragged. The bookshop may as well have had tumbleweeds blowing through it. The weather and recession had chased the tourists away, and after doing the returns, Shaun had spent the time playing spider solitaire and thumbing through the new releases – he was an expert at turning the pages without creasing a spine. The nights were drawing in, and he decided to lock up early. Máirín, his boss, would never know. She was thousands of miles away in Australia helping her daughter deal with the latest in a long line of personal crises, and had left him in charge. And besides, it was Thursday. He always left early on Thursdays to visit his mother. He cashed up, then went into the office at the back of the store to collect Daphne, who despite being safely ensconced in her basket, had somehow managed to shed all over the latest batch of Michael Connellys. She perked up as he shook her lead, then whined with impatience as he buttoned up his greatcoat.

As he was locking up, Terry, who ran the cafe next door, bustled out to waylay him. His heart sank. Terry's tongue was hinged at both ends; he might never get away.

'There was a man hanging around the shop earlier, Shaun. When you took the dog out at lunchtime. Asked after you.'

'A customer?'

'Couldn't say. Didn't like the look of him, but.' Shaun wasn't surprised. Terry didn't like the look of anyone – Shaun included. He was always screwing his mouth into a disapproving cat's arse whenever they ran into each other. Could it have been Brendan? Doubtful. Brendan was paranoid about anyone spotting them together and only communicated by text message. 'There was something rough about him,' Terry continued.

'Rough how?'

'Stank of drink and you should have seen the hair on him. Looked like Elvis's dead brother come back to life. You know someone like that? I haven't seen him around the town before.'

'God no. Did he say what he wanted?'

'He didn't. You don't owe anyone money, do you?'

Shaun bristled at the question. 'No.' He was behind on one of Daphne's vet bills, but they'd hardly send the bailiffs around for that. There was always the possibility that someone from his past, a spectre from the murky 'lost months', might appear. There was always that dread. Daphne was straining at her leash and Shaun let the dog drag him away. Terry and his intrusive questions could get stuffed.

He and the dog usually walked the two kilometres to Rathnew, but the cemetery closed early in October so today they took the bus. When they were safely through the gates, he let Daphne off the lead and headed for his mother's plot at the end of the family row. It was a fair walk. An early death was part of the Ryan legacy, along with odd-shaped ears and a smoking habit, and his relatives had colonised the place like bindweed. Shaun dug out the moss between the stones. It was a soothing, mindless task and one he looked forward to. While Daphne did her business on the grass next to his grandparents' dual plot, Shaun lit a Vogue, and leaned towards the headstone to exhale. Bringing his dead mother a nicotine fix had become a weekly ritual, daft as it was. Not only daft – costly. It had got him back on the cigarettes again, and the habit was eating into his escape fund. At least he hadn't yet resorted to talking to her.

A cough, then: 'Howya.'

Shaun started, looked up to see a man approaching. A shoe-polish black quiff and skin so white he could have just rolled off an embalmer's table. Reddish stubble sparked his jaw and he was tugging on a roll-up like it was his sole source of oxygen. The hair was a dye-job and a poor one at that; there were black smudges around his ears. Must be the man who was hanging around the shop – Terry's description was spot on. Had he followed him here? Shaun stood and weighed up the situation. There was no real aura of threat coming from the fellow, but Shaun's radar for trouble jangled all the same. He whistled for the dog in case he had to make a hasty getaway. As usual, Daphne ignored him.

'Were you at the book shop earlier?'

'I was. Place was locked up, and some nosy arse kept eyeing me up so I left.'

'Did you want to see me about something?'

The man jabbed his cigarette at the headstone. 'That what killed her?'

'You what?'

'The fags. That what killed her? Saw what you were doing. Good of you to do that. Eileen always liked a smoke.'

'You knew my mother?'

'I did. Couldn't believe it when I heard she'd passed over. Must have been hard for you losing her so young.' He sniffed and swatted a hand under his nose. There was a slur in his voice and he stood with his feet apart, weaving slightly. 'Had a mouth on her, didn't she? She was always back-chatting the teachers at school. Always gave as good as she got.'

'There's no way you were at school with her.' Shaun had every right to be dubious. His mother was thirty-two when she died and judging by Elvis's jowls and sunken eyes he wouldn't see fifty again.

'Nah, but I used to knock about with your uncle.'

'Donny?'

'Not that cunt. Teddy. You're the spit of him, you know that?'

'I've heard that before.'

'Bet you have. Knew you had to be Eileen's kid the second I saw you in the town. It was like going back in time.' The man wiped a hand on his jeans and held it out. 'John McKinnon. Johnny.'

Shaun didn't recall his mother mentioning anyone called Johnny, but after a hesitation he reached out. Johnny's palm was hot, and he was giving off the sour milk stink of the dedicated drinker. 'Shaun.'

'Good to meet you. Was it cancer that took her?'

'Aneurysm.'

'That's too bad. Sorry, son. Sorry.' The breeze tickled Shaun's fringe, but Johnny's pompadour remained impervious. 'She was full of life when I knew her, full of spark. Wish I could have made it to the wake, only I've been away.'

'Is that why you wanted to see me? Because of my mother?'

'Just wanted a word.'

'About what?' Shaun waited for the request for cash. Johnny looked the type to use any tenuous connection to hit someone up for a loan.

Daphne deigned to return and sniffed at Johnny's shoes – two-tone winklepickers that poked like knives from the bottom of his turn-ups. Before Shaun could warn him, he stooped to pat her. She snapped at him, but he barely reacted.

Shaun clipped the lead onto her collar and yanked her to heel. 'Sorry. She doesn't like men.'

'Well, who can blame her? What's her name?'

'Daphne.'

A snort. 'Daphne? No wonder she's got one on her.' Specks of ash fell from his fingers as he crushed the rollie. 'Daphne an old girl is she? Got some grey on her muzzle there.'

'Twelve. She was my mother's dog.'

'Ah right. Eileen was mad for animals. Always bringing in the strays. Daphne a stray?'

'She was.' Erin from Shaun's old estate had found Daphne running loose in Rathnew, the dog's ears a mess of cigarette burns, but couldn't keep her as she clashed with Beyoncé, Erin's

German shepherd. To save Daphne from euthanasia, his mother had taken her on, and now she was Shaun's – or Shaun was hers, depending on how you looked at it. Beyoncé was long gone, but Daphne had clung on, a small mutt who resembled a rusty wire brush on legs, her eyes now clouded with cataracts.

'Eileen had a good heart, son. A good heart.'

Greedy as he always was to hear tales about his mother, Shaun was still picking up a dodgy vibe from Johnny that had nothing to do with the man's dress sense. 'I'd better get back. Got to feed the dog. Nice meeting you.' He moved away.

'Did Teddy come back for Eileen's funeral?' Johnny called after him.

'What?'

'Did he pitch up? For the wake, like.'

Was the man messing with him? The light was fading fast, and Shaun couldn't read Johnny's eyes. Maybe he didn't know. 'Teddy died twenty years ago.'

'The family still sticking to that story, are they?'

'What?'

'The story, son. That your uncle died in an accident. Where was it again?'

'Galway.'

'That's it. He didn't die, son. They lied to you.'

'Are you trying to be funny?'

'Teddy didn't die. He left. He's in New York. Was last time I heard from him anyway. That would have been around '95 or so. Could be anywhere now.'

'You're talking bollocks.' Intent on another sniff at those shoes, Daphne fought Shaun's attempts to drag her away. He gathered her into his arms; he'd deal with the dog hair later.

'You seen his grave then, have you? Got a death certificate?'

'I'm not listening to this shite.' But all the same, a splinter of doubt niggled. Shaun ignored it and picked up the pace.

'He's not dead. I'm not messing with you. Ask your auntie Janice. Ask Donny. See if you can get the truth out of them. Teddy's out there somewhere. You should track him down.'

Shaun broke into a jog, only risking a glance over his shoulder when he reached the cemetery gates. Johnny was a distant, unsteady silhouette. There was relief as he hit the pavement, then irritation that he'd ignored his instincts and engaged the man in conversation. Daphne sighed and tucked her head into the crook of his arm. She loved being carried, thought it was her due, and now he'd set the precedent she'd only drag her heels if he put her down. A soft rain began to fall, turning the oncoming car lights into golden blurs. Shaun slowed and let his mind pick at the mental splinter. He and his mother *hadn't* been to see Teddy's grave, but he was certain they'd planned to go when he was younger. Why hadn't they gone in the end? Money issues, probably. They never went anywhere. And why was he giving credence to the words of a man who looked like he'd happily drink booze off a banshee's bollocks?

A gush as a bus choked with condensation whooshed past. It would be twenty minutes till the next one. He'd have to walk it.

Arms aching from carrying Daphne, he made it back in double-quick time. As usual, the shop had the aura that it was holding its breath – *books are not absolutely dead things* – but he didn't pause to drink it in. He hared up the stairs to his room, breathing in the comforting scents of dog and damp. The room was too small to air out properly. It wasn't built for long-term habitation. Máirín had let him use it after he was ousted from his aunt Janice's house, and it had become a home of sorts. Ablution-wise there was only a sink and an unpredictable lavatory down the hall, but he used the showers at the leisure centre or had an all-over body wash when he needed it.

He chucked Daphne's ready-cooked chicken slices into her bowl, and dragged his mother's suitcase out from beneath the bed. He'd been too messed up to save all of her belongings, but he'd managed to salvage the Ceil Chapman dress she'd found online and only wore on special occasions, and the blue cardigan she was wearing when she died. He dug out the photo album and flicked through it. Most of the photos were of him and his cousins, petering out after he was ten and everything went online.

He paused at the faded image of his mother just after she gave birth, red-faced and shell-shocked – the moment she'd decided to keep him. She was honest about that and of all her stories that was his favourite. There was only one photograph of Teddy, sitting with his siblings on a corduroy couch. His mother aged around twelve with a corona of auburn hair, Janice with her pug face and button eyes already raging at the world, Donny, the eldest, who even back then had the look of a diminutive Christopher Lee, and sixteen-year-old Teddy perched on the edge of the sofa, a cigarette held nonchalantly in his fingers. Caught side-on, he was the only one laughing. Shaun removed the photo and went to the mirror. He and Teddy had the same ears, crooked mouth and a similar haircut: short back and sides and a long fringe. *Brideshead Revisited* hair. Shaun hadn't looked at the photo for years; he must have unconsciously copied it. Uncle Teddy. Tragic Teddy. The black sheep of the family, 'like us', his mother used to say, although this label never seemed fair to Shaun. Janice's husband Keith was prosecuted for defrauding the council and Donny was a borderline psycho. His mother's stories about Teddy had dried up over the years, but he'd always put that down to grief. And hadn't they started to trickle away just after the aborted trip to Galway? Was this the source of the niggle?

Alive. Couldn't be. He'd have known. His mother would have told him. But still . . .

He sat on the bed and Googled Galway cemeteries. There were two Edward Ryans listed in Bohermore; one who'd died in the sixties, the other in the early 2000s. No Edward Shaun Ryan. Sensing his guard was down, Daphne flaunted the rules and jumped up next to him. Knowing it was stupid, he opened Facebook. He'd killed his profile after his mother died – her page was still linked to his and he couldn't bear the facile 'she was such a lovely girl' comments – and searched for Edward Shaun Ryan, using New York as his starting point. Most had profile pics rather than avatars (although there were a slew of Darth Vaders for some reason), and he trawled through them searching for a glimmer of familiarity, a kink in an ear, that crooked grin. He tried Teddy Ryan, Eddie Ryan, Ed Ryan, Ted Ryan, Edward John Ryan, TJ Ryan, Irish Ted, every permutation of his uncle's name he could come up with. He couldn't settle, wished he could talk it out with someone – which wasn't like him at all – but his only options were Máirín, who even if she wasn't in a different time zone had enough on her plate, or Brendan, his on-again, off-again shag and a habit he'd been trying to break for both of their sakes.

'It's bollocks isn't it, Daphne?'

She cracked her jaws and rolled onto her back.

The dog was his last tether to this place and when she died the plan was to escape to London. It was where he and his mother were supposed to go after he finished school. Where Teddy had lived for a while before he came back to Ireland and supposedly died. But perhaps now there was another option.

Giving into a nicotine lure, Shaun went to the window. He lit up and funnelled smoke into the rain. The town was winding down for the night. The estuary's black mass undulated beyond the street, the hiss of traffic punctuated by the occasional bark of laughter. Tentatively, alive to the pitfalls of false hope, he allowed himself to dream, dredging up safely stereotypical images from *The New York Trilogy*, *Breakfast at Tiffany's*, *Triburbia*. Pictured himself in a loft apartment, sitting at a breakfast bar while an older version of Teddy cooked him an American breakfast – pancakes, maybe. There was a copy of the *New Yorker* on the counter, and they were arguing good-naturedly about which show to catch that evening. The place smelled of coffee beans and old books. As he closed the window, he caught his reflection in the glass. Shaun Edward Ryan; Teddy Shaun Ryan. Mirror images. 'Mad.'

His uncle Keith answered the door, still dressed in his pyjamas although it was going on for midday. 'Well, well. How's Wicklow's answer to James Joyce?' It was the closest to wit the poor sod could manage, and Shaun responded with his usual weak laugh. Keith had aged since Shaun last encountered him: thread veins were turning his nose into a glowing light bulb. 'The boys are at work, Shaun.'

'It's not them I'm here for. Need a word with Janice.'

'Ah, right, right. She's in the kitchen. I'll leave you to it.' He winked. 'Good luck.'

Shaun breathed through his mouth as he went through to the kitchen. The room held the odour of countless bland meals that somehow managed to taste of the passive aggression that went into their production. Janice was bent over the sink, furiously peeling potatoes and muttering to herself. She started when she saw him. 'Shaun? What's happened? Why aren't you at work?'

'Took an early lunch.' He'd locked up the shop and left the dog in the room, along with (hopefully) enough chew toys to keep her busy. She'd only howl herself stupid if he brought her along. She'd never forgiven him for the indignity of being relegated to a kennel in the yard when they stayed with Janice after he lost the house.

She looked him up and down. 'And still in those old clothes, I see.' Shaun didn't bother commenting on this. 'I suppose you'll be wanting a sandwich.'

'No, you're alright.'

A snort that could be relief or censure. 'Now what is it? I've got the tea to do for tonight.' He'd never seen her still for more than a couple of seconds. 'She's like a great white,' his mother used to say, 'she'll die if she doesn't keep moving.' On the counter sat a trio of onions and a slab of defrosting mince – the makings of one of her anaemic cottage pies.

'When did Uncle Teddy die, Auntie Janice?'

'Why are you asking that? You're not going funny in the head again are you?'

'Ran into a man while I was visiting Mam yesterday.'

'Did you now.'

'John McKinnon. Said he used to be friends with Teddy.'

The hand scraping the potatoes paused. Colour bloomed on the skin at the nape of her neck. 'He's back is he? Stay away from him. He's nothing but trouble.'

'He says Teddy isn't dead. He says he's in New York.'

'Don't believe a word that gobshite says.'

'So Teddy is dead then.'

'Of course he is.'

'Where's he buried?'

'You know where. Galway.'

'There's no record of him. I checked. They've got a list online.'

Scrape, scrape, scrape.

'He's not there, Auntie Janice.'

'Well . . . they made an error then.'

'Is he dead or not?' Something shifted inside him – he'd never seen her this cagey. 'Did he die in an accident in Galway or not? I can check. I can apply for a death certificate. It's easy to do.'

She pointed the peeler at him. There was calculation behind her eyes – and what could be fear. 'Don't you bloody dare.'

'Why not?' This came out as a whisper. 'Did he die in Galway or not?'

She slammed the peeler onto the counter. 'For the love of . . . No. No he bloody didn't. Happy now?'

He couldn't seem to swallow and there was a static buzz at the base of his skull; the shape of this, of what it could mean, was too huge to absorb. 'But why say he did?'

'There were reasons.'

'What reasons?'

'Keep your voice down,' she hissed. He hadn't raised his voice; he rarely did. 'You'll upset Keith. You know how fragile he is.'

'Well?'

'There are things about Teddy you don't know.'

'Like what?'

A moue of distaste. 'Things.'

'I know he was queer if that's what you mean.'

'Don't use that word, Shaun.' Janice plucked a knife out of the drawer and began attacking an onion as if it were an enemy's head.

'But what has that got to do with anything? Keith's sister Nessa lives with a woman. And what about me?'

'That's different.'

'How?'

'Nessa doesn't flaunt it. You don't flaunt it.' She turned to look him up and down again. 'Much.'

'*Flaunt* it?'

'Oh don't look at me like that. You know what I mean. It was a different time back then. You couldn't go around showing off about it and not expect trouble.'

There were a couple of LGBTQ societies in the area now, and it had been a while since Shaun had dealt with outright taunts, but there were also lads like Brendan who would rather poke a potato peeler in their eye than come out. 'It can't have been that bad. It was the nineties, not the nineteen-fifties.'

'People would turn a blind eye if you kept it quiet.'

'And he didn't.'

'I blame that gobshite. He was the one who dragged Teddy off to London.'

'John McKinnon went to London with Teddy? Mam never said.'

'Well he did. Teddy was different when he came back. Came into the house and told us he was gay and we had to deal with it. Broke your granddad's heart. He was always wild, but . . . not like that. He couldn't keep his mouth shut about it. Got into fights, goaded people, told them to get out of the dark ages. Sending him away was the best thing for him. The safest thing. And he wanted to go.'

'Why New York? We don't have family there as far as I know.' Unless that was another Ryan family secret. 'He could've just gone back to London.'

'He always wanted to go there. He was always talking about it. That was the deal.'

'The deal?'

'If the family paid for his ticket then he wasn't to come back.'

Shaun took a moment to digest this, the questions crowding in on each other. 'So he was targeted by the local Neanderthals and sent away to America. But why say he was dead?'

She swiped at her eyes, red from the onions. 'So your mam wouldn't go after him.'

'What?'

'She was always "Teddy this" and "Teddy that". Idolised him. When he left for London she was beside herself, begged him to take her. Then there was the shame of it, you know. Your grandparents had just found out their sixteen-year-old daughter was pregnant with you, and after Teddy had all his . . . after that trouble he had, your granddad said Teddy was dead to him. I'm not saying it was the right thing to do, but it's the way it is.'

Shaun could believe that of his grandparents. They'd died within six months of each other when he was ten, and right till the end treated him and Eileen as if they were pariahs. He remembered his mother whistling 'Ding-Dong! The Witch is Dead' after she returned from his grandmother's wake.

'And everyone believed he was dead?'

'Why wouldn't they?'

'How could you have a funeral if there wasn't a body?'

'They said they had it down in Galway where your granddad's sister lives. No one spoke to her.'

'But if he came back then everyone would know you were lying.'

'He wasn't going to come back.'

'Why? He could have come back after his parents died.'

'Well he didn't, did he?'

'Did Mam know he wasn't dead?' She would have been in Dublin when Teddy returned from London, she and her pregnancy hidden away like a dirty secret.

'Not then. She was furious that she couldn't go to the funeral. Your grandparents only told her when they heard she was planning to go and visit the grave in Galway.'

Teddy's non-existent grave. 'She never told me.' She'd always been honest with him – too honest sometimes. He shelved this betrayal; it could bruise him later.

'She was trying to protect you.'

'From what?'

'The stories about him, the rumours. She worried about you. She knew what you were. That you were the same as him.'

And then he was back there, age eleven, walking home from school, feet scuffing the pavement, lost in a daydream – picturing himself at Hogwarts, waiting for the Sorting Hat to be placed on his head – so absorbed he didn't notice Aidan Sullivan and his gang lurking outside the shop until it was too late. 'Hiya freak.' Cheeks burning, he ducked his head, jumping into the road to avoid being swiped by an elbow. Aidan coming close, breathing cider fumes into his face: 'Fucking weirdo. My dad says your uncle was a fucking fag, and it runs in the family.' One of them, Dylan Carey maybe, saying: 'Just leave him be.' Sitting in the lounge that evening with his mother, plates of fish fingers and chips balanced on their knees, feeling the force of this new information pushing up and out of his throat: 'Mam, am I a fag like Teddy?' Eileen freezing, her fork to her mouth, blood rushing to her face – like Janice she was a chameleon, showed every emotion on her skin: 'Where were you hearing that?' She got it out of him, and must have told Janice about the taunts, because his aunt sent his cousins around to sort out Aidan Sullivan and the others. They left him alone after that. Everyone left him alone after that, but Eileen never encouraged him to hide who he was – the opposite. Janice was talking bollocks.

'Did she look for him? Did any of you?'

She slammed a pan on the hob in answer.

'Have you heard from Teddy since then? Johnny says he heard from him in '95 or thereabouts.'

'No.'

'What about Donny?'

'Don't bother Donny with this. He's only just moved back from Spain and he's got enough to deal with, what with the kids and that bitch of a wife.' Shaun didn't push this. He'd rather not have anything to do with his uncle Donny; his mother never had a good word to say about him.

'But it's been twenty years.' Longer. Twenty-two. 'You'd think he would've come back for Mam's funeral. You'd think he would have checked up on us over the years.'

'Ah well . . . He must have decided to get on with his life, leave all of us behind.'

'And who can blame him? You all threw him away.'

Oil hissed as it hit the pan. Onion pieces skittered and sizzled. Janice's skin flamed. 'Don't look for him now. Leave it be. He would have been in touch or come home if he wanted to. How will it look if people find out that the family was lying all these years?'

The tension stretched. 'I'd better go.'

'Wait.' She followed him to the door. 'Shaun, you'll leave this alone, won't you?' Desperation – something he'd never seen from Janice. Sloughed of her usual bluster, she seemed smaller, older. 'Leave it alone. You'll cause the family a world of trouble if you go poking around in this. You did without him your whole life, why dig it up now?'

'How can I leave it?'

'Shaun. I'm begging you. Have I ever asked you for anything?' Guilt-tripping: the nuclear weapon in Janice's arsenal. 'If you won't do it for me then do it for your mam's memory. Leave it be.'

'Okay.'

'You swear on your mother's grave?'

'I swear.'

But his mother wasn't superstitious and neither was he.

Missing-Linc.com

Matching Unidentified Bodies (UIDs)
With Missing People

How to join | FAQs | Current UIDs | Success stories | Rules

NEW ENTRY

Name: 'GI Doe'

Description: The remains of a white male were found near the banks of the Black River, Jefferson County, NY, on 07/17/96 four miles outside the boundary of the Fort Drum grounds.

GI Doe is thought to have been in his early to mid twenties. Approx 74 inches in height, 155–170 pounds. Blond hair (highlighted). Traces of glitter make-up found on his skin. Dental reports inconclusive. Decomposition was advanced.

Multiple stab wounds from a serrated knife to the torso and upper thighs. Classified as a homicide. GI Doe thought to have died from a month to six weeks prior to discovery.

A single Adidas tennis shoe was found a hundred yards from the body, as well as part of a ripped T-shirt with a (partial) photo of a white, blond-haired man on it, see links.

See link for forensic portrait artist's 3D rendering of GI Doe.

Case sourced from NamUs.

DNA was entered into CODIS in 2010.

Agency contact: Sondra Nell at Jefferson County Coroner/ Medical Examiner's Office

Thread dated: August 22/2017

Ratking1 [admin]: As always, read the description above, then add any possible missing person matches into the thread below. Follow the links to see the original report as well as a map of the body dump site. Feel free to share on SM.

I will pass on any relevant information to Sondra Nell at the ME's office.

Marlborowoman: Flagging up a missing guy from 1989. Brunner, Jacob [see link]. Last seen in Queens, NYC. Blond hair, same height, 25 years old, so on the outer edges of the age range??

Mommydearest [moderator]: Checked your link and Brunner had a lumbarized first sacral vertebra. This is not in GI Doe's description.

Marlborowoman: Description is sketchy. Not much to work on.

Vladtheromantic: Thinking about the glitter stuff and dyed hair. Thinking maybe he was gay.

Bisontastic: Stereotype much?

Vladtheromantic: You don't think this is a good point?

Ratking1 [admin]: Could be useful to flag up any gay men who went missing around that time.

Lorrainegrey2: **[message deleted by moderator]**

Bisontastic: **[message deleted by moderator]**

Vladtheromantic: It could be a hate crime. Look where GI Doe was found. Military guys aren't known for their tolerance. Just saying.

Lorrainegrey2: **[message deleted by moderator]**

Ratking1 [admin]: A reminder to all on this thread, hate speech will NOT be tolerated. [**Lorrainegrey2** has now been blocked from the site. I WILL name and shame.]

Vladtheromantic: Is LE looking for other similar suspicious deaths in the area? The mutilation could indicate a serial killing. Flagging up a similar case on the site [see link]. This boy was killed in Minnesota but same victimology.

Keysersoze: Different MO in the Minnesota case.

FacetiousB: Don't serial killers stick to locations they know?

Dotspot: Not always. Bundy killed people in multiple states.

Ratking1 [admin]: A reminder that our priority is to IDENTIFY our UIDs ONLY. Please focus your energies on this. WE ARE NO LONGER A SLEUTHING FORUM.

Thread dated: August 24/2017

Crowroad: Hey, RE the t-shirt. Shared it on twitter & I'm thinking the guy on it could be Billy Idol (for those of you born after 1990 Billy Idol was a pop star back in the day ☺).

See link for comparison pics??

Ratking1 [admin]: Good catch. Can you check if Billy Idol was on tour round about that time? Could be a tour T-shirt. (Remember this is how Grateful Doe was identified). I will pass this information on to the coroner's office.

Crowroad: Thnx ☺. You thinking GI Doe could be a groupie? I'm on it.

Mileycircus: Closest US tour date to body discovery was in '91 in LA. Not gonna help us.

Thread dated: September 1/2017

Mister.Tonyface: Been reading up on the camp near to where GI Doe was found. They have a ton of training sessions & bring in like, military from all over the world. Could be one of those guys?

Ratking1 [admin]: There are no missing person reports of military personnel foreign or otherwise going AWOL at the time. **Mommydearest** has ruled this connection out.

Mister.Tonyface: Yeah I posted that without thinking! Should've known they would check that big time. My bro was in the military.

Thread dated: October 10/2017

Ratking1 [admin]: **UPDATE ON GI DOE**
Thanks to all of you who are still working on this. There are currently 22 possible mispers. **Mommydearest** has the list on a separate thread.

Thanks to **Crowroad**, the T-shirt has been identified as a Billy Idol screen-printed shirt circa '87. The coroner's office assures me this information has been passed on to LE.

Vladtheromantic: Why don't they do an isotope test on GI Doe so that they can find out where he was from? Read about this case on Reddit where a girl's severed head was found in like, Wisconsin or somewhere and they couldn't identify her and no one knew her in the area so they tested the isotopes in her bones and they could map where she'd been for like the last few years and they found out she was from Florida.

Ratking1 [admin]: Agreed. I have enquired why this has not been done.

Ratking1

The phone chimed out its hourly alarm and Chris automatically swiped it to silent. It was the third time she'd ignored the reminder to do her pressure relief, but screw it, she'd make up for it later. The site had been flatlining lately and she needed to keep up the momentum. It wasn't unusual for UIDs to be identified by their clothing, and they were getting some real traction on the GI Doe case.

A chat message popped up on screen – Mommydearest, checking in as usual: **<Coroner's office got back to you RE isotope yet?>**

<Nope>

<They should have the decency to keep us updated. We're trying to help them here>

<You know how it goes. Sometimes they appreciate our help, sometimes they don't & might not have funds to do it anyway>

<BTW I've ruled out the Winterson guy, Kelvin Michaud and the kid from Wyoming as matches for GI Doe. They were long shots anyway>

<Gotcha. I'll let you know the second Sondra gets back to me>

<Coolio. I'm here>

Chris smiled at this. He was always here, always online. She'd never met Mommydearest – aka Louis Bartlett – who said he was an ex-dispatcher from Tulsa who'd quit his job to care for his elderly father and had a thing for old Joan Crawford movies, but she'd done her due diligence and his Facebook profile seemed to verify his identity and story. Most of her moderators burned out pretty quick, but he was working out. Chris suspected he was on the spectrum, which worked in her favour; he was almost as obsessional as she was.

The trailer's screen door banged open, then came the sound of stumbling and a muttered: 'Oh *shit*.' Chris had heard the bikes roar in a couple of hours ago and knew Jeanie would show up sooner or later.

Jeanie clacked into the office space, a bottle of Coors in her hand. 'Hey, Chrissy Chris.'

'Hey.'

'Whatcha doing?'

'Usual.'

'You eat well today?'

'Course.' If a tube of Pringles and three pieces of toast counted as 'eating well'.

'Come on over to the house, have a drink with us.' She shook the bottle, and beer frothed over its lip. She sucked it up, droplets spattering onto the floor.

'Can't. I'm in the middle of something.'

'Aw, don't be a party pooper.' She waggled her fingers. 'Devin's got some good grass.'

'Nope.'

'C'mon, honey, for me. *C'mon*.'

'I've got no interest in being a freak show tonight.'

'Honey, you're not a freak.' She grinned. 'Okay, so yeah, you're a bit of freak, but I can't stand the thought of you being out here all by your lonesome and me having fun. Pretty please? Please with some coke on top?'

Sometimes it was easier to let Jeanie have her way. And Chris should get out. Time had disappeared into its usual black hole today. 'If I come for one will you get off my back?'

'Sure I will.' Jeanie gave Chris one of her wicked grins, then headed out to wait for her at the edge of the path that led to the main house. The land around the trailer was mostly desert scrub, and without the path Chris would be stranded. It wasn't perfect: the tar melted when the temperature hit the nineties, and the rattlers sometimes took to lying on it at night, but it was better than nothing.

'Got to pee – see you inside.' Typical Jeanie, now she'd prised Chris out of her cave, she couldn't wait to get back to the action. She skipped ahead in her ankle boots, adjusting the straps of her top. Chris took her time. The solar lights set along the path were haloed with bugs, and the grassy scent of weed and the sounds of music and laughter floated from the main house. It was a larger gathering than usual: a row of bikes snaked alongside her truck and Jeanie's Pinto. Mack's customised chopper wasn't among them, but that was no surprise. He always warned her in advance whenever he planned to rock up. She trailed on past her father's old workshop. The tools nailed to its exterior were being devoured by rust, as were the sculptures he'd cobbled together out of scrap, bottle glass and bike parts. Chris kept meaning to restore them; she'd better get on it soon before they crumbled into nothing.

A small group of Jeanie's cronies were gathered on the porch, boots up on the railing. An audience, but she was long past getting self-conscious. Devin, Jeanie's latest, called out a greeting and Chris gave him a wave. He wasn't the brightest, but she'd checked him out and he wasn't affiliated. He was currently working at a hot rod customising and detailing shop and seemed to be getting his shit together. Then there was Paula, who worked the meat counter with Jeanie at Family Dollar. Paula was okay; had a history of bad checks and low-level dealing, but she wasn't malicious and watched Jeanie's back. A ratty little guy in a leather vest nuzzled at Paula's neck – another new man. Like Jeanie, Paula got through them faster than corn through a duck's guts.

As Chris reached the bottom of the ramp, someone called: 'Need any help?' It wasn't Devin, he knew better than that by now. A big bearded guy she hadn't seen before gazed down at her.

'Nope.'

Like the path, the ramp was the result of half-assed construction. Its slats were beginning to warp, but the gradient didn't give her any trouble. She ended up directly in front of the big guy's crotch.

'Get you a beer?' he asked without introducing himself.

'Sure. Thanks.'

He disappeared into the house.

'Hey, Chrissy.' Paula snaked an arm around the ratty-faced guy. 'This is Michael.'

He stared at the chair. 'How did you end up in that thing?'

Paula nudged him. 'I told you not to ask that.'

'It's fine.' Chris gave him the measured smile she reserved for assholes. 'You sure you want to hear it?'

'Yeah.'

'It's really bad. Graphic, even.'

'I can handle it.'

'Okay. You know SeaWorld down in Florida?'

He frowned. 'Sure.'

'You hear about the orca they had there at one time?'

'That killer whale?'

'Yep. Went crazy after being in captivity for so long.'

He whistled through his teeth. 'Fuck, man. No way . . . did that thing get you or something?'

Devin hooted. 'She's fucking with you, dumbass.'

Paula leaned over to give her a fist-bump. Michael didn't laugh along with the others, but that didn't worry Chris. Paula could handle herself. She'd dealt with far worse than the fallout of a bruised ego.

The big guy returned with Chris's beer. Not in the mood for a crowd, she moved to the far side of the porch. He followed, asking: 'Okay if I join you?'

She nodded at the porch swing. The paint on it was peeling – he'd be lucky not to get an ass full of splinters.

When he sat, the chains creaked. He had to be six five, nudging three hundred pounds. 'I'm Scott.'

'Christina. Chris.'

She let the silence stretch. He'd joined her; it wasn't on her to break it. Not that it was silent exactly. Jeanie was blasting out her

Stevie Nicks at full volume again, and Devin was hooting at something Paula was saying. She took in Scott's shaven head, Jethro Tull T-shirt – not what she would have expected from someone in Jeanie's crowd – biker boots of course, and arms covered with ink. The light wasn't great, but she could make out a competent skull, flames, and an eagle that had the whiff of the eighties about it, probably one of his first. Nothing that screamed white power or hinted that he'd been in for a stretch.

He cleared his throat. 'How long you been living here, Chris?'

'I was born here. Been back five years or so. I was in Vegas for a while.'

'Yeah? Doing what?'

'Show girl.'

He nodded as if he were taking her seriously. 'At one of the casinos?'

'Man, *really*?'

He smiled, masking his mouth with his hand. 'You're screwing with me.'

'It's a habit.' A bad habit, drove Jeanie crazy, drove everyone crazy. 'You? Haven't seen you around here before.'

'Just got a job with Devin over at Barrick Customs. Moved here from Henderson.'

'You a mechanic?'

'Body work mostly.'

Another silence. She waited for him to make his excuses and head off to find a less prickly companion, or do a Michael and start in on the personal questions.

'Hey, so your sister says you're some kind of PI?'

'Ha. No.'

He drained his beer, belched. 'Scuse me. So if you're not a PI, what are you?'

'I'm nothing. I run a website is all. More of a forum.'

'Yeah? What kind of website?'

'The kind that specialises in unidentified remains.'

'Remains?'

'Bodies.'

'You messing with me again?'

'No.'

'You work for the coroner or something?'

'Nope.' He appeared to be genuinely interested. She should tune down the bitchiness. By now, most people would've turned the conversation onto themselves. 'You really want to hear?'

'Yeah.'

'So what we do is list the details of UIDs – unidentified people – on the site, and our members try and match them with the profiles of people who've gone missing.'

'Oh wow.' He smiled, covering his mouth with his hand again. 'Hey, I heard about that kind of thing—'

Devin called out: 'Hey, Scotty! Tell Chris how much you can bench press.'

Scott squirmed, muttered, 'Screw you, Devin.'

'Chrissy, you should see his biceps, man. He's like the Terminator.'

Chris caught Michael's eye and he twisted his mouth into a sneer. Her first assessment was right: *Asshole.*

Paula lit up a joint and told the others to leave them alone.

'Don't mind them,' Scott said as if he knew them better than she did.

'I don't.'

'I was going to ask, by unidentified people, you mean like the Lady of the Dunes? Girl that was found murdered on the beach somewhere?'

'Yeah. Provincetown.' Impressive. It was a famous case, but he was the first person in Jeanie's crowd who'd mentioned her – or shown any interest in the site.

He leaned forward, elbows on his knees. 'Didn't they think she was murdered by the mob?'

'Whitey Bulger, yeah. There are a ton of theories.'

'She ever been identified?'

'No, but there are hundreds of people working her case. The ones we feature are mostly the unglamorous ones. The ones that don't get so much attention.'

'People send them to you?'

'Sometimes. Usually I pick them off coroners' websites or harvest them from the bigger sites like the Doe Network or whatever.'

'So what are you working on now?'

'We feature lots of them at the same time. You never know when you're going to get a tip or a lead. Might have a lead on one of them now.'

'Go on.'

Chris's beer was almost finished. She was getting a faint buzz on, and the knots in her neck were loosening. 'Okay, so we're working a body that was found in '96. Name of GI Doe.'

'That's some name.'

'He was found near a military base. They all got names. So there's GI Doe, Big Foot Doe – he was found next to Route 244 in Oregon with his head caved in – then we've got Dog Doe—'

'*Dog* Doe?'

'A dog's collar was found in the vicinity where he was dumped. A neighbourhood woman said she saw a dog around there afterwards, a husky.'

'Freaky.'

'Yup.'

'So this GI Doe . . .'

'We're thinking he might've been gay, the victim of a hate crime.' His expression didn't change. 'That's just speculation though.'

'How did he die?'

'Stabbed multiple times. He's been on the site for a while now, so it would be great to match him up.'

'You do mostly men?'

'It's not a misogyny type deal. If you're a white co-ed you're going to get far more attention than say, a minority or some random guy.'

That wasn't entirely true. There were a few women on the site. One in particular. Only, she wasn't a UID. She was a missing person. Been missing since eighty-six. Left the house one morning without saying goodbye, and never came back.

'How did you get into this, Chris?'

'There are tens of thousands of unidentified bodies out there. Someone's got to do something.' Now she was coming across like a martyr. 'It's nothing big. Just somewhere where people can talk about this stuff.'

'You make money off it?'

'Nope.'

'But you've solved cases, right?'

'We don't solve anything. It's identification we focus on.'

'Nuh-uh. Not true,' Jeanie said. Chris had been so absorbed in the conversation she hadn't noticed her sister creeping up on them. 'She has solved a case. Lots of them.'

'Oh yeah?'

'Yeah. She's like . . . what the fuck. Y'know. Sherlock or some shit.'

Chris drained her beer. 'Okay. That's me done.'

'You want another?' Scott asked.

'Nope. Got to get back.'

'Well it was cool to talk to you.'

'You too.' And it was.

It took a few manoeuvres to turn around, and this time he didn't offer to help. With a 'see you around' he headed into the house. Thankfully, Michael and Paula were nowhere to be seen. Jeanie stumbled after her as she navigated the ramp. 'He's cute, right, Chris?'

'He's not in any way cute. You trying to set me up again, Jeanie?'

'Hey listen, his kid has that . . . multiple . . . fuck . . . that wheelchair disease.'

'Multiple sclerosis?'

'Uh-huh.'

'That's why you wanted me to come over? To set the cripple up with the cripple's dad? And just so you know, MS isn't a goddamned "wheelchair disease".'

Jeanie did her little girl pout. 'Don't be mad at me, Chrissy.' Devin ran up behind her, grabbed her waist and pulled her on top of him. She squealed.

'Yeah, yeah. Night.' For all her faults, Jeanie just wanted her to be happy. And in Jeanie's world being happy had to involve a man.

Exhaustion hit the second she reached the trailer, but instead of doing her exercises or hitting the sack, she returned to the office and scanned the site's inbox. Bookended by the usual slew of membership requests from spambots, there was another message from Mommydearest, this one with a link attached:

<Saw this circulated on http://longlostpeeps.com/. One of ours? Hair color different but timescale/height/weight matches GI Doe?>

She clicked on it and scanned the text: 'Looking for my uncle Edward Shaun Ryan. Goes by Teddy. He left Wicklow County in Ireland in 1995 and might be in NYC. To my knowledge he hasn't contacted the family since then. His current age would be 42. Irish, slender, five foot five (approximately), gay. If you have any information please contact wicklowboy22@gmail.com. Thanks.'

She enlarged the image beneath it, a blurry shot of a dark-haired kid that had clearly been cropped from a larger photo. His head was tilted at an angle, three-quarters of his face visible.

It wasn't GI Doe. She had a good eye for faces – you had to, doing this. Chris leaned back in the chair, the pressure cushion letting out a soft sigh, and scrubbed at her eyes. It wasn't GI Doe, but she reckoned she knew who it might be. '*Shit.*'

Rainbowbrite

Alerted by the slam of the front door, Ellie slid her laptop to the side of the breakfast bar and covered it with a copy of *Us Weekly*. Noah mumbled a greeting, stalked to the fridge and started foraging through it. He had the inward look he always got whenever he was replaying the day's events over and over, and she waved him away. 'Sit, Noah. I'll make you a grilled cheese.'

'Thanks. Where are the kids?'

'I've let them have some TV time.' He raised an eyebrow: *Again?* But she could tell he was too tired to argue. 'You okay with Swiss?'

'We not got American?'

'No. Didn't get to the store. Boys had hockey practice after school.' It was only a small lie. 'You want to talk about your day?'

'Later.' He sat and watched while she separated the cheese slices. He'd talk when he was good and ready and she knew better than to press him. She heated butter and oil in the pan, then dropped in the sandwich. The scent of melting cheese and toasting bread filled the kitchen. Ellie thought about making one for herself, but she'd been grazing all day. She'd finished the kids' waffles that morning, then made inroads into the pound cake she'd bought on the sly at the Stop & Shop yesterday.

The house phone rang. She went to get it, but Noah leaned across and plucked it off the wall. He listened, then said: 'For you.'

'Who is it?'

'Didn't say.'

She took it from him, tucking it under her chin so that she was free to flip the sandwich. 'This is Ellen.' Probably one of those pollsters, most people used her cell.

'It's Chris.' Ellie couldn't place the voice. It was low, husky, could be male or female.

'Excuse me, who?'

'Chris. Chris Guzman. From Missing-Linc.'

Ellie would be less shocked if Jesus were on the line to her. Noah mouthed: 'Is it your dad?' She covered the handset. 'No. Nothing like that. Can you watch the pan?'

'El—'

'Just watch the pan.' She hurried out, making for the den.

'You still there?' Chris said.

'What do you want, Chris? How did you get this number?'

'It's listed. Would have emailed or sent you a Facebook DM but you blocked me.'

'Do you blame me?'

'I wasn't the one who screwed up.'

'What do you want?'

'I need to send you something. You got your iPhone or laptop handy?'

'Why?'

'Get online.'

Chris's tone was as bossy as her online persona. Back when they were colleagues, Ellie had tried and tried to get her to FaceTime or call so that they could chat in person, but she'd resisted. She'd never said why. 'Wait a sec.'

Noah shot her another questioning look as she raced into the kitchen and grabbed her laptop. She gestured at the pan – the bread was blackening. Back in the den, out of earshot, she balanced the device on Noah's desk. Her insides were on spin-cycle. 'Okay. I got my laptop.'

'You still got the same email?'

'Wait, I'll unblock you.'

There was dead air between them while she did so. Seconds later, an email with no subject line and a link came through.

'You get it?'

'Wait a sec, Chris.'

She clicked on the link – a request for information about a

long-lost uncle – and homed in on a cropped, fuzzy headshot of a young man.

'Well? Is it him?'

She opened her mouth to ask, 'is it who?', then took in the shape of his face, his ears, and that indefinable something. 'Oh. Oh my *Lord*.'

'Well, is it? The hair's different.'

She was about to answer, then stopped herself. She'd got herself into trouble before by being too hasty. 'I'm not sure.' She told Chris she'd call her back, then hung up.

Ellie leaned over the desk and breathed in. Next, she checked her reflection in the den's small mirror. Her cheeks were crimson, her neck blotchy. She flapped a hand in front of her face in a vain attempt to cool it down as she made her way back to the kitchen.

'Who was that?' Noah said when she entered the room. The sandwich was sitting untouched in front of him. Ellie drifted to the stove, and took the pan to the sink as an excuse to get her emotions in check. She was getting better at hiding things, but this was too big.

'Chris. From Missing-Linc.'

'What the hell did she want?'

'There's been an update on the Boy in the Dress. We might have an ID for him.'

'Thought you'd left the site?'

'I have. This lead literally just came in.'

'You said you were through with all that.' His voice was low, laced with disappointment.

'I know. But you know what this could mean, don't you?'

'I can't deal with this right now.'

'Noah—'

'You said you were done.'

'I *am* done.'

'No you're not.' He got up.

'Where you going?'

'Need a nap. It's been a helluva day.'

'What about your sandwich?'

'Lost my appetite. You said you were *done*, Ellie.'

She couldn't argue with that. He didn't know she'd been late collecting the boys from school a couple of times because she'd got caught up checking the photo archives on Lost&Found.com. He didn't know that she sometimes got up at three a.m. to trawl through the UnsolvedMurders threads on Reddit, or that she'd joined Websleuths. After the upset with Chris, after it had started taking over her life, she'd promised she wouldn't do it any more. But like a dog returning to its vomit – or like an alcoholic or one of those meth addicts – in the last couple of months she'd regressed.

A howl came from the TV room. She stormed through to find the twins tussling on the rug. Potato chips crusted the gaps between the couch's cushions, and the air was thick with the funk of popcorn and boy socks.

She pulled them apart. 'Stop that right now, you hear?'

They both crossed their arms and pouted.

'Where's Dad?' Philip whined.

'He's having a nap. You're not to disturb him. We had a deal. I said you could have an extra hour of TV time if you behaved.'

Sammy wriggled out of her grasp. 'But Philip won't let me watch *Adventure Time*.'

'It's not his *turn*, Mom.'

'It is, you liar. Liar, liar, you're a goddamned liar.'

'Sammy! No cursing.'

Another pout. 'Sorry, Mom. But it's *my* turn to choose.'

'Okay, okay. How about a compromise? You want one of your movies? How about *Sing*? You both like that.'

'No.'

She bribed the boys with promises of ice cream after supper and games on the iPad if they kept it down, and spent the next ten minutes getting them to compromise on a movie. Bad parenting 101, but she'd deal with the guilt later.

Back in the kitchen, she made a decaf with extra sugar. How long was it since she'd been on Missing-Linc? Had to be months.

It was as painful as visiting an ex's Facebook page and seeing they were happier without you. But she couldn't put it off forever. Chris was waiting. The case was archived, and it took several seconds to scroll through to it. Re-reading it brought on a mixture of sorrow and guilt – she'd abandoned the Boy in the Dress after she left the site. Dumped him. She dragged Noah's plate towards her and picked at the sandwich, not quite ready to compare the photograph with the composite drawing. The boy wasn't her first case, but it meant more to her than the others she'd worked on. Meant more to her than the first case that got her hooked, the mystery of Steven and Miranda Shepherd, the couple who'd disappeared while they were camping in the Catskills. She'd read about them on one of the news sites when she and Noah were living in Roseville, a few months before Noah got the job at St. Cloud correctional and they'd moved here. The Shepherds were a seemingly happy couple who'd disappeared without a trace while on vacation. When a couple of hikers came across their tent, their dog was tied up outside it and their camp stove was still alight. Looked like they'd been taken by aliens. That case woke something up in her. She was on forums day and night swapping theories and digging into the couple's online profiles. Noah encouraged it at first. She'd been down for a while after the boys started school, and he reckoned it was good for her to have something to do other than look after the house. It was the Shepherds who'd brought Ellie and Chris together. She'd joined Missing-Linc and, later, applied to be a moderator. That was back when the site also did sleuthing. That was back before it started taking over her life.

Ellie didn't hear about the boy online, but via Lisa, one of the moms at the boys' karate class. She and Noah had just moved into the area, and she was saying how nice it was to be in a small town with one of the lowest crime rates in the country. Lisa said, 'Uh-huh, I know, right? Last big murder I heard about was that boy who died back in the nineties.'

'What boy?'

'That gay boy. They think he might've been a drag queen like that RuPaul.'

'How come?'

'Body was found wearing a prom dress. Weird, huh?'

'They find out who killed him?'

'Couldn't tell you. They might've, but I don't recall reading about it.'

The second Ellie got home she'd started digging. There wasn't much, but she tracked down a couple of archived articles about the case. She'd flagged it to Chris, who agreed to feature it on the forum. But it was always her case. And not just because she found it: the boy was personal. He'd been dumped in the reserve where she took the boys after church. Five miles from their home.

She'd built up the content, taken photos of the dumpsite where the boy was found and uploaded them, and after the sheriff's office shut her down, it was she who'd unearthed a photograph of the dress from the *Herald*'s archives at the library.

She shivered. The sandwich was finished, and she hoovered up the last of the crumbs with her finger. She scrolled down past the description page. No one had commented on the case for almost a year, and her username jumped out at her, a window into the past. Old Ellie. Happy Ellie. Thin Ellie. Rainbowbrite Ellie.

Thread dated: July 17/2016

Rainbowbrite [moderator]: Could everyone share the pic of the prom dress on social media? Might help lead us to the Boy's identity, or to whoever did this horrible crime.

Zanzibarb: Done! Is there a clearer picture of it?

Rainbowbrite [moderator]: Thanks Zanzibarb ☺ I'll keep asking the county if they can provide us with a better one and more details about material, size etc. I'll also check with the *Herald* and try and locate the original pic.

Zanzibarb: It might not be a prom dress. It could be a bridesmaid's dress.

Rainbowbrite [moderator]: Good point!! Here's the description I'm using BTW: 1950s style, pale pink (faded?), fitted bodice, flared skirt, knee-length, satin and tulle most likely, size around 8–10.

Zanzibarb: Hand made? Or could be vintage?

Rainbowbrite [moderator]: It's so hard to tell isn't it? ☹

MaydayMayday: That dress is some freaky serial killer shit right?

Bobbiecowell: Don't jump to conclusions. Not sure the dress is a signature.

MaydayMayday: Why would someone dress him up like that if it wasn't like a personal thing?

Bobbiecowell: This scene was staged. The killer attempted to mask the Boy's identity and knew what he was doing. Don't let the dress derail you. He's done it before. We should look for similar cases we can link up. Could be that the dress is a misdirection. Perp wanted LE to focus on it, take the investigation down a particular route.

MaydayMayday: Perp?? You trying to sound like you're LE or something?

Bobbiecowell: 20 year vet. NYPD. Retired.

Rainbowbrite [moderator]: Great to have you on the team Bobbie!!!!

Bobbiecowell. He'd worked the case as diligently as she had. They'd corresponded privately for a month or so about it. It used to give her a thrill every time she received one of his emails – a real-life detective talking to *her*. Noah used to tease her about that, too: 'You're in a good mood, El, got another message from your boyfriend?' Bobbie had some interesting theories, thought it might be linked to the unsolved murder of a young man in Louisville, even attempted to use his contacts to prise more information out of the county. Then the shit hit the fan, Ellie was kicked off the site, and she lost touch with him. Not true. She hadn't lost touch – she'd disappeared. If it did look like there was an identity for the boy, then he deserved to know.

Ellie couldn't put it off any longer. She clicked on the link, and compared the composite portrait with the photograph. At first glance there was a definite resemblance – the Irish boy had the same asymmetrical features and skewed mouth. She shut her eyes, opened them, then looked again. Doubt crept in. It could be because the photograph showed someone bursting with life, the hair was shorter and darker and it wasn't a full-face profile like the composite image.

But her gut said it was him. Could she trust her gut? It had been wrong before.

She tiptoed upstairs to check on Noah. He was snoring lightly. Then she made the kids some more popcorn to keep them busy. They were best friends again, sitting side by side, inches from the screen.

Her armpits began to dampen as she dialled Chris's number.

Chris picked up immediately. 'Is it him?'

'I think so.'

'You only *think* so?'

'That composite wasn't the best.'

'Yeah, but there's something there, right?'

'Right. Do you still have that guy who was good at facial recognition on the site? That artist who used to work for Disney – the one who does the age progression stuff? He might be able to compare the photograph with the reconstruction and say for sure.'

'Contacted him already. He's been AWOL from the forum for a while, but he gave it a look. Says the angle isn't ideal for a comparison. Mommydearest has tried with open source software, but it's not a hundred percent. And it doesn't match with anything on Google Images.'

'Who's Mommydearest?'

'New mod. He's thorough, knows what he's doing.'

'Right.' Despite Ellie's efforts, loss stained her voice.

'According to the description, this Irish guy was last seen in New York. That's a long way from Minnesota.'

'He could've travelled here easily.'

'Yep.'

'Do we know why he wasn't reported missing before now?'

'No.'

'Chris . . . Why did you come to me with this?'

A pause. 'Didn't seem fair not to. You worked him for months. It was your case.'

'I appreciate that. Look, what happened last time . . .'

'You fucked up.'

'Well now, there's no call to use that kind of language. How many times have I apologised?'

More dead air, then: 'You're right. The past is the past, Ellie. Let's get over it.'

'You mean that?'

'I mean that.' She sighed. 'You got to swear not to put any of this out there. I don't want this plastered all over Twitter. Not till we're sure.'

'I won't. I *swear* I won't. Jeez, Chris, c'mon, you can trust me.' Ellie was now gripping the handset so tightly her fingers ached.

'So the first step is to contact the guy who posted the pic. The nephew.'

'Oh . . . oh. He thinks his uncle's alive.'

'Yeah. We can't string him along. I ask again, how sure are you that the pic is a match?'

We. Like she was part of this again. 'Um, eighty, ninety percent?'

'Which is it, eighty or ninety?'

'Eighty.'

'Either way, Teddy Ryan should be officially listed as missing. I've checked Interpol, Irish missing person sites and NamUs and he's not on them.'

Ellie paced, blood fizzing like Alka-Seltzer. 'Listen, if it is this guy and we do have an ID, we should work this case. You should think about opening it for sleuthing.' More dead air. She'd blurted it out without thinking. But she was right. She knew she was right, and she'd paid for her past mistakes. 'You still there, Chris?'

'I moved away from that after the Callie Forrest fuck-up. That guy's life was ruined because of what—'

'I get that. I *do*. But we were a good team. If it is this guy, we should work it. Stenton County dropped the ball on the investigation, and there's no guarantee that they'll look into it even if they do get an ID.' Chris didn't reply, and again Ellie was left listening to the *whoompf* of her pulse in her ears. 'This could be big for Missing-Linc, Chris. Let me in on this. If you don't do it, Reddit or one of the other sites will and you'll lose out.'

'You threatening me?'

'*Threatening* you? No, of course not! Do I sound like I'm threatening you?'

'The site's not about that any more.'

'But . . . Don't you miss it?'

'No.'

And then Ellie said something she knew she'd regret: 'You found your mom yet, Chris?'

Click.

Bobbiecowell

'Driving while you're on your phone is *dang*erous. I could be *kill*ed.'

'You're right, Tasha.' Pete dropped the iPhone onto his lap.

'Who are you messaging anyway? Mom?'

'Work stuff.'

'Why do you have that look on your face if it's just *work*?'

'What look?'

'Like you were *smi*ling.'

'Was I? Work must be going well then, huh? Hey, you want to stop for a vanilla shake?'

'No. It's un*healthy*.' She blew on the passenger side window and ran a finger through the cloud on the glass, knowing full well this annoyed the hell out of him. 'Why are *you* picking me up anyway?'

'I told you. Your mom's working late again and I offered.' It didn't hurt to bank the brownie points with Margie. 'How was band practice?'

'Like *you* care.'

He tightened his grip on the steering wheel. He could cope with the insolence, but her verbal tic, that emphasis on a random syllable, really needled at him. A while back he heard himself using it on a client: 'See, the basement needs *clad*ding to stop the *damp* from getting *in*.'

He flicked on the radio, turned it up too loud, tried to lose himself in some bubble-gum song. Tasha slid out of the truck the instant he pulled to a stop in the driveway. He took his time. The house was one of the few properties in the area that wasn't overlooked by the neighbours, and today the Sound was the rare, azure blue of a real-estate agent's brochure. The lines of the bridge sliced across the water, disappearing into the haze on the other side. Vista View was as safe as it got, and he'd chosen it carefully. If he had to leave, he'd miss it.

Tasha pushed past him as he disabled the alarm, and with a last disdainful glance made for her room.

'Remember the rules,' he called after her in Cheery, Unflappable Pete's voice. 'No games until after you've done your homework.'

'You're not my *dad*, you can't tell me what to *do*.' Her door slammed. If he did move on, it would be because of Tasha and he had no one to blame but himself. He knew the score when he hooked up with Margie, broke his rule about never getting involved with women with kids. Tasha was tenacious; hadn't deviated from her campaign of passive aggression since he'd moved in. And she was smart, toned it down when her mom was around.

He wiped down the kitchen counters then flumped into the leather recliner Margie had bought him as a moving in gift. The subreddit he was absorbed in earlier had fallen off the front page, and in any case no one was getting worked up enough to make it worth pursuing. As he scrolled through his Twitter feeds, a message alert came in. A forwarded email from one of his linked accounts – one he hadn't used for months:

From: Ellen Caine <rainbowbrite66@gmail.com>
To: Bobbie Cowell <bobbiesammycowell@gmail.com>

Hi Bobbie, sorry I haven't touched base for a while. Hope you're doing just great. I wanted to let you know we might have an identity for the Boy in the Dress. Thought you should know seeing as you were so involved in the case. It's confidential for now, but I know I can trust you to keep it to yourself!!! ☺

Best, Ellen (Rainbowbrite!!!)

A punch in the gut; the room faded. He was sucked into the depths of the chair, inhaled into a bottomless hole, his blood pulsing and roaring. He rode it out, shook his hands, and focused on the portrait of Tasha and Margie above the fireplace: filled his vision with Margie's bleached smile and Tasha's bored, faraway gaze. Little by little, things realigned. His breathing steadied, the fist in his solar plexus unfurled.

Here it was again, bobbing to the surface, a bloated corpse that refused to stay weighted down. The case was featured on other sites, but those weren't open for comments, and they didn't have a Rainbowbrite poking and prodding and digging and pushing. Interest in the case had died when she'd drifted off the site. He read the email again, then logged on to Missing-Linc as Bobbiecowell. He'd been dipping his toes into other cases occasionally, but there were no new updates on the Boy's page. One of his old messages jumped out at him: **<These things take time. H e'll slip up eventually. These guys always do>**

Oh the irony.

A workout session might help, but there were other, more effective ways to de-stress.

Pete removed his boots and socks, unlocked the bifold doors and headed out onto the deck. The deck he'd built. The deck that had got him here. The railings, each hand-turned; the slats, perfectly aligned. *Artisanal craftmanship at its finest.* The moment he'd decided this would be his next stop was imprinted in his memory: the chafe of the knee pads, the thunk of the nail gun, the sun warming the back of his neck, and the seductive glimpse of his future self lounging on a recliner, taking in the view and sipping a morning cappuccino. Working on Margie had been a slog – she was smarter than the average bear – but he'd chipped away at her defences. He'd spent years honing that craft, too.

There was a loose tack at the edge, and he held onto the rail and stamped on it until it popped through his heel's calloused skin. A spike of pain, then a low throb.

The house phone was ringing. It cut off, and a door banged. Through the tinted glass he made out Tasha approaching.

'. . . *yes*, I'm doing my homework, Mom. Yes, he's here. How would I know why he isn't answering his phone?' She handed him the receiver. 'She wants to talk to *you*.'

'Thanks, Tash!' he said, loud enough for Margie to hear.

Tasha grimaced. 'Ew, why is there *blood*?'

'Did she just say blood?' Margie said.

'It's nothing. Stubbed my toe.'

Tasha mouthed: 'You're *gross*,' then ran off.

'I tried your number, Pete. There was no answer.'

He made himself smile – it'd come through in the words: 'Must've run out of juice. How's work, hon?'

'I'm ovulating.'

'Great!'

'You don't sound pleased.'

'I am. You know I am, Margie.'

'Really?'

'*Really*, hon. Why wouldn't I be?' The chickens were coming home to roost all at once. He was the one who'd planted the seed, building the fantasy that he was in it for the long haul. Painting a picture of an older, stable father who was good with his hands, a real partner who'd haul his weight, leaving her free to pursue her career. He'd assumed she wouldn't go for it; misjudged that one. She was forty-four, the last chance saloon. He paced, leaving more dime-sized spots on the pale wood. It would stain; he'd skimped on the sealant.

'Have you thought about what I said? About you getting checked out? It's just with the chemo you had back then . . .'

'I have. And you're right. Gotta build up to it though. You know how I feel about doctors.' He could only push this line so far. He had the scars to prove it, but it was making him weaker in her eyes – *surely your love for me is more powerful than your phobia, Pete?* 'I'll do it, Margie.'

'Really? I'll come with you. You don't have to do this alone.'

'You're sweet.'

A pause. 'Did you hear back from any of those estimates?'

She couldn't help herself. As if money was an issue. 'I did.' *Smile.* 'They want to negotiate, so the margin might be too slim. Got to do the numbers.'

'That the kitchen remodelling one? In Ruston?'

There was too much noise in his head to concentrate. This was how mistakes happened. *Wrap it up.* 'Yeah. Oh hey – my phone's ringing in the house. Could be them now.'

'Thought you said it was out of juice?'

'Must've been mistaken. Hurry home now, you hear?'

'I will.'

'Bye, hon. Love ya.'

'You too.'

He double-checked the call was disconnected. Paranoia – another sign he was losing his grip. Stupid. *Stupid.* He waited for the foot to stop bleeding, then went inside, filled a bowl with cold soapy water and mopped up the deck. The blood had dried in places, and he had to pick at it with his nails. Shouldn't have done that. Not with Tasha around. As he cleaned, he let his mind off its leash and allowed it to travel down the alleyways that were usually out of bounds. He could do this. He could control this. He was *good* at this, he'd just lost the knack. It had been a while.

Softly, softly, catchee monkey.

Back inside, he composed a message to Rainbowbrite: **<A wesome to hear from you after so long. H ow are the twins doing? A n ID? H ow sure are you?>**

No answer. He tried again, this time remembering to ape Rainbowbrite's tendency to over-punctuate and litter her messages with emojis. *Flatter the subject by mirroring their style of communication.* **<You have a name? Would appreciate being kept in the loop! ! ! ☺>**

Nothing.

He crept along the hallway and listened at Tasha's door. There was no sound from within. She could be getting up to anything in there, hacking the Kremlin, hounding schoolmates to suicide on Facebook. Fairly confident that he wouldn't be disturbed, he padded down to the basement, through his workshop – ordered, neat, the tools greased and cared for – and into the side room. It was full of what Margie called his 'boy toys': snowboards, mountain bikes, camping gear – all carefully battered as if they were well loved and used – his weights, gym mat and, hidden in plain sight, his stepfather's old lockbox and its dangerous cargo. The gun safe was Margie's only claim to the space. Her firearm fetish and NRA membership were the only things about her that didn't add up. She said she'd caught the bug from an old college friend who used to blow off steam at the firing range, but there was something more there. In every other way she was as liberal as you could get. Pro-choice, a Democrat, campaigned against the unfair treatment of immigrants.

He sat cross-legged in front of the safe and placed the phone within easy reach. When it finally buzzed he made himself wait for exactly a minute before he read the message.

<H ey Bobbie! Isn't it A MA Z ING? It's an Irish guy and it's lookin good! ! ! ! Got to keep it q uiet for now until it's confirmed. Twins are good they love their new school still! H ow are you?>

He closed his eyes, regulated his breathing, then picked at the scab on his heel until the wound started leaking again.

Wicklowboy22

<I knew your uncle he died of aids it was slow>

<F or only a small fee I can locate your missing relation and I guarantee a successful outcome I have many satisfied customers>

<he's a cute twink lemme know if u find him;) >

<I make 3 0 0 0 0 dollars a month working from home! F ind ou how by going to CV r.7 7 .org>

<L ooking for hot guys? Check out www.menhoney.org.net>

<H e looks familiar. Think I've seen him hanging around bed stuy>

Shaun had replied to that one, only to get a request for three hundred dollars to cover 'travel expenses and incidentals'. He'd posted his 'have you seen my uncle?' appeal on every 'get back in touch' site he could find, and the email account he'd set up for the purpose was full of spam and worse. He refused to let it get him down – it had only been a couple of days.

He'd thought about printing some 'have you heard from this man' posters and putting them up around the town, like the missing person flyers he'd seen scattered around the estuary, but decided against it. Janice would lose her shite if she saw them, and in any case the chances of Teddy resembling his younger self were slim. He could be the size of a house by now; he could be addicted to plastic surgery and unrecognisable. Twenty-two years and not a word. And saying he was dead to stop his mother going after him . . . Shaun knew his grandparents could be brutal, but that was beyond the pale. Janice was holding something back, he was sure of it. Could Teddy have got himself into trouble with the guards, gone on the run? Why else wouldn't his mother have told him he was alive?

Shaun had propped the photo of his mother and her siblings next to the till, and his eye kept being drawn to it. *You're just like him, Shauny. Teddy reincarnated.* His mother's words. He'd been mining for the things she used to say about Teddy, and they were trickling back. Antsy, he went into the shop's tiny kitchen for a fortifying brew. Daphne flapped her tail half-heartedly as he passed through the office. It was small, the hope, a seedling of a thing, but he'd been allowing himself to nurture it. His escape fund, depleted by vet and phone bills, was only sitting at three hundred and sixty euros. Not enough for a flight to JFK and the other costs this would entail. He couldn't ask Máirín for a raise, the shop was barely breaking even, but when she returned from abroad and picked up the slack, he could always take a second job. And who knew, perhaps Teddy would pay for his flight. The dog was an issue, but Máirín might watch her or he could get Daphne a pet passport and take her with him. His fantasies of this possible new future were shifting dangerously close to maladjusted daydreaming. He'd been picturing himself as a clerk in a Greenwich Village bookstore, a barista in a Williamsburg deli. He'd even gone so far as to plan his wardrobe: a tartan scarf in winter (he'd always wanted one), a vintage linen shirt with rolled up sleeves in summer.

He laced the tea with extra sugar, and returned to the shop. A familiar figure was pacing up and down outside the window, smoking and glancing nervously at the door as if he were a porn shop customer steeling himself to go inside. It was Johnny. There was relief that he didn't have to track him down, and a sliver of disquiet – Johnny was right about Teddy but that didn't make him less of a weirdo. At least today Johnny was looking less like a recently disinterred fifties throwback – clean-shaven and wearing a zip-up leather jacket that Shaun recalled seeing in the Oxfam shop window. Johnny caught his eye and gestured for Shaun to join him outside.

Shaun poked his head around the door. 'Are you not coming in?'

'Having a smoke, aren't I? Thought you'd come and find me before now, son. You speak to Janice?'

'You were right. Teddy went to New York.'

'Came clean did she?' He coughed, a phlegmy nightmare of a thing that should be used in an anti-smoking ad. 'Janice isn't so bad. Sorry I told you like that. I wasn't in my right mind that day.'

'I've been trying to find him online.'

'Any luck?'

'Not yet.'

'Keep trying, son. Shall we go for a drink?'

'I don't drink.'

'I do.'

Shaun considered. He had to pick Johnny's brain – might as well do it now. And he had to take the dog out at some stage. 'I can't leave the shop for long.'

'I know a place.'

Shaun retrieved his coat and the dog's lead, and flipped the 'back in five minutes' sign on the door. Daphne went straight for Johnny's shoes, but this time, when he bent to stroke her, she didn't snap at him, surprising them all. 'Will you look at that?' Johnny said.

Terry from the cafe wasn't around to gawp at Shaun's companion, thank God, but as they walked up towards the main road, a pair of elderly women approaching on the other side nudged each other. 'Hey, Elvis!' one of them called: 'Give us a tune!'

Johnny paused and for a second Shaun was afraid he was going to rage at them. Then he twisted his mouth into a passable Elvis sneer, posed and said: 'Ladies, Elvis has left the building. Ahhh thank-you-very-much.'

The women screamed with laughter.

They walked on, and Johnny shook his head. 'I'm always getting that.'

'Can't think why.'

'Alright, son. No need to be sarcastic. You're one to talk. What do you call that get-up? English country gentleman?'

Shaun shrugged. Máirín said he dressed like Truman Capote, which he chose to find flattering. He always wore a vintage linen shirt, tweed suit and waistcoat – all natural fibres, they knew how to make clothes fifty years ago. It was his only outward quirk and another link to his mother, who was a fiend for vintage.

Johnny was making for a nondescript doorway slotted between a struggling estate agency and the long-dead toyshop. 'In here.'

Shaun had passed the pub a thousand times, but had never been inside it. Unlike the bars that depended on the tourist trade, this had a defiant lack of 'olde worlde' charm: all Formica tables, laminate flooring and strip lighting that wouldn't look out of place in a morgue. Apart from an elderly man curled over a flat pint in the corner, they were the only customers. Johnny slapped a palm on the bar. 'Hoy! Service.'

A short-haired woman with arms like a wrestler's emerged from a back room. She checked them out through myopic eyes. 'Oh it's you, John. You going to behave yourself today?'

'Might do. This is Shaun. Shaun, this is Molly, queen of all she surveys.'

The woman gave him a nod that was as dour and unwelcoming as the pub itself. 'From Máirín's shop?'

'That's right.'

'What'll you be having?'

Johnny ordered a pint of Bulmers and a double Bushmills. Shaun asked for a Diet Coke.

When the drinks were slopped onto the counter, Johnny patted his pockets. 'Bit short this month.'

Shaun paid, and Johnny raised his pint glass. 'Cheers.' Molly drifted back to the room behind the bar.

Time to pry. 'Janice says you went off to London with Teddy.'

'Got out as soon as we could. You ever thought of getting out of here? Eileen was always talking about it. She was desperate to come with us to London.'

'Can't. I've got the dog.'

'That's your excuse is it?'

'It's not an excuse.' But it was. He wavered between resenting Daphne and dreading the thought of her not being around. 'Mam never mentioned you.'

'Hated me, didn't she? Blamed me for taking her brother off to London like that. Was the other way round, but. He was the one who pushed for us to go. Stubborn bastard.'

'You and Teddy were close then?'

'Best friends. Since we were thirteen.'

You are the company you keep. What did that say about Teddy? Not a lot, but people could change. 'But you were never . . . you know.'

'Never what?'

'Together.' *Please God no.*

Johnny choked on his pint. 'Christ Jesus no. What the fuck made you say that? I look like a queer to you?'

'Had to ask it.'

'No you bloody didn't.'

'But you always knew Teddy was gay?'

Johnny shrugged. 'Told me a couple of months after we arrived in London. Didn't have a clue until then. He chased girls same as I did, said he'd ridden Maureen Murray, and maybe he had. He came out with it one night after we'd been drinking. "I've got something to tell you, Johnny. I like men." I thought he was messing with me at first. When I found out he was serious, I lost it.' Johnny leaned in close, the sour milk stench less potent today, and tapped a scar above his eye. 'Teddy did that. He was wiry, built like you, but he was a scrapper, gave as good as he got. And he was right to do it. Took me a while to get my head around it. It's the way I was brought up, see.'

'Janice says he only came out to the family when he returned from London. They were mortified. Said he was getting into fights about it.'

'That sounds like him, alright.'

'He was violent?'

'Like I say, always gave as good as he got.'

Shaun put this to one side to pick over later. He knew Teddy was a tearaway, but violence didn't gel with his mother's stories. 'Did he leave London because he found out Mam was pregnant?'

A shifty look came into Johnny's eyes. He knocked back the whiskey. 'Let's go and have a smoke.'

Shaun followed Johnny down a corridor that reeked of the gents' and out into a walled-in gulag of a place, the floor a graveyard of cigarette butts. Shaun lifted Daphne onto the solitary bench and offered the packet of Vogues to Johnny.

'What the hell are these?'

'Eileen's brand. I'm used to them now.'

'Go on then.'

The slender cigarette looked ridiculous in Johnny's hairy fingers. He ripped off the filter, held it between his thumb and forefinger like a gangster and lit up. 'Not bad.'

'You were saying why Teddy left.'

'You were right about it being because of your mother. He heard Eileen had got herself knocked up and been sent away by the family. He was going back to help her. That's all I know. Week or so after he left I called home, heard he'd been killed in a car accident. That almost finished me off.'

'How did you know he was sent to New York?'

A pause. Johnny stroked Daphne's head and she nudged his hand for more. 'He sent me a note. Only short. He wasn't much for writing. Said that he was alive, not to listen to the shite the family were saying about him and that he'd gone to New York. He was always saying he wanted to go there. Had a thing for the States, we both did.'

Hope kindled. 'Did it have an address on it?'

'No, just a . . . whatdoyoucallit – poste restante. He said he was staying at a YMCA.'

'Have you still got it?'

'Come over to the house and I'll give it to you. You can see for yourself.'

'I have to get back to work.'

'I don't mean now. Tomorrow evening if you like. We can have a drink.'

Shaun checked the time – he'd been gone too long. One more question: 'What was Teddy like?'

'He was loud. In your face. You were never bored with Teddy around. He was a real one for getting people to do what he wanted.' His voice faltered.

'He was manipulative?'

'You could say that. And wild. Did Eileen tell you about the time he got up on the roof of the school?'

'She did.' The Teddy tales were trickling back into his memory, too. 'It's a wonder she didn't look for him.' Or maybe she had. He might never know: her computer and its search history were long gone to the hard drive in the sky. 'What did Teddy want to be?'

'Be?'

'As a career?'

Johnny snorted. 'Career. Back then all we wanted was enough cash to get the next drink. What do you want to be?'

'I don't know.' Eileen had always encouraged him to be whoever or whatever he wanted to be, but this had backfired when he announced to the class he wanted to be a poet. They'd ripped him to pieces for that, and he'd come home crying. 'Ignore them, Shauny,' she'd said. 'You'll be out of here soon. We both will.' But they never got the chance to leave, because then Eileen's brain exploded and Shaun gave up on dreams of being a writer, gave up on dreams of being anything. 'Am I like him in other ways?'

'Don't know you well enough to say. You've got a quieter way about you. And you work in that book shop. That's a good thing. Never knew Teddy to read a word. Eileen was different. Animals and books. That was her thing.'

'Who else did he hang around with? Maybe they've heard from him.'

'Back then it was me, Teddy and Pat Carey. Donny and his crowd on occasion.'

'I was at school with some of the Careys.'

'Bunch of cunts.'

'They weren't so bad.' They'd left him alone for the most part. 'Would he have got hold of Pat over the years?'

'Last person he would've got hold of. Fell out with him before we went to London.'

'Why?'

'Pat was a difficult bastard. Thought he was better than everyone else.'

'I'll have to talk to Donny then.'

Johnny looked away. 'Heard he's back.'

'Yeah. He is. He's moved to Brittas Bay.' The last time Shaun had encountered Donny was at Eileen's funeral. He and his wife Carmel had flown in and out on the same day, tanned, flashy and fully up themselves. Shaun had a vague memory of Donny inviting him to stay with them in Spain, but it could be false. He couldn't remember much of that day other than feeling the bite of Máirín's rings as she squeezed his hand and concentrating on the plaster of Paris Jesus that hung above the lectern. Someone had ineptly retouched Jesus's stigmata – his palms were dripping with blood the colour of strawberry jam – and the only thing that kept him from howling was imagining how hilarious his mother would've found that.

'Why didn't you challenge the family about this before, Johnny?'

'Like I said, cut my ties with the place. Been away.'

'In London?'

'In London. No reason to come back till now.'

Time to go.

Johnny gave Shaun his address – which was just around the corner from Janice's estate – then said: 'Get me a top up on your way out, son.'

Jack Devilly slapped a copy of *Beyond Black* on to the counter. 'This any good?'

'It's in the "staff recommendations" section.' Shaun turned his attention back to the shop's monitor screen.

'But is it any good?'

'Why else would it be in the staff recommends?'

'I know *that*.' He shuffled. 'But is it any *good*?'

'No, you're right. That's where we put all the shite.'

'Thought so.' Jack went triumphantly back to the main display. Máirín threw him out of the shop whenever he appeared, but Shaun didn't have the heart to oust him. He was harmless enough, but had been known to shoplift on occasion.

Keeping half an eye on Jack, Shaun went back to running through the new messages in his 'wicklowboy22' account. Most had been automatically relegated into spam, thank God. Delete, delete, delete, then:

From: ratking1@missingLadmin.com
To: wicklowboy22@gmail.com
RE: Edward Ryan

To whom it may concern,
I run a forum that specialises in identifying the remains of missing people. Edward Ryan has a resemblance to an unidentified man on our site who was found deceased in 1996.

I understand that this is a sensitive matter and I apologise for contacting you like this.

Has Edward Ryan been officially reported missing? I have done a cursory search and he is not listed on Interpol or NamUs (National Missing and Unidentified Persons System).

I've attached a link to the composite portrait of our John Doe.

It is important to stress that until a DNA test has been done, an identity cannot be confirmed. The autopsy report lists a broken arm, so it is possible that X-rays could potentially be used to confirm an ID.

Regards,
Chris

It was more articulate than the others, more convincing. He re-read it, then let the cursor hover over the link, warning bells jangling. *Don't do it. No turning back.* But how could he not? *Click.* A face looked back at him, empty eyes, as soulless as a mugshot.

'What about this?' Jack waved a copy of *The Spinning Heart* in his face.

'Out.'

'But . . .'

'Out. *Now.*'

Jack stuffed the book down his trousers and then ran out of the shop. Shaun let him go.

He looked again, clicking back and forth from the dead-eyed portrait and the photo propped on the till. *It's him; it's not him; it's him; it's not him.* It came over him at once: nausea, numb fingers, an elevated pulse rate.

He stood, flexed his hands. Paced into the children's section, stared up at the inept *Matilda* mural his mother had painted when she'd first started working here. He returned to the counter. Now he couldn't feel his fingers at all; the nerve endings may as well have been severed. It had been years since he'd had a panic attack, he'd lost the knack of dealing with them. Icy sweat, bitter saliva. *Out. Air. Fresh air. Now.*

He was dimly aware of the door banging behind him, vaguely aware that his feet were taking him over the bridge, following the path that snaked past the estuary. He picked up his pace, shoes sliding on the slick concrete, but he kept going, only slowing to a jog when his lungs began to ache. On past the half-finished playground and skate park, all the way to the underpass where the kids came to smoke and drink. Breath now coming in shallow gasps, he bent double and stared down at the broken bottles and cigarette ends. The walls here were scrawled with graffiti. He used to come here and look for his mother's name among the curse words and declarations of love, and his father's, before he met him and realised Eileen was right about him being a waste of space. He did so now, looking for Teddy's name, too.

It might not be him. The picture of that head with its bland, dead eyes was nothing like the photograph of Teddy.

Dead. Teddy hadn't been in contact because he couldn't. His twenty-two years of silence explained. Cold comfort. And what the hell was Shaun doing out here? He was being histrionic – he'd never actually known Teddy. His overreaction wasn't from grief or shock. It was the loss of the hope of it. *You're Teddy reincarnated, Shaun.*

He picked up a stone and hurled it at the wall, the action bringing him back to himself. Now he could feel the damp in the air; he'd left without his greatcoat, without the dog. Had he even locked the shop?

He hurried back, this time following the path that looped parallel to the estuary. Beyond the chain-link fence, a plastic bottle bobbing downstream kept pace with him. In the distance, the top of the old stone church rose to meet the sky. From here, the town looked picturesque, unsullied, a world away from the boarded-up shops and scars of recession. Teddy could have walked this way a thousand times. As he reached the first bridge a poster on a lamppost caught his eye. It was of a missing man, Keith O'Neill. Last seen two years ago. Another lost soul.

Daphne was waiting by the door, shaky with separation anxiety. He was shaking too, but that could be because he'd left without his coat.

'Sorry, girl.'

Shaun busied himself around the shop, reorganising the stacks, dusting the storeroom, but it didn't help. It was too quiet for a Saturday afternoon, and for once he didn't want to be alone. He gave in, broke the rules and texted Brendan – he was never the one who initiated their hook-ups. Thought for a second, then added: **<bring vodka>**

'Can you leave that?'

'Sure.' Brendan placed the bottle back on the side table.

The first effect of the alcohol, a woolly euphoria that Shaun had missed and dreaded, was making way for his old friend melancholia. There was a reason he didn't drink. It changed his personality, drew him into dark places. Inviting Brendan over had been a mistake.

'Are you okay, Shaun?' He must be in a state if Brendan was picking up on his distress.

'Fine, darling.' He wrapped himself in the duvet and prayed for Brendan to hurry the hell up. It wasn't like the man to linger – *Eats, Shoots and Leaves* was more Brendan's style – but he'd been pottering around the bed for the last ten minutes, arse winking ridiculously whenever he bent to retrieve a piece of clothing. Shaun feigned a yawn. 'Isn't Ashling expecting you back?'

'Told her I'm working late.'

'Ah right.' Stymied – Brendan wasn't one for taking a hint.

'Oh, almost forgot,' Brendan dug in his man bag and lobbed a packet of Vogue Slims onto the bed. 'Bought you these as well.'

'That was thoughtful.'

'Can't come here empty-handed, can I?'

'Why not? I'm not a rent boy, darling.'

Stop it. The camp act Shaun used on Brendan and only Brendan had more of a hollow ring to it than usual. *End it now.* He should, knew he should, made this resolution every week and never went through with it. Their set-up was too convenient: a functional outlet safe from the dangers of emotional involvement.

On with the trousers – black, conventional, very *Brendan* – then a pit-stop to inspect his hair in the mirror above the sink. Bland Brendan. Safe Brendan. Short back and sides, loved his mother, one of the lads, did well at school, looked after his body, went to mass. *Married* Brendan. Shaun was his only dirty secret. 'How're you fixed for next weekend? Ashling's got a thing with the girls next Saturday. She won't be back till midnight.'

It was only a matter of time before Ashling found porn on her husband's MacBook or followed him here. Shaun barely knew her – she'd been four years ahead of him at school, one of the anonymous hair-flicking masses – but no one deserved this. Rationalising that she must know about Brendan's dual life and was turning a blind eye to it didn't cut it any more, although that might be true. Brendan was as useless at dissembling as he was at taking a hint. Shaun reached for the bottle.

Concern was now etched all over Brendan's large flat face, dripped from his cow eyes. A new side to the man, or one that Shaun had never bothered to see. Shaun knew every inch of Brendan's body, but never dug deeper than the surface. 'You sure you're okay? It's just . . . I've never seen you drink before, and you've been knocking that stuff back like it's water.'

'First time for everything.'

'Did something happen at work?'

'No. Work's fine.'

'Is it me?'

'What?'

Brendan perched on the corner of the bed. 'Have I done something to piss you off?'

'No.'

'If you need to talk to someone, you can always—'

'I'm *fine*.'

'Okay, okay.'

'Sorry.' He wasn't sorry. He wasn't sorry at all. He bit back the rest of what needed to be said. The vodka sat in his guts like muck in a drain.

'I'm here if you—'

'Look, Brendan, can you not just take the hint and fuck off?'

Daphne whined; Brendan flinched. Without looking at him, Brendan grabbed his jacket and stalked out.

Shaun closed his eyes, felt the world move. Opened them, reached for the drink and his phone.

The Boy in the Dress. There was something callous about that name. Callous and anonymous. Drinking from the bottle, he brought up the page. At the top of the site there was a link to 'success stories'. There were only three. A man who'd been hit by a car in the late nineties and who was eventually identified by a tattoo on his ankle; a Mexican fellow whose remains were discovered in scrubland outside San Antonio and whose family recognised his facial reconstruction; and a man known as Underground Doe who was found lying in a culvert and who was identified by his surgical scars.

Shaun scrolled through the photographs of the place where the boy's body had been found. With its patches of dirty snow it could be anywhere. The pic of the dress was blurry, but it looked to be a stained rag of a thing. The whole thing was tawdry. Tawdry, cruel and sad. Underneath it strangers were discussing the boy's death as if it was some sort of game.

The body of a young man was found . . . .

You're the spit of him.

The room spun. He couldn't rest. He needed to know.

From: wicklowboy22@gmail.com
To: ratking1@missingLadmin.com
RE: Edward Ryan

This is Shaun Ryan you left a message on my email. How sure are you that this is my uncle? Is this him?

From: ratking1@missingLadmin.com
To: wicklowboy22@gmail.com

Hi Shaun,
Thank you for responding to my email.

It is important to stress that until a DNA test has been done, an identity cannot be confirmed. We have done a facial comparison using open source software and there are some similarities to your uncle's bone structure but this is not a definitive match.

If Edward Ryan has not been officially reported as missing then I encourage you to do so immediately. It is possible that you will have to contact multiple agencies, including Interpol and

Irish authorities to do this, as well as authorities in the state where he was last seen. It is unlikely that NamUs or the relevant authorities will conduct a DNA test until he is officially listed as missing.

Regards,

Chris

From: wicklowboy22@gmail.com
To: ratking1@missingLadmin.com

how long will a dna test take?

From: ratking1@missingLadmin.com
To: wicklowboy22@gmail.com

I can't give you a time frame on this as this varies from case to case and it is likely in this situation that multiple agencies will be involved.

To speed up the process it would be helpful if you could provide more details about your uncle's height/weight/appearance/identifying marks at the time he was last seen. The coroner's report lists a fracture to his left arm and a scar in his groin area. Can you confirm your uncle sustained these injuries?

Regards,

Chris

From: wicklowboy22@gmail.com
To: ratking1@missingLadmin.com

I don't know if he ever broke his arm. I don't know anything about him. can't wait for all this. do you think it's him? I need to know now just tell me how sure you are.

From: ratking1@missingLadmin.com
To: wicklowboy22@gmail.com

As all we have to go on at this stage is a possible similarity between the photograph and our UID's facial reconstruction, it would be negligent of me to comment further on this.

Again, I encourage you to report Edward Ryan missing in order for an official identification to be undertaken ASAP.

Regards,

Chris

From: wicklowboy22@gmail.com
To: ratking1@missingLadmin.com

Why cant you give me a straight answer I need to know now?

From: ratking1@missingLadmin.com
To: wicklowboy22@gmail.com

I understand that this is distressing for you.

I have answered your questions as clearly as I can.

Regards,

Chris

From: wicklowboy22@gmail.com
To: ratking1@missingLadmin.com

Why are you doing this I've seen your website and its like some sort of twisted game but this is peoples lives

From: wicklowboy22@gmail.com
To: ratking1@missingLadmin.com

Its okay for you you're just doing this as a sick hobby mendacious and cruel you are

From: wicklowboy22@gmail.com
To: ratking1@missingLadmin.com

Cold you're cold you don't know how this feels. its brutal to play with people like this what sort of a monster are you?

From: ratking1@missingLadmin.com
To: wicklowboy22@gmail.com

I understand you are distressed by this situation but there is NO CALL to insult me.

I will not enter into further correspondence if you continue to be abusive.

Regards,
Chris

From: wicklowboy22@gmail.com
To: ratking1@missingLadmin.com

sorry

Ratking1

It wasn't the first time Chris had received vitriolic emails from a searcher. It went with the territory; people lashed out when they were in pain. Didn't mean she had to take it. Didn't mean it didn't affect her when it happened.

It was the small, defeated 'sorry' that bit at her, and this: *You don't know how this feels . . . What sort of a monster are you?*

Sorry.

She should leave it alone. She knew she wouldn't.

From: christinaguzman123@gmail.com
To: wicklowboy22@gmail.com

Shaun, I understand if I came across as insensitive to what you are going through. I am not. This is my private email. If you would like to talk further add me to your contacts or we can WhatsApp.

If he didn't respond, at least she'd tried.

Mommydearest was on moderator and pending membership duty tonight, so now would be a rare chance to watch one of the shows Jeanie was always talking about or get some goddamned sleep. But she couldn't drag herself away from the screens. She cleaned the monitors with a tissue, then scanned the rest of the admin inbox. Scattered between progress reports from Mommydearest were five emails from Ellen. They were all along the lines of, 'I'm so sorry Chris, please forgive me for saying that about your mom,' and got progressively more desperate – the latest one was all in caps. Chris sent her a short message accepting her apology. Would she have done that if Shaun hadn't got to her? Nope. It was a cheap way of making herself feel better. Not that she'd done anything wrong. There was no easy way to break the kind of news she'd relayed to Shaun – but could she have softened the blow?

The message alert bleeped, and a pop-up appeared at the corner of the screen: **<this is shaun>**

<hi>

<sorry for ranting at you had a drink don't usually drink>

<No problem>

<I have to know. Is it him?>

<I'm going to sound like a stuck record here. There's a resemblance there but we can't be certain without a formal ID>

<A nd to be sure I have to go to the guards?>

<The first step is to officially file a missing person's report yes>

<ok>

<Can I ask why he wasn't reported missing before now?>

<We were all told he died in an accident years back the family lied about him & I recently found out they were lying & he might be in NYC>

Chris whistled through her teeth. This was a first. The majority of the long-term UIDs tended to be the missing-missing, the folks who'd fallen through the cracks: the unwanted child who'd been passed around so many relatives that it was years before anyone realised he'd been snatched; the woman with mental health issues whose family had disowned her and whose bones sat for decades in the anonymity of a coroner's cardboard box; the family man who'd crossed the border to look for work, and ended up in a mass grave in Brooks County. **<Why did they lie?>**

<family shite. part of it was because he was gay and my grandparents couldn't stand that and said he was dead to them and sent him away>

<A religion issue I'm guessing?>

<that's part of it too. They also didn't want my mother going after him because she was pregnant at the time. they lied to her too>

Jesus – and she'd thought *her* family history was a soap opera. **<must have been a shock for you learning all this>** Bland, safe, noncommittal.

<Do you run the website?>

He was changing the subject and Chris knew better than to pry until she knew exactly what she was dealing with. **<yep I started it>**

<Why do you do this? What do you get out of it?>

She gave him the standard answer, which was partly true: **<I lost my j ob a while back and it keeps me busy>**

<Who are you?>

<ex cuse me?>

<who are you as a person where do you live?>

<My name is Christina Guz man and I live in Nevada U S>

<las vegas?>

<nope town on the outskirts of Death V alley, about 1 0 0 miles from V egas. Not much to do here unless you're into rocks>

<death valley. apt seeing what you do>

This made her smile. **<didn't think of it like that before. Who are you?>** She added a smiley face emoji. She hated all that shit, but if she was going off script then she might as well go the whole hog.

<shaun ryan I work in a book shop in Wicklow>

<how old are you shaun?>

<2 2 >

She checked Facebook again – there were numerous Shaun Ryans on there, but a brief scroll yielded no matches for someone around that age in Wicklow.

<what time is it in Ireland?> Her phone buzzed with a text from Mack. She deleted it unread.

<4 a.m. Something like that. I can't sleep. What time is it there?>

<2 2 .1 3 >

<Do you want me to leave you alone?>

She was always telling the mods not to get involved or make promises, but screw it, they could be close to getting an official ID on the boy. **<I'm cool to chat if you are>**

<I never do this>

<Do what? Chat to strangers?>

<& drink. Don't know if I'm ready to know all this about teddy. I j ust found him and now he's gone again. My mother died 6 years ago & all I have left is Daphne>

<Is Daphne your girlfriend or sister?>

<No the dog>

Ha. **<I love dogs. What breed is she?>**

<some kind of terrier. the way that dress boy was killed. It's brutal. cant understand why anyone would do that in the comments they're saying it could be a serial killer>

<that's one theory>

<do you think he suffered horribly?>

What to say to that? Another message appeared, saving her from answering:

<in the snow like that. I looked up how far it is from new york it's a long way>

<Could he have gone to MN for work?>

<I don't know. There's a lot I don't know about him. So you're sure he's the Boy in the Dress then?>

<not saying that. J ust spit- balling here. Do you know where he was staying in NYC? Do you have family there?>

<no. a friend of Teddy's said he was staying at a YMCA >

<which one?>

<dont know>

Chris did a quick search. There were twenty-two YMCAs in NYC. Even if they did pin down where Teddy was staying, it was unlikely anyone would remember an Irish kid from two decades ago, but it was a start. **<how about the dress? any connection to him? Belonged to a relative maybe? Was Teddy into fashion? Drag maybe? Was he transitioning?>**

<I don't know. Teddy could still be alive couldn't he?>

<It's wise to manage your ex pectations>Now she was sounding like some dead-eyed grief counsellor. He wouldn't want to hear that hope could keep you going, but it also brought you to your knees. **<There's something else we can do to speed up the process and get more certainty. If we had a full- face photograph of Teddy we could forensically compare it to the drawing using open source facial recognition software>** She was on safer ground with this. Practical help.

<I only have that one but I'll see what I can get. can you use my DNA ?>

<Mitochondrial would be best. Is his mother still alive?>

<No. Died years back>

<Sorry>

<it's ok she was a right old cow. he's got a brother and sister but I don't know if they will help as they were in on the lie and don't want it coming out. It's enough to wreck your head>

<You find ways to cope with it. We can all be resilient if we choose to be> *Thank you, Dr Phil.*

<You must think I'm weak. I never knew him so I should get over myself>

<You're not weak Shaun. U ncertainty is a bitch. Do you want me to make a page for him on the site? I won't link it with the Boy in the Dress case until we have clarity on that> Mommydearest would make the connection in seconds, so would the others most likely. The reconstruction portrait wasn't the best, but there was something there. He didn't respond. **<We've got good people on the site who can share it. I can use your ex isting info as a base>**

<I don't want people talking about him like he's a thing or a game>

<We can disable the comments. We could mention the YMCA connection. L ong shot, but you never know who might come forward> Now who was sounding desperate? She was coming across like Rainbowbrite on a sugar high. She *wanted* this. And not just because Shaun needed answers. It had been a while since they'd made an ID. She was buzzing, felt like she'd just knocked back a double espresso. **<We can help. It'll be handled sensitively I promise>**

No answer. After five minutes she gave him a nudge: **<You still there?>** Could be that he'd passed out. She waited another five minutes. Then another. She was about to log off when the alert came in:

<ok>

'Hey.'

There was someone looming over her. Jeanie? Mack? Adrenaline blasted through the sleep fug and the figure came into focus. It was Scott – that goddamned guy from Jeanie's party. 'How the hell did you get in here?'

'The door was open. I knocked but there was no answer.'

'That doesn't give you the right to just barge on in.'

'Jeanie said it was okay to come in.'

Typical. 'Course she did.'

'Brought doughnuts.' He brandished a jumbo-sized Dunkin' pastry box.

'I see that. You leave any in the store?'

He grinned without showing his teeth. 'Didn't know which ones you like, so I got a selection.' The shock of being woken so abruptly fizzled away, and Chris's body showed the first signs of the high price she'd be paying for falling asleep in the chair again. She rolled her shoulders, trying and failing to ease the crick in her neck. 'What time is it?'

'Getting on for eleven.'

'Shit.' She wiped a palm over her face, brushing away a crackle of dried drool at the corner of her mouth. After she'd created the page for Teddy, she tried to switch her mind off with a couple of episodes of *Storage Wars*; didn't remember dozing off. 'Why are you here?'

'No reason. Just dropped in to say hi.' Today he was in a sleeveless Hawkwind tee, and in the light he looked older, his beard flecked with grey.

'You couldn't call first?'

'Didn't have the number. This was a bad idea. I can see you don't want me here.' He rubbed his free hand on his jeans, an oddly endearing show of nervousness from such a big guy, then turned to leave.

'Wait. You want coffee?' She was going soft. First Shaun, now this. Or maybe she just wanted a doughnut.

'You want me to make it?' Eager – too eager. Big red flag.

'Nope. Just give me a few, okay? Need to clean up.'

He stepped back to give Chris space. The aches and pains would drip feed their poison all day, but that was no one's fault but her own and she didn't show the discomfort on her face. Locking the bathroom door behind her, she risked a glance in the shaving mirror she'd set up at a low angle next to the sink. As expected she looked like crap. Her eyes were rimmed with red, and there was a seam of grease at her roots. Jeanie kept nagging her to dye out the grey, but once you started doing that you were stuck in a cycle. She brushed her teeth and dry swallowed her medication. She considered applying some blush – there was an old compact somewhere – but screw *that*.

When she emerged, Scott was hulked over the sink doing the washing up. The trailer was a double-wide, but the place seemed to shrink with him in it.

'You don't have to do that, Scott.'

'It's okay. I like doing it.'

The kitchen was the only area she hadn't yet converted, and she gripped the counter and got up from the chair to reach the coffee granules. 'I've only got instant.'

He was staring at her, as she knew he would. 'You can . . .'

'Stand? Yeah. I got limited movement.' Very limited, but he didn't need to know that. 'Don't look so shocked.'

'I'm not shocked.'

'You should see how people react if I get out of the chair to grab a box of Wheaties in the store. They either act like they're witnessing a medical miracle or think I'm some kind of charlatan.'

'I don't.'

'Good. Can you get the milk?'

He passed her the carton and she sniffed it. It was okay-ish. There was nothing else in the fridge, but he didn't comment on this. He collected the mugs from the draining board and waited while she made the coffee. The silence should be far more uncomfortable than it was. Her stomach rumbled, and she picked out a doughnut dusted in sugar. 'How come you're not working today, Scott?'

'It's Sunday.'

'Shit. Really?' She'd lost track of time again.

He grinned. 'Really.' Scott helped himself to the box. 'Hey, I joined Missing-Linc.'

'When?' Apart from Charlie, Jeanie's kid, no one she knew in real life had joined up. She wasn't sure how to feel about this.

'Last night.'

'What name did you use?'

'Aqualung. No one had taken it.'

'Yeah? Not sure there are that many Jethro Tull fanatics on the site.' Mommydearest must have verified it.

'I checked out GI Doe. And Dog Doe. Are you Ratking1 or Mommydearest?'

'Ratking.'

'You like rodents or something?'

She polished off the doughnut and licked her fingers. 'You know the book *Mrs. Frisby and the Rats of NIMH*?'

'Wasn't that a movie?'

'Both. It was my favourite book when I was a kid. Took it from there.'

'So why aren't you Rat Queen?'

'You get less hassle on the site if they think you're male.'

He considered this for a few seconds, then: 'Hey, how did that lead pan out? Were you talking about the T-shirt GI Doe was wearing?'

'Got side-tracked on that. Something else came up. Long story.'

'I got time.'

Maybe she was compromised by lack of sleep, maybe she just needed to talk, but she ended up telling him about Shaun, Teddy Ryan and the Boy in the Dress connection. He let her speak without interruption, his second doughnut forgotten in his hand. 'I think I pushed him too hard. Came on too strong.'

'Sounds to me like he needed to talk. You're trying to help him, right?'

'Right.'

'It would be different if you were using his story to get clicks or were monetising it.'

'Charlie, Jeanie's kid, says I should at least sign up with an affiliate, get the site to pay for itself. He says I'm stuck in the dark ages.'

'Why don't you?'

'I've got a donate button.' Not that anyone ever donated. Site was too small for that. 'And I get by.' Just.

'So they think the killer put a dress on the body?'

'Not just a dress. A prom style dress. And they're not sure if that was staged or if the Boy was wearing it at the time of death.'

'That's messed up. You reckon the killer was making a statement? Punishing the boy for, say, being a drag queen or whatever?'

'Could be. Could be that it belonged to the boy. Who knows? Could've belonged to the killer's girlfriend or sister.'

'And you and this . . . Rainbow . . .'

'Rainbowbrite.'

'Yeah, you and Rainbowbrite are sure it's this missing Irish guy?'

'Not a hundred percent, but close enough.'

'Can you bring up the guy's page so I can see it?'

'Bring the doughnuts.'

He followed her to the office space and took a pair of reading glasses out of his pocket. In an instant he went from biker guy to studious eccentric. He waggled his eyebrows. 'What do you think? Sexy, huh?'

She rolled her eyes and grabbed another doughnut. She enlarged the pic of the composite image and the photo of Teddy Ryan, and displayed them side-by-side. Scott shuffled behind her to get a view of the screens. He smelled faintly of smoke and bike oil. She caught her breath as he brushed against her shoulder, then told herself not to be so goddamned stupid. 'So what do you think? Reckon they're the same guy?'

'You know . . . there's something there. The shape of the face, right?'

'Right.' She could hear him breathing over the roar of the Lenovo's fan.

'That's a long time to be missing. That's a long time for whoever killed him to be out there. Did the cops have a suspect?'

'Rainbowbrite lives in the area where the Boy was found and says the cops dropped the ball on the case. She reckons they assumed the kid was itinerant, a drifter or a sex worker maybe.'

'He was definitely gay?'

'That's what they're assuming.'

'Sounds like that GI Doe case. Young gay guy killed in the nineties.' Scott moved to the other side of the desk, and sat on the chair Jeanie sometimes used when she visited. 'You mind?'

'Go ahead.'

'You think the two cases could be connected?' He leaned forward, eager again, as if he were the first person to come up with that theory – the rookie who'd cracked the case.

'The crimes took place in different states. Different MOs. GI Doe was stabbed, the Boy had a cranial fracture. Then there's the dress – there was nothing like that in GI Doe's case.'

'They were both gay. Sounds like a type to me.'

'Don't know that for sure.'

'But they could be linked, right? Those sickos, they . . . what's the word? They escalate.'

'That's what everyone wants it to be. Some Hollywood Hannibal Lecter shit. Tie it all up, catch the guy and it'll end with a shoot-out in a basement somewhere. But that's not going to happen, and even if it did, it's not going to secure an ID for the Boy in the Dress.'

'But you want to solve it, right?'

'Wrong.' A lie. She couldn't forget last night's caffeine jolt. 'Shit, I don't know. Maybe. I had a bad experience a while back with one of the cases.'

'What happened?'

'Things got out of control. People got hurt.'

He waited for her to continue. She rarely talked this much, hadn't even told Charlie all the details. Rationalising that if she didn't tell him he'd only look it up, she reeled it out dispassionately:

'Couple of years after I started the forum, I had a medical thing I had to attend to, left a moderator running the site. She got a message from a guy saying that his daughter had been driven to suicide after being hounded by a stalker, and the cops weren't following it up. The mod took it seriously – the father was convincing. She looked into it, posted the stalker guy's name online, and it got spread around. Reddit picked it up, other sites too. He was hounded at work, harassed online, ended up taking an overdose. Only, turns out that the father was lying and this guy was some random neighbour who didn't even know the daughter, and he wasn't the first person they'd accused of stalking her. Their way of dealing with their daughter's death, I guess.'

'A false accusation. Like those guys who were accused of the Boston marathon bombing even though they were innocent. Internet were convinced they'd done it.'

'You got it. Once the narrative's out there and people run with it, it's like shit on a blanket. And the rumour started on the site. My site. When I got back, it was too late. Kicked the mod off, thought about shutting it down.'

'That's why you just do UIDs.'

'Yep. Safer.'

He took his time working through this. 'Okay, so tell me about the cases you solved. The ones Jeanie mentioned.'

'I didn't solve anything. She was exaggerating. They're on the site – you can see them for yourself. Most of them are down to dumb luck.'

He reached across the desk. She reared back. 'What the *fuck*?'

'You got some sugar on your nose. Sorry, didn't mean to be—'

'What do you want from me, Scott?'

'Me? I don't want nothing.'

He hadn't mentioned the kid with MS and she wouldn't dig, but there had to be a reason why he'd shown up at her door. 'We both know that's not true. If you're looking to get laid you're out of luck.'

'You always like this?'

'Like what?'

'Confrontational. Like you're always gunning for a fight.' He'd lost his hang-dog demeanour. There was no anger there, more curiosity – as if she were a strange object he was trying to identify.

'Always? You don't know me. Don't think you can just come in here and pass judgement on me.'

He flipped the box's lid and made a show of inspecting the remaining doughnuts. 'Just speaking as I find.'

'Well keep your opinions to yourself. I didn't ask you to come over here. You just barged in here like . . . like some creepy-ass goddamned stalker freak.'

'A creepy-ass goddamned stalker freak, huh?'

'Yeah.'

'That's what you think of me?'

'Yeah.'

He stared at her; she stared back. He didn't have the flat gaze of a psychopath, but he could kill her just by sitting on her. Then he threw his head back and laughed. There was no hand shield this time, and far as she could tell, there was nothing wrong with his teeth. 'Yeah, but I'm a creepy-ass goddamned stalker freak who bought doughnuts. That's got to count for something, right?'

'That's it? That all you got to say?'

'That's all I got to say.' He stood.

'You one of those guys who's looking for someone to fix?'

'I've got enough of my own problems. Don't know anyone around here apart from Devin. Liked talking to you the other night is all.' He shrugged. 'I'm not going to bug you, Chris.'

And with that, he walked out.

'You know I can't run after you, right?' she called after him.

The screen door banged in answer.

Wicklowboy22

The egg white popped and flapped in the hot oil, and Shaun's stomach twisted itself into a defensive knot. He needed to soak up the alcohol with something, and unless he resorted to digging into Daphne's food, it was eggs or nothing. It'd been years since he'd fought a hangover and he'd lost the knack of dealing with the nausea, and worse. The lurch of morning-after remorse: he had enough of a bond with Drunk Shaun's memories to know that he'd embarrassed himself, revealed too much. Whatever Chris's motives, she was kind to humour the lush, must have thought she was dealing with an illiterate wastrel. It was mortifying. He slid the eggs into Daphne's bowl and blew on them to cool them.

While the dog lapped up his discarded breakfast, he clicked onto the page Chris had made in the early hours. There wasn't much to it: a photo of Teddy, his description, and a mention that he'd stayed at a YMCA in New York. True to her word, the comment function wasn't enabled. The idea of strangers discussing Teddy as if he was nothing more than a problem to be solved had a blemish of voyeurism to it, a salaciousness that didn't sit right.

Or maybe he should just get over himself. Teddy was either dead or he wasn't. *Uncertainty is a bitch.* He found two aspirin in the pocket of an old leather jacket – a relic from the brief period when he'd tried to fit in – and dry swallowed them. He'd been pootling along for years. Living vicariously through books. Using the dog as an excuse to live a life trapped in amber. Embracing the role of the eccentric loner, slamming the door whenever anyone tried to get in. Even if Teddy was alive he was hardly going to waltz in here and whisk him off to a life of artisanal coffee and Greenwich Village loft spaces, was he? He could mope around all day or be proactive. Chris had mentioned that a full-face photograph of Teddy could help provide more certainty. He was seeing Johnny that evening, so maybe he'd have one. Then there was Pat Carey and Donny. Johnny was adamant that Teddy wouldn't have contacted them, and while Shaun's opinion of the man had improved, he wasn't about to take his word as gospel. If this went any further he'd have to talk to them at some point. For now, Janice was the safest option. Lighting a fortifying cigarette, he scrolled to her number. Keith answered on the tenth ring. 'She's at mass, Shaun,' Keith said, his words punctuated by the smacking sounds of whatever he was eating for breakfast. 'Then she's got the church supper. She won't be back till six.' Shaun hesitated, then asked for Donny's number and address. It took an age for Keith to track them down. Shaun killed the cigarette on the window ledge – the nicotine was only making his head swim – and rinsed the pan in the room's tiny sink. Before he could talk himself out of it, he tapped in his uncle's number. It went straight to a 'no longer in use' message. There was relief at the stay of execution, annoyance that he was giving in so easily.

Eggs inhaled, Daphne was now watching him intently, her whiskers jewelled with yolk teardrops.

'What shall I do?'

She cocked her head as if she was seriously considering the question, then padded to the door.

Brittas Bay was a half-hour drive away. There was just enough battery life left in the phone for one more call.

'Brendan?'

'Huh?' In the background Shaun heard the mosquito whine of Ashling saying, 'Who's that?' Brendan mumbled something Shaun couldn't make out, then: 'What is it?'

'Need a favour.'

Brendan cruised past the entrance, pulled up on the verge and killed the engine. They'd driven past Donny's place twice already, the sat nav confused by the warren of narrow lanes that wove around it. The majority of the neighbouring properties were abandoned holiday homes, most of which sported faded estate agent boards. Its gilded electric gates and high walls gave nothing away.

The sea whispered behind scruff-topped dunes; a gust of wind rattled the windscreen. The buffering from the open back window and the bass thunk of Brendan's choice of road music – some nineties techno – still reverberated in Shaun's ears.

Brendan shifted in his seat. 'Right then. What's going on?'

Brendan had barely said a word on the drive. It could be that he was battling his own post-booze malaise or was still smarting from Shaun's dismissal of him the night before, but whatever the cause, Shaun wasn't sure how to deal with this new, serious un-Brendan other than to drop the camp act. 'Nothing's going on.'

'Bollocks. First you're drinking and now you're calling me on a Sunday morning. You never call me. You can talk to me, you know.'

If Chris was right about the identification, then everyone would have to know sooner or later. But he and Brendan weren't confidants; they'd never been that. 'I told you. I fancied visiting my uncle.'

Brendan looked at his lap. 'How long will you be?'

'Not long. He might not even be in. Don't worry, no one will see you here.'

'I'm not worried.' But he glanced in the rear-view mirror all the same.

'Will you watch the dog?'

'Yeah.' Daphne was the only one who'd enjoyed the journey. Brendan had insisted on covering the back seats with towels to protect the leather, but she'd scrabbled them into a nest after five minutes then spent the rest of the journey with her head out of the window.

Time to go. He climbed out of the car. 'Shaun?' Brendan called after him.

'What?'

'Be careful.'

'He's my uncle.'

'Cal says he's an arms dealer.'

'That's bollocks.' Was it? For all Shaun knew Donny *might* be an arms dealer. Whenever he'd asked Janice about the source of Donny and Carmel's wealth, she'd changed the subject. His mother had rarely spoken about Donny, other than to rage about him joining her parents' campaign to pressurise her into giving Shaun up for adoption.

The wind nipped at the top of his ears, and he could detect a faint odour of rot beneath the salt. Lack of sleep had given the world a too-bright, unreal clarity. All he could make out through the gate's bars was a sea of smooth-tarred driveway snaking away to the left. He pressed a button on the intercom, but got nothing back but a static pop. He gazed into the black eye of the camera placed on the post next to him. Another reprieve. He was about to return to the car when a woman's voice crackled out of the intercom: 'Who is it?'

'Shaun.'

'Who?'

'Shaun. Donny's nephew.'

A pause. 'Oh Christ. Didn't recognise you. Hold on, I'll get Donny.'

A squeal of laughter and a girl of about eight or so and a younger boy came racing up to the gate. Janice had told him the names of Donny and Carmel's kids, but for the life of him he couldn't dredge them up. They'd had them later in life after a long campaign of IVF – remembered Janice griping about the cost of that.

'*Hola!*' the boy said. His nose was clogged with yellow snot, and he was dressed in a grey suit and white shirt, which gave him the look of a miniature banker.

The girl elbowed him. 'No Spanish remember? Dad said.' That jab must have hurt, but the boy didn't react. She glared at Shaun through flat grey eyes. 'Who are you? Are you a molester? You look like a molester.'

'I'm your cousin.'

'No you're not. Iain and Cal and Deon and Jeanette are my cousins.'

'I am too.'

'Hoy! Leave him alone.' A paler version of the man Shaun remembered from his mother's funeral came walking purposefully down the driveway. His hair was thinning at the temples, his eyes were the same predator grey as the girl's and he was wearing a slick dark suit, complete with black shirt and tie, as if he fancied himself a Bond villain.

'Who's this, Dad?' the girl asked.

'This is Shaun. My sister Eileen's son.'

'Eileen's dead,' the boy said solemnly.

'She is.'

'Is he the one Auntie Janice says has a banjaxed head?' the girl piped in.

Shaun didn't allow the hurt to show. He didn't have a banjaxed head after Eileen died: he had a broken heart.

'Banjaxed.' The boy whispered wonderingly. 'Banjaxed *head.* What's that mean?'

'It means his head is messed up, right, Da?' the girl said.

'It can mean that.'

'Is that why he looks so fucking weird?'

Donny went as if to give her a clip round the ear, but it was a token gesture, there was pride in his eyes. 'The mouth on you! Get inside. Your mother's waiting for you.'

The girl didn't flinch. She shot Shaun a cruel smile and ran off, the lad in tow. Donny gave Shaun a shrug. 'Kids. You know what they can be like.'

'Ah no, it's fine. Sorry to just drop in like this. I tried to call but the number was out of use.'

'Which number?'

'Keith gave it to me.'

'Yeah? He isn't the brightest, probably gave you my old one. You almost missed us. We were just going out.'

'Shall I come back another time?' Part of him prayed for Donny to say 'yes.' Donny wasn't a large man, but he held himself as if he were coiled, ready to strike. Shaun couldn't find a trace of Eileen in him.

'About Teddy, is it? Janice said that bastard Johnny had been blabbing about him. Would have come to see you before only I've had things to deal with. Been back and forth to Malaga so often I should have shares in fucking Ryanair.'

Shaun managed a weak smile.

'Ah Christ. You're here now, you may as well come in.' Donny clicked a remote and the gates drifted open. He stalked ahead like a strutting cockerel and Shaun was forced to jog to keep up with him. The driveway curved past a pristine garage and on towards a split-level structure. The top half of the building was a paragon of gleaming glass and beige paint, the underbelly a mish-mash of flaking plaster and crumbling orange brick. The garden had that same split personality: rectangular concrete planters filled with grey pebbles sat uneasily alongside wind blasted lawn. 'You have a lovely house,' he said to Donny's back.

'Carmel's insisting on doing it over from scratch. It's like living on a fucking building site.'

'What's it like being back?'

'Shite.'

Through the front door and along a wide corridor with tiles as slick as water. Most of the doorways were sealed with plastic and the place reeked of paint. There was no sign of the kids, or anything that might belong to them. They ended up in a perfectly white kitchen. The surfaces were bare and the cupboards and counters melded seamlessly into the floor. The brightness of it drilled into Shaun's eyes; the lack of a reference point made him feel like he was floating and brought on another wave of nausea.

Donny dipped into the fridge and handed him a can of imported beer.

'No thanks, Donny. You're alright.'

'Go on.' Shaun took it, although he hated anything that tasted of hops. Donny didn't get one for himself – a petty show of power. Shaun took a sip and tried not to gag. It frothed in his gullet then settled.

Donny's phone piped out the Nokia tune. He killed the call, cursing under his breath. It rang again. 'Fuck's sake.'

A clack of heels and Carmel entered the room. She was in a short-sleeved red dress as if she was about to go out for the evening; a splash of colour against the white like blood on a sheet. She was thinner and blonder than Shaun remembered, her forearms rippling with tendons. She shot Donny an unreadable glance, then tottered over to kiss Shaun on the cheek, enveloping him in a cloud of scent. There was something of the eighties about her vigorously styled hair. 'How are you keeping, Shaun? I wish I'd known you were coming over. We were just off to take the kids to see my parents.'

'He knows that,' Donny said. 'Where are they?'

'Upstairs. I've told them we'll only be a minute.'

'Let's get this over with then. Come on into the lounge.' Donny waved Shaun through an adjoining door and into another pale space. A chandelier dangled from the ceiling. Giant silver-framed mirrors hung on every wall. He was hyper-conscious of the threads in his turn-ups, the scuffs on his shoes. Conscious of his banjaxed head. There was nothing of character here, nothing of their years in Spain. 'Sit.'

A white leather couch sucked him in. Carmel perched on the end of an ottoman, and Donny sat opposite Shaun, hands dangling between splayed legs. Shaun couldn't hold his gaze for more than a few seconds. He'd seen eyes like that on the psychos that frequented the travellers' bars outside Rathnew. 'Janice told you to leave this Teddy business alone. You'd better not have been spreading it all over town.'

Sip, block out the taste, swallow. Hair of the dog: it was already numbing the hangover and bringing with it a helpful distancing effect. He took another gulp. He was going to have to dig deep for this. He looked to Carmel. 'Did you know?'

'Know what?'

'That Teddy isn't dead.' Shaun caught himself. He *might* be dead. 'That he didn't die in Galway, I mean.'

'Course she knows,' Donny said.

'Am I the only one who doesn't know?' It came out sounding bitter, and why shouldn't it?

'The kids don't know, nor do Janice's. And why should they? It's ancient history.'

Shaun had a sudden urge to chuck the can at Donny's face. He breathed in, numbed his fingers on the tin. 'Did Teddy ever get in contact with you over the years?'

'Not a word.'

'What about his friends? Johnny said he used to hang around with Pat Carey.'

'You stay away from the Careys. They're a brutal lot.' The irony. 'I'd have known if Teddy had contacted anyone.'

'How? You were in Spain all those years.'

A sneer. 'Use your head. Dead man coming back to life? It would have been all around the town. I would have heard.'

'That's right, Shaun.' This from Carmel. 'We would have heard.'

Donny slapped his thighs. 'Is that it? You'd best be going then—'

'I might have found him.'

'What?' An instant of what looked to be genuine shock – a slackening of jaw muscles, a widening of the eyes – before Donny's mask slid back into place. 'Bollocks you have.'

'It's not bollocks. Only . . .' He faltered. He hadn't planned on blurting it out like this, hadn't planned on bringing up the Boy in the Dress at all. The idea was to dig for information, ask for a photograph of Teddy. He couldn't backtrack now. Donny might be a borderline sociopath, but his brother could be the victim of a murder. 'This might be hard to hear.'

'Go on.'

Another sip, then Shaun rambled through a potted explanation of posting his 'have you seen my uncle' plea and receiving the email from Chris. He skimped on the details, couldn't quite bring himself to say the word 'murdered.' Floundering, he brought up the screengrab of the boy's face and handed his phone to Donny.

Donny's expression didn't betray much, but once again, Shaun caught a ripple of something beneath the surface. 'What the fuck's this?'

'A portrait of the boy they found in the mid-nineties. The people on this website reckon it could be Teddy. We'll need DNA to—'

'Bollocks.'

Carmel snatched the phone out of Donny's hand. She scrolled through it, fingernail poised. 'Oh for the love of God.'

Shaun tightened his hold on the can. 'They're not sure it's him. I'll have to report him missing to the guards, then we can—'

'No, no, no, no,' Donny's eyes bored into his. 'You're not to get the guards involved.'

'But he might be *dead*.'

'That's not him.'

'But we should be sure, shouldn't we? Do you have a recent photograph of him? We could use that—'

'I am sure. You think I don't know my own fucking brother's face when I see it?'

Carmel was still transfixed to the phone. 'God, I can't believe it. Jesus. What's this about a dress?'

Donny's phone rang again. He glanced at the screen, then jabbed a finger in Shaun's direction. 'Stay there. Got to take this.' He stalked out, barking, '*What?*' into the receiver.

Carmel glanced at the door. 'Christ, Shaun. I can't get my head around all this.' Janice was always calling her a 'flighty cow', but there was some heart there and she must be tougher than she looked to stick with Donny all these years.

Speak. 'Have you always known that the Galway story was a lie?'

'God no. What do you think of me? My mother was furious she wasn't invited to his funeral. She would have travelled there. We all would have gone. No, it was after Eileen went down to Galway. I knew something was up. She had it out with your grandparents and it was a fight to end all fights. And you should have heard me raging at Donny for lying to me all that time. Eileen couldn't believe they'd send him away just to stop her going after him. She wouldn't speak to us after that.'

'Is that the real reason he left?'

Her surprise at the question appeared to be genuine. 'Course it was. What else could it be?'

'From what Mam said they were close. I can't believe he'd leave her like that.'

Carmel adjusted her skirt, gave him a sympathetic smile. 'I liked Teddy, Shaun. Always liked him. He could make me piss myself laughing. But he had a selfish streak. Donny said that when he was offered an opportunity to go to New York, he leapt at it.'

Selfish. Another smudge marred his childhood's idealised Teddy portrait.

She looked to the door again. 'Now listen, be careful. Donny won't like any attention on the family. Not now. He won't want the guards getting involved. Donny can be . . . you don't want to get on the wrong side of him. You know that.'

'Talking about me?' Donny came back in. 'You'll be going then, Shaun.'

He got up, noting with vague surprise that he'd drained the can. In a small act of defiance he crushed it and left it on the glass coffee table.

Donny escorted him to the front door and out into the sea air, a relief after the paint fumes and blandness. Shaun was formulating a 'See you then' – he wasn't quite sure *what* to say after that scene – when Donny pincered his shoulder, the grip firm enough to hurt through his coat's heavy fabric. 'Going to tell you something now, Shaun. It's not Teddy. Can't be. I spoke to him just the other week.'

Shaun twisted out of his grasp, turned, tried once again to read Donny's eyes. The shutters were down – impossible to be sure if he was telling the truth.

'Teddy's got himself into a bit of bother on that side of the pond. Asked me to keep it quiet. Not even Carmel knows about it.'

'What kind of trouble?'

'Drugs. Hard drugs. He was always wild, and he got in with a bad crowd over there. He's gone into hiding. If the cops are looking for him, well . . .' Donny shrugged. 'Wouldn't like to say what might happen to him. So no running off to the guards. Leave it be. Are we clear on this? Am I getting through to you?'

Shaun swallowed, tasted sour hops and old pennies. 'Yes.'

'Good. Now off you fuck, there's a good lad.'

Shaun looked straight ahead as he made for the gates, aware of Donny's eyes on his back. Brendan was leaning against the car, as far away from Daphne as her lead would allow, puffing ineptly on one of Shaun's Vogues. Shaun had never seen him smoke before, and this added another element of surrealism to his already bizarre morning.

'Go okay, Shaun?'

He swallowed again. 'I don't know.' Daphne jumped up at him, and he gathered her up and returned her to the back seat. The windows were all misted up.

'Can you not just tell me what's going on?'

'You won't believe it.'

Brendan dropped the cigarette into the road. 'Try me. For fuck's sake, I care about you, Shaun.'

Not this, not now. 'Let's get back.'

They climbed into the car. Shaun's left knee jumped involuntarily, and he couldn't seem to click the seat belt into its slot. Brendan leaned across and did it for him. His hair stank of nicotine. He'd had more than one cigarette.

'Thought you didn't smoke?'

'Don't usually. Saw them in the car and . . . Ah Christ.' He shrugged, tried to smile – nothing but a shadow of the usual insensitive, broad-brush Brendan. It was a little like sitting next to a stranger. 'You're not the only one who's having issues. I've been thinking . . . I'm thinking about telling her. Ashling, I mean.'

'I know who you mean.'

'But then I keep thinking about what everyone will say. My mother would . . . She loves Ashling, she's always on at me to have some kiddies. You're braver than I am, Shaun.'

'I'm not brave.'

'You are. You don't care what people say about you. Look at how you dress.'

A tap on the passenger window made both of them jump. Brendan glanced at Shaun, then clicked on the power and slid the window down. Donny peered in at them. 'Well now, isn't this cosy? Brendan Irvine, isn't it? I was at school with your da.'

The colour drained out of Brendan's face. 'I was just giving him a ride.'

'What you get up to in your private time is no business of mine.' Donny's laser beam gaze shifted to Shaun. 'Meant to say. Where do you think John McKinnon's been all these years?'

'Working in London.'

'Is that what he calls it? Lying bastard. He's been banged up in Belmarsh.'

'What for?'

'He's been gone twenty years, what do you think for? Murder.'

Shaun may as well have been pinioned to his seat. 'Who did he kill?'

'Ask him.' Donny slapped the door panel. 'And don't be a stranger now. I'll get Carmel to invite you both round for dinner when the house is finished, give you the grand tour. You can advise us on the furnishings. You lot are good at that, aren't you?' With a wink aimed at Brendan, Donny slithered away.

A minute of silence passed, and then Brendan said: 'I can't see you any more Shaun.'

'I know.' The only thing filling Shaun's head was: *murder*.

Rainbowbrite

Ellie's hands reeked of Clorox. She'd scrubbed the bathroom and the den and made a hotdish for supper. She'd shaved her legs and squeezed herself into the only good dress that didn't bite into her waistline. Noah usually called her when he was on his way home, but he hadn't yesterday and there was nothing today.

While she waited, ears straining for the sound of Noah's Subaru, she revisited the list of dressmakers and retailers she'd compiled back when the case was first posted on the site. She'd flag it on Twitter again, and it might be worth visiting the high schools in the area to check out their prom pictures from the early nineties – there was no Facebook back then, so she'd have to look through the yearbooks. If they had an ID for the Boy, maybe this time the sheriff's office would let her see the dress, or at least put out a clearer photograph of it. Bobbiecowell wasn't convinced it was a major piece of the case, but it was good to have him back on the team, and he seemed upbeat about the possible ID. There was still a chilliness coming from Chris, but she'd accepted the apology, which was a start. And if Chris wouldn't sleuth the case, other sites would.

The shudder of an engine came from outside. She stowed the laptop, and composed her face. Noah took his time scuffing off his boots.

'I made your favourite for supper, and I fetched a—'

'Ellen, shush now.' Ellen, not Ellie or El. She toyed with her wedding ring. A cold hole opened up inside her.

He sat. 'We need to talk.'

'I know.'

'I've been thinking. This stuff you do, this online stuff. We got to have some balance here.'

'I know—'

'Let me finish.'

'Okay.'

'Now see, I get why you got to do it. I know looking after the boys and the house isn't enough for you.'

'They are enough.' A lie. She'd tried to fill her days, she really had. Began making a quilt, bought one of those teach-yourself-Spanish courses. Nothing stuck, and it was too late now to join in with the activities that vacuumed up the other stay-at-home moms' empty hours. She'd made sacrifices for the Boy in the Dress. The parents at the school, so welcoming at first, no longer invited her to join them in their activities – she'd made excuses too often. Even Sherry, whose son Danny was best friends with the twins, treated her distantly. 'I could look for a job, Noah. Go freelance. Reckon I could canvass the local businesses.' She wasn't the world's most adept bookkeeper, but she was okay.

'You could do that. You want to do that?'

'We could use the extra.'

'We're doing fine.' Since his promotion they were keeping up with the house payments, and his health insurance wasn't bad. 'We agreed it was the right thing for the boys to have someone at home. I never had that. You never had that.'

'I know, but—'

He held up a hand. 'I'm still talking here.' A different tone to the one he used with the boys or when he was mad. Must be how he talked to the juveniles at the facility. Not patronising exactly, but firm. It should rile her, but she was too desperate for the air to clear. 'See, I know why you got to do this online stuff. It's an outlet. Know what that case means to you, and I used to support you, didn't I?'

She nodded.

'But it took over. Things started to slide. And I don't mean the house. I don't care about that. After you had all that bad blood with Chris, and how upset you were, it was right for you to shut it down. Know that couldn't have been easy, and I appreciate you making the effort. But it hasn't all been good.' He didn't spell it out. Didn't need to. In the last year, she'd put on twenty pounds. 'And I know you've been doing it behind my back.'

'How?' A surge of anxiety, swiftly followed by resentment – how could he know that? She'd been careful. 'You been spying on me?'

'We've been married for twelve years. You think I don't know when you're hiding something? Last few months, you've been as jumpy as someone fooling around on the sly.'

'I didn't mean to hide it from you.'

'Yes you did. And you've got to admit things haven't been great between us for a while.'

'That's my fault.'

'It's not. It's on both of us.' He took out his phone. 'Got something for you.'

'What?'

'Texting you a number.'

'A number? Whose number?' For a cold second she was certain he was going to suggest marriage counselling.

'Eric-Lee White. Guy from work.'

The name wasn't familiar. 'Why would you give me his number? Did I meet him at one of the cook-outs?'

'Eric used to be with Stenton County. He knows about the case.'

'The Boy?'

A nod.

'He *worked* the case?'

'Not directly I don't think, but he knows about it and he's got some things to say about it.'

'And he'll talk to me?'

'Off the record or whatever you call it. But sure he will. I didn't tell him you might have an ID, just so you know. That's up to you.'

'Oh Noah . . .' The ice inside her thawed. Only . . . 'How long have you known him?'

'A while.' He looked away.

'How long?'

'Year or so. Something like that.'

'You didn't think to tell me this before? You knew how hard I tried to get someone from the sheriff's office to talk to me.'

'I know. Thought you'd get it out of your system. Thought you'd move on. Get into something new. I was wrong.'

It was up to her to decide how to take this. Excitement elbowed everything else aside.

'Got to make a deal here though, El. You do this, you don't let it take over your life. Not for my sake. For the boys' sake. And yours. You know you got an obsessive streak when it comes to this stuff.' He held out a hand. 'Deal?'

'Deal.' Ellie glanced at her laptop, already formulating the email she'd send to Bobbie – and Chris. This lead might convince Chris to open the case for sleuthing.

'Where are the boys?'

'With Sherry. She says she'll give them supper.' She'd have to reciprocate this time; made a mental note to invite Danny for a sleepover.

He grinned. 'So we got how long?'

'A while.' She smiled back at him, the last of the tension dribbling away. It was going to be fine between them – for now at least, and if she was careful. It wasn't the first time they'd been through this dance.

Noah muttered, then shifted in his sleep. Ellie stilled until his breathing steadied. It was past midnight, and messaging Bobbiecowell in the early hours was definitely nudging the boundaries of 'letting it take over her life'. She tapped in the rest of the message: **<. . . used to work with Stenton County & knows the case & I'm meeting him this week for coffee. Seeing as you were L E, you got any advice for me? What should I ask that kinda thing?>**

<Wow! Nice work. Got to be careful here, not accusatory. They dropped the ball on this case so this guy might be defensive>

<A nd they've been stonewalling ever since. You know that, you tried them too>

<Gave it my best shot. Got nothing. You know why this guy left the dept?>

<Noah didn't say>

<Might have an ax e to grind so not everything he might say could be true>

<I guess. But Noah says he's a good guy>

<O k. A sk if they had any suspects. If anyone was on the radar>

<I will>

<They been told about the possible ID yet?>

<They will be soon as Teddy Ryan is reported missing>

<That not been done yet? There's a page up on the forum listing him as missing>

There was? How had she missed that? **<Chris didn't tell me about that>**

<Chris?>

<O h! Ratking's real name>

<What's Ratking like? H e doesn't give much away. Control freak right?>

<Chris is a woman ;) >

<Women can be control freaks too;) >

<She can be a real pill sometimes>

<I'll bet! >

<Shouldn't have said that. Chris can be tough but she knows what's she's doing. F eel bad for saying that now! I And she did. She shouldn't gossip about Chris, whatever had happened between them.

<I won't tell her you said that. You can trust me>

<Thanks ☺>

<She know you're meeting this guy?>

<I'll see how it goes first>

<H ey j ust a thought. I could be on the line with you while you talk to him in case you need backup>

That brought her up short. It could be useful, but also . . . this was *her* thing. *Her* lead. **<Maybe nex t time, don't want to spook him>**

<Your call>

<Don't want you to think I don't appreciate it. You've had some great thoughts on the Boy. TBH I'm kinda nervous about it☹>

<You'll be fine. Way I've seen you handle yourself on the site, you'd make a fine cop>

<H a. Thanks ;) but not true> Noah threw an arm over her chest, almost knocking the phone out of her hand. Holding it above her head she tapped in: **<Gotta go. Will report back letter>** *Stupid autocorrect.* **<I mean later! ! ! ! >**

<L O ☺ okay, night. Great talking to you and good luck x >

A kiss – the first time he'd sent her one. Didn't have to mean anything, lots of people ended their messages like that, but still, heat rushed to her cheeks. She typed one back, then deleted it.

Bobbiecowell

Pete pressed the knife's tip into the webbing between his thumb and index finger until a blister of blood formed, then ran the wound under the cold tap. He watched, semi-hypnotised, as the pink stream joined the soup beneath the unwashed mugs. The hole closed up in minutes and became lost in the pores around it. He hadn't done more than nick the surface. *Coward.*

The pain didn't help. Nor did working out until his muscles tore and he threw up from the exertion. He'd moved the lockbox into the truck, but who was he kidding? He should cut his ties now. That would be the smart thing to do. Walk away. He was careful – used sophisticated VPNs and mostly stuck to one device, ensuring that all syncing functions were disabled – but engaging with Rainbowbrite and lurking on the site was a needless risk.

Rainbowbrite. She was the update queen, couldn't go more than a few hours without uploading a photo of some boring kid excursion on Facebook. He'd been tracking her for over a year now. She'd put on weight since they first worked the case together, and had developed a thing for floral tops in summer and pink puffer jackets in winter, which gave her the look of an inflatable doughnut. There were endless snaps of her boys playing hockey, doing martial arts and splashing around in the lake, half-naked. He should get Bobbiecowell to talk to her about that. You never knew who might be looking. In contrast, Noah, the husband, a deputy warden at a juvie facility, had a minimal online presence. And then there was Ratking1. Chris. A woman – but he knew that, had for months. It had taken him seconds to discover the Missing-Linc domain was registered under 'Christina Guzman'. She was camera shy, the site's Twitter and Facebook pages were run under the same Ratking1 avatar, and all he'd come up with so far was an archived article from the nineties about a stock-car racing teenager with the same name. She was a hard taskmaster, wasn't aware or didn't care how many members had quit due to her bitchery, but he reckoned he'd unearthed her weakness. And she hadn't even tried to hide it.

Back away, walk away.

Not yet.

There was no way Bobbiecowell could convincingly dissuade Rainbowbrite from talking to the cop – not when he'd supposedly 'used his contacts' to extract information out of Stenton County last year. But if he played his cards right then he could use this to his advantage. She was the poster girl for low self-esteem, wouldn't be hard to use her as his canary in the mine; train her to squawk if there was trouble heading his way. And he had other contingency weapons he could deploy if he had to. He'd had over twenty years to prepare for this. He'd hold his nerve for now, do what he could to channel the stress, and reassess once Rainbowbrite reported back.

It was too late to message her again, but he drafted one all the same. It helped take the edge off, preserved the illusion that he was in control: **<hey Ellen ask him if he can use his contacts to get a look at the file x x >**

Back to the sink, back to the knife.

'Who's Ellen?'

He turned to see Tasha standing barefoot in the darkened kitchen, holding his phone. Fighting the urge to lunge at her, he faked nonchalance. 'Hey, Tash. Can't sleep?'

'*Ob*viously. Who's Ellen? Is she your *girl*friend? Are you cheating on Mom?'

'Of course not.' Pete held out his hand for the device. 'You shouldn't look at other people's stuff.' It was password protected, but the message was up when he left it on the counter. Would she have seen his username? She swiped and frowned – the screen must have gone into sleep mode.

'If she's not your girlfriend, why would you send *kiss*es?'

'Do that to everyone. Habit.'

'And what do you mean by a *file*?'

There was no time to work out all the angles. *If in doubt, keep as close to the truth as possible.* 'I'm working on something with her. Nothing to do with your mom.'

'Like what?'

If I tell you I'll have to kill you. 'I'm part of an online group. Grown-up stuff.'

'Like porn?'

'No! You're too young to know about that.'

'I am *not*. What stuff?'

'Websleuthing. We're trying to solve—'

'I *know* what websleuthing is.' She handed the phone over. 'Show me.'

The screen was dark, waiting for him to input his password. He was signed on to Missing-Linc as Bobbiecowell, so he logged out, refreshed and let her glance at the GI Doe header. 'I can't show you all of it. It's pretty gross.'

'Gross how?'

'Pictures of dead people.'

She eyed him with a new respect – fleeting, but it was there. 'Does Mom know?'

'Nope. She'll think it's dumb.'

'What's the case?'

How far should he go? And if she blabbed to Margie, so what? There was no shame in solving cold cases online. 'We're trying to identify the body of a young man who was killed twenty years ago. No one knows who he is.'

'How come?'

'There are lots of bodies out there that never get identified. People get lost in the system.'

'Don't their families look for them?'

'Might not know they're missing. Might think they don't want any contact.' *Might have lied about them dying so that no one hunts for them.* Good old Rainbowbrite had spilled that juicy bit of intel, which explained why Teddy Ryan had remained unidentified for so long – a mystery he'd wondered about, off and on, over the years.

'That's sad.'

'Yeah. You want me to make you some hot milk?'

'Gross.'

'Hot chocolate?'

She nodded. No 'yes please, Pete'. His father would have whipped him for that. 'What's up with you, Tasha?'

'Nothing.'

'You can't sleep. Something must be up.'

'*You*'re not in bed.'

'Yeah, but I told you why I was up.' He dropped two marshmallows into the mug, then caught her eye and added a third. 'Whatever it is, it might help to talk it through.'

'No it *won't*.'

'Suit yourself.' He shrugged and turned back to the phone.

A minute passed, then: 'Some of the girls at school are being *mean*.'

'Which girls?'

'*All* of them. Brittany and Olivia started it.'

'Aren't Brittany and Olivia your best friends?' He was on shaky ground here. Tasha rarely had kids over for sleepovers, but those names sounded familiar.

'They *were*.'

He could make it worse for her, or he could help. 'What are they doing?'

'Saying mean stuff about me.'

'That's tough. Trust me. I've been there.'

'You were bullied?'

'Yeah.' He could reel out some anecdotes, but that might be overkill. 'You told your mom?'

'No.'

'How come?'

'She'll only go and talk to Brittany's mom and then it will be a whole big *thing*.'

True. Margie could be tough, smashed through her firm's glass ceiling like it wasn't even there. He wouldn't put it past her to take Brittany's parents to court for emotional damage. 'You spoken to Ms Albright about it?'

A withering look: '*She* won't do anything.' Also true. Pete had met the woman briefly after one of Tasha's tedious plays and remembered a vacant thirty-something who picked at her late-onset acne. 'Anyway, they're not doing it at *school*.'

'Online?'

She nodded.

'Facebook?'

'Everywhere.'

'Doesn't your mom monitor your Facebook?'

'All the parents do. We're not stupid.'

'I get it. They use different accounts?'

A shrug – *duh*.

'What are they saying?'

He waited. She let out a shuddering sigh. 'So for a social science project we had to come up with an idea to raise money for this sick kid from Africa who is like a really good artist and has a really rare disease and needs to come here for treatment and I wanted to do a crowdfund and give people rewards like sending them a print of one of her drawings to say thank you when they donated but Brittany and Olivia said no we should do a bake sale.' She paused to draw breath. She'd lost the annoying emphasis, and for once sounded like a regular kid. 'And I said their idea was lame and boring because it is and now they're saying I think I'm better than everyone else.'

'That's not so bad. I gotta say, your idea *is* way better than theirs. No wonder they're on the defensive. They're just jealous.'

She toyed with the teaspoon. 'They also told everyone that I got my period already which isn't true and that I'm a freak and I smell bad and everyone's laughing at me now.'

'Mother*fuckers*.'

Her mouth dropped open.

'I know it's a really bad word, but am I wrong?'

She stared at him warily. Then she shook her head and gave him a rare smile.

'I get why this would shake you up.'

'Everyone believes it.'

'You've got two choices here, Tasha. You can ignore it, hope it goes away, or do something about it.'

'Like what?'

'You're smart. You can figure this shit out.'

'I *can't*.'

'You ever hear the phrase "the enemy of my enemy is my friend"?'

'No.'

'You get what it means?'

'I'm not *stu*pid.'

'Have they ever been mean about anyone else?'

A nod. 'All the time.'

'To kids' faces or behind their backs?'

'Behind their backs mostly.'

'It would be a real bummer if everyone found out what they were saying about them, wouldn't it?'

She chewed her lip, working through it. The gears grinding behind the scenes. 'Yeah.'

'Let me know if I can help.'

She wiped away a chocolate moustache. 'Okay. Don't tell Mom.'

'Pinky swear.'

'Huh?'

'I won't.'

'I won't either. Tell her about your thing, I mean.'

'You can if you want. Don't want you to have secrets from your mom. She'll just think it's dumb anyway.'

'I *won't*.'

'Okay. Night.'

Secrets were always dangerous, but it was the first time she'd treated him with anything other than disdain. He returned to the sink and the knife. No. No more. He was on this journey now. He had to get off the train or drive it.

Wicklowboy22

Shaun's post-hangover coma was broken by the *knock, knock, knock* of his mobile juddering against the table lamp. He reached for it, expecting to see Brendan's name, steeled himself for a barrage of contrite bollocks, but the screen showed a number with an unfamiliar prefix.

'Hello?'

'That you, Shaun?' An Irish voice with an American edge. Kicking away the duvet, Shaun was on his feet in an instant.

'Yes.'

'This is Teddy, your uncle. Donny says you're looking for me.'

The thump of his pulse, a jumble of questions – what to ask first? 'Where are you? Are you okay? Why didn't you come home when Mam died?'

'I can't come back to Ireland.'

'Donny says you're in trouble. What sort of trouble?'

A hush of traffic in the background. 'Stop looking for me. I can't have the cops looking into it.'

'Can I come and see you? In New York?'

'Not right now. Isn't safe. And tell that website to take that stuff about me down. I don't want to be found.'

'How do I know this is really you? How do I know that—'

'Do what I say or you'll never hear from me again.'

The call cut off.

Fingers trembling, Shaun scrolled to 'received calls', praying that he had enough credit left to ring back. An American woman coldly informed him that 'this caller is not available.' He tried again, then again, saved the number and Googled the code.

Rainbowbrite

The two cappuccinos Ellie had already consumed were playing on her bladder. There was no time to go to the bathroom – Eric was due to show up any minute. To take her mind off it she ordered another Danish. The coffee shop was one of those new places tacked onto the mall like a chrome and glass barnacle, and the twenty-something barista gave her a patronising 'Are you sure you should eat that?' glance as he dropped it onto the plate. She thanked him sheepishly, hating herself for it, and safely back at the table, picked at the pastry and fiddled with her phone. Bobbiecowell had sent another two messages asking for an update. She started to write back: **<he's not here yet ☹ hope he isn't going to cancel. Do you think I should—>**

'Ellen?'

She jumped, dropped the phone onto the table and looked up to see a well-built fellow staring down at her. 'Yes. Hi. Hi. Mr White?'

'Eric.'

'Hi. It's so good to meet you. Thanks a bunch for agreeing to meet me. Can I get you a coffee or a sandwich or something?' She was babbling like a teenager on a first date.

'I got it.' He ordered a black coffee, then sat. He was mid-fifties or thereabouts, sixty pounds overweight, with tired denim eyes and one of those bushy cop moustaches. Noah had had one for a while and Ellie used to tease him about it, called it his *Forensic Files* facial hair.

'It's really generous of you to do this, Eric.'

'Noah's a good man.'

'He is. I'm super lucky.' He didn't return her smile. 'I'm sure your wife would say the same thing.'

'I'm divorced.'

'Oh! Oh well that's . . . that's lovely too.' *Oh for Pete's sake.* Her cheeks were burning. His unwavering gaze was making her feel irrationally guilty – she got the same thing whenever she saw a traffic cop.

'Noah says you're interested in the boy who was dumped out by North Park.'

'That's right. I've been looking into the case for a while now, ever since we moved here. It's not just me, there's a team of us, one of them's even a retired detective from New York.' She wiped her palms on her thighs, gave herself a mental shake. The barista brought his coffee, and Eric dismissed him with a nod. 'I've tried getting information from Stenton County but they said the files were closed to the public on account of the case was still active, so . . . Noah said you were with the sheriff's office when he was discovered.'

'This off the record?'

'I'm not a journalist, but anything you say . . . I won't put it online if you don't want me to.'

He sipped his coffee, grimaced. 'If you do, it can't have my name attached.'

'I won't mention you, I promise.'

He thought for a minute, seemed to be sizing her up. He'd be good at interrogations. 'Okay then. I was first on the scene.'

Ellie wasn't expecting *that*. 'Oh . . . That must've been just awful.'

'Wasn't the best morning I ever had. I'd only been with the department for a couple of months. Patrol deputy.' He looked inwards. 'Saw the dress first of course, a dirty pink colour. The boy was face down, arms outstretched as if he was caught midway doing one of those snow angels. The fella who found him, Carl Faberson, said he'd gone after his dog, thought it was just a bundle of old clothes at first. I secured the scene, waited for the others to show up. Sandy Eversham was the lead on that.'

She didn't recall reading anything about a Sandy Eversham

in the *Herald*'s coverage. Most of the statements about the case came from the sheriff. 'Do you think Sandy would talk to me?'

'Doubt it. Sandy's been dead since '98.'

'Oh I'm so sorry. Were you close?'

'Yeah.'

'Was it cancer?'

He looked away.

'Sorry, Eric. Ignore me. I'm prying.'

He cleared his throat. 'You want me to go into how the investigation proceeded?'

'Please.' The nerves were under control – she needed to stop interrupting and let him talk.

'Right away we knew it was going to be a tough one. Sandy was the first one who put his hand up, said the department didn't have the experience for this type of investigation. The only serious crimes he'd worked before were domestic in nature. He wanted a state investigator involved, maybe the FBI, but the chief said no, the county could handle it. There was an election coming up, see, didn't want it to look like he wasn't on top of things. It didn't help that there was some confusion at the outset. Boy's remains were degraded, and we assumed the body was female until the coroner said otherwise. Then, no one had an idea who this boy was, and no one had seen him around the area before as far as we could tell. Sandy cross-checked missing person reports, came up with nothing, and there was nothing but that dress in the way of evidence.'

'And the man who found the body, Mr . . . what was it, Faberson?'

'He was never a suspect. Heard he drank himself to death five years back. So there's him, and then Sandy. Seems like this case has the kiss of death to it.'

Ellie made herself wait for him to continue.

'Initial working hypothesis was that the kid was involved in the sex trade, got picked up by the wrong person.'

'Why did they think that?'

'Way the kid looked, I guess. Dyed hair, that dress. Coroner said there was some indication the boy was sexually active.'

'Could he have been sexually assaulted?'

'That was inconclusive.'

'And there was no foreign DNA at the scene?'

'The body was exposed to the elements for a long time. Months, the coroner reckoned.'

'How about on the dress?'

'Couple of dark fibres they reckon could've come from a car's interior. Never identified them as far as I know.'

'If they thought the boy was . . . I was wondering if the case wasn't high profile because of . . .' He waited patiently as she stumbled over her words. 'I guess I'm trying to say . . . was there prejudice in the department at the time?' It was a fair enough question. The county could be conservative.

'I know what you're getting at. There were some who held those views, talk that the queer boy got what was coming to him, that kind of thing. Sandy wasn't one of them. Sandy stuck with it. He was the one who got the funds together to get the composite done, put out pictures of that dress in the media. He spent months checking in with local dressmakers, visited stores that sell that kind of garment.'

'I've been doing that too. I've also been looking at old prom and wedding photographs.'

'That's good thinking.'

'The dress has to be the connection.'

'Could be. Sandy wanted to send the file to one of those profilers from the FBI.'

'See . . . see that's what I think too – that the boy might have run into a serial killer. We've got another case on the site that happened around the same time. Gay man murdered. And Bobbie, he's the guy I told you about who was in the NYPD, he thinks there are other cases that could match up as well.' She was leaning so far forward she was squashing the Danish with her elbow. 'Bobbie thinks the killer had done it before, and by the time he got to the boy he'd got smarter, maybe used the dress as a misdirection.'

'That's a stretch. Sandy couldn't find any other cases that

matched up at the time. Like I say, fact we didn't know who the boy was stymied the investigation.'

'We might know who he is.' She waited for his reaction: nothing but mild interest.

'That so?'

He remained a closed book as Ellie told him about Teddy Ryan.

'Why was this Irish kid in the area?'

'We don't know for sure. The last place he was seen was New York.'

'You told the sheriff's office?'

'Teddy has only just been reported missing – or . . . I don't know for sure if he *has* been reported missing. I guess they'll be told soon.'

He ran his thumb and forefinger over his moustache. It sat on his top lip like a coffee stain, free of the grey peppering his crew cut.

'Did Sandy have any suspects?' One of Bobbiecowell's questions.

A long pause. 'Sandy came to the conclusion it had to be someone who knew the area. You seen where the boy was found? Back then it was difficult to get to, way back from the trails. You'd need local knowledge for that.'

'The killer knew to mask the boy's identity, remove the fingertips. Do you think he wanted to delay an identification because he was connected to the boy in some way?'

'Good a theory as any. Whoever did this went halfway, then stopped. If you wanted to be sure, should've hacked off the guy's feet, removed the teeth.'

'And not leave the body out in the open like that. Did Sandy think the killer wanted the boy to be found?'

'That I couldn't tell you.'

'Mr White – Eric – if you don't mind me asking . . . why did you leave the department?'

'There were things that didn't sit easy with me. Politicking. No accountability. I'm no saint, but you got to do the job. Stayed longer than I should have.' Another of those assessing looks: 'This case mean a lot to you?'

'Yes.'

'Why?'

'Where the boy was found . . . it's so close to where we live. I take my boys to that park next to the reserve all the time. And it's so sad. The thought of that boy lying there all that time. No one reporting him missing. No one *caring*.'

'Sandy cared.' He sighed. 'I promised him I wouldn't let it go. Wouldn't let it get buried. But I did. I took the easy route.' He shrugged. 'But I'm the one who has to live with that.' He checked his watch, frowned.

'Do you think the county'll do the job properly this time? Reassign it? Things have moved on since then. We've got CODIS, more sophisticated DNA techniques. They could retest the dress, see if they can pick up something. Those fibres could be pinned down, give us a solid lead.'

'Dress is gone.'

Had she misheard him? '*What?*'

'Checked a few years back. It's not in evidence.'

'How can that be?'

'Happens all the time. Things get thrown out, damaged, misplaced. There was one case back in the seventies where a deputy took it on himself to squirrel away evidence. Locked it away in a drawer, and it was only found months later. He was jostling for position in the department at the time, wanted any kudos for himself.' He looked straight at her. 'That's just one of the ways it can go missing.'

'Are you saying . . . Could Sandy have done that?'

'Couldn't say.' He knocked on the table, and finally gave her a smile. 'Gotta go. Good luck, Ellen.'

She watched him leave, then finished the squashed Danish. She didn't leave a tip.

Bobbiecowell

The doorbell buzzed, and he jumped before he could stop himself.

Margie gave him a look. 'What's got you so wound up?'

Smile. 'Nothing. I was wool-gathering is all. Sit. I'll go.'

The stress wasn't going to give up that easy. Rainbowbrite was talking to the ex-cop right this second and no amount of rationalisation could erase the paranoia. Pete worked out religiously, waged war against his body's inclination to snap back into its natural shape, but he'd never survive incarceration. Couldn't let that happen. *Couldn't.* He opened the door, smothering the irrational certainty that he'd see a cop car skewed on the driveway, a team of boiler-suited tech guys picking through his truck, but it was only Gary, Tasha's father, and his leased corporate-mobile.

'Hey, Pete. How's it hanging?'

'The usual. To the left.'

Gary laughed and Pete chuckled along. He could afford to be magnanimous. He was the one who'd got the girl, the house, Gary's old high-end life. As he waved Gary in, he caught a whiff of cologne and mouthwash – Daddy Dearest was drinking on the sly again. And judging by his baggy chinos and Nikes, the asshole was also regressing even further into the nineties. *A wasp without the sting.*

Margie shouted from the kitchen: 'Gary! Need to talk to you.'

Gary gave him a collusive, long-suffering look and Pete played along, although he loathed all that brotherhood crap.

'I'll let Tasha know you're here.'

Gary clapped him on the shoulder. 'Cheers, bud.'

Leaving Gary to his fate, Pete made for Tasha's room, glancing at the phone before he tapped on her door: nothing from Rainbowbrite. 'It's Pete.'

'Come in.'

She was perched on the bed, her overnight backpack next to her. The room had all the character of a show home. No clutter, devices lined up on the desk, the books colour-coded on the shelves. OCD central.

'Your dad's here.'

'Can't I stay here?'

This was new. 'It's your mom's night out.'

'He'll only give me pizza again.'

Cry me a fucking river. 'You'll survive. How's it going? You sort out your situation?'

'Yes.'

He waited for more. Nada. 'How did you do it?'

'I screengrabbed some of their comments and sent them to everyone and now everyone *hates* them especially Monica Tallis because Olivia said that she looked like a pig. She does look like a pig but *still*.'

'Won't they snitch on you?'

'They know it's me but they can't prove anything.'

'Proxy – different – account?'

A nod.

'Smart.'

'They deserved it. They started it.'

'That's true.'

'I'm not bullying them, I'm telling the truth. They were the ones who bullied me by lying. I also gave them a bad rating on Savvy.'

'Savvy?'

A flash of the old Tasha as she rolled her eyes at his ignorance. 'It's an *app* where you can rate your friends. You can like, leave comments telling them what they should do to make themselves better. Everyone has it.'

Jesus. 'And what did you say?'

'I said they should be nicer and stop telling lies. And that they're stupid and *boring*.'

'Nice work.'

'They're trying to be my friends again because everyone *hates* them now.'

'You going to make up with them?'

'I don't need friends.'

'Everyone needs friends, don't they?' He did – once.

'I don't.'

'Well, play it carefully. You got to be subtle about this.' The sound of Margie and Gary's raised voices trickled in from the kitchen.

She plucked at the duvet. 'Can I ask you something?'

'Sure.'

'Do you love Mom?'

She'd wrong-footed him again. He sat next to her. 'Course I do.'

'I mean like *really* love her.'

'Your mom's done a lot for me, helped me get my life back on track.' It sounded convincing. It should. It was partly true.

'The last time I was at his house Dad said you were only using her for her money.'

Oh, did he? As tempting as it was to expose the home truths Margie had revealed about Daddy Dearest – the DUI, the dalliance with the intern, the subscription to the grubbier areas of Pornhub – there was more traction to be had if he took the moral high ground. 'Got my own money. I'm with your mom because she's the best thing that's ever happened to me.'

'Okay.'

'Do you believe me, Tash?'

A shrug.

'It's normal to resent anyone who comes into your parents' lives. I'm not trying to take your dad's place, and I get why you'd want them to get back together.'

'I *don't* want them to get back together. They just fight all the time.' On cue, the Margie-Gary soundtrack upped a notch in volume.

'It's still tough. I get that.'

'How would *you* know?'

'My folks split up when I was a kid.'

'Why?'

'Same reason. Sometimes people just don't get along.'

'Were you sad?'

'Not really. My dad was an asshole who used to drink a lot, and then my mom got remarried to a guy who actually gave a shit about me.' He waited for her reaction – couldn't tell if she was buying this crock of shit or not.

'You curse a *lot*.'

'That a problem?'

'No.'

'Well you tell me if it bugs you. I can tone it down.'

'Did you solve that case yet?'

'Not yet. But we might have a solid identification for the victim.'

'How did he die?'

'I don't want to give you nightmares.'

'I won't get nightmares. Dad lets me watch *American Horror Story*.'

'Okay . . . He was hit over the head.'

'Did his brains come out?' There was nothing salacious about the question. It was clinical, verging on disinterest.

'Not that I know of.'

'Was there lots of blood?'

Yes. 'Could've been. His body wasn't found for a while.' He hesitated. He shouldn't go any further – he knew he shouldn't. He heard himself say: 'The body was found wearing a prom dress.'

She nodded – no big deal. 'The boy wanted to be a girl. Like Malika's brother.'

'Maybe. Could be whoever killed him dressed him like that after he died.'

'Why?'

'Maybe he was trying to tell the police something. Leave a clue.'

'Maybe he wanted the boy to look pretty.'

'Maybe.' The kid was too sharp. *Back up, back up.*

The door crept open. Margie and Gary smiled down at them with the forced brightness of people trying to hide that they'd just been at each other's throats. For a second Pete felt like a kid again.

Tasha sighed. 'Hi Dad.'

'Did you finish your homework?' Margie asked.

'Yes.'

'All of it?'

'Yes. Pete helped me.' A lie.

Margie gave him a sharp glance, and Gary said: 'Cheers, bud. That was good of you.' He capped this off with a nauseating double thumbs-up.

'Hey, no problem.' It was tempting to give Highway Patrol a call. Let them know that Gary would shortly be hitting the road with a skin-full of booze and a kid in the back seat. But if he deprived Gary of his driving licence then Margie – and he – would be forced to do all the kiddie-lifting.

While Margie saw them out, Pete went to the kitchen and poured himself a glass of cranberry juice. Time for a brief self-interrogation:

Okay there, Pete. Just why the hell did you reveal that to Tasha?

He'd given her enough to find the case online. She'd no doubt look it up the second she was ensconced in her father's pathetic bachelor pad. Something made him do it. An urge to confess? No. Not that. Since their middle-of-the-night heart to heart, her attitude had changed towards him and he wanted to keep that going. Who knew he'd be so eager to gain the respect of a pre-teen sociopath-in-the-making? He snorted a laugh.

'What's funny?'

Whoops. Margie was back. 'Something Tasha said to me.'

'Oh yeah? What?'

Yeah, Pete, what? 'It's nothing – a dumb joke. I guess I'm just relieved we're getting on better.'

She leaned against the counter and smiled. 'You really help her with her homework?'

'Help's not the right word. Math has changed a lot since I was in middle-grade.'

'Tell me about it. She seem happier to you?'

'For sure.'

'Huh. And there was me thinking she's been more intense lately. I was saying to Gary that we should think about taking her to a child psychologist.' So that was what the fight had been about. The asshole wouldn't want to cough up for that.

'I don't think that's necessary.'

She stiffened. Control-freak Margie didn't appreciate unsolicited parenting advice, even from him.

'But what do I know? You're her mom. You know best.'

She softened. 'You've put in a lot of effort with her. Not everyone would.'

'You're worth it.'

She rolled her eyes.

'It's true.' And it was. Of all the women he'd hooked up with in his long career of hopping from state to state, she was at the higher end of the spectrum. Not in terms of looks – a juddering blue vein wormed into her collarbone and she was emaciated to the point of starvation – but in intellect and stability. That had its downsides of course: Margie may be talented at self-deception, but she was smart, too smart, and he'd had to up his game. Suspecting she'd do a background check on him before he moved in, he pre-empted it by coming clean about his one and only conviction for fraud – probation, no jail time. He went by his given name, and he'd learned over the years how to cover his tracks. He kept the phone with him at all times, but the MacBook was fair game. On occasion he left it open in case she was tempted to snoop, updated his search history every so often: this week it was fertility in cancer survivors and some vanilla porn for realism. Then there was his Gmail account with its roll call of fictitious friends with matching Facebook accounts. There was Millet, an old school buddy who was having a tough time with his wife, and Kev, a workmate who kept in touch sporadically. Had to preserve the illusion that he had *some* friends. She wasn't social – another plus – but he'd be dumb to underestimate her.

'Do you think we should tell Tasha we're trying to get pregnant?'

'Let's not rock the boat. See where we're at after I've been checked out.'

She considered this. 'Okay. You ready?'

'Born ready.'

'You want the Glock?'

'Sure.'

He knew from experience that his snot wouldn't run clear for days: the cordite was already stinging his nostrils. Margie could easily afford to join a higher-end range, but for some reason she dug this Puyallup shithole run by a family of monosyllabic in-breeds. In the adjacent lane a group of teenage girls were shrieking and shoving each other. The safety standards were as lax as the ventilation.

He glanced at his phone while she finished the clip. Still nothing from Rainbowbrite, although she must be through talking to the cop by now. His last message – **<You okay? Getting worried about you ☹☹>** – was sent at six-thirty her time.

Margie was impervious to the smoke, the stink, the noise (even the ear protectors were sub-standard). He ran through his IBS pantomime, grimacing, touching his stomach and mouthing: 'Got to use the john.' She made a moue of sympathy, but her real attention was on the target. If he played it right, upped the symptoms, he might avoid the rabid sex session that always followed this outing.

The Neanderthal behind the counter gave him the key grudgingly. The bathroom was exactly as expected: cramped, grubby, and with a poster parody of the Nike sign on the door: 'Just Shoot It.' Using his foot he closed the pan's lid, covered it with a copy of *Guns & Ammo* and sat. There was no movement on Rainbowbrite's Facebook page – a reassuring sign that she wasn't just blanking him.

His phone vibrated, but it was only a message from a client in Ruston requesting an estimate. He'd go in too high: he deserved a break. After a year of proving to Margie that he was a workhorse, taking every job that came his way, he reckoned he was due some downtime – just as well seeing as this coincided with the new interest in the case. Another message alert came in. Bingo. *Atta girl.*

<v sorry bobbie to worry you phone died then had to have family time promised Noah no phones at dinner>

<Hey!!!!! Relieved yr okay! No problem. How did it go? You learn anything?>

<OMG the dress isn't in the evidence it's gone>

He had to read it twice before it registered. **<It's gone missing? Really????>**

<REALLY Eric looked for it a few years back says this happens all the time>

Someone banged on the door. 'Busy in here,' he called. **<That's too bad. Is he SURE it's missing????>** Too much, too desperate, but it was too late. He'd pressed 'send'.

<Yes. I'm so bummed ☹>

<Me too ☺☺> Whoops – smiley faces instead of sad ones, his subconscious taking over. **<I meant: ☹☹☹. SO BUMMED TOO>** The *relief*. It was like being plunged into a warm bath after being chilled to the bone. **<They have any suspects?>**

<no but he said the original investigator was convinced the killer must have had local knowledge>

Local knowledge. Close, but no cigar – that wouldn't help them. **<Could be>** Pete paused to check his pulse rate. It was steady. Good. **<Pity about the dress but great work!!!! Told you you could do it. What else did he say?>**

<lots more to tell you but got to get the boys to bed. Speak later?>

<don't you mean letter??;)>

<LOL bye for now>

<Xx>

A small, guilty **<x>** came in response. The first one. Another triumph.

He yanked the chain – as expected the flush was weak – and washed his hands. *No dress. The dress is gone.* He looked in the mirror, leaned in until his nose almost touched the glass. Behind the relief, the elation, there was a shadow of something else. *Regret.* Madness. If the dress was AWOL, he was home free. Did he *want* the house of cards to fall? He stared into his eyes: 'Do you?'

Another thump on the door. He opened up, came face to face with a guy in a Hawks tee and camo pants. The man moved to shove past him, but Pete held his ground. The guy outweighed him by fifty pounds, but the way Pete was feeling right now he could push the gun-nut's eyes into his sockets, crush his windpipe. Picking up on this, the guy stepped back. Pete leaned into him, said, '*Love* your pants,' winked and walked away.

Wicklowboy22: Please can you take down the page you made for Teddy thanks

Ratking1: What's up? You getting cold feet? Have you reported him missing? If you can't face it, I'd be happy to do it. Or ask a friend. You don't have to be related to a misper to file a report

Wicklowboy22: He called me

Ratking1: Holy. Fuck. You spoke to him? He give you proof of identity?

Ratking1: Shaun? You there?

Ratking1: We should chat about this. You there?

Ratking1: Shaun?

Ratking 1

'Wake up.' Chris prodded at his shoulder.

'Ugh.'

'Jeanie will be up soon. She's got the early shift.'

'So?'

'So you know the rules. You gotta get out of here.'

'Aw, c'mon.'

'Up. I've got things to do anyway.'

'Jesus, Chris. You're such a buzzkill, you know that?' Mack rolled out of bed and hopped into his jeans. She preferred it when he didn't talk, but he was okay, played the game – left his bike down the road out of Jeanie's sight and hearing. Last thing she needed was her sister dropping hints about Mack moving in. While he scrambled around for his belongings, she checked her phone. It was three p.m. in Ireland and there was still no response from Shaun. She'd keep trying. Someone was messing with him. Had to be. She wasn't yet prepared to accept she might be wrong about the ID. Knew in her gut it was Teddy – the dates matched up, and Shaun had flat-out told her that his family were cagey about Teddy. If they'd been lying about him dying, could be they didn't want twenty years of deceit exposed.

'Heard that new guy was around here,' Mack said. 'That Scott guy.'

'Not your business.'

'You screwing him too?'

'Not your business.'

'Yeah, yeah. You seen my boots?'

'Nope. Why do you care who comes around here anyway? You're seeing other people.'

'Not right now I'm not.'

'Bullshit.'

'Whatever.'

'What's Scott like?'

'He's okay. He's cool.'

'Has he been talking about me?'

'Nope.'

'So how do you know he's been around?'

'Devin said.'

He headed into the bathroom. He'd be a while – he had a vain streak. She took the opportunity to shrug over to the edge of the bed and into the chair. There was no way she'd let him see the effort that took. She waited for the dizziness that always came over her when she first got up to fade, realigned, then made for the kitchen. She'd clean up and get dressed when she was alone.

She already had the coffee on when Mack emerged, his hair slicked back. He retrieved the boots from under the bed, and with a 'see ya', clumped out.

Chris placed the flask into the cup holder, went into the office and ran through her morning ritual, checking new reports and UIDs on NamUs and scrolling through last night's activity on the forum. Scott's 'Aqualung' avatar jumped out at her. He was working one of the possible mispers on the GI Doe case, and was up till the early hours messaging with Mommydearest. She scanned through: one misplaced apostrophe, but otherwise his grammar and spelling were perfect – good for him.

As expected, Mommydearest had immediately made the Teddy Ryan/Boy in the Dress connection, but he knew to keep this on the down low until they had confirmation. If there was an ID, the bigger sites would pick it up and they had more resources: ex-profilers, coroners, pathologists, PIs, cops. But they didn't have Shaun – a direct line to the victim. They didn't have Rainbowbrite who lived in the location. And Ellie was right. Chris had missed this. She *wanted* this. Speaking of which, in her email there were several DMs from Ellie begging for a Skype call. She could wait. She'd filled Ellie in on Teddy's family situation days ago, including the intriguing nugget that his family had lied about him dying. She scrolled down, pausing at an email from a generic account, subject line: 'NOT DEAD'.

Rainbowbrite

'. . . so after I got the lead from Eric, I looked up the Evershams but the house was sold in 2000 and I can't find where his widow might have moved to.'

'Can I speak now?'

'Sorry, Chris.' Ellie had launched straight into it, barely said hello.

'Where are you going with this?'

'Well . . . I had this lead and I thought—'

'A lead,' Chris snorted. 'Go Nancy Drew.'

'I wouldn't have told you if I'd known you'd be so snippy about it.' Ellie glanced at her webcam image in the corner of the screen. Her sweaty face glowered back at her. Chris refused to put her cam on, so it was a little like talking into a void.

'Okay, okay.'

'I only told you seeing as we're so close to getting an ID now and seeing as you might open the case to sleuthing, and I know how you feel about . . . I didn't want to do anything behind your back.' Not true. She'd asked for the call because she wanted to show off. Guilty Ellie looked back at her now. It was no wonder Noah busted her for going behind his back with the sleuthing; she couldn't hide a thing. She clicked off the webcam.

'We got bigger issues here, Ellie. I got a message from Shaun asking us to take the case off the site. Says his uncle has been in touch with him.'

'Oh . . . oh jeez. *Really*?'

'Yep. And that's not all. Someone saying they're Teddy Ryan contacted the forum, demanded we take the page off the site. I sent a message to the originator asking for proof of identity, but got nothing back. Get this: IP is in Ireland. I've got Mommydearest on the case trying to be more specific about the locale.'

'Have you told Shaun?'

'Been trying to. He's ignoring my messages. If this is a troll, and it's either that or one of Shaun's family screwing with him, then this would mess with his head.'

'Pretending to be a dead man . . . That's such a cruel thing to do. Do you want me to call the coroner's office and tell them about the possible ID?'

'Let's give Shaun a couple of days. He's vulnerable and I don't want to push him. There's no rush on this.'

Sammy was yelling something from the TV room. She got up to shut the door. The twins could sort themselves out. 'What if it's the killer? Pretending to be Teddy, I mean.'

'Teddy was found in Minnesota. The messages I'm getting are from Ireland. Thought your main theory was that the Boy was offed by a serial killer? You saying it's an *international* serial killer now?'

'The killer could have followed him there, then returned to Ireland.'

'That's . . . never mind.'

'What are you going to do?'

'Page isn't getting any traction. One of the perks of being a small site. I'll suspend it for now until I hear from Shaun again.'

'Shouldn't you keep it up on the site and try and lure the fake Teddy into a trap?'

A sigh.

'No, listen, Chris. There was that cold case last year on Reddit. You must've read about it. Woman was murdered on a hiking trail in Australia, and everything pointed towards the husband being the perp. Guy came on the site to defend himself against the accusations going around, and law enforcement told the forum's mods to let him talk. Husband slipped up, revealed details only the killer could know and dug his own grave.'

A beat, then: 'Give me the name again. Eversham?'

'Sandy Hector Eversham.'

'Okay. Stenton County, right?'

'Yes.'

'We got a date of birth?'

'December 24th, 1955. He died January 7th, '98.'

The clatter of fingers on a keyboard: 'Okay. We got a Louisa May Eversham remarried in 2000 to a Gerald Zachary Jensen. Could be the wife.'

'Could be.'

Tap, tap, tap. 'Gerald Zachary Jensen died in 2008. Jensen was registered to an address in St. Joseph. Could be his wife is still there.'

'Did you get that from the voters' registry?'

'Yep.'

'That's only fifteen miles from where I live.'

'Seriously, we should get confirmation on the ID first.'

'That's what Bobbie says. But I dunno, Chris, even Eric said the sheriff's department didn't care about the case, except for Sandy of course and he—'

'Slow down. Who's Bobbie? I thought your husband was called Noah.'

'Bobbie Cowell. The ex-cop. He worked the case with me when we first posted it on Missing-Linc.'

Another round of tapping. 'Oh yeah. Him. He was really pushing the serial killer angle. How much have you told him?'

Ellie squirmed. 'You can trust him, Chris.'

'How much have you told him?'

'Some.'

Chris cursed under her breath.

Say it. 'Listen, Chris, you can say no, and I know how much you hate doing this stuff, but Bobbie would really like to meet you. Shall I see if he's around? He's usually online and I could add him to the call.'

'We can't do this via email?'

'We can, but . . . It would mean a lot to me. I know we can't open it up to sleuthing yet, but there's no reason why we can't discuss it between ourselves. He's also looked into Stenton County. Eric said they've got a history of hiding evidence and Bobbie's been following that up.'

'Shit. Okay.'

'Really? Thanks . . . Hang on.'

Ellie sent Bobbie a Skype message, and then added him to the call. She'd prepped him – she knew Chris would be resistant to this – and he'd been waiting. A flash of disappointment that he'd also disabled his video link. 'Hey, Bobbie.'

'Hey! Awesome to finally talk to you, Ellen.' His voice was low, gravelly, how she'd imagined it. *Manly.*

'This is Chris. Chris, this is Bobbie.'

'Good to meet you, Chris. Really admire what you do on the site.'

'Thanks.'

'Chris has found an address for Sandy Eversham's widow.'

'You got to be careful there, Ellie,' Bobbie said. 'Say he did keep something back and she's been hoarding it for some reason, by going after it you could mess up the chain of evidence.'

'If there is something there I don't have to touch it. I'll be careful.'

'Safer to leave it to the authorities. You don't want to be given the third degree by some opportunistic defence attorney if the case ever goes to trial.'

'You were with law enforcement, right, Bobbie?' Chris asked.

'NYPD.'

'You don't have a New York accent.'

'Wasn't born here. Grew up all over.'

'Why did you leave LE?'

'Put in my twenty. Decided to get out.'

'A detective?'

'Second grade. Narcotics, then serious crimes. Usual career trajectory.'

'Which district?'

'I'd rather not say.'

'Why not?'

'Value my privacy.'

'Fair enough.'

Ellie breathed out. Chris's interrogatory tone had been making her twitchy. And Chris couldn't take issue with Bobbie's desire for privacy – she was the most private person Ellie knew. 'Tell her about Stenton County, Bobbie.'

'So the county has a low crime rate, but even worse solve rate, especially Part One crimes. You heard of the Waverly case, Chris?'

'No.'

'Okay, so Miranda Jo Waverly, a local teenage girl, went missing in the late seventies. Cops assumed she was a runaway, didn't bother looking too hard for her. Her body was found six months later in a rural area. Found a hunting knife in the vicinity, which they reckoned could've been the murder weapon. Hard to tell for sure as decomp was advanced. Girl's stepbrother confessed to the crime, but the knife was long gone and wasn't used as evidence in the trial. Turned up several months later when one of the deputies quit and his replacement moved his stuff in. This might be the piece of evidence your contact was talking about, Ellen. Lucky they got the confession. They've got a habit of botching cases and they're not going to like the Boy's case being dragged up and waved in their faces.'

Ellie could kiss Bobbie. 'That's why we should work on this. This is what I've been saying all along. We can't trust them with this.' Another volley of shouts came from the TV room. 'Sandy thought it had to be someone with local knowledge. See, back then, to get to the area of the reserve where Teddy was found, you used to have to go far in, take one of the tracks only the rangers use in the summer.'

Chris huffed agreement. 'Could be. You checked the sex offender registry, right?'

'I did that last time around.' That had resulted in months of paranoia; just the thought of it made her want to take a shower. 'There's no one local with a history of crimes against boys.'

'It'll help if we can profile the victim,' Bobbie said. 'Find out if Teddy Ryan had a history of sex work, drugs maybe. I'd be happy to talk to Shaun Ryan if you like.'

'I've got that covered.' Chris's snippy tone was back.

'Well let me know.'

Move it forward. Ellie was now feeling like a host trying to rescue an awkward dinner party. 'Tell her about the new one you found in Seattle, Bobbie.'

'New one?' Chris asked.

'Victim.'

'You mean your serial killer theory. How does that fit in with the local knowledge angle?'

'We have to look into everything, Chris. Go on, Bobbie.'

'Okay. So far we got three unsolved homicides with similar characteristics. All occurred in the nineties, blond guys aged nineteen to twenty-five. There's GI Doe, Boy in the Dress, and a kid who was found in Louisville – Maxwell Davis. Been looking through cold cases, and there's an eighteen-year-old boy killed in Seattle in '95 who matches the victimology. White, slim. Stripped and dumped.'

'Was he identified?'

'Yeah. He was local. Known to frequent gay venues. Disappeared one night after talking to an older guy at a bar. White guy, fifties.'

'How was he killed?'

'Ligature strangulation.'

'So a different MO to the others.'

'Reckon this guy killed them in different ways. Made some of them look like hate crimes, or like mob killings or whatever.'

'Ligature strangulation. That's rare.'

'Relatively, yeah.'

'And personal. Implies the guy knew this kid.'

'Wow. You know your stuff, Chris.'

'Can you crawl any further up my ass, dude?'

'*Chris,*' Ellie was up and out of her seat.

Bobbie laughed good-naturedly. 'It's cool. Sorry, Chris. Didn't mean to come across all star-struck.'

Ellie sat back down. 'Do you have be so rude, Chris?'

'Calm down, Ellie.'

'It's just . . . Bobbie's trying to help us on this.'

'Okay, okay. Bobbie, I'm sorry if I offended you. Look, is that it? I gotta go.' And with a blip, she was gone.

She and Bobbie spoke at once. 'Sorry, you go.'

'Ladies first.'

'I didn't think she'd interrogate you like that.'

'I'm a big boy, I can handle it.'

'She's so *aggressive*.'

'Don't sweat it. She comes across the same on the site. So do you.'

Ellie laughed – a mortifying squeal of nervousness. 'I do?'

'Yeah. And I mean that in a good way.'

'You sound the same too.'

'That a good thing?'

'Yes.' *What are you doing?* She touched her face: her cheeks were burning as per usual. 'There's something you should know. Shaun Ryan wants the case off the site. He's been getting calls from someone saying they're Teddy.'

A pause. 'You're kidding.'

'No. And Chris says the site has been getting messages from someone saying they're Teddy, too. Chris is sure it's trolling. The IP address is in Ireland. I said to her it could be the killer doing this, but she says that's just dumb.'

'It's worth bearing in mind.'

'It's dumb. I know it is. It's just . . . I really want to get this thing solved.'

'Of course you do. You've been working it for months.'

Except for when she took her time out. Should she bring that up? No. 'I still think I should talk to Sandy's widow. How can it hurt? If she's got something I could just let law enforcement know.'

'Hang fire on that for now, Ellie, see how the county reacts when they got a possible ID. Could be they'll surprise us and follow it up.'

Ellie. It made her feel light inside. 'You're right.'

'It's great to be working with you again. Can't say that enough. I've missed you. Can't tell you how good it is to finally hear your voice.'

The door opened, Noah peered in, gave her a look, then left.

'You still there, Ellie?'

She swallowed. She could practically taste the guilt. 'I'm here. Only . . . I'd better go.'

'You okay?'

'Of course. I'm . . . I have to see to the boys.'

'Gotcha. Say "hi" from me. And Ellie . . .' he'd lowered his voice. 'Hope we can do this again. And soon.'

'Yes.'

She killed the call, stayed where she was until the flutter inside her stilled. She hadn't done anything: this reaction was way out of proportion – *wasn't it*? Bobbie wasn't this friendly and flirtatious when the case was first put up. They'd been messaging constantly this time around. In the last couple of days she'd spent more time online with him than she had with the boys and Noah combined. She pocketed her phone and made for the TV room. The twins were nowhere to be seen.

She took another moment to compose herself before she joined Noah in the kitchen.

He was seated at the breakfast bar, picking through a work file. 'Heard a man's voice.'

'That was Bobbiecowell.'

'Your ex-cop?'

'We were Skyping with Chris. Are the boys okay?'

'Almost killed each other. Sent them to their room for a time out.'

'Not what you want to deal with when you come home.'

'Why not? I'm their dad. What's for supper?'

She hadn't even thought about that. 'There should be something in the freezer.'

'Relax. I'm not getting at you. Eric was asking about you.'

'We should get him over some time.'

'I'll ask him. Reckon he's lonely.'

She dug through a stack of ice crystals and Häagen-Dazs until she came to a family-size Hawaiian pizza. 'Pizza okay?' She didn't remember buying it; could've been there for months. Her phone beeped. Bobbie again: **<Mean it. Great to hear your voice! Xx>** Shame joined the guilt: she wasn't wholly innocent – she'd sent him an 'x' in response the other night.

'Earth to Ellie?'

'Sorry.'

'I said pizza's fine. I got time for a shower?'

'Sure.' She waited for him to leave the room, then typed 'robert cowell + cop + nypd' into Google. Something she should have done months ago.

Rainbowbrite: Why were you so hard on bobbie?

Ratking1: Told you. Accent didn't match the story. I offend him that bad?

Rainbowbrite: He says not. Don't take this the wrong way but does his verification check out? Can't find a retired NYPD detective called robert cowell anywhere online. He's not on FB

Ratking1: He tell you it was his real name and not his user name?

Rainbowbrite: No just got that impression I guess ☹

Ratking1: You smelling catfish?

Rainbowbrite: I think he's okay. We've been talking for a long time now & he's always been super helpful and smart

Ratking1: Checked him out. VPN he uses is high end. Paid bucks for it. Doesn't have to be suspicious. Most members use them

Rainbowbrite: I don't

Ratking1: Yeah but you're all sunshine and light and don't think The Man is spying on you. Bet you don't even tape up your webcam

Rainbowbrite: OMG I don't!!!

Ratking1: What's got you jangling?

Rainbowbrite: It's dumb

Ratking1: Spit it out.

Rainbowbrite: I think he was coming on to me. Flirting ☹

Ratking1: Welcome to the internet dude. Tell me he hasn't been sending you dick pics . . .

Rainbowbrite: No!!!
OMG Chris

Ratking1: Lots of people like to big themselves up, pretend to be cops on the site. And if he's harassing you then we'll block him. Want me to unleash Mommydearest on his ass?

Rainbowbrite: Not harassment. Think I might have given him the wrong idea which is on me. Don't worry shouldn't have told you. I'll talk to him

Ratking1: You sure?

Rainbowbrite: I'm sure.
Thanks

Ratking1: Hey Shaun, you OK?

Ratking1: Site's been getting messages from someone saying they're Teddy Ryan. IP is in Dublin. Could be the same person who called you?

Ratking1: My gut says someone is trolling you & us

Ratking1: You know anyone who might do this?

Wicklowboy22: Teddy's brother Donny doesn't want the guards involved or coming anywhere near the family or his business

Ratking1: Why? He shady?

Ratking1: Hate to bug you Shaun but we should talk about this. Whoever is doing this is a cruel asshole

Wicklowboy22: Teddy called me from a New York number checked the code 646

Ratking1: Cell or terrestrial? Can you send it? Might be able to trace it. Or you try it. Use Reverse Google to find the address

Wicklowboy22: Looked like a cell. It's disconnected now

Ratking1: He give you proof of identity?

Wicklowboy22: He says he won't contact me again until I take everything down & I'm not to go to the guards as he's in trouble in the US & can't get involved with the police

Ratking1: Yeah well that sounds as hokey as shit to me

Ratking1: Sorry Shaun but had to say it

Ratking1: Why not be sure it's him?

Wicklowboy22: Can't decide if it's better to know he's dead for sure or have the hope he's out there

Ratking1: It's better to know

Wicklowboy22: Is that what other families say?

Ratking1: Know from personal experience. My mom went missing when I was a kid

Wicklowboy22: Oh jesus I didn't know. Did you find her?

Ratking1: She's listed on the site. www.missing-linc/guzman/

Wicklowboy22: She's very beautiful. Is that you with her in the photograph?

Ratking1: Nope. My sister Jeanie. 6 years older than me. Pic was taken 2 months before Mom left for the last time

Wicklowboy22: What will you do if you never find her?

Ratking1: I'll keep looking until I can't any more

Wicklowboy22: That sounds lonely

Wicklowboy22: Sorry not sure what I meant by that

Ratking1: Lonely works. It doesn't have to be lonely

Wicklowboy22: Is this the real reason why you started the site?

Ratking1: Yeah

Wicklowboy22: Do you have any leads?

Ratking1: She was in and out of our lives when we were growing up and then one day she didn't come home at all. Sometimes that's the way it is. If the Boy is Teddy you should know. Rule it out. Go to the cops, or at the v least get another pic we can compare. Worth a shot right?

Wicklowboy22

Johnny came to the door dressed in a vest and tracksuit bottoms, the pompadour drooping like a dying animal. 'Missed you the other day, son. Thought you were coming over?'

'You're a murderer.' Shaun let it blurt out: there was no other way to say it.

No surprise, only resignation: 'Who told you?'

'Donny.'

'That bastard.' As Johnny stooped to pet the dog, his vest rode up, revealing whorls of silver hair on his back. Shaun couldn't take his eyes off them, found himself thinking, ridiculously: *the hairy back of a murderer*. Daphne rubbed her head against Johnny's palm, then attempted to slip past him and into the warmth of the house. Shaun yanked her to heel.

'Why didn't you tell me before?'

'Why do you think? You wouldn't have given me the time of day.'

'Who did you kill?'

'Are you not coming in?'

'Tell me first.'

Johnny leaned against the doorframe. 'Not much to tell.'

Shaun waited for him to continue. He'd been sick with the thought of it. He'd searched for 'jonathan mckinnon + murder + 1995' but there wasn't much to go on – not everything was put online in those days. In his darker moments he found himself wondering if Johnny could have travelled to the US and killed Teddy for some reason, but talked himself out of that convoluted bollocks before it could take root. He'd thought again about calling Máirín, confiding in her about his visit to Donny and the Teddy call, but something held him back. Oddly enough, he didn't have that issue with Chris. There was truth in the cliché that it was easier to talk to strangers, even if she was convinced Teddy was the Boy in the Dress. Shaun knew in his heart that she was right – especially as the site was also receiving messages from a local IP address – but he couldn't quite sever every strand of hope that Teddy was out there somewhere.

Johnny focused on a point over Shaun's shoulder. 'Happened just after I heard Teddy had been killed in that accident. I was in a bad place, told you that. A girl I was seeing asked me to come over to her place, some dive in Camberwell. We went for a drink and a fellow made a play for her. I wasn't having that, and things turned ugly. He ended up dead; I ended up banged up. Didn't plan to do it, but I was a violent sod when I was on the drink.'

'How did you kill him?'

'You don't want to hear that.'

'I do.'

'Glassed him.' He tapped his neck – a chilling, matter-of-fact gesture. 'Hit an artery. Like I say, it wasn't planned.'

The indistinct sound of a woman's voice came from within the house.

Johnny looked over his shoulder, called: 'Coming, Mam.' He turned back to Shaun. 'I've got to get her out of the bath. Can you not judge me in the fucking house?'

Johnny hadn't mentioned a mother before, but so what? That was the least of his omissions. 'I've got the dog.'

'Bring her in.'

Rationalising that Johnny was hardly going to slaughter him with his mother present, Shaun let Daphne drag him inside. He couldn't leave here empty-handed. He needed that letter Johnny had mentioned, as well as a photo of Teddy for Chris.

The layout echoed the tiny bungalow he'd shared with Eileen; the bedrooms, kitchen and lounge tacked onto the hallway as if designed to minimise privacy. It was in better repair than theirs had been – the laminate flooring gleamed, the walls were a bright, crisp white – but it smelled the same, of bacon and cigarette smoke, which brought on a pang of nostalgia. Daphne sniffed at the skirting boards.

'Go on in the lounge,' Johnny said. 'I won't be long.'

As Johnny opened a door at the end of the hallway, Shaun caught a glimpse of a naked, elderly woman clinging to a metal bath rail, all bones and skin. Johnny closed the door behind him, but Shaun heard him saying, 'Ready, Mammy? And one, two, three, up.' He shivered: a man who'd glassed someone – *killed* someone – had no right to sound so compassionate. Daphne took the lead again, pulling him into a living room with a busy carpet and drawn curtains. A flat screen took pride of place next to a vintage drinks cabinet, and while the couch and armchair were baggy with use, the room was clean and well cared for. He went over to the framed photographs on the sideboard. There were several depicting a young guy with Johnny's hair, shirt collar up, a cigarette dripping from his lips – a moody, cut-price matinee idol. Johnny wasn't conventionally handsome back then, but he'd had something. It was obvious why he clung to his youth.

Daphne rolled on the rug, and Shaun perched on the end of the sofa. A clock ticked softly in the background – what he thought of as an 'old lady' sound. It was soothing, and for the first time since he'd received the Teddy call the tension loosened its grip.

A door opened and shut, a shuffle of footsteps, and then a woman inched into the room, tiny frame hunched over a wheeled walker. Johnny came in behind her, watching her every move. He helped her over to the armchair, and she gave Shaun a bright, gummy smile.

'This is Shaun, Teddy's nephew. Spit of him, isn't he?'

Wet blue eyes flicked from Shaun to Daphne. She smiled again, nodded, and said, 'Ahhh.'

'She's recovering from a stroke.' Johnny raised his voice. 'Have a bit of trouble with words, don't you, Mammy?'

'Do.'

Shaun stood. 'Nice to meet you, Mrs McKinnon.'

'Idee.'

'She says to call her Bridie.'

The fingers on her left hand were furled into a fist, and Johnny took a cotton bud out of his pocket and gently cleaned between them. 'Won't be long until you're back to normal and giving me shite for not doing the washing up, will it?'

Bridie let out a sound that could be a laugh.

Before Shaun could stop her, Daphne jumped up onto her lap. He fumbled for the lead, hadn't realised he'd allowed it to slip off his wrist. 'God, sorry.'

'She's alright, son,' Johnny said and Bridie flapped her good hand at him. A tear snaked down her cheek as she patted Daphne's head.

Johnny turned on the TV. 'Come on in the kitchen,' he said to Shaun. 'Can't smoke in here. Shout if you need anything, Mammy.'

Shaun moved to collect the dog.

'Leave her. You love dogs, don't you, Mammy?'

Bridie nodded.

'You sure? She can be a handful.'

'I'm sure. Let's go.'

Shaun kept a wary eye on Daphne as he followed Johnny out of the room. The dog stayed where she was. She loved a lap, used to spend all evening curled up with Eileen, and she was already shedding over Bridie's flannelette nightgown.

The kitchen had the same comforting, old-fashioned aura. The linoleum and melamine were worn with use, but every surface was spotless. Whatever else Johnny might be, he was a talented housekeeper. Johnny lined up an ashtray and a bottle of Bushmills.

'When did you get out of prison?'

'Year ago. Was in a halfway house for a while, then got permission to come home and look after my mother when she had her stroke. There's no one else. Drink?'

He shouldn't, he hadn't eaten anything since breakfast, but he needed something to shore him up. 'Thanks.' There was so much to say, so much to ask, he couldn't hold it all in his head. Decided to start with: 'Did Teddy ever break his arm?'

Johnny froze, midway through unscrewing the bottle. 'Why the fuck would you ask that?'

'Did he?'

Johnny eyed him, then slopped whiskey into the glasses. 'He did. Roller-skating, years back, when we were kids. Down by where we used to go knacker drinking. Got us all to sign his cast and we covered it with bad words. Your nanna was livid.'

The hope gave a last dying flutter. Shaun took a sip, blocked out the taste, waited until the liquid burned all the way into his stomach. 'What about his groin? Did he ever injure that?'

'His groin? Why the fuck are you asking this now?'

'I've got something to tell you. About Teddy.'

A snort. 'I'm beginning to get that, son. I'm not a total fucking numpty. Have you found him?'

'Yes. No. Maybe. Long story. You'll want a drink. It'll be hard to hear.' *Even for a murderer.* And wasn't 'hard to hear' the same phrase he'd used with Donny?

'Hard to shock me.'

We'll see. He took another fortifying sip, then launched into it. The words came out sounding flat. It could be the booze cushioning him, or perhaps he was too tired to feel much of anything, but it was easier to relate this time around than he thought it would be. Other than to ask 'what the fuck is websleuthing when it's at home?' Johnny let him talk without interruption, his gaze focused inwards, chain-smoking roll-ups and Shaun's Vogues and grinding each butt into the base of the ashtray. Shaun ended the spiel with the composite portrait show and tell.

Johnny stared at the image on the phone's screen, then handed it back. 'That it?'

'That's it.'

Johnny breathed in, breathed out, then bent over the counter as if he'd been punched. 'Jesus fucking Christ. I knew it. I *knew* something had happened to him. Knew he would have been back, son. They chased him away but he would have been back.' He took a drink, ran a hand through his oily hair. 'Murdered. Some fucker killed him. Christ.'

'You think it is him then?'

'Course it fucking is.'

'But what about the call I got from New York?'

'Wasn't him. Donny's talking bollocks. Teddy was never into drugs, hated the fucking things. When we were in London, you couldn't go anywhere without someone handing you a spliff or shoving an E down your neck. Teddy hated all that, said it turned people into tossers. Christ.' He banged his chest. 'Blood's pumping like a bastard.'

'I told you it would be hard to hear.' He didn't recall finishing his drink, but somehow, his glass was empty. And now there was an emptiness inside him too, as if Johnny's delayed, emotional response was enough for both of them.

'You weren't wrong. Could have built up to it, but. Jesus.' He slopped more alcohol into their glasses. 'And Donny doing that. He's a hard bastard, alright. Trying to cover up his brother's murder because he doesn't want the guards poking into his business.'

'Is he into gun-running?'

'You what?'

'Donny. Is that what he does for money?'

'How the fuck would I know? He's your uncle, not mine. Haven't seen the bastard for twenty years.'

It was a shadow at the back of his mind, something he hadn't yet dared to verbalise. 'Could he have killed Teddy? Or . . . had him killed? He got someone to call me from New York, so there's something he's hiding. What if Teddy found out something dodgy about his business and threatened to go to the guards?'

Johnny snorted. 'Donny wouldn't do that. Not to his own brother. And as for Teddy grassing him up, there's no chance. You've been reading too many of those thriller books.'

There was no way that Johnny could know this for sure, but Shaun allowed himself to believe it – for now. 'Was Teddy into drag?'

Now Johnny choked on his drink. 'The things you're hitting me with. Where's this coming from?'

'The boy was found wearing a dress.'

'What the fuck are you talking about?'

He'd left out this detail – he couldn't go into everything – and he gave Johnny a rundown. 'Was Teddy into that?'

'Cross-dressing you mean? No.' He paced, a bear in the kitchen. 'No. Never a sign of that. Jesus. A dress? What kind of a sick bastard would do that to him?' His lips were trembling, but Shaun couldn't tell if this was from anger, grief or disgust.

Keep going. 'You said you had a note from him. Can I see it?'

'Oh Christ, yeah. Wait here.'

Shaun should really check on Daphne, but he remained where he was, unwilling to move in case it threatened the numbing equilibrium. Johnny returned and handed him an envelope with torn edges. 'It came to the house when I was locked up. Teddy couldn't send it to where we were staying in London on account of we were squatting.' The writing on it was childish, borderline illegible, the postmark ripped away. 'This was inside it.' Johnny handed over another envelope, this one sealed and addressed simply, 'To Eileen.'

The floor dropped, righted itself. 'You didn't say he'd written to my mam as well.'

Johnny looked at his socks.

'Why not?'

No response.

'You didn't open it?'

'No, son.'

'Why didn't you send it on to my mam?'

'Didn't know it even existed. I wasn't here when it came to the house, was I? When I got sent down, I didn't have the heart to tell my folks. I lied to them, didn't I?'

'For twenty years?'

'I told them I was working overseas. Don't think they believed it, but then you don't want to think the worst, do you? Had to come clean a couple of years later, but by then the last thing on their minds was a two-year-old letter. Found it with my things when I got home. Thought about confronting your family as soon as I got back, course I did, but then I saw you at the shop and . . . you know.'

'You followed me to the cemetery that day?'

'No. I was visiting my da. I couldn't come back for his funeral on account of bad behaviour. Why I got extra time. Never been good with authority. Seeing you then was . . . what's the word I'm after?'

'Serendipity?'

'Jesus, you've got a brain on you haven't you?' He glanced at the letters. 'Go on. Read them.'

Fingers now as numb as his insides, Shaun couldn't feel the paper. He shook out his hands one by one, praying that the booze would keep the panic attack at bay. He started with Johnny's. The writing was smudged, little more than a scrawl:

> john
> Im in new york and can you give this to eileen and tell her I'll rite to her soon for longer when Im sorted. Tell her that Im not dead like they said and not to listen to anything the fuckers say and I was coming back to find her but they wouldnt say were she was & tell her to keep this letter sekret. Can you do that? Old times sake. She can write to me at General Delivery New York, NY 10001–9999 america and I'll keep checking it before I leave here to see if shes send something. Ill try calling the house again but they wont let me talk to her Staying at a ymca at the minute and I'm okay need money but okay sorry how we left things
> Cheers ted

Johnny was watching his every move. 'What about the other one?'

As he tore into the second envelope, of all the things Shaun could have been thinking about, it was a scene from *Charlie and the Chocolate Factory* that came into his mind – his favourite scene, the one where Charlie ripped through the wrapping off his last, precious chocolate bar to find a golden ticket beneath. *Mad*. 'Shall I read it out?'

'Yeah.'

'"Eileen, I'm alive. Don't listen to what those fuckers say to you. I'm not dead, wrong of me to let them get away with that. I'm sorry I just left it burns at me and I had found a clinic for you in Camden but it's too late for that now."'

He looked up. 'Teddy was going to help Mam have an abortion.'

Without being asked, Johnny lit a rollie and handed it to him. The filter was soggy, the smoke harsher than he was used to. He gagged; the room swam, the floor dipped once more. He knocked back the last of his drink, teeth clinking against the glass. So much for his mother's story that she fought to keep him. He dared to dig beneath the numbing cocoon to see if this new twist had the potential to mess him up. If Teddy hadn't been sent away, Shaun might not even exist. What would he have done in her position? The same, probably. How would he ever know?

'Go on.'

The words danced on the page, and he rubbed at his eyes. He stumbled through the rest: '"I tried to call the house many times but Da answered. Met this guy JT a while ago he said he could get some work for me where he lives but it's a long way but anyway so I'm going there in a bit to get organised so you can come to me if you want to I'll look after you fuck em I'll rite again when I'm fixed up. I shouldn't have left you but I did. If you want to keep the baby and not do adoption then I'll bring you here when I'm sorted out. I'll go through Johnny with the letters as Mam and Da will stop anything from New York he's a bastard but you can trust him. Love you and please write to me soon so I know you are okay."'

Silence for as long as a minute. 'Is this all he sent? He says he was going to write again.'

'Never got a reply, did he?'

'And she never got this. It was better when I thought he'd died in an accident.'

'The truth always comes out.'

'You forgot the part about it setting you free.'

'Didn't set me free.'

There was something he was forgetting. 'Have you got a photograph of him? Taken as recently as possible?'

Johnny took a wallet out of a kitchen drawer, and pulled out a folded photograph. It was creased, faded at the edges, but the image – young Johnny and Teddy leaning against spiked railings, glaring into shot, cans of lager in their fists – was clear enough. It was what Chris needed. There was a mocking, defiant quality in Teddy's eyes that wasn't evident in Eileen's old photograph.

'Had it on my wall for years when I was inside. Got the shit ripped out of me for that.'

A sob blarted out before Shaun could stop it, an odd, toady sound. He wanted nothing more than to slide to the floor, shut his eyes, fade away. Shaun heard himself saying: 'Would he have liked me?'

Johnny tipped the dregs of the bottle into his glass. 'Can I give you some advice, Shaun?'

'Yes.'

'Some sick bastard killed your uncle and you have to go after justice. So for the love of Christ, toughen the fuck up.'

Bobbiecowell

He'd made capellini with clams, Margie's favourite. It was good – it was always good – but his appetite had deserted him. As he picked over his food, he picked over the interesting fact that someone pretending to be Teddy had been trolling Shaun and the site. It wasn't unknown for assholes to impersonate missing people in order to screw with family members – he'd briefly considered doing so before he came to his senses – but it was an unexpected twist. And that wasn't the only thing that had him on edge. He'd been sloppy. That Skype call had been a mistake, should have guessed Ratking would question his Brooklyn cop persona, and he'd woefully misjudged Rainbowbrite's level of self-worth. He'd shelved his plan to entrap her into a compromising online romance, and it was going to take some fancy footwork to dance back into her good graces. He needed her. Dissuading her from visiting that cop's widow was another miscalculation – if she were doing the digging then at least he'd be forewarned if there was something there. That goddamned dress. *There today, gone tomorrow.* It was like being on death row and getting a reprieve from the Governor. Or was it? He couldn't discount the shadow of regret he'd felt when he learned this major piece was potentially out of play. If he were a true deviant or a pop-up character on *Criminal Minds,* he'd take the next flight to the Twin Cities, pay Sandy Eversham's widow a visit, see for himself. Erase the evidence and whack the widow – take a leaf out of Bobbiecowell's mythical serial killer playbook and make it look like a mob hit or a suicide. *Ha de fucking ha.*

Margie was saying something. He looked up and smiled. 'What was that? Miles away.'

'You always are these days, Pete.' Waspish.

'Sorry, hon.'

'I was saying that an email came from the school today. A letter about cyber-bullying. There was something about an app called "Savvy". Do you know anything about this, Tash?'

The kid was also pushing her food around her plate. 'No.'

Pete shot her a collusive glance. He had to admire Tasha's brevity. He would have been tempted to elaborate and bolster the lie with another.

'How about your friends?'

'No one's said anything.'

'We haven't had Olivia for a sleepover for months. Why don't you invite her this weekend?'

'Maybe. Can I be excused, Mom?'

'Pete hasn't finished eating.'

He shrugged. 'Fine by me.'

Tasha took her plate over to the sink, then slunk off to her room.

Margie watched her go. 'I'd better keep a closer eye on her.' His phone trembled and she clucked her tongue. 'Better keep a closer eye on you too. Work?'

'Yeah.' A message from Rainbowbrite – *finally*. **<no new updates>**. It was dry, but better than nothing. 'Think I've lost the Ruston job.'

'Is that why you've been so distracted?'

'Feel bad that I'm not contributing to the household as much as I should lately.'

'We get by.'

'On the upside, I've got a couple of bites. One in Seattle. Could be good, a complete remodelling job.' Best to lay the groundwork now – just in case he needed to nip away at short notice. *Oh really? And just where are you planning to go, Pete?*

'Seattle?'

'I might not have a choice. Things are tough in the trade at the moment.' A lie. New requests for estimates were coming in daily.

'I make more than enough.'

'I've got to contribute. Isn't right otherwise.' He sighed and pushed his plate away. 'I made an appointment at the clinic.' He'd been holding this little nugget back in case he needed the brownie points.

'You did?'

'Told you I would.'

'When for?'

'Wednesday. Three-thirty.' Halloween. *How apt.*

'I can shift things around.'

'I can handle it by myself.'

She smiled. 'That a euphemism?'

'Could be. After all, it *will* just be me and my hand in a room with a jar.'

'You make it sound so romantic. Well you're not going by yourself. We're in this together.'

'Not gonna lie, it'll help knowing you're there.'

'Come here.' He got up, and she pulled him down for a kiss. 'Mmm. Garlic.'

'You love garlic.' He moved away and started packing the plates into the dishwasher. 'You go relax, I'll do this.'

'You sure?'

'Of course.' He always did it. *Actions speak louder than words.*

'Thanks. Been a tough day.'

He waited until he heard the sound of the TV, then got to work. Time to plaster over the cracks. **<Hey, Ellie. You've been quiet. You okay? I do something to offend you? ☹>**

He rinsed the pasta pot, wiped the counters, and when she still hadn't replied, nudged her again: **<This is hard to say, but I'm guessing I made you uncomfortable. Came on too strong. Am I in the right ball park?>**

<Yes ☹>

<Thought so. Guess it's because we have a connection you know? Read too much into it. Won't happen again>

<I was flattered kind of but I don't do that kind of thing. I'm happily married>

'Pollyanna,' he said under his breath.

'You say something, hon?' Margie and her supersonic hearing. The perils of an open-plan house.

'Talking to myself,' he called.

'You coming through? *Atlanta*'s on.'

'Won't be long.' Back to Rainbowbrite: **<I get that. Feel terrible ☹>**

<Is Bobbie Cowell your real name?>

Here we go. **<User name>**

<What is your real name?>

<What's with the questions? Is this coming from Chris?>

<No>

<My real name's Mark>

<Mark what?>

<Starmer. You won't find me on Facebook ☺ I don't do social media> A minute passed. Then another. **<Know you're looking me up so while we're clearing the air about stuff I got something else to tell you. Haven't been entirely honest with you. Reckon it's time to come clean>**

He waited. Who could resist that juicy morsel? Not Rainbowbrite, for in came: **<What u mean????>**

<I was a cop but not a detective. Beat cop & then a desk jockey. Bigged myself up to impress you. Say the word and you won't hear from me again. Know I let you down. Not cool> He deployed the first missile: **<I'm this guy: cache:https//:nypost.com/NYPD-officer-shot-apprehending-suspect>**

He'd almost given up hope of finding someone who fitted the criteria – ex-LE, alive, but with no social media presence – when he'd stumbled upon a cached article from the late nineties featuring Officer Mark Starmer from Bed Stuy, Brooklyn. Starmer fell off the radar a while back, and would now be in his early sixties. It was older than Pete would ideally like his Bobbiecowell persona to be, but hey ho. It was chancy – if Rainbowbrite even scratched the surface, tracked this guy down, Bobbiecowell would be toast.

Then he'd have no choice but to leave this alone or spend months gaining her trust under a new avatar. He had a couple of sleeper alter egos who popped up occasionally on the site and social media, but they were one-dimensional in comparison.

<You were shot????>

No trademark 'OMG!!!' Time to go to DEFCON 5. **<You want to see the scar?>**

He took a close-up picture of the keloid bump on his abdomen, careful to keep the shot tight. Last thing he wanted was Rainbowbrite querying the remarkable shape Mark Starmer was in for a sexagenarian. She wasn't a doctor – the scar where the drain was inserted could easily double as a healed gunshot wound, or act as proof for any number of conditions if he was careful about it. It had worked so far with Margie. The years he'd spent fighting cancer were more dramatic and useful than the truth – peritonitis. He *had* almost died – a defining moment in his life, but cancer had more weight.

<Thanks for sending me this you didn't need to>

<I did. Should have done it way back>

<Are you okay now?>

<Got some problems but who hasn't? You think badly of me for saying I was a detective? Always wanted to be, but couldn't cut it>

<It's okay. I get why you would. You were still a cop ☺>

Annnnd the emojis were back. She was thawing. **<You can still call me Bobbie;)>**

<Why Bobbie?>

If you only knew . . . **<Name of my first lieutenant. Looked up to him. You want to Skype, hash all this out?>** A gamble – she'd seen Mark's photo now. If she went for it, she'd be dumb not to ask him to use the webcam.

<No it's okay. Are you married?>

<I was once>

<Divorced?>

<She died> *No. Too much, delete, delete.* **<Messy break up. Years ago. Still hurts. She found someone else>**

<I'm so sorry. Do you have children?>

<One. She's all grown up>

<What does she do?>

<She lives in England. She married a doctor> Where did that come from? Jesus – if he didn't rein it in he'd have to start making a spreadsheet.

<Oh wow! England!! Where??>

<London>

<Do you visit her?>

<No. Money's too tight. Pension's small. Can I tell you something else?>

<Of course>

<I got issues. I'm kind of a shut in>

<Agoraphobic?>

<Not that bad but yeah borderline. PTSD. The site helps. Makes me feel like I got a purpose. Again, really sorry if I shook you. You're the first person I've connected with in a long time>

<I understand. It's the internet right? ☺ Should have set the boundaries straight away>

<LOL. Won't happen again. Sorry again from this lonely old man ☺ Hey, any more info on that troll who was messing with Shaun?>

<Chris thinks it might be someone from Shaun's family who doesn't want the cops looking into their business>

<A criminal element?>

<Maybe. She's not sure>

<She knows her stuff. Would've thought she was LE;)>

<I know right?>

<Hope we can get over this>

<We can ☺>

<Thanks for being so understanding>

He'd patched this up for now, but it would be a while until the circle of trust was whole again. It was a wake up call – he had to be more careful. If he was going to continue driving this train, then shunting Rainbowbrite along – or shutting her down

– was a priority. He hadn't yet attempted to derail Chris, but maybe it was time to set that in motion too.

Before he went through to join Margie, he leaned over the sink and breathed in. Invisible fingers trickled over his scalp, the feathery touch of ASMR. There was no paranoia. No fear. No stress. And then it hit him: he was enjoying this.

Rainbowbrite: Hey Chris I checked out Bobbie

Ratking1: And?

Rainbowbrite: He was a beat cop not a detective

Ratking1: So it was ego shit

Rainbowbrite: He's got PTSD and has some other issues

Ratking1: So not boyfriend material then?

Rainbowbrite: LOL

Ratking1: You sure he's kosher?

Rainbowbrite: He told me some stuff about himself in confidence. I can show you if you like?

Ratking1: You know what in confidence means Ellie?

Rainbowbrite: Just saying ☺

Ratking1: Ok if you've checked him out that's fine by me

Rainbowbrite: Thanks ☺ Anything from Shaun?

Ratking1: Still trying

Ratking 1

She didn't have dark days often: wouldn't – couldn't – allow herself to wallow. Whenever she felt one coming on she left the house before the tentacles dragged her too deep. A drive to the store and the obstacles this entailed were usually enough of a distraction to get her through, but as she glided through the supermarket doors it still dogged her.

The email had come into her private admin account during the early hours, no message, just a heading: RE: RIP Eliza Guzman. Going against her principles – trusting her antivirus software was up to the job – she'd clicked on the attachment. Up came a doc pasted with scores of dead women's faces, all of Mexican descent. Most she'd seen before, recognised them from coroners' websites; some of them had even been identified already. There was a taint to it. A subtle viciousness. This wasn't someone attempting to trace her mother, more a calculated effort to taunt her emotionally. The message originated from a generic email account, 8754272@yahoo.com, and the IP trace hit a VPN rabbit hole – her tormentor knew what they were doing. She'd replied to it, but her response had bounced back. She'd told very few people about her mother, but it wasn't impossible to make the connection. She'd riled a good number of members over the years with her zero tolerance policy for infighting – more than likely it was from a blocked member harbouring a grudge. That didn't take the sting out of it.

Music also helped. She chucked a punnet of oranges into the basket on her lap, her only concession to healthy eating, and chose Iggy Pop, 'Funtime', as a soundtrack. She tended to go shopping at night, when there were fewer people around, and apart from an elderly man who was inspecting the cantaloupes with a myopic intensity, she had the place to herself. The darkness finally began to loosen its grip, and her mind turned to her last interaction with Shaun. Telling him about her mom was a calculated decision, an attempt at not-so-subtle emotional manipulation, but he'd flipped that back on her. *Lonely. That sounds lonely.* Of all the things he could have said, he chose this. Sharp of him. And her sense of ownership over the Boy case was growing. She wanted this. *Too much.*

'Funtime' segued into 'Baby' as she moved to the snack section. She was stocking up on ready-made salsa and chips when Scott came around the corner and into the aisle. It was too late to pretend she hadn't seen him; their eyes locked.

'How's it going, Chris?' If he felt any antipathy towards her he didn't show it. More than she deserved. She'd treated Bobbiecowell like crap as well, although maybe that was warranted.

'Hey.' She removed the ear buds, killed the soundtrack.

A teenage girl sloped up behind him. She was overweight, tall, bowed her shoulders, scrunching in on herself.

'This is Kelly. My kid.'

Kelly looked down at her Converse and tugged on her top. 'I'm not a *kid*, Dad.'

'Are to me. This is Chris. Runs that website I was telling you about.'

Chris smiled at her. 'Hi Kelly. Cool name.'

The girl didn't meet her eyes. 'Thanks. I like your hair.'

'Yeah? My sister Jeanie says I should dye it.'

'No ways.' The girl tapped through her phone, and showed Chris a photo of a skeletal model with long silver locks. 'Silver and grey are still the best.'

'You think?'

'I'd love to have hair that colour.'

'You can have mine if you like. Started going grey when I was thirty.' And eight years later it had taken over the black. She kept it long – easier that way. Cut the ends herself whenever she could be bothered.

Scott was watching them, bemused. 'I was telling Kelly about the sculptures at your place.'

'Yeah?'

'Kelly wants to be an artist.'

'*Dad*.'

'What? It's true isn't it?'

'She doesn't want to hear about that.'

'Sure I do,' Chris said. 'What kind of artist?'

'Not sure yet. Graphic, maybe. Illustration. I don't know. I like sculpture too.'

'Cool.' Chris hesitated. 'You can come over and see them if you like.'

'Now?'

'Sure, if you want.' Where was this coming from?

'Your mom's expecting you back,' Scott said.

'I can call her.'

'Yeah. Let's not do that. Can you go get the pancake mix?'

Kelly looked from Chris to Scott. 'I get it. You want to talk. Nice meeting you, Chris.'

'You too.'

With a last shy glance, Kelly shuffled away.

Chris spoke first. 'Seems like a good kid.'

'She is. Got self-esteem issues, but hey, I was a mess at that age.'

'Jeanie mentioned she had a medical condition. MS?'

'Scuse me?'

'Said she had MS.'

'She had meningitis when she was a kid. She's got some issues with her hearing, but that's it.'

'Shit. Sorry. Jeanie's always getting stuff mixed up. Sometimes I think she does it on purpose.'

'It's all good. It's why I moved here. Her mom got remarried.'

'A bad situation?'

'No. He's a good guy. My dad wasn't around when I was growing up, and I don't see why she should go through that.'

They fell into silence. This time, it was on her to break it. 'About what I said when you came over . . .'

'Forget it. Shouldn't have just shown up like that. You finish all the doughnuts?'

'Fraid so.'

'Doesn't show.'

'I run it off.'

He laughed and shook his head. 'You're dark, you know that?'

'I know it. Seen you've been busy on the site.'

'Yeah. I'm kinda getting into it. Listen. I got to run Kelly home. You mean it about bringing her over to see the sculptures some time?'

'Sure. Give me your number.'

They exchanged texts, and he lumbered away. Scott wasn't her type – if she even had a type any more – but she had to admit running into him had buoyed her up.

She was over by the dairy when the message from Shaun came in: **<Will this help?>** Linked to it was a scanned photograph – a full-face shot of Teddy, creased but usable. Adrenaline extinguished the last of the bleakness, and despite knowing Scott was long gone, she found herself looking around for him, eager to share the news.

Mommydearest: I ran the pic

Ratking1: AND??

Mommydearest: Can't be 100% because we can't be certain of the reconstruction's accuracy

Ratking1: Tell me something I don't know. Is it a match or not?

Mommydearest: Would put it at 70%

Ratking1: Sorry to tell you this Shaun but we ran the pic you sent through the software and we're 100% sure it's Teddy

Wicklowboy22: I knew it was him. Do I go to the guards tomorrow and report him missing?

Ratking1: That's the first step

Wicklowboy22: Do I tell them we think he is the Boy in the Dress?

Ratking1: Yeah. Not sure how it'll work but reckon they'll liaise with Stenton County Sheriff's dept & go from there

Wicklowboy22: I read through the comments again. Everyone is saying it wasn't investigated properly

Ratking1: An ID might put a fire under their asses get them to reassign it ASAP

Wicklowboy22: You think they will?

Ratking1: We can help. Got a lot of good people on the site. We can put pressure on the cops & look into things

Ratking1: Might be coming on too strong here but we can feature it on the site. Work it

Ratking1: Think about it, don't have to make a decision now

Wicklowboy22: Don't need to think about it. Someone killed my uncle and I have to go after justice

Ratking1: I'm opening the case for sleuthing

Rainbowbrite: OMG!!! Really? ID official?

Ratking1: Not official but gonna do it now

Rainbowbrite: OMG Shaun okay with this???

Ratking1: Yeah. He's going to liaise with me on this

Rainbowbrite: When will it be live????

Ratking1: Soon. Will send out a notification. You want to help moderate?

Rainbowbrite: OMG yes please!!!

Ratking1: OMG okay

Rainbowbrite: OMG so Chris says ID is definite & she's opening the case for sleuthing!!!

Bobbiecowell: Fantastic news! when?

Rainbowbrite: Tomorrow!!!

Bobbiecowell: Awesome!! ☺☺

Rainbowbrite: I know right? even if this goes big & the other sites pick it up we'll have an edge because we'll have Shaun. Chris says he's going to help with info

Rainbowbrite: Feel bad saying that like we're using him or something ☹

Bobbiecowell: Don't feel bad, know what you mean ☺ Shaun's not the only edge we got. We've got you

Bobbiecowell: That wasn't me hitting on you again BTW ☺!!! Just saying you're the one who championed this case. You should let Shaun know that

Rainbowbrite: Nice of you to say that *blushes*

Bobbiecowell: Speaking as I find. BTW been thinking. Reckon you should go & visit Mrs Jensen to see if Sandy did stash evidence

Rainbowbrite: REALLY? Chris is still adamant cops should do that

Bobbiecowell: I won't tell her if you don't ;) Would be good to know if there's anything to it & might be a while till they reassign it. If there is something we can discuss where to go next

Rainbowbrite: Okay. That's good thinking ;) I'm going to be busy helping mod the site but will think about it. What changed your mind?

Bobbiecowell: Guess I'm just tired of whoever did this getting away with murder

PART TWO:

FOUND

Missing-Linc.com

Matching Unidentified Bodies (UIDs)
With Missing People

How to join | FAQs | Current UIDs | Success stories | Rules

NEW ENTRY

Name: 'Boy in the Dress'

Description: On 4/15/96, a dog walker discovered the remains of a white male on the outskirts of North Park, Millar Town, Stenton County, Minnesota. The body was found wearing a pink prom-style dress.

The Stenton County coroner performed the autopsy. The Boy is thought to have been in his early twenties. 72 inches in height, approx 120–130 pounds. Blond hair (highlighted). Dental showed teeth 16, 17 and 32 as antemortem loss or never formed. Signs that the left forearm was fractured several years before. Fingertips severed post-mortem. Scar tissue present in groin area from possible old injury.

Body was in an advanced state of decomp. Signs of recent animal and insect activity to the face, eyes, and extremities. Cranial fracture, blunt force trauma. The appearance of ice crystals in the heart confirm that the body froze over the winter months, and most likely was covered with snow around late October.

Death categorised as a homicide.

Dress has no identifying labels. See link for a photograph featured in the Stenton County Herald.

We have new information that the dress is missing from evidence.

A composite facial reconstruction portrait was done in 1997, see links.

The case is open but as far as we know has not been reassigned.

<u>**Thread dated: October 28/2017**</u>

Ratking1 [admin]: We have an unconfirmed match on this case and we're opening it up for sleuthing.

Our misper is Edward 'Teddy' Ryan, an Irish national. Teddy was openly gay, 22, and left Ireland in March 1995 to travel to NYC. Looking to track his movements from then until October 1995.

Teddy was staying at a YMCA somewhere in NYC. [There are 22 YMCAs in NYC].

From correspondence he sent to friends in Ireland, we know he was planning to leave NYC in order to visit someone called 'JT' to find work. We do not know where JT was/is located.

I am in touch with a family member and will liaise with them regarding additional info and any questions that may come up. Please be as courteous as you can. Comments will be pre-moderated. NOTE: a grieving family member will be reading our posts.

Teddy Ryan has only recently been reported as missing. According to our contact, a 'garda family liaison officer' (cop) will pass information to the family. Most likely, Teddy Ryan's X-Rays will be accessed and used as a possible means of confirming the ID.

We currently have two photographs [see <u>link</u>]. **Mommydearest** has matched them to the composite image.

Crowroad: REALLY interesting. Why has he only been reported missing recently?

Ratking1 [admin]: Reasons are complex and personal.

He went to New York in 1995 after a family dispute. As mentioned above, he was gay and this caused some friction.

Rainbowbrite [moderator]: Hi everyone!!!! So good to be back. So many familiar faces! And new ones!

Marlborowoman: [message deleted by moderator]

Vladtheromantic: [message deleted by moderator]

Mommydearest [moderator]: Please keep comments relevant to the thread. Personal conversations should be limited to DM.

Rainbowbrite [moderator]: Right!! Sorry!! (also Hi Mommydearest, I've heard so much about you!!)

I would encourage you all to look at the earlier threads here to see our theories. Me and Bobbiecowell did a ton of work on it.

Vladtheromantic: You reckon we could be looking at a serial here?

Bobbiecowell: Reckon the perp is a 'marauder' style killer. AKA a hunter.

Aqualung: You think? The dress seems to make it more personal. A fetish killer maybe? I've done some research, and for e.g. the killer Jerome Brudos had a thing for high heeled shoes & staged his scenes with them.

Dotspot: Can always spot a newbie, they smell like Wikipedia pages and overenthusiasm. (That's my way of saying welcome on board, Aqualung lol).

Vladtheromantic: Teddy Ryan has a similar profile to GI Doe.

Bobbiecowell: So far, I've flagged up four cases with similar victimology, listed here [WARNING: NSFW]. And yes, I've included GI Doe as one of my similar victims (well spotted Vlad). With site's approval I can post a route map where each victim was discovered. All are within 20 miles of popular trucking routes.

Ratking1 [admin]: Go for it.

Mommydearest [moderator]: Will set up a sub thread for this and others we decide to follow. @Ratking1 Coolio by you?

Ratking1 [admin]: @mommydearest Yup

Bobbiecowell: Thanks ☺

Bisontastic: If you post that map Bobbie then I'll check trucking companies, see which ones used that route during our approximate timeline.

Marlborowoman: Must be thousands.

Bisontastic: That's why I'm the resident masochist with a hard-on for eighteen wheelers.

Pennywise: The dress might not have a connection to the killer at all. Could have belonged to the victim.

Aqualung: And why a prom dress? That feels symbolic of something. Do they have proms in Ireland?

Ratking1 [admin]: They do not commonly have proms in Ireland. It's a very American tradition.

Aqualung: Any bloodstains on it?

Rainbowbrite [moderator]: Can't tell from the quality of the crime scene photos :/ unless we get our hands on that police report we'll never know.

Thenightman: Can't believe it's missing from evidence.

Crowroad: You can't believe that small town cops are incompetent and bungled the case? Reeeeeally? Wonder if it has anything to do with it being a gay victim hmmmmmmmmmmmmm . . .

Bobbiecowell: Did Teddy Ryan lead a marginal lifestyle? Any history of drugs, homelessness, sex work? I don't mean to offend the family with this question. It can help to profile the victim.

Ratking1 [admin]: I've asked the family contact and Teddy Ryan was not into drugs.

Dotspot: Employment history? Would have been hard to find work as a foreigner, might have resorted to sex work?

Ratking1 [admin]: Family has no knowledge of what Teddy was doing for money while over here.

Anniehall: Was he into drag?

Ratking1 [admin]: Teddy was not known to be into drag.

Keysersoze: Any sign of defensive injuries?

Bobbiecowell: Nope. Whoever killed him overpowered him.

Keysersoze: Height and weight suggest that wouldn't have been hard to do.

Ratking1 [admin]: Family member says Teddy Ryan knew how to fight.

Dotspot: The perp must be a strong, adept guy then.

Aqualung: Or took Teddy by surprise like a coward.

Bisontastic: OR Teddy didn't see it coming because he knew the perp. Trusted him. Removing the fingertips suggests the perp didn't want Teddy to be identified. Knew it would link back to him?

Crowroad: Good point. Curious about this JT guy. Last known location was New York but his body was found in Minnesota. Possible theory: met this JT in NY. Then met his death while hitchhiking to visit JT in MN?

Mileycircus: Might've visited JT THEN met his death. Murder-by-Stranger is far rarer than being killed by someone you know.

Crowroad: Either way this JT guy is a person of interest. I'll look into NYC arrest warrants, see if anyone matches the initials and timeline.

Mileycircus: Shot in the dark but I'll do the same for Minnesota.

Vladtheromantic: Good thinking. We should also compile a list of perps who were active at the time & who might be incarcerated now.

Mister.Tonyface: Think you just volunteered for that job Vladdy :P.

Mister.Tonyface: Just a thought but was the sex offenders' registry active at that time?

Bobbiecowell: MN sex offenders list went public after the Wetterling case. Already looked into that. No offenders resident in the area at that time.

Aqualung: Convinced the dress is key & has significance for the killer. Say the killer put the dress on the body to stage it, we thinking it could belong to a GF/Sig other? We know what era it's from? Don't know much about dresses but it looks like something out of the 50s.

Rainbowbrite [moderator]: I agree! That style has never been out of fashion which sucks for us ☹ Would be just great to track it down.

Dotspot: Good luck with that guys reckon it'll lead all the way to a dusty thrift store in New York . . .

Aqualung: Do we know what size it is?

Rainbowbrite [moderator]: I've always thought it had to be a six? Sizes have changed over the years. @aqualung it looks like you are just as obsessed with finding it as I am!! Do you want to DM me? Hijacking the thread with this and then will post anything new we dig up?

Wicklowboy22

Funny how a mind could shift: he'd gone from thinking of the people on the site as salacious monsters to something akin to allies. The theories and questions had been coming in thick and fast all afternoon, Chris holding his metaphorical hand throughout. He wouldn't say they were friends exactly, but there was no doubt they shared a bond of sorts and he now understood why she'd cultivated such a brittle carapace. His mother's death may have broken him, but there was a finality to it, whereas Chris had lived with decades of howling uncertainty. And in the days before he'd learned Teddy's true fate, he'd only experienced a taste of how bitter hope could be; she must live with that daily.

He'd have to go and see Janice. Couldn't put it off any longer, not now he'd been to the guards. At least that hadn't been as traumatising as he feared. It had taken him ages to build up the courage to go into the station, wore out the pavement as he paced back and forth, smoking Vogue after Vogue, nicotine burning his tongue. He'd half expected to be treated as a charlatan – the story was outrageous on so many levels – but Neil, the guard who took the report, had listened patiently as Shaun unreeled the story, then asked him to wait while he went to consult with a superior. Neil's phlegmatic attitude helped, as did his honesty about the fact that he wasn't certain about the procedure.

A tourist – British, nervy – came up to the counter with an armful of highbrow travelogues and a guilty-pleasure thriller entitled *His Body of Evidence*. Shaun went through the small talk motions, mind straying back to the discussion. He bagged up the goods, and returned to the monitor the second the fellow left the shop. Something was niggling at him, a question he hadn't thought to ask Neil: Teddy's body. *Teddy's remains.* Where were they? Chris might know. He dropped her a message and she responded immediately – she could type like the wind: **<Not sure. But they won't release anything until case is solved. Rainbowbrite might know. Want me to put you in touch? She was the one who found the case in the 1st place. Lives near to where Teddy was found>**

Rainbowbrite. What a name. Her comments on the site were fulsome and upbeat and he'd been picturing her as a teenager dressed in sparkles. **<Yes please>**

<Thanks for doing this today Shaun. Must have been difficult for you>

Was it? Not really. He hadn't resorted to boozing since that night at Johnny's, and despite spending the day watching his uncle's life being picked over by strangers, he'd maintained an even keel throughout. **<It was easier than I thought. Least something is happening>**

<Sure you won't join the site? You can stay anonymous>

It was the third time she'd pushed him to sign up. He wasn't a joiner, never had been. He was more comfortable staying on the outside, looking in. **<I'll think about it>**

He was cashing up when a pop-up message appeared on screen. Rainbowbrite. Chris worked fast, or maybe these people had nothing else to do all day: **<Hi Shaun, I hope you don't mind me messaging you like this!!! I'm so so sorry about your uncle. I've been working on the case for a long time now and I live near to where he was found so if there's anything I can do to help then please let me know. Chris says you are wondering where he was buried. I tracked that down when I first started working on your uncle's case & he is in the Park Central cemetery Stenton County Lot 987, Plot #17. Burial #25987. I am very sorry to say there is just a marker there no headstone. I can take some photos of it if you like?>**

The kindness of strangers. A flare of mixed emotions took him off guard: anger at Donny and Janice for slinging Teddy on the dung heap; misplaced guilt and shame that it was left up to a stranger on the internet to find out where his uncle was laid to rest. So much for keeping on an even keel.

The message box blinked. He wasn't sure how to respond, settled on an inadequate 'Thanks'.

<If you need anything else or want any more info please let me know thinking of you ☺>

He should take a break from this, start on the Halloween display, a task he'd been putting off. There wouldn't be a story hour this year – that was Máirín's thing, not his – but he should make a bit of an effort. He collected the box from the storeroom. The light outside was drawing in, and the old-fashioned glass lampshades filled the shop with a greenish, Victorian glow. The cosy atmosphere and the simple task of draping novelty spider webbing across the sconces helped banish the emotional pall. He stood back to inspect his handiwork, then made for the display window to hang the origami ravens he and Máirín had made last year.

The door tringed. Typical – someone always came in whenever he cashed up early. He turned, 'You'll have to be quick, we're . . .' He couldn't hide the dismay as Donny stalked in, brushing rain from his sleeves, bleak eyes boring into his.

'You've been to the guards.'

Speak. 'Did they come and see you? Neil said it would take a few days before a Garda family liaison officer was—'

'I've got contacts there. You think I wouldn't find out? I told you to leave this alone.'

'I was waiting to be sure, and then I was going to—'

'I told you to leave it alone. It'll be in all the fucking papers.'

Toughen the fuck up. He drew on the anger he'd felt just minutes before, but fear was taking over and he couldn't muster more than an echo of it. 'Teddy's dead. He's *dead*. He was murdered. That's more important. Don't you care?'

'Don't you fucking say that to me.'

'Did you get someone to call me from New York and pretend to be him?'

A sneer. 'Course I did.'

'Why would you do that? What are you hiding?' And then, before he could stop it, out came: 'Did you kill him?'

The air seemed to freeze between them. '*What* did you just say to me?'

'You know people in New York, you got someone to call me.' His voice had gone up an octave. 'Is it because you're a—'

Donny shoved him up against the bestsellers, gloved hand forcing his left cheek into glossy spines, body pressing into his. Shaun heard himself cry out, attempted to wriggle free, but Donny only increased the pressure. The fight trickled away, leaving him limp, nothing but prey, waiting for the inevitable. 'Are you mad? Kill my own fucking brother?' Donny was close enough for Shaun to smell his breath, feel spit flecking his skin. Blood boomed in Shaun's ears; he'd never been so aware of his heart before. 'What the hell is wrong with you, Shaun?'

The scrabble of claws on wood, a yell from Donny, the pressure eased. A yelp.

Daphne.

Shaun turned, saw the dog, tail tucked between her legs, cowering next to the box of decorations. Donny was going in for a kick – his second? – and Shaun came alive, acted on instinct, slammed his shoulder into Donny's spine. Donny stumbled, rounded on him, face a study of hate. Shaun automatically raised his arms above his head, waited for the blow. It didn't come.

Donny adjusted his coat, flexed his fingers, wiped his mouth. His eyes were dead. 'You're going to regret this, Shaun. You don't know what you've fucking done. Stay away from us. You're not part of this family any more. I wash my fucking hands of you. So does Janice.' He made for the door, paused. 'You should get that fucking dog put down.'

Then he was gone, slamming the door behind him with enough force to rattle the glass.

A beat of empty time, then Shaun dropped to his knees and ran his hands over Daphne's body. She was shaking, but she didn't wince as he pressed down on her limbs. The rage came then, an impotent, delayed force that sapped his breath. He buried his face in the dog's fur, and whispered, 'I've never been part of this fucking family.'

Rainbowbrite

She was just looking. And she couldn't stop looking. It was a ranch-style property, set on a leaf-dusted plot just like hers, wouldn't stand out if it wasn't for the life-size mesh reindeers and sleigh on the lawn. The skeletons of Christmas past, waiting to bc garlanded with lights. The neighbouring houses were all sporting jack-o'-lanterns, another reminder that she didn't have long before she was due to show up for the school run. The back of the car was full of pumpkins she'd bought at the last minute for the boys' classroom display – she'd offered to carve them out of guilt months ago – and they'd been rolling around in there, thunking against each other like severed heads.

She tapped her fingers on the steering wheel. A closer look wouldn't hurt anyone – there was no sign of life from within. Ellie climbed out of the car, crossed the street and moved to the edge of the lawn. A gang of mildewed elves congregated around the porch steps like cheerful muggers, and a plastic snowman lay face down, shrouded with leaves. The breeze tickled her hair, icy with the promise of snow, and she shivered. No one knew she was here. She hadn't even told Bobbie. Going behind Chris's back felt a little like cheating, but after messaging with Shaun, there was both a new urgency and a conflicting, sobering reality to what she was doing. Whatever she did – whatever they all did on the site – had the potential to wound someone. After what had happened with the Callie Forrest case, she shouldn't need reminding of that.

A hoot sounded from behind her, and she stepped back to make room for an elderly Cadillac to pass. The driver's window hummed open, and a woman with bright red hair and sloppily applied blue eye shadow gave her a Bette Davis glare: 'You're two months early.'

'Scuse me?'

'Won't be Christmas for another two months.'

Ellie's brain caught up. 'It looks like you're all set up here.'

'Used to clear it away every January. Now we leave some of it all year round. Makes it easier.'

'That makes sense.' *Back away, or dive in.* Shoving the doubt aside, she gave the woman her best smile. 'Are you Mrs Jensen?'

'You got it.'

'I'm . . . my name is Ellen Caine. Can I talk to you for a sec?'

'You selling something?'

'No. Well, see . . . this is difficult. I don't want to bother you with this, you seem like such a nice lady, but . . . ah, I'm just going to say it. I've been looking into an old case, a murder that happened back in the nineties that your husband Sandy was working.'

The woman's eyes turned into blue slits. 'Sandy's passed on.'

'I know, and I'm sorry for your loss there.'

'You don't look like law enforcement.'

'I'm not.'

'If you're not police, what are you? A reporter?'

'I'm looking into the case in a private capacity.'

'A PI or a looky-loo?'

'Bit of both. Kinda.'

'Why should I talk to you?'

'You don't have to.'

'Is it the boy who was found in the dress?'

'Yes. We think . . . we think we know who he is.'

The woman nodded, and the window closed. Not sure what else to do, Ellie remained where she was as the car cruised up the driveway and came to a stop. Mrs Jensen staggered out, a grocery bag in her arms. She was tiny, barely five feet, and her oversized purple coat brushed the ground. 'How did you hear about me?' she called.

Ellie took this as her cue to approach. 'A guy who used to work with Sandy. Eric-Lee White?'

'Thought so. He came around here a while back.' She gave Ellie a long, intense once-over – her eyes were quick and sharp, and a shade lighter than the make-up – then pursed her lips. Her cheeks were plastered with beige foundation; fuchsia lipstick bled into the lines around her mouth. Ellie was almost certain that the hair was a wig. 'You may as well come in. Cold out, and you look like you could use some coffee.'

'Really? That's so good of you.' She didn't have time for this, but how could she pass up the opportunity? 'Let me help you.'

Mrs Jensen handed over the bag. It was heavier than it looked and clinked. The entranceway was crammed with boxes, and Ellie was forced to turn sideways to squeeze past them. She was about to ask Mrs Jensen if she was moving out, then took note of the writing on their sides: 'Santa head #2', 'porch left window front lights'. The place was ill-lit, smelled of dust and soup and seemed to stretch on indefinitely. Ellie followed Mrs Jensen into a kitchen diner that was roomier than it first appeared – every surface was laden with pickle jars, coffee bean cans, and magazines, which created the impression that the walls were closing in. Mrs Jensen removed a stack of *Family Circle*s off a chair, and gestured for Ellie to sit. She shrugged off the overcoat to reveal a hand-knitted sweater decorated with miniature roses.

'I love what you're wearing.'

'Did it myself. Keeps my hands busy while I'm watching the box.' She retrieved the bag. 'Let me pack this away, then I'll put the coffee on.'

Mrs Jensen opened the fridge, which Ellie put at the same vintage as its owner, and upended the bag's contents into it – more pickle jars and slabs of cheese – slamming the door at the last second to prevent anything from spilling onto the floor.

'Can I help?'

'No, no. Won't take me but a minute.' She moved another pile of magazines further along the counter in order to get at the kettle. The stove was spattered with grease, and the floor couldn't have seen a mop for years, but Ellie quite admired Mrs Jensen's blatant disrespect for domestic order. She always felt compelled to apologise for the state of her kitchen, even if she'd just cleaned it.

She tried not to glance at the clock. If she stayed any longer than five minutes she'd be late for the boys, but she couldn't just come out with it. 'Do you put on a Christmas display every year?'

'Uh-huh. We got into it after Jerry – that's my second husband – died. My son Jared always liked Christmas and it gives him something to look forward to.' She riffled through a cupboard, another ode to disorder and junk, took out a photograph album and handed it to Ellie. 'Here.'

It was full of photographs and newspaper cuttings showing the house in all its Christmas glory, twinkle lights cascading over its facade, candy canes ringing the porch, and the corpse of the snowman and the reindeer skeletons brought to life with the power of LED strip lighting. Ellie didn't have to fake her admiration – it was genuinely impressive. There were several pictures of Mrs Jensen standing in front of the display next to a hulking middle-aged man with a broad face. The son? 'Is it open to the public?'

'Get people driving all the way from St. Cloud to see it.' She flicked on the kettle. 'Cream and sugar?'

'Both, thanks.'

'Hmmf.' Approval or disapproval? Ellie couldn't tell.

'I'll have to bring my boys over to see it.'

A practised dart into the fridge to retrieve the milk. 'How many kids you got?'

'Two. Twins.'

'Bet they're a handful. How old?'

'Seven.'

'That's a good age.'

'You didn't say we had visitors, Momma.' A man wearing lace-up boots and an 'Obama 2008' T-shirt filled the doorway. He was larger than he looked in the photographs, and had his mother's small, bright eyes, although his didn't seem to settle on anything for more than a second. 'I'm doing important things and I can't be disturbed.'

'That's too bad.' She nodded to Ellie. 'We got company. You forgotten your manners?'

His shoulders drooped. 'Sorry.' He crossed the kitchen with more speed than Ellie would have given him credit for. 'Hello there, ma'am, I'm Jared John Eversham-Jensen.'

'Hi Jared. I'm—'

'Can I see your ID please, ma'am?'

'Scuse me?' Ellie blinked.

'Gotta verify your identity, ma'am.'

Ellie was aware that Mrs Jensen was watching her closely. 'My driving licence okay?'

'Uh-huh. That's fine.'

He looked at it and handed it back. 'Sorry to trouble you, ma'am. I like your name. Ellen. Like Ellen Barkin, the actress. She was in *The Big Easy*. And Ellen Ripley, the character from the Alien franchise. "Get away from her you bitch."'

'*Jared*.'

'It's a *quote*, Momma, from *Aliens*. Gale Ann Hurd was the producer on that. Carrie Henn who played Newt never did any acting after that.' He jabbed a finger at Ellie. 'Did you know that?'

'I didn't.'

'Uh-huh. And you were born in '87. A gallon of gas cost eighty-nine cents then.'

'Wow. I didn't know that.'

'It's the truth.' He rubbed the tips of his fingers together very fast, glanced at the album.

'I've been looking at the photographs of your Christmas display. Real impressive.'

He broke into a smile. 'You think?'

'I do. It's quite something.'

He came close – too close – leaned across her and flipped through the album. He smelled of chewing gum and sweat. 'I made that. And that. You think we should have a Mrs Claus or is that too dumb?'

'I've always liked her.'

'Me too. See, Momma?'

'We'll talk about it later. Go on now, Jared.'

'Gotta go.' He saluted. 'Nice to meet you, Ellen-not-Barkin.'

'You too.'

Mrs Jensen watched him go. 'He gets agitated sometimes, but he's a good boy.'

'I can see that. Smart, too.'

'He likes facts. Spends all day on that computer of his.' Mrs Jensen brought the coffee to the table, and sat opposite. Ellie's mug was decorated with a decal of Lionel Ritchie and the words: 'Hello, is it tea you're looking for?'; Mrs Jensen's coffee smelled strongly of alcohol. 'Tell me about this boy. You said they found out who he was. Local?'

'He was from Ireland.'

'Ireland? Don't think Sandy ever thought he was a foreigner. What's your interest in this?'

For once, Ellie paused to think before she spoke. Mrs Jensen was no fool – Ellie had picked that up straight away – and while she may have invited her into her kitchen, she was staring at her with the same level of shrewd intensity Ellie had received from Eric. 'I live local, over in Millar Town, and started looking into the case as a . . . I don't want to say a hobby, but it interested me. Then evidence came to light that pointed to the boy being a missing Irish guy, and now we're really close to getting an official ID.'

'Who's this "we"?'

'Me and a group of people who are looking into the case.'

'Eric part of that?'

'No. Not as such. He's a friend of my husband's. They work together.' Mrs Jensen gave nothing away. 'Things moved on, and I got to know the victim's family. Well the dead boy's nephew. He's hurting.' It wasn't an exaggeration. Shaun *was* hurting. 'We think if the case gets reassigned it'll help him get closure.'

A sniff that could be disapproval. 'Closure, huh? Sandy had to fight the department all the way on that case, couldn't get the resources he needed. They just wanted it to go away.'

'That's what Eric said. According to him Sandy was the only one who seemed to care about the case. He said it might be worth talking to you to see if you had any more information we could use.'

'Did he now. Like I said, Eric came sniffing round here a while back. Thought Sandy might've taken some of the evidence. Hidden it away. Is that what you're here for too?'

Ellie swallowed. She took a sip of coffee, barely tasting it. 'Yes. Did he?'

'Well now, that would be going against procedure, wouldn't it?'

That isn't a *no*. 'If you do have anything, I mean, if you happen upon anything, I—'

'That case ate Sandy up. Couldn't stand the thought there was someone out there who was capable of that. Jared was around the boy's age back then. Jared's always been vulnerable, easy prey, ever since he had his head injury. Reckon that's what got to Sandy. I can't help you with this. I don't want all this brought up again, people coming to my door. Sandy's death almost killed Jared. Same as when his stepfather died. He has his Christmas, and the rest of the time we keep ourselves to ourselves.'

Mrs Jensen breathed out and seemed to deflate. Ellie squirmed inside. She had no right to be here, intruding on someone's pain like this. She stood, risking a glance at the clock – it was worse than she thought, she wouldn't be able make it in time even if she went by helicopter, and it was all for nothing. 'I get that. I'm so sorry for bothering you. Thank you again for the coffee.'

'Welcome.' Mrs Jensen got to her feet.

'Oh don't trouble yourself. I can see myself out.'

There was no time to absorb the disappointment or deflect the guilt; Ellie was scrolling to Sherry's number before she was even out of the front door.

It was going on for two a.m. and she was only halfway through the pumpkins. She'd nicked her thumb twice, and the breakfast bar was awash with seeds and pulp. She'd meant to start it after supper, but got sidetracked brainstorming with Aqualung, which took the sting out of the day. After what had happened with Bobbie, she was careful to keep her dealings with him strictly business, had to fight her natural inclination to chit-chat or bombard him with personal questions. Aqualung had suggested they source dressmaking catalogues from the nineties, and they'd been scrolling through eBay looking for vintage-style patterns that could match up. He reckoned they shouldn't get hung up on the colour, but should concentrate on the style in case it was a mass-produced item, although it looked bespoke to her. They'd both agreed that it could be useful to buy a dress that resembled it, spread that around on social media alongside the grainy image. The dress had to be the key; she was sure of it.

'Ellie.'

It was the second time today she'd been caught off guard, *caught in the act*. 'I know, I know. You don't need to say it.'

Noah's eyelids were puffy, his hair flattened to one side. 'It's two a.m.'

'I *know*.' She flicked a glut of sinewy pulp from her fingers, kept her eyes down.

'Meant to tell you earlier, Eric was asking after you. I invited him over for supper, so you'll have to tell me when would be a good time.'

'Any time would be good.'

'Yeah? Says the woman carving pumpkins in the middle of the night.'

She was making a mess of it too – she'd sliced right through the cat template.

'You're quiet. What's eating you?'

Should she tell him? She still hadn't told Bobbie about going to see Mrs Jensen. Couldn't figure out if it was because she'd failed, or because the self-doubt was back. 'Nothing's eating me. I don't have to talk *all* the time.'

'What about your boyfriend? That cop? You told him?' His tone wasn't accusatory, but there was an edge to it.

'He's not my boyfriend.' There was a vestige of guilt whenever she thought about sending Bobbie that kiss, but she had no intention of ever confessing that. Besides – it wasn't *that* big a deal. 'In any case, he's much older than I thought he was.'

'Not going to take that how it sounds.'

'Huh? Oh. I haven't got the time to fool around even if I wanted to. Think he's lonely, wants to have a purpose.'

'Sounds like someone I know.'

'I'm not lonely. I've got you. And the boys.'

'We hardly see you.'

She opened her mouth to say, 'You want me to quit?' then stopped herself. She wouldn't quit. Not now the case was on the site, not now they were getting so close. She couldn't let one setback get her down. And the more she replayed her encounter with Mrs Jensen, the more she was convinced the woman was hiding something. She hadn't flat-out *denied* Sandy had held back something, had she? If only she'd thought to leave her number. Should she visit her again? Chip away at her, gain her trust? Mrs Jensen didn't have it easy, and she was protective of her son, so whatever Ellie decided, she couldn't go in like a bulldozer.

Noah was still staring at her, half-exasperated. She was sick of it. Sick of being judged. Sherry's stony face when she'd finally made it to her place to collect the boys was enough admonishment for one day. She'd promised to have Danny for a sleepover soon, but that wasn't enough to make up for the countless times she'd dropped the ball. 'I'm not a child, Noah, stop looking at me like that.'

Without another word, he left, shutting the door firmly behind him. Remorse came then; he hadn't accused her of anything – the opposite in fact. Mentioning Eric had clearly been an attempt to forge common ground. *She'd* picked this fight. Exhausted, frustrated at herself for taking it out on him, she grabbed a handful of seeds and threw them at the door.

Rainbowbrite: I went to see Mrs Jensen yesterday. Sorry I didn't tell you when I was going. Wasn't sure how it would pan out ☹

Bobbiecowell: And?? You find anything?

Rainbowbrite: No. She says Sandy didn't keep anything back ☹ ☹

Bobbiecowell: ☹ That sucks. You believe her?

Rainbowbrite: I think so

Bobbiecowell: Only think so? You're a good judge of character Ellie. What does your gut say?

Rainbowbrite: On the fence ☹ might have to accept this is a dead end

Bobbiecowell: No such thing as a dead end. We'll get there. You got to have faith ☺

Rainbowbrite: Thanks. You always cheer me up ☺ I haven't told Chris

Bobbiecowell: Wise ☺

Wicklowboy22

'It's a certainty then,' Johnny said into his pint glass.

'It is. The X-rays match. They'll be putting out a press release and an official announcement soon.'

'Janice and Donny won't like that. Serves them right. Their brother dead all these years and them trying to cover it up.'

'They didn't know he was dead.'

'You sure about that?'

'I'm not sure about anything.' Janice still wasn't answering his calls, and after his run-in with Donny, Shaun hadn't mustered up the courage to go round there. And now that Donny had played the next-of-kin card, insisting the guards funnel any information directly to him, Shaun was out of the loop. He'd only heard about the official identification because Neil from the guards had had the decency to call him with the news. Daphne shifted on the bench and eyed them with a level of passive-aggression that put Janice's to shame. They were back in the gulag, and a pit stop in a pub's smoking area was a poor substitute for her usual lunchtime walk.

Johnny gestured for a Vogue, and lit up while staring moodily into the distance. 'Where's your da these days? Colin Benchley, isn't it?'

Thrown, it took Shaun a second to recalibrate. 'What made you ask that?'

'Came into my mind.'

'He's in Dublin.'

'See much of him?'

'We're not in touch.' An understatement. Colin hadn't even

bothered to come to Eileen's funeral. His mother was honest about Shaun's conception – the result of a cider-fuelled shag behind the GAA clubhouse – and hadn't objected when he'd eventually asked to meet his father. She'd warned him not to expect much, and she was right. There was a generosity to Eileen, but during their one and only meeting, at a McDonald's of all places, Colin did nothing but talk about himself. Shaun barely thought about him these days; pretended that part of his genetic make-up didn't exist.

'She was a nice-looking girl. How come she didn't find herself a man?'

'Didn't want one.' A long-term relationship would have messed with their plans to escape. There were a couple of online dates that she'd laughed about with him and Máirín, but nothing serious. 'It's you and me against the world, Shaun.' And Shaun had carried on that tradition, hadn't he? Kept himself to himself, shut himself off from anything or anyone that could anchor him here, and all for some nebulous dream that he'd escape one day.

Johnny let out one of his trademark grunts that could mean anything. Breaking the news about the identification wasn't the only reason Shaun had offered to buy him a drink: time to get down to business. 'What sort of work did you and Teddy do in London?'

'Where's this coming from?'

'We're trying to track Teddy's movements. Figure out what he may have been doing in New York.'

'We?'

'I told you. The people on the website.'

'Ah right. So what's London got to do with that?'

'He might have done the same kind of work.'

Another grunt.

'So? What did you do for money?'

'Bar work, odd jobs. Cash in hand.' A cagey look came into his eyes.

'What aren't you telling me?'

'I don't want you to get the wrong idea about him.'

'Anything we can use will be helpful. We've got next to nothing to go on.'

'Ah fuck it. He's dead. Isn't going to hurt him now, is it? From time to time he was a house boy.'

'A what?'

'He worked in men's houses, doing the cleaning and things. He used to advertise in a thing called *Fruit Camp*, a mag they used to have back then. Found a copy of it in his bag. That's how I found out he was a shirt-lifter. No offence. Why we fell out.'

'I thought you said he came out to you one night?'

'Lied, didn't I?'

'He was a rent boy?' He was aware he should be shocked at this, but the exhilaration at uncovering a potentially useful clue trumped everything else.

'Ah God, Jesus no. I know how it sounds, but it wasn't like that. Teddy swore he didn't let them touch him. And he could handle himself if anyone tried to take things too far. After I got over myself we used to laugh about it. This one fella he worked for, he liked him to vacuum the place wearing nothing but a pair of legwarmers.'

'So he could have been doing this in New York?'

'How the fuck should I know? It was easy money.'

It was an avenue. Teddy could have hooked up with the wrong client, run into trouble. Shaun hesitated, then gave in to the urgency to send the information to Chris. Johnny watched him wryly as he tapped away at his phone.

'That's what got me the most when I got out. People glued to those fucking things all the time.'

'You should get one.'

'Too old for all that shite.'

'Better get back.' Daphne shook out her fur and jumped down from the bench the instant he reached for the lead. Still glued to the phone, he stopped at the bar on the way out to buy Johnny a refill. He knew the drill by now.

There was a woman browsing through the poetry section, but as it was obvious she was only getting out of the rain, Shaun turned back to the monitor. The new house boy information was setting the comments section on fire, and had already spawned a volley of theories about killers who harvested their victims via personal ads. Bobbiecowell was suggesting this could provide a possible link to other murdered men who shared Teddy's 'victimology profile'. There were four on the list, two currently unidentified. One of them, GI Doe, could be Teddy's cousin – *his* cousin. He'd only been to the man's page once, couldn't bear the photos of the forensic sculpture and its dead-eyed gaze.

The doorbell pinged, and a woman ushered a pair of bickering kids into the shop. He was about to turn back to the screen, when recognition hit, bringing with it a surge of panic. *Carmel.* He peered past her, but Donny was nowhere in sight.

She shook out her umbrella, blithely spattering droplets over the hardback display. 'Alright, Shaun?'

'Hi.' Wary – and why shouldn't he be?

Carmel nudged the kids. 'Say hello to your cousin Shaun. Where are your manners?'

'Hola,' the boy said with a wave.

'Can we buy a book, Mam?' the girl asked. She looked to Shaun. 'I like stories about monsters.'

'There's a surprise,' Shaun said under his breath. Carmel shot him an amused glance. 'The children's section is in the back.'

The boy gazed around, entranced.

The girl tugged on Carmel's designer coat. 'Can we, Mam?'

'Go on. But look after your brother.'

'Come on, Declan.' Surprisingly gently, the girl took her brother's hand and led him away.

Carmel didn't move. 'Donny said he came to see you.'

'Thought he was going to kill me.'

'Don't take that to heart. His bark is worse than his bite.'

'It didn't feel like it. He kicked the dog.' Or tried to. He still wasn't sure if the blow had landed. He prayed that she'd stay in her basket in the back. He didn't want her anywhere near Donny's offspring.

'Ah well, it's the shock of it, isn't it? Finding out your only brother is dead. And the *Gazette* called this morning wanting him to comment on it, which gave him a face like a smacked arse all day. Janice is seething, thinks you're the devil incarnate.'

'What's she saying?'

'The old bitch won't speak to me, you know what she's like, but she's on the phone to Donny all hours of the day and night.'

'Have the guards told you anything else? Has the case been reassigned?'

'The guard who came over didn't say much. He was all formal, said he was after delivering an official death notice. Donny wouldn't let him in the house. He had to do it outside the garage. Now listen. I've been reading through that website you showed us when you came over.'

'Oh right.'

'I've got something for you. You were after a photograph of Teddy?'

'I got one from Johnny.'

'I saw that. I've got another one. I can't be sure, Shaun, but I think Teddy sent it to Donny when he was in New York.'

Shaun just stared at her.

'Found it in the safe. Donny doesn't know I've got it yet, but I thought it might help in some way. Do you want it or not?'

'I want it.'

She rooted through her bag, which Shaun estimated must be worth more than he made in a year and was capacious enough to house one of her kids. 'Where did I put it now? . . . Ah. Here it is.' She handed him a large glossy print. Blood booming in his ears, he placed it on the counter, and stared down at Teddy, shirtless, not an ounce of fat on him, looking triumphantly into the camera and lifting his middle finger. The hair resembled the Boy's – longish, highlighted strands. A crowd of scantily clad men were frozen in time in the background, one wearing nothing but angel wings and a thong. Every time he looked at a new photograph of his uncle he was forced to adjust his childhood image of the man.

'Was there a letter with it, anything that could tell us where he was living or what he was doing?'

'Just the photograph.'

'Can I post it on the site?'

'Do what you like with it. Put it on the site, give it to the guards.'

'You aren't worried that Donny will know where it came from?'

'That's my problem.' A hardening of the eyes – he was right to assume there was another side to her. 'I can handle him. Do what you have to do Shaun. Teddy was family.'

'Thanks for doing this.'

'You're alright.' She slung the bag over her shoulder. 'Better check on the kids, make sure Caitlin doesn't have her brother in a headlock.'

'Wait . . . Why would Donny keep it? I thought he hated him.'

'He was his brother. Donny's a hard man, got that from his father. But he's not all bad. Why else would I stay with him?' *Money*, Shaun thought but didn't say. She moved off, then looked over her shoulder. 'Look on the back of it.'

He didn't buy Carmel's explanation for why Donny had kept it all those years, but the reason Teddy had sent it to his brother couldn't be clearer. Scrawled on the back of it were the words: FUCK YOU DONNY.

Bobbiecowell

The room and its contents were almost exactly as he'd envisaged: white walls, an outdated TV, soft porn DVDs, and a stack of magazines with greasy pages. There was also a questionnaire to fill in, paper towels, a sink, the specimen jar and a selection of wipe-clean hospital furniture that reeked of disinfectant. The only outlier objects were a brazenly un-erotic print of a stag on one wall, and the room's keyring, a life-size plastic doughnut covered in multi-coloured sprinkles. According to the nurse who'd signed him in, the clinic had resorted to this novelty item after countless clients pocketed the key in their haste to leave. At least they'd held off on the Halloween decorations, although the clinic's waiting room, where Margie was waiting for him among his fellow masturbators and their sidekicks, was a riot of leering pumpkins and skulls.

He'd been here for ten minutes already, and nothing was happening. He flicked through the magazines, which catered for all tastes as long as you were straight and into vanilla, then delved through his mental Rolodex, digging up images that he could usually rely on whenever he had to perform with Margie.

Nothing.

Time was ticking. *Go big or go home.*

He shut his eyes.

And then it floated into his mind: an image of *her*, the moment he knew it was over – the moment she knew. A snapshot he kept locked in a vault, because using it, what that said about him, was too close to the bone. He should block it out, shove it away, but he was feeling something now, an electric tingle, a low pulse.

Just this once.

He was done in seconds, and it took everything he had to stifle the cry that reverberated up from some hidden primeval hole and exploded out of his throat. Shaken, breathless, he counted back from fifty until his heart rate slowed. Body thrumming with the aftershock, he capped the jar, gave the stag the finger, and exited. He handed over the paperwork and the doughnut, and a sea of faces looked up as he returned to the waiting room. He half-expected his audience to break into a round of applause.

Margie hurried over and squeezed his arm. 'How did it go?'

'About how you'd expect.' He'd crossed a line, strayed into territory he swore he'd never revisit. He hadn't felt anything that intense for years.

'And now we wait.'

'Not much else we can do.' More than likely, it was a pointless exercise. He'd never been tested before, but at least two of the women he'd hooked up with over the years played fast and loose with birth control for reasons of their own. He knew for a fact there were no mini Petes peppered around the Midwest or California – made sure of that before he moved on. But who knew, maybe his swimmers *were* viable.

'Thanks for doing this, Pete.' She was more subdued than she should be.

'You okay?'

'Yeah.'

'Still wondering if we're doing the right thing?'

'I'm good.'

'Sure?'

'Sure.'

She wasn't sure. It was his own fault for not keeping his finger on the pulse, allowing himself to get carried away delving into the mess his old self had caused. Past Pete – that cowardly, hopeless fuck-up – would drag him down like a waterlogged dress if he wasn't careful. Must. Do. Better. And Margie wasn't the only one who needed work.

<Happy Halloween! What are the boys going as?>

<Batman! Both of them. OMG they look so cute!!!!>

<Superheroes, huh?> He'd half-expected Tasha to dress up as Kim Jong-un or Aileen Wuornos, but she'd decided to go as an eyelash of all things. He paused, then added: **<Pauline always went as a princess ☺>**

<Which one?>

Good question. He Googled 'Disney princesses', and worked out how old his mythical daughter Pauline was supposed to be. **<Cinderella>**

<OMG she's my favourite!!! Can you send me some pics??>

<I'll have to scan them. Didn't have digital in my day ;)> *Nice catch there, Pete.*

<Too funny to think how different things were back then and you had to go get pics processed!!! These days it's so immediate>

<Yeah, and like the other morons you immediately parade your kids all over Facebook for the perverts to enjoy> He deleted this before the temptation to send it became too strong. **<Things were much slower back then in the dark ages>**

<LOL!!>

Jesus, this Rainbowbrite small talk was stultifying, but it was a necessary evil, especially as her new message-buddy, Aqualung (Aqualung!) was crowding in on his turf. He was reluctant to let his canary in the mine flit away; who knew when he might need her? He didn't have long before Margie and Tasha were due back from the school's Halloween bash. **<How are things progressing with the dress?>**

<We think we should go on eBay, find a similar one we can use for a clearer pic>

<That's good thinking>

<Thanks! You're doing GREAT too ☺>

Couldn't argue with that. He was now the site's official geographical profiler and Serial Offender Guru, still hawking his line that Teddy Ryan was just one of the many victims who fell foul to a travelling homophobic sicko. To be fair, it was staggering how many young gay guys *did* go missing or were murdered back then. **<How's Chris?>**

<The usual ☺>

No mention of the Missing Mom email and how it might be affecting her. Was Rainbowbrite even aware of Chris's AWOL family member? Had he got it wrong? Guzman was a common name; might just be a coincidence. But his gut said different. Eliza Guzman was the only missing person on the site. The others were UIDs. Had to mean something. **<How's Shaun doing?>**

<Broke my heart to send him those pictures of where Teddy is laid to rest. Kinda brought it home to me, you know?>

<I do. So sad>

<Do you think it's dumb to offer to take flowers to Teddy's grave? There's no headstone, just a number. It's so lonely there>

<That would be a v kind gesture. You're a good person>

<I'm not! But thanks for saying that. Wish we had more to tell him ☹ Wish we could track down JT & find out what Teddy was doing in Minnesota>

Ah, the elusive JT. He knew what Teddy was doing in Minnesota, and he'd deploy that bomb if he had to. The doorbell went. He tapped in: **<BRB!!>**

A kid dressed in a store-bought Thor costume and its bored father looked at him expectantly as he opened up. He vaguely recognised them, but the dull, smug families who populated the block all blended into one. 'Trick or treat,' the kid said, shaking its plastic greed bucket.

'Gonna take the second option.' He dropped an apricot bar on top of the stash of Reese's Peanut Butter Cups and Haribo packets. As expected, the kid eyed it unenthusiastically and muttered a tepid, 'Thanks.'

'Hey, don't blame me. Lady of the house is doing her bit to fight childhood obesity.' The adult could lose a few pounds. Pete waited a beat, then said: 'No offence.'

The guy wasn't sure how to take it, chose the cowardly way out and guffawed as if he were in on the joke.

Pete shut the door before the man could start in on the small talk, automatically checking the phone. There was another missive from Rainbowbrite, this one far more interesting: **<OMG have you seen the site? New pic of Teddy>**

He went straight there. Bare-chested Teddy pouted at him from the front page, cocky, self-assured, crackling with life. A blip of panic, an urge to flee to the truck to check the lockbox was secure, and then sense returned. The photograph was vastly different to the spoils in the box. It wouldn't help them. He gazed into Teddy's eyes, and something stirred deep inside, an echo of that primeval howl he'd felt in the room. The stain of his old self bled up from beneath the layer of the new – it wasn't going anywhere.

Mommydearest: Hi Chris sent the pic to Rhonda St George. She's a big name drag queen and was part of the club scene in the 90s

Mommydearest: She tweeted it. Sent you a screenshot

Mommydearest: It's now been retweeted 28K times & #JusticeForTeddyRyan is trending

Mommydearest: Site being linked all over

Mommydearest: Where are you Chris? This thing is blowing UP

Ratking 1

For once Chris was making an effort to hide her true feelings. Much as she'd rather stay ensconced in her 'woman cave' (as Jeanie had taken to calling it), she couldn't beg off her sister's birthday party without feigning serious illness. She grabbed another beer from the cooler bucket, and hung out by the door – her only option, unless she wanted to drown in a sea of crotches. The place was heaving, Led Zep cranked up, the air blue with smoke. All the usual suspects were here, including Devin, Paula and Michael – Paula's rat-faced squeeze with the attitude. Over in the corner Mack was leaning against the wall, flirting with a dark-haired woman. He caught her eye, and gave her an ironic salute. She looked away. She was itching to check her phone. She'd promised Jeanie she'd stay away from the site for a couple of hours, but there was now a 'Boy in the Dress' thread on Reddit, and the urgency to stay relevant was growing. Then there was the new pic Shaun had sent through. If they could track down the name of the club, identify the partygoers in the background, then who knew where that would lead?

Charlie, Jeanie's kid, who'd driven down from Santa Monica for a couple of nights, pushed through the throng and stooped to give her a hug. 'Hey, Auntie.'

'Don't call me that. It makes me sound old.'

'You are old.'

'Nice. Least you've stopped calling me Professor Xavier.'

'Hey, I was like, fifteen. Any case, it was a compliment.'

'It's good to see you. You're looking cute.'

'Thanks to you.' He ran a hand over his scalp. She'd suggested he shave it to hide the fact that at only twenty-six he was losing his hair, and it suited him. He hadn't taken her advice about ditching the preppy gear, but she admired him for that – at least he stood out among the crowd of leathers and beards. He was the poster child for kids turning out the opposite of their parents.

'See the site's going well.'

'You been checking up on it?'

'Here and there. You thought any more about monetising it?'

'Maybe.'

'Is Mom behaving herself?'

They glanced over to where Jeanie was sharing a joint with Paula. 'Depends what you mean by "behaving".'

'Charlie,' Jeanie shouted, waving him over. 'Come and meet Michael.'

He clinked his bottle against hers and gave her a long-suffering look. 'Back in a minute.'

'Immigrant Song' started up and someone cranked up the volume. She shoved the beer between her thighs, turned, and made for the door. She'd freeze her ass off on the porch, but it was better than being deafened by Robert Plant, and she'd be free to check the site without Jeanie giving her a hard time. Scott came thumping up the ramp that led to the path as the door banged closed behind her, and she *really* didn't like the way her heart lifted as he neared.

'Hey. You leaving already?'

'Taking a breather. It's packed in there.'

'I can hear that.'

'How's Kelly? You still haven't brought her around.' Even out on the porch she had to raise her voice to be heard over the music.

'Yeah. Wasn't sure you were serious about that.'

'I am. She's welcome.'

'You made a good impression on her. She thinks you're cool.'

'Was it the hair or the attitude?'

'The hair. We both know your attitude sucks.' He delivered this deadpan, then smiled to take the sting out of it, stopping himself from covering his mouth with his hand at the last second.

'Can't argue with that.' She passed him her beer and he took a sip and bounced it back. 'How's life on Team Prom Dress?'

'Good. Well, kinda. This sleuthing stuff gets addictive, doesn't it?'

'Yep.'

'Never thought I'd know so much about tulle.'

'Tulle, huh?'

'Yeah. And boned corsets – ask me anything.' He turned serious. 'Dress has to be the key to finding the guy. Got a gut-feel on that.'

'How are you and Rainbowbrite getting along?'

'We're good.'

'You told her anything about me?' She hadn't meant to say it. Might as well admit to having a deep-seated insecurity.

'Nope. Don't know anything about you, except you run the site and live in a trailer.'

'And don't get out much.'

'And like chips and dip.' He cocked his head. 'That you ringing?'

He was right. She dug out the phone, checked the caller ID: Mommydearest. He'd never called her before, shared her preference for non-verbal communication. 'Hey.'

'Chris, Chris? Finally. Where have you been?' Distress strangled his voice, made him sound about twelve years old. 'The site's gone dark. It's crashed.'

'I'll call you back.'

She hung up, logged on to the site, got a '503 server unavailable' page. Either the servers had slowed to a crawl or she'd been hacked. She looked up at Scott, who was watching her intently. 'Can you go get my nephew for me? You can't miss him. Twenties, losing his hair, preppy-looking.'

'On it.'

She texted Mommydearest: **<Dealing with it>**

<okay coolio hurry> The poor guy was melting down. In the last ten minutes he'd sent her scores of messages, each one more panicked than the last. She skipped these, scrolled to an earlier tranche, came to: **<we're being linked all over. Going viral>** Scott returned, Charlie in tow.

'The site's gone dark.' Mommydearest's panic was infectious – now she was beginning to feel like a hysterical pre-teen. 'Can you come to the trailer, check it out?'

'Mom'll kill us if we leave her party.'

'Yeah, that's too bad. Blame it on me.'

'I will.'

She was only aware Scott was following them when she heard him say: 'There are no handles on the back of your chair.'

'Yeah there's a reason for that.'

'So people don't push you around?'

Charlie laughed. 'No one pushes the professor around.'

'Huh?'

'Ignore him.'

She let them in, and Charlie took a moment to inspect the trailer. 'Looks exactly the same. I've seriously got to buy you some art or something.'

'Fuck that. C'mon.'

Charlie moved what she thought of as her 'guest chair' around to her side of the desk, and went straight to the site's back end. 'Thought so. CPU is overloaded. You've been hit by the hug of death.'

'The what?'

'You're getting too many hits. I keep telling you to upgrade. You need to switch servers or this will keep happening.'

'Can you fix it?'

'Yeah, "fix" isn't strictly the right term. You should seriously think about updating it. Site's like something out of the nineties. Got to move with the times.'

'We've got a Facebook page.'

Charlie didn't comment on this.

Scott hovered. 'Anything I can do?'

'Wouldn't mind a coffee,' Charlie said.

'Sure.' Scott looked to Chris. 'Okay if I do that?'

'Thanks.'

Charlie peered after him. 'Who *is* that guy?'

'That's Scott.'

'Yeah?' He turned back to the screen: 'You need to keep this one.'

Bobbiecowell

It was a runaway train and there was nothing he could do to stop it. It should be reigniting the stress, but he was oddly calm. There was something beautiful about it. He'd created this. *He'd* set this in motion. Most of the US was sleeping, but the rest of the world had taken up the gauntlet. #JusticeForTeddyRyan had been trending on Twitter for hours, and the list of bandwagon celebs howling for justice was growing. Over on Missing-Linc, back from the dead, there were scores of new comments beneath every Boy in the Dress update. Among the outrage ('Dept guilty of blatant prejudice why else would they screw this up so badly?') were reams of '**[message deleted by moderator]**'. The cops would have real pressure put on them to reassign the case, but he refused to let that worry him. There was only one link to him, and that was circumstantial at best.

Despite the unexpected drama, or perhaps because of it, he kept being drawn to the photographs of the dumpsite. Rainbowbrite was no Annie Leibovitz, but she'd captured some of the atmosphere. The trees that were there in the nineties had been cleared to make way for a picnic area and a network of hiking and mountain biking trails, leaving it more bereft than he remembered – *lonelier*, somehow – and he zoomed in, focused on a Mountain Dew can some asshole had dumped in the snow. Tar skinned the jogging track running parallel, the narrow road now severed by a parking lot and ablution block. Flanked by knotty undergrowth, shadowed by overhanging branches, it once led deep into the reserve, and tempting though it was, he hadn't allowed his mind to travel along its rutted surface for years. Would she still be there? Perhaps her bones had been scattered long ago, lunch for a coyote, supper for the bugs. He'd read that squirrels were especially talented at dispersing body parts.

He shook himself out of it, returned to the main page, scrolled to where Teddy was living it large in the club, unaware that thanks to Pete, one day he'd be immortalised as the poster boy for hate crime and inept police work.

It would be easy to take it too far. His past self was reckless, acted without thinking things through. He'd vanquished the stress, but the urge to up the manipulation, play God, see how far he could push this was seductive, akin to standing on a high bridge, looking down and allowing the lure of gravity to tempt him over the edge. It would be easy to connect with Shaun – *hey Ellie okay if I give Shaun my condolences in person?* – but he'd bide his time on that. Shaun wasn't on Facebook or Instagram, so he was smarter or less social than the average bear, but Pete had unearthed a photograph of a fragile guy standing behind the counter on the Wicklow Books website. It wasn't a close-up shot, but the resemblance to his uncle was unmistakable.

'Can I have a hot chocolate?' This time he didn't jump as Tasha, his witching hour nemesis, crept up on him.

'Can't sleep?'

'*Obv*iously. So, can I?'

'If you say please.'

'*Please*.'

'Okay. You get the milk, I'll do the rest.'

'Okay.'

She waited while he decanted milk into a mug, then jumped up to sit on the counter. He'd be dumb to trust their growing bond – it was born out of collusion. 'So what's up? Your frenemies still giving you a hard time?'

'No.' She swiped her iPhone, and handed it to him. He saw with no surprise that she'd called up Missing-Linc's Boy in the Dress page. 'That's what you're working on.'

'That's right.'

'Can I join in?'

'Your mom won't like that.'

'I won't tell her.'

'You have to be over eighteen to join that site. They're strict.'

'They have a Facebook page. I can follow that. And they're on Insta.'

'Can if you want.'

'Which one are you? Are you Mommydearest?'

'Not telling you.'

'Crowroad, then. If I guess the right one, will you tell me?'

'Nope. Hey, I gotta keep *some* mystery about me.'

He handed over the hot chocolate and she blew on it, swinging her legs. 'Who do you think killed him?'

'Not much to go on so far.'

'Some of the people are saying it's a serial killer.'

'You know what that is?'

'*Duh.* I looked it up on Wiki. There are loads. Where did they all go?'

'Scuse me?'

'There were like, hundreds when the Boy in the Dress died, but not so many any more.'

'Lots of theories about that.' He'd made it his business to delve into this subject a few years ago for obvious reasons. He didn't conform to the usual trajectory: bed-wetting, animal torture, setting fires, peeping, exposure, sexual assault. Then murder. That wasn't him. So what was he? *An outlier.*

'Like what?'

'Could be that potentially violent misogynists – that's women-haters – have a new outlet now, thanks to the Internet.'

'Like trolls?'

'Yeah. Really bad trolls. Means they're free to unleash their inner demons without ever having to get up off their lardy asses.' To be fair, there might be truth in what he was saying; there was no doubt his current online life was giving him a thrill.

'But what about women who are killers too?' The question could have come straight from Breitbart.

'Rare for women to perpetrate mass killings.'

'How come?'

'Less testosterone, maybe. Social conditioning.'

'Why else aren't there so many men being serial killers?'

'Some experts say there were lots of serial killers in the seventies and eighties because their fathers were messed up from the wars way back when – we're talking World War II, Vietnam, Korea – and they took it out on the kids when they got back home. Bad role models, I guess you'd say.' He paused while she took this in. 'Could be better law enforcement techniques catch them before they get the chance to go on a spree. These days we have CCTV, sophisticated forensics, DNA, watchlists, ViCap.'

'ViCap?'

'The Violent Criminal Apprehension Program. It's a database where cops can look for similar crimes in other states. It's not always effective though as it relies on them inputting info. Some don't bother.'

'You know a lot about this stuff.'

Forewarned is forearmed. 'Am I boring you?'

'No.'

'Could be that there are just as many as there ever were. Could be the FBI are moving away from catching lone sickos in order to concentrate their energies on terrorist activity. Could be that mass shootings are the new outlet for later generations rather than serial killings. Could be that the killers have got smarter.' *What a lecture.*

'Smarter how?'

'By only targeting people who won't be missed. Sex workers, drug addicts, runaways. You could go on for years wiping out these folks and no one would ever know.'

'Do you think Teddy Ryan was killed by a serial killer?'

'As it happens, I don't.' There was something deliciously ironic about contradicting mouthy ol' Bobbiecowell, who was still pushing his serial killer line with the subtlety of a brick.

'Who then?'

'I think Teddy Ryan knew his killer. More than likely met him in New York. Killer panicked, drove him across the US, deliberately dumped him in a different state to confuse the cops.'

A slow nod. 'Washington state had lots of serial killers.'

Including the poster boy for sociopathic crime. '*Used* to have lots of them. Look, Tash, you mustn't get too hung up on this, or let it scare you. Most murders are committed by family members. Stranger killings are rare.'

'Why were there so many *here* though?'

'No one knows for sure. Back in the day there were a lot of deprived areas around here, cops weren't such great quality, could be they let them slip through the net. Could be the weather. Could be something in the water.'

Not his water. In any case, he wasn't a serial killer. You didn't earn that label if you'd only killed two people.

She slid off the counter and took the mug to the dishwasher. 'So, how *are* things with your frenemies?'

'I don't care about *them*.'

'Don't blame you. All good otherwise?'

'I'm going to get a prize for coming up with the GoFundMe idea. We've raised like, hundreds of dollars now and lots of other schools are doing it too so there will be enough money for the sick girl to come out here.'

'That's great, Tash. Congratulations.'

'I don't care. Awards are *stu*pid.'

'Still, gotta say, that's got to mess with . . .' A mental scrabble for the names . . . 'Brittany and Olivia.'

'Yeah.' A brief, icy smile of satisfaction. She was human, after all.

'Your mom didn't mention this.'

'I haven't told her.'

'Why not? She'd be proud.'

A shrug.

'It's a good thing you're doing. Helping out someone less fortunate. Can I see the GoFundMe page?'

She sighed and flipped through her phone. 'Here.'

It was slick, illustrated with photographs of a wizened kid

holding up a piece of artwork and smiling bravely around a breathing tube: images designed to tug on liberal heartstrings. Tasha may have all the empathy of Ted Bundy, but she knew what she was doing.

A tug of that gravitational lure; the seed of an idea.

Bobbiecowell: Keep thinking about Shaun wanting to know where Teddy is buried

Rainbowbrite: Felt SO BAD sending him those photographs. Like his uncle is nothing but a number. Must be SO upsetting for him

Bobbiecowell: You think it would help if he could visit & see it for himself? And getting a family member out there might push the county to get off their asses too

Rainbowbrite: OMG I didn't think about that. Shall I ask him?

Bobbiecowell: Can't hurt ☺ Here's a crazy idea. How about setting up a GoFundMe or crowdfund for him? Always seeing them being set up to support victims' families

Bobbiecowell: Or is that dumb?

Rainbowbrite: It's not dumb!!!

Ratking1

Scott was due to show up any minute and she kept checking the time like a needy asshole. How had this happened? In the course of a week – apart from Thursday, when he'd taken Kelly to a movie – Scott had become a permanent fixture, rocking up to the trailer each evening after work. Jeanie wasn't helping the situation, kept showing up uninvited, dropping hints and prying for information.

The left-hand monitor screen was flickering. She smacked it back to life, her go-to fix for tech, and cracked a yawn. She'd hardly slept in the last two days, resorted to deleting her pressure relief alarm – couldn't stand the guilt of constantly ignoring it. It was impossible to keep up with the number of new members waiting to be verified, and requests for interviews had started rolling in from podcasters and bloggers. Now that the social media behemoths were stealing the case's oxygen from the site, it would be dumb to turn them down. There was no choice but to ease up on her control freak tendencies. She decided to delegate these to Ellie – she'd found the case in the first place and Mommydearest, the only other person she trusted, wasn't exactly Mr Charming. She dropped her a line, braced for a slew of sparkly responses. She wasn't disappointed:

<Me??? You sure? OMG chris!!!>

<Why not? You know the case better than anyone and we've got to keep the site relevant>

<Thanks for trusting me chris ☺ ☺ BTW you see my email RE Shaun/GoFundMe??>

<Thinking on it>

<Okay it was bobbie's idea but he didn't want to take the credit. Will you let me know what you decide??>

<Wilco. I'll forward the interview requests now>

<SO EXCITED>

<Really? I can't tell>

<LOL>

The grumble of an engine – she'd become attuned to the rattle of the truck's blown silencer – and then Scott slammed his way into the trailer. Completely at home, he sat opposite and handed her a stuffed bagel. 'Ham and cheese. Didn't know if you liked mustard.'

'I do, thanks.' Her stomach growled. If it wasn't for him and Jeanie she'd be surviving on oranges and out-of-date salsa.

On with the glasses, out with his vintage MacBook (another surprise – she would have pegged him as a Microsoft guy), and off with the jacket. It had become a routine. 'I've been thinking. Could it be a cult killing?'

'Where's this coming from?'

'Satanism was a big deal around that time. I was reading up about how in the nineties all these blond chicks had to dye their hair black cos so many girls were getting killed on Halloween.'

'Don't talk shit.'

'It's true. Just saying, has anyone looked into it? They reckon Teddy was bumped off around that time.'

'Knock yourself out. Not sure Rainbowbrite's home town is a hotbed of Satanism though.'

'Yeah.'

'Thought you and Rainbowbrite were working the dress angle?'

'We are. You know we are. Just saying we should keep an open mind.'

'Fair enough.'

He mimed having a heart attack. 'You just conceded something?'

'I know. Stop the presses.' They shared a smile. 'Your friend Rainbowbrite has suggested we set up a GoFundMe for Shaun Ryan, wants to fly him out here so that he can see where his uncle is buried. She reckons getting a family member over here could be our way in to getting more info out of the county. She tell you that?'

'Nope.'

'You think it's a good idea?'

He considered. 'Yeah.'

'Okay.' It might drive more traffic to the site – help keep the momentum up. 'I'll give her the go-ahead, tell her to check in with Shaun.' Would he be up for that? She'd been forced to cut down on their messaging sessions, another casualty of the case blowing up. She missed their daily interactions, and not just because he was the site's trump card. Maybe she should set up a chat group. Keep it small to discuss plans – keep Shaun in the loop and onside. As expected Ellie was all over this idea too, fired back immediately: **<Can we invite bobbie?>**

<Seriously? Won't his ego get in the way?>

<He apologised for misrepresenting himself & the GoFundMe was his idea. In any case he's a HERO>

<????>

<It's why he retired he was shot in the line of duty there was an article about him & everything although he asked me not to tell anyone so PLEASE don't tell him I told you>

<Sounds like more bullshit you verify this?>

<Yes!! I saw his scars!!! He sent me a pic with a date stamp on it & everything I can forward it to you??>

Chris blinked. *Okay.* **<Don't want Shaun bombarded with people tho. Just him and if he steps out of line he's gone, deal?>**

<Deal. And Aqualung? Mommydearest?>

<Let's keep it small for now>

<Okay, just us and THANK YOU>

She scanned the 'reported comments', deleting the now ubiquitous 'what about all the straight menz who been murdered?' screeds and the variations on 'so tired of everyone pushing this gay agenda shit!!!' Now that she'd delegated the running of the social media accounts to Mommydearest, she couldn't rely on him to shovel all the dirt. He may be as taciturn as she, but he had a hidden talent for networking: there wasn't a drag queen in New York he hadn't contacted in his hunt to discover the elusive JT. Yet, despite the vast number of people insisting they'd been Teddy's best friend, no one had come forward with more photographs. The majority of the 'I knew him briefly! He was great & Irish!!' Teddy tweets had the whiff of climbing on a bandwagon about them. Nothing specific; nothing personal. Nothing – so far – that could help them.

Across from her, Scott squinted at his laptop, pecked at the keyboard, and sat back – the king of two-finger typing. She was picking up on his quirks, the way he sometimes silently mouthed what he was about to write, tugging at his beard while he searched for the right word. He caught her staring. 'What? I got mustard on my face?'

'No.'

He grinned. 'You have.'

She laughed, turned back to the screen. And *boom*, just like that, her mood plummeted. Lurking in the inbox, like a rattler curled on the path, was another 'RE: Eliza Guzman' email, sent from a different, equally untraceable generic account. She knew she should just delete it; knew she wouldn't.

This time, there was a byline: **<Hey, what if she took a trip to Mechicho?>** and an attachment containing a map of Ciudad Juárez – the notorious area where countless murdered women had been dumped in the desert.

She hammered a response: **<WHO THE FUCK ARE YOU?>**

It bounced back.

'Chris?' She looked up. It was Scott's turn to stare at her. 'You okay? You were looking kind of lost for a moment there.'

A moment where she considered spilling her guts. It passed: saying it out loud would be an admission that it was hitting home, a sign of weakness. 'All good.'

MissingLinc#TeddyRyan

BobbieC, Rainbowbrite, Ratking, You

Ratking
This is a closed group please do not invite anyone else 3.32PM

BobbieC
Appreciate being invited ☺ 3.32PM

Ratking
@BobbieC wasn't my idea you got Ellie to thank for that 3.32PM

BobbieC
@Rainbowbrite thanks! And great to finally 'meet' you Shaun ☺ 3.33PM

You too Bobbie 3.34PM

Rainbowbrite
@Shaun so what do you think about the GoFundMe? It was Bobbie's idea ☺ ☺ Chris & I think it's genius!!! 3.34PM

BobbieC
Aw shucks. Can't take all the credit!!
3.34PM

Do you think people will really donate? 3.35PM

Rainbowbrite
Absolutely!! 3.35PM

Feels like I'd be taking charity
3.36PM

BobbieC
You got to remember that people like doing things like this. They want to help. You'll be doing them a favor ☺
3.36PM

Rainbowbrite
OMG Shaun I've just thought if you come to MN you can stay with me!!!
3.37PM

I couldn't do that 3.37PM

Rainbowbrite
I insist!! I'll have to check with Noah first but I know he'll be thrilled!! 3.38PM

Ratking
Let's not get ahead of ourselves. Haven't even set the thing up yet
3.39PM

BobbieC
@Ratking Happy to help just let me know what you need 3.39PM

Ratking
Thanks 3.39PM

BobbieC
We'll have your back Shaun. Also wanted to say that you're doing great work on your side. Can't be easy finding out all this new info about your uncle & seeing us all discussing him
3.40PM

It's not as hard as I thought. Getting used to it 3.40PM

Rainbowbrite
And the case is still trending!!! So many people want to help. I hope you are ignoring the troll comments Shaun & concentrating on the good things
3.41PM

I'm trying to 3.42PM

BobbieC
Seconded. There's always gonna be assholes. Don't let them grind you down. Just morons hiding behind a screen getting their kicks by being cruel
3.42PM

Rainbowbrite
So true ☹ ☹ OMG gotta go doing a skype interview now with krimi.com for a podcast!!! Wish me luck & thanks chris for asking me to do this!! think about what I said shaun
3.43PM

BobbieC
Good luck!
3.43PM

Good luck 3.44PM

@BobbieC how sure are you that Teddy was targeted by the same guy who killed those other boys?
3.47PM

BobbieC
Just conjecture for now. Wish I could give you certainty on that but all we know for sure is that whoever is behind this could still be out there 3.48PM

Ratking
You going to sign up on the site now, Shaun? 3.48PM

Not yet. Is that alright? 3.49PM

Ratking
Sure. Not pushing you. See what else you can dig up on your side. Now the case is viral should get more info on Teddy but every bit will help 3.49PM

BobbieC
Seconded 3.50PM

Bobbiecowell

She was one of *those* people. Humourless, entitled, saw everyone else as a bit player in the Movie of her Life. She wanted maple wood cabinets, 'ethically sourced of course' (*of course*, he told her), and all the appliances must be integrated (*of course*). The original kitchen couldn't be more than a year old; bespoke, had some real craftsmanship to it. He'd struggle to match that quality – if he took the job on. Which he wouldn't. She clacked ahead of him as if she had something far more important to do, even though she was the one who'd called him in for the estimate. The house was huge, cold and had the atmosphere of Hitler's bunker. Must have cost over a million. He pictured her rattling around in it, obsessing over the exact placement of the Eames chair. She kept twisting the wedding ring on her finger. Divorced. A bitter divorce, he reckoned, and this house was her prize for ditching the asshole. She was exactly the type he would have made a play for back in the day.

He was only here at all because Margie had been within earshot when the call came in, and he had to show willing. It was the right decision. The woman would only call back and bug the shit out of him. He gave the client his spiel, and engaged in a detailed discussion about storage space and the hidden shelving she wanted in the 'entertainment room'. He drifted off while giving the impression that every word she said was the gospel.

That GoFundMe suggestion was the gift that kept on giving. Not only had it cemented his place in the circle of trust, it had given him a direct line to Shaun. He didn't seem to possess his uncle's brashness and spark, but people were always different online. Could be a carbon copy for all he knew. Time would tell. He'd have to watch what he said – it was a group chat, after all – but he'd learned his lesson about the pitfalls of hubris after the disastrous Skype call. *Softly, softly, catchee monkey.* Rainbowbrite must have told Ratking about his Mark Starmer persona and the man's tragic, heroic history by now. Would it hold? Maybe, maybe not. Ratking had her hands full modding the site, so she might not bother digging too deeply. He'd play it by ear, subtly continue to plaster over the cracks. Was that why he'd suggested the funding idea? To nudge his way into the clique?

No.

'. . . do you agree?' the client came to the end of whatever she was saying.

'Absolutely. You got great taste. Most of my clients . . .' a self-deprecating chuckle. 'They don't have your kind of vision.'

She smiled – taking this as her due. Like Margie, she was too skinny, Botox propping up her facial muscles.

He paused to check out the picture windows that framed the Sound. 'Great view.'

'Yes.'

'Mind if I take a closer look?'

'Be my guest.'

He approached the doors that led out onto the deck, and ran a finger over the lock. 'Hmmm.'

'What is it?'

'It's not really my place to say.'

'Please do. Is there some sort of problem?'

'No. It's just . . . like I say, not really my place to say.'

'I'm asking you.'

'Well, I'd suggest you might want to up your security. This type of lock? It would take an intruder less than a minute to get through it.'

'I have an alarm.'

'Yeah. Forget I said anything. Not my business. Now, you said you wanted to discuss more options for integrated appliances.'

'You think the house is unsafe?'

A shrug. 'It's just with the spate of attacks that have been happening in the North End area—'

'Attacks? What attacks?' She immediately checked her phone. Unable to think for herself without Google. One of *those* people.

'I didn't mean to alarm you. Probably nothing to worry about.'

'What attacks?'

'Couple of home invasion attempts, sexual assaults.'

'Why haven't I seen this on the news?'

'Heard it from a law enforcement connection. Could be they've asked for a media blackout. Usual MO if they've got a suspect in mind.'

'Oh no.'

'Like I said, I wouldn't worry about it.' *You should worry about it.* Petty crime was how eighty-one percent of serial killers started their careers.

'How do you know all this?'

'Like I say, got some contacts here. Before I moved to Tacoma and changed careers, I was with the LAPD.'

'Really?'

'Uh-huh. Detective division.'

'Why did you leave?'

'Shot in the line of duty apprehending a suspect.' He lifted his shirt and showed her the scar on his abdomen.

'Oh my God.' She touched her throat, and now there was a gleam in her eye. 'I feel bad, I never offered you a refreshment. Can I get you some coffee or something?'

This woman probably didn't know where her own coffee machine was. It would taste like crap, and he never drank bad coffee. Besides, he'd had enough. Giving himself – and her – a cheap thrill wasn't cutting it. He was aching to get back to the truck and the shiny new group – a serious case of FOMO.

Cue regretful smile. 'Thank you, but no. I have a couple more appointments I have to get to.'

'More clients?'

'Yes. Gonna have to take on some more staff if this keeps up.'

'But you will be able to fit *me* in.' A hint of desperation.

'I'll make it my priority.'

She saw him out, and he made himself stroll nonchalantly back to the truck. He drove a couple of hundred yards down the street – ensuring he was out of her sightline – parked, then reached for the phone.

Shaun wasn't online, but Rainbowbrite had left a group message regarding a new profile of the Boy in the Dress's killer that had appeared on one of the larger sites, reputedly from a hot-shit ex-FBI profiler. It was linked to Missing-Linç, and he went straight there. He scanned the comments first – Mommydearest had left one of his characteristically terse statements that Pete suspected was aimed at Bobbiecowell: **<this contradicts our thoughts on the perpetrator being a hunter/serial killer>**

He knew the profilers would slither out of the woodwork sooner or later. Part of him had been looking forward to that, wanted to see how wrong they were. Whoever had written it had peppered it with buzzwords straight out of *Criminal Minds*: 'latent urges', 'unsub', 'signature', blah blah. Probably an armchair wannabe; Pete could sniff out a fellow fake at a hundred paces. Still, it was getting a lot of traction. He made himself comfortable, began to read: '. . . the unsub is white, early thirties, blue collar, familiar with the area.' As Tasha would say, *duh*. He read on: the killer had 'latent homosexual urges of which he was ashamed' – *wrong, nice try* – and apparently the 'way the body was positioned and clothed' pointed to an attempt at 'undoing' the crime. This was 'a sign, possibly, of remorse. A sign that the unsub knew the victim personally.' *Undoing*. Wrong again. The scene wasn't staged. Down, down, and then: '. . . the unsub is a "soft shouldered guy" who wanted to be the wearer of the dress.' Right about the soft-shouldered comment – back then, not so much now – but wrong about the dress.

The killer *wanted to be the wearer of the dress*.

An unexpected gush of rage, and he slammed his fist on the steering wheel. No, no, *no*. A jogger in lycra and earphones came running up, and shot him a curious glance. He would've liked nothing more than to kick open the door, catch the asshole in the thighs, but instead he bent over the passenger side and pretended to riffle through some paperwork.

How could they get away with this crap? Christ, if he could only put them straight. He shut his eyes, held his breath for six seconds, breathed out, did it again. The fury abated, and he continued to read.

The killer 'may have dumped the body in a place that holds emotional resonance as a sign of remorse.' He had to admit – grudgingly – that there was truth to that. The summer he'd spent at his grandparents' place on the outskirts of Millar Town was the happiest of his life. Second grade – before it all went to shit. The neighbourhood kids had accepted him into their gang, and they'd spent weeks playing softball and war games in the reserve, staying out until the light died. He was *someone* back then. He hadn't been back there since '97, the week after he was discharged from hospital. He hadn't been able to go all the way in – a group of teenagers were hanging around the new hiking trail information board, huffing cigarettes and pretending they weren't freezing – but he made it within a hundred yards. Close enough. It was then, the air searing his windpipe, the soundtrack of adolescent posturing in the background, still weak from a month of subsisting on saline and hospital dreck, that he made the decision to reinvent himself, scour away Past Pete's impulses and needs. Would he have carried on if he hadn't got sick?

He didn't know.

Had he even stopped?

He didn't know that, either.

Wicklowboy22

He'd been nervous about broaching the subject of heading to the States with Máirín, but in the end he needn't have worried. The news about Teddy had made it all the way to Melbourne, and she'd called him the night before – forgetting the time difference – to gobble up all the details. He missed her. They weren't friends exactly, she was his boss and twice his age, but she'd given him his mother's old job and somewhere to stay when everyone else had written him off. 'You have to go out there, Shaun,' she'd said. 'Don't worry about the shop, we'll close it if we have to. I'll be back for the Christmas rush.'

So that obstacle was out of his way.

He was prevaricating between excitement and – if he was honest – trepidation. Other than that fateful trip to Galway, he'd never been further from home than Dublin. After he'd finished with Máirín, he'd stayed up researching flights and watching *Fargo* in an attempt to get an idea of what small-town Minnesota entailed. His passport was valid – a legacy from Eileen, who'd drummed the importance of 'always being ready to bug out' into him – but he couldn't just flit off at a moment's notice. It wasn't just the shop – what would he do with the dog?

His phone buzzed for attention. Requests for comments about his uncle had been showing up in his Wicklowboy Gmail account all morning, including one from the *Daily Mail.* Either Neil from the guards had leaked his details, or the reporters had done their homework. Online, everyone who was part of the NYC party scene in the early nineties seemed to have known Teddy, and their messages were being retweeted all over. Máirín had been full of that last night too: 'Did you see, Shaun, that actor, the one who was in, what was it called now . . . the one with the robots . . . he's retweeted a message from the Arklow LGBT whatsit society. Who would have thought your uncle would become such a celebrity?'

Dead celebrity.

Peppered between these were multiple texts from Brendan: **<WTF???????? Cal told me about yr uncle. Is this why you wanted to see Donny??? He says Janice is freaking TF out>**; **<Can I see you Shaun?>**; **<Forget I said that>**; **<Thinking of you tho>**.

Shaun deleted them, and scanned through the #JusticeForTeddyRyan thread on Twitter. There were several tweets saying: 'he was the life & soul of the party R.I.P.'

The life and soul of the party. *You're Teddy reincarnated.* Only he wasn't, was he? Physical resemblance aside, he couldn't be more different to the extrovert scrapper that Johnny and the New York queens described. He knew for a fact that wasn't him; tried on that lifestyle just after his mother died, spent six months partying and drinking in a futile attempt to numb the shock of her abrupt death. Blew the cash his mother had saved for their escape fund on trips to Dublin, lost the house, lost himself in sordid sex, booze and MDMA binges. He was still paying for that. He'd missed his final exams, ended up leaving without a certificate, raged at Janice until she'd threatened to have him sectioned, and worst of all, neglected Daphne. If Máirín hadn't offered him his mother's old job he didn't know what he would have done. The growing dissonance between his childhood image of Teddy and the actual person didn't mean they weren't family, didn't mean he should stop digging for information. And, as Chris reminded him daily, they *needed* more information.

His lunchtime excursions to meet Johnny at the pub were becoming a habit, so much so that Molly the morose barmaid greeted him by name and poured him a Diet Coke without being asked. It was too rainy to smoke out in the gulag, so they were huddled around the bar, Daphne curled within lunging distance of Johnny's winklepickers.

'What are they saying he was?'

'A club kid. Part of a gay subculture and party scene during the late eighties and nineties. Drugs were a big part of it. I thought you said he wasn't into that?'

Johnny sniffed. 'Told you. He hated drugs. Who says he was into this?'

'Here.' Shaun showed Johnny the photo of Teddy posing in front of his backdrop of glitterball queens. 'He sent this to Donny. Carmel found it and gave it to me.'

'Look at the fucking state of him. And he sent this to Donny, did he? The bastard must have loved seeing his brother like that.'

'Carmel said Donny kept the photograph for a reason.'

'Yeah. Guilt. Families. They cause nothing but shite.'

He wasn't here just to buy Johnny drinks and disappoint Daphne. 'Do you have Pat Carey's address?'

'What for?'

'I should go and have a word with him. Teddy sent Donny that photograph and wrote to you and Mam; for all we know he sent something to Pat, too.'

'Told you. They fell out before we went to London.'

'Why?'

'Told you. Never said.'

Shaun wasn't picking up any caginess this time. 'It's worth asking all the same. You haven't seen him since you've been back?'

'God no. Haven't been looking.'

'He can't be that hard to track down. Where was he living when you knew him?' The Careys he remembered from school were feral kids who never seemed to go home, even at night and in the winter.

'Rathnew. Three streets from my mam's. Heard he got married. Don't know where he's living now.'

Molly emerged from the back, waving a custard cream. 'Alright to give the dog a biscuit?'

'That's kind of you. She can be fussy though.' An understatement, the dog's food bill was higher than his.

As expected, Daphne turned her nose up at it.

Johnny shook his head. 'What do you feed her? Steak?'

'That's terriers for you,' Molly said. 'Know what they like.'

'Hey, Moll,' Johnny said. 'You know where Pat Carey is these days?'

'Try Toolan's. Seen him in there loads.'

Johnny downed his drink and stood. 'Come on then.'

'Now?'

'Unless you'd rather sit here and watch the dog acting like a spoiled shite.'

As they strode up the high street and on towards the smoked glass windows and garish signage of Toolan's, the wind changed direction, slanting drizzle into Shaun's eyes, and threatening to dislodge the solid black mass on top of Johnny's head.

'Wait here,' Johnny said, before diving through the doors and into the bookies.

The shop's doorway was no match for the weather, and the dog pressed against his legs and stared up at him balefully. Shaun tucked his chin into his coat's scratchy tweed collar. He'd be facing worse than this if he made it to Minnesota. Maybe he should discuss the pros and cons of going with Johnny. There was no one else.

After what felt like an age, Johnny emerged. 'Not here.'

'Ah well, thanks for trying. I'll—'

'Well, well.' Johnny narrowed his eyes, nodded to a stringy fellow who was crossing the road, wearing nothing but a T-shirt on his top half, head bent, bow-legged. 'What's that word again, son? Serentipity?' Before Shaun could respond, Johnny barked: 'Oy. Pat.'

The man looked up, jerked when he clocked Johnny. 'Ah fuck.'

'How are you keeping, Pat?'

'What's it to you?' Another wreck of a man: the sunken eyes and hollow cheeks of the prematurely aged; his skin a raw network of broken veins. Shaun must have seen him around the town before, but hadn't absorbed who he was.

'Lost your manners along with your teeth?'

'Fuck off.'

This was going very bad, very fast. It would be up to Shaun to salvage it. 'Hiya, Pat. I'm Shaun, Teddy's nephew and—'

'I know who you are. I've got nothing to say to you.'

'All we're after is information on Teddy. Did he ever—'

'Information?' He weaved up close. 'I'll give you that all right. Teddy was nothing but a fucking pervert.' Pat hawked a glob of brown phlegm, which narrowly missed Daphne's back. 'He got what was coming to him. That pervert faggot got—'

With a shocking, casual grace, Johnny stepped forward, grabbed Pat's shirt, then headbutted him. Pat squealed, reeled, clamped a hand over his face, 'You—'

Johnny lunged again, and without pausing to second-guess, Shaun grabbed for his arm. Johnny rounded on him, eyes glazed, a sneer distorting his mouth. A cold second when Shaun was certain Johnny was going to strike – he wasn't even *seeing* him – then Daphne yipped, recognition sparked and Johnny pulled the swipe.

Behind them, Pat was scrambling away, muttering: 'You'll fucking pay for this.'

Shaken, sick to his stomach, Shaun gathered the dog in his arms and turned away.

'I wouldn't have hit you,' Johnny called after him. 'Don't have it in me. Come on, son. Don't be like that.'

Head down, Shaun kept on walking.

MissingLinc#TeddyRyan

Rainbowbrite, Ratking, Wicklowboy, You

Hey Shaun, see you're online. Gotta be late there. Everything ok? 5.02PM

Know we don't know each other, but here if you need an ear 5.04PM

Wicklowboy
Something happened today. It shook me up 5.10PM

To do with Teddy? Okay if I call him that? Seems too familiar . . . 5.10PM

Wicklowboy
Everyone on twitter's doing it 5.11PM

Wish I'd met him. Seems like he was quite a guy. Big personality. You take after him? 5.12PM

Don't feel like you have to answer that! Well here if you want to unload. 5.15PM

This is hard to say, but it's always the people left behind who hurt the most. Get that you're having a hard time. It's ok to admit that 5.20PM

Wicklowboy
Someone I thought I knew shocked me today 5.25PM

Family? 5.25PM

Wicklowboy
Someone else 5.26PM

You know what they say, you can never really know someone. This kind of thing can bring out the worst in people 5.27PM

You're handling it well. Bet you're stronger than you think 5.28PM

Wicklowboy
Thanks 5.28PM

How are the plans coming along?
5.29PM

Wicklowboy
Plans? 5.29PM

For coming out here.
GoFundMe's over $1000 now.
Got to tell you, it'll make a
helluva difference having a
member of the family out here.
5.30PM

Wicklowboy
With the police you mean? There's so
much publicity now will that really
make a difference? 5.31PM

Publicity helps, but can't count on
that. 5.31PM

Wicklowboy
Do you miss being with the police?
Ellie said you were a detective 5.33PM

Just a beat cop. Overstated my importance. Showing off, you know? Ellie's forgiven me for that though, hope you can too. Still working on Chris ;) 5.34PM

Rainbowbrite
Hi guys!!! Am I interrupting? 5.34PM

@Rainbowbrite Course not. Always great to hear your voice!! 5.35PM

Rainbowbrite

. . . among the sleuths who first championed the case is "Rainbowbrite", aka Ellen Caine (33), a stay at home mom who lives 'within walking distance' of where Edward Ryan's body lay, undiscovered for months. In stark contrast to the grisly discussions held on the Missing-Linc forum, Ms Caine's online persona is as sparkly and relentlessly positive as her alias suggests. However, she is not as positive when it comes to the subject of Stenton County's handling of the case. 'They just didn't care,' she told us. 'Teddy Ryan might never have been identified if we hadn't followed up on it.'

A spokesperson from Stenton County Sheriff's Office strenuously denied accusations that the case was mishandled and says that the sheriff's office is working closely with the Minnesota Bureau of Criminal Apprehension to form a cold case unit. Led by Stenton County Sheriff's Office Commander Patricia Stillson, the county says it will be liaising with authorities in Interpol and Wicklow County, Ireland. 'We will look closely at the case and review all evidence.' The county refused to comment on allegations that vital evidence has gone missing, nor would it discuss the possibility that Edward Ryan was the victim of a hate crime.

It was Ellie's fourth interview, but she still got a thrill seeing her name in print like that. Mommydearest had already posted it on the site's Facebook, Instagram and Twitter accounts. She hadn't wanted to like him – he was a far more efficient moderator than she could ever hope to be – but she had to admit he was a real find. She sat at the breakfast bar and picked at the crusty remnants of the mac 'n' cheese she'd made from scratch. From *scratch*. She was proud of herself. The boys were in bed at a reasonable hour for once, which only took a minor amount of bribery to achieve, and Danny was coming for a sleepover at the weekend, so that should mollify Sherry. She *could* do this, after all. Noah wouldn't have anything to carp about when he got home from the late shift. His dinner was warming in the oven; the house was clean. He was never online, thought it was dumb, so it was unlikely he'd discover the true extent of her balancing act unless Eric or someone else filled him in. Things were going okay. Not great – she was mostly living on caffeine and adrenaline – but okay. And much as she wished she could share this with him, after pumpkin-gate, she didn't want to risk another showdown. It was easier to pretend she was doing less work on the case than she actually was. Capping an almost perfect day, a message came in from Bobbiecowell congratulating her on the interview. She smiled.

<Thanks so much Bobbie! ☺ You really think it's okay & I didn't say too much?>

<You sounded v professional and best of all gave the county the kick up the ass they needed ☺>

<You think they're serious about the task force??>

<Who knows? You asked your contact?>

<I will. I've been thinking, shall I go to the county and try to talk to them again? They might speak to me now that they're getting all this bad publicity>

<Won't hurt to try>

<I'll let them know that a family member is going to come out here which might also convince them to talk>

<Good idea ☺ you see the GoFundMe's hit $1500??? That's got to be enough to get Shaun out here right?>

<All down to you>

<Aw shucks *blushes*. You picking up that Shaun is reluctant to come out there?>

<Yes. Doesn't like the idea of charity, but saw that convo you had with him. Good of you. A real father figure!!>

<Paula would disagree. Wasn't the best dad. Too busy working, regret that ☹>

<Don't you mean Pauline?>

<I do! See? Crap dad. Not really – that was auto correct ;)>

<You're making up for that now>

<I'm not, but bless you Ellie for being so kind. Hey, when are you thinking about going to LE?>

<Tomorrow maybe?>

<Just look after yourself. Came up against a lot of bad cops when I was on the job>

<One day you'll have to tell me all your war stories!!!>

<I will!!! Boy, I've got some doozies ☺>

She wrapped it up – she couldn't spend all night chatting with Bobbie. She and Aqualung had business to conclude. He'd found a dress on eBay that was ticking towards the end of its auction. Bidding was at two hundred dollars. She should really check with Noah before she splurged their savings, but what he didn't know wouldn't hurt him. She still hadn't mustered up the courage to ask him if Shaun could stay with them; she'd spring that on him when everything was finalised – it was her house too. And tomorrow she'd visit the sheriff's office – *make* them talk to her.

'. . . we should liaise with each other. We've done a ton of work on the dress, and we're in contact with Shaun Ryan, Teddy's nephew? He's going to come out here, we're doing a crowdfund on that, he doesn't have the resources to pay for himself.' Crimson-cheeked, sweaty-palmed, Ellie was back to her old babbling ways. When she'd arrived at the front desk and asked for a meeting, she'd steeled herself for a long wait or a refusal, already building up a steam of righteous indignation. Five minutes later, Commander Stillson herself came out to greet her – disarming

Ellie further with her dishevelled, homely appearance and approachability. Ellie had been on the back foot ever since.

Stillson unbuttoned her jacket, a creased affair that was dandruffed with crumbs. 'Scuse me getting comfortable. They always put the heat up too high in here. Go on.'

'I'm trying to say that you can use us – the site, I mean – as a resource. Lots of departments are doing that now.'

'Uh-huh. Crowdsourcing. Can work. I had a partner who got involved with one of those websites a few years back.' She crinkled her eyes. 'He had a name for you guys. What was it?' She tapped her teeth, 'It'll come to me. Which one of these forums are you connected to again?'

'Missing-Linc. With a "C".'

'Gotcha. Clever name.' Stillson turned to her laptop, tapped away. 'Mmhmm. You guys *have* been busy.'

'What about the dress?'

'What about it?'

'Have you got any new information? Did you track it down?'

'Interested in how come you know about that.' Stillson paused. 'Ellen. Pretty name. My sister's an Ellen. You go by Ellie or El?'

'Ellie.'

'Okay for me to call you that?'

'Sure. Yes, of course.'

'So Ellie, who told you the dress wasn't in evidence?'

'A contact.'

'You're not going to give me a name?'

'I . . . I can't.' Could she be legally compelled to? *Woman-up Ellie.* 'That doesn't matter. The fact is that the department allowed it to go missing. It's a vital piece of evidence.'

'Can't argue with you there.'

'Have you interviewed any of the incarcerated killers who were active around this time to see if they could be involved? I can give you some names. And then there's JT. Teddy's friend? He was on his way to see him, or at least we think he was, when he was murdered.'

'Listen, Ellie, appreciate all the good work you're doing, but I can't discuss the case with you. You understand that, right?'

'I do. It's just—'

'Super. Well thanks for coming in. Leave your details and I'll be in touch if I need you.' With a last disarming grin, Stillson turned to her screen.

Knowing full well she'd been given the bum's rush, but with no other option than to take it, Ellie gathered her things. She was at the door when Stillson said: 'Doe Nuts. Knew it would come to me. *That's* what he called you guys.'

Bobbiecowell

Ms Albright blinked very fast and scratched at a scaly patch on her chin. 'As I said, we thought long and hard about whether or not to bring this to your attention.'

'So why did you?' Margie snapped.

'Maybe it's best if I . . . It was something Tasha brought up during Debate and Engagement Hour.'

Gary chuckled. 'Debate and Engagement Hour? Sounds like my marriage.'

Margie sighed, Ms Albright smiled weakly and Pete pretended he hadn't heard. He should be feeling like a third wheel stuck between Margie and her mouth-breathing ex – he was only here at all because Tasha had asked him to go along – but he was the one with whom Ms Albright made the most regular eye contact.

'As you know, we're eager to instil in our learners a critical engagement with the wider issues facing society. The idea is for them to choose a topic that interests them, and then use it as the basis for a class debate. Tasha's choice of topic was . . . unusual.'

'Well don't keep us in suspense,' Margie said in a tone that could freeze blood.

'She asked the class to debate why there are fewer serial killers in today's society then there were in the 1980s.'

Margie stiffened. 'I see.'

Pete turned the laugh into a cough.

'Why *aren't* there so many killers?' Gary said, a frat boy to the tee. Today he was dressed like a reject from *The Breakfast Club* in Keds and a hoody.

Margie hissed: '*Gary.*'

'What? It's interesting.'

Ms Albright's fingers strayed back to her chin. Pete longed to slap her hand away, sensed that Margie wanted to do the same. 'On every other level Tasha is an exemplary student, but in today's climate . . . well you can understand why we would be concerned. It's school policy to address any worrisome behaviour.'

Margie wasn't going to let that pass. 'I hope you're not implying Tasha may have violent tendencies.'

'Not at all. Could she have picked it up online? The school's website has guidelines about approved entertainment viewing and online influences.'

'I monitor that closely. Gary? What about when she's with you?'

'Sure, sure.' The man couldn't lie to save his life.

Pete gauged the room. Should he get involved? Why not? 'Not sure I'm understanding the problem here.'

Ms Albright twitched. 'I explained that the topic wasn't suitable—'

'I get that. My point is that here we have a student, an exemplary student, who I believe you have recently rewarded for outstanding selfless behaviour, and you're punishing her for thinking outside the box.'

'Well . . . well, we're not *punishing* her exactly.'

'Seems that way to me. You called us in here, didn't you? Seems like you're trying to shut down debate. Censor an above-average student's development.'

'That's not it at all.'

'If Tasha picked this topic in order to say, regale the class with tales of violence and gore, that would be one thing' – he wouldn't put it past her – 'but what if her intention was to use it as a jumping-off point for a discussion about, say, how patriarchal attitudes and toxic masculinity historically manifest into instances of male violence that then impact society on a wider scale?' Pure, unadulterated word salad.

The scab gave way to a bead of blood. Ms Albright glanced at her fingers and wiped them on her skirt. 'I'm not following you, Mr . . .'

'Kazinski.' He sighed as if she'd really disappointed him. 'The fact that you're not following me is concerning. I'm not Tasha's father, so let me know if I'm speaking out of turn here, Gary' – Gary nodded, mumbled something inaudible – 'but from the debates I've had with Tasha, it's obvious that her sensitivity and level of engagement are way above average. Heck, she's smarter than ninety percent of the *adults* I know. And from what you've said, Ms Albright, I'm wondering . . . perhaps this environment isn't challenging enough for her?' A peripheral glance at Margie to see how she was taking this meddling. She gave nothing away – appeared to be too intent on watching Ms Albright as the woman squirmed through the implications of losing one of the school's brightest, fee-paying students.

'Oh no. No. We *do* value Tasha. That's not what I'm saying at *all*. Perhaps we did misunderstand her.'

'Perhaps you did.'

Margie stood. 'Are we done here?'

'Yes. Thank you for coming in. We do value Tasha, she's a wonderful student, and a very . . .' Margie sighed as the woman fished for the right adjective '. . . *kind* person.'

Pete made sure he was the first to exit the room. Tasha was waiting on a bench outside, and he gave her a surreptitious thumbs-up before Margie and Gary joined them in the hallway.

Margie got straight into it. 'Where did you hear about serial killers, sweetie? Was it something you saw online?'

'I don't want to say.'

Pete held his breath. This could go either way.

Tasha looked down at her Mary Janes. 'I saw something about them on Netflix when I was at Dad's house.'

'I knew it.' Margie rounded on Gary. 'You know you're supposed to monitor her TV time. What were you thinking?'

Gary spread his arms. 'I can't watch her twenty-four seven.'

'She's your *child*.'

Pete jumped in, back to saviour mode: 'Let's go wait in the car, Tash. Give your folks a chance to talk.'

'Good idea,' Margie said, pressing her lips to hold in the vitriol

Pete knew would be fired at Gary the second he and Tasha were out of earshot.

Feet squeaking on the polished hardwood floor, they passed collaged walls boasting of 'Our achievements!!' That and the school's aura of restrained propriety made the relatively innocuous place he went to seem like Attica in comparison.

He held back until they were safely inside the plush leather interior of Margie's status-mobile. 'Why didn't you tell your mom the truth, Tash?'

'Snitches get stitches.'

'Where the hell did you hear that?'

'It's a *meme*.'

'Course it is.'

'If I tell her everything then she'll be mad at you.'

'Now she's mad at your dad.'

'She's *always* mad at him.'

'True. You might want to reconsider your choice of debating topic in future. Just saying.'

'I know. I only said it because it interests me and all the other subjects are *bor*ing. Like, everyone picks climate change or why we shouldn't be online all the time or why people are getting like, really fat.'

'Yeah, well, some interests are best kept on the down low.'

'I *know*.' She sighed. 'There's a GoFundMe for Teddy's family now. I saw it. Did you tell them to do that because of me? Was it your idea?'

'Nope. Wish I had. That came from Rainbowbrite.'

'Rainbowbrite is *such* a lame username.'

'I know, right?'

'I want to give them some money.'

'I'll do it for you.'

The doors swung open; Margie emerged in a flurry like Glinda the Good Witch; Gary sloped out exuding the demeanour of someone who'd just had their ass handed to them.

'Sorry, Mom,' Tasha whispered when her mother had slid into the driver's seat and shut the door.

'You don't have anything to be sorry about. I'm proud of you.'

Margie slammed her seatbelt into the slot and glared after Gary as he reversed, jerkily, out of the parking lot. Not for the first time Pete reckoned it was a good thing he'd been extra attentive lately, ignoring his phone despite the constant itch. When Margie was in a mood there was always some collateral damage. She gunned the engine and reversed out like a getaway driver.

He brushed her thigh. 'Hey, sorry if I stood on any toes back there.'

'It's fine.'

'What did you do?' Tasha's bright little eyes peered at him in the rear-view mirror.

'Pete stood up for you,' Margie said. 'Told that – told Ms Albright – that you're too smart to be treated like that.'

'Oh.'

He caught Tasha's eye and she gave him a half-smile.

Back in the house and fresh from his triumph, he locked himself in the bathroom to check on the latest developments. Rainbowbrite had rallied from her predictably fruitless excursion to ferret info out of the county, and had uploaded several photographs showcasing the dress she and Aqualung sourced on eBay. The bodice wasn't far off, but the pink frills were way off base. Again he reminded himself not to fall into the temptation of pushing things too far with Shaun – he'd have to watch that. In any case their brief one-to-one hadn't given him the thrill he thought it would.

Otherwise, interest in the case was beginning to wane. The bandwagon celebs were showing signs of moving onto the next hot thing, and even the Facebook groups' righteous indignation had dimmed now that Stenton County had reassigned the case. It should be a relief. It wasn't. As Tash would say: *bor*ing. And just what *was* he planning to do if Shaun did come out to the States? Why suggest the GoFundMe at all if he didn't – deep down – have something in mind? *The Websleuth Massacre*. Jesus. That was all hypothetical, and going off half-cocked smacked of Past Pete's thoughtless actions. No. But all the same, he needed an outlet. The Boy in the Dress was his production; he was the goddamned director here. *He'd* decide when the show was over.

Should he deploy one of his bombs? They were supposed to be his Patriot missiles, only to be released if the enemy threatened the gates, but they were too good not to use. Risky? Sure. Should he? No. Was he going to do it? *Hell*, yes.

Bobbiecowell couldn't go near it, but one of his sock-puppets could always step up. Keysersoze? Nope. That one had been dormant for too long, but could act as back-up. Dotspot would do.

Enter, stage left, JT.

Thread dated: November 10/2017

Dotspot: hey guys screen-grabbed this pic from twitter you seen it yet?? 100% sure that's Teddy on the left there. Need to ID the guy he's with.

Vladtheromantic: HOLY. SHIT. Good catch. That's the same club from the other photo. You asked whoever posted it? Did they know Teddy?

Dotspot: contacted them but no reply yet. Their profile is sketchy but could be the other guy in the photo?

Vladtheromantic: Gonna scan & run through images now . . .

Keysersoze: way ahead of you. So we got a bunch of possible matches including THIS guy: facebook.com/John.Tremain

Vladtheromantic: Initials match.

Ratking1

She should delete it. Delete it right now. It had only been up this long because Mommydearest had finally succumbed to burnout and taken a break. As little as a week ago she would have gone on a banning and deleting rampage, but the temptation to let it play out held her back.

Scott snapped his fingers. 'Hello? Earth to Chris?'

Chris looked up. 'Think we've found JT.'

'No way.'

'Yes way.'

He nudged his glasses higher on his nose, then clicked away from whatever he and Rainbowbrite were working on. 'Shit.'

The photograph dominated the JT sub-thread: Teddy Ryan, grinning savagely, arm slung around a good-looking black guy who was holding up a hand as if trying to deflect the camera's eye. Apart from the pair she'd received from Shaun, the photograph Dotspot had harvested from Twitter was the only other pic of Teddy anywhere online. Another coup for the site, but the comments below were straying into murky territory.

Vladtheromantic: Arrest warrant here for 04. Criminal negligence.

Dotspot: This is interesting . . . guy was in the military worked in the catering corps. Could be a connection to GI Doe?

Bobbiecowell: How did you get access to military files?

Dotspot: Imma vet too

Vladtheromantic: Holy crapola. He ever at Fort Drum?

Dotspot: Unclear.

'Whoa,' Scott said. 'Fort Drum. This could be a link to GI Doe. This could be *big*.'

Mommydearest might be out of the loop, but Rainbowbrite wasn't. A DM came in: **<Chris??? You seen this? Aren't you on modding duty?>; <Chris??? Hello???>; <PLEASE!? I'M AT THE STORE RN BUT IF YOU DON@T REMOVE IT THEN I WILL!!!>**

'I've got to delete this,' Chris said to herself as much as Scott.

'But what if he's the killer?'

'Told you. We don't post names. Can't.' She came to her senses, got to work. Not long after came the inevitable:

Dotspot: Looks like the mods here have an agenda. Thought you wanted to sleuth this case?? Why do you keep deleting? Other sites are going to run with this if we don't!!!

'Shit.'

'Anything I can do?'

'Nope.'

Ratking1 [admin]: You all know the rules. No unsubstantiated accusations are allowed. Doxing can RUIN LIVES.

Dotspot: A life has already been ruined. Screw this. Thought we were here to find JUSTICE for Teddy Ryan.

Bobbiecowell: Ratking is right. Cool it.

Dotspot: You kidding dude? You're the one saying the killer wiped out GI Doe as well. YOU GOT A LINK BETWEEN THEM NOW. WTF????

Bobbiecowell: An <u>UNSUBSTANTIATED</u> link.

Dotspot: Yeah but that's why we should work it dumbass. Whose side are you on? Fuck THIS. I'm out. So long and thanks for all the SHIT. Going somewhere where they CARE.

She had minutes to act before this blew up.

Using the connection she'd forged with a veterans' website during the GI Doe case – which nudged the edges of legality – she unearthed a John Edwin Tremain who'd enlisted in late September '95 in West Virginia. Same guy? Maybe. If Teddy had been murdered in October in Minnesota, how likely was it that JT had hooked up with him, killed him, then dumped the body in a different state? The base at Dawson was a two day round trip from Minnesota. Add another couple of days if he'd picked Teddy up in New York.

'Were you ever in the military, Scott?'

He blinked. 'Nope. My brother was though.'

'Far as you know, they get time off base during training?'

'Nope. Gotta stay there until graduation far as I recall.'

'Ten weeks, right?'

'Right.'

'Think JT might have an alibi.'

She pulled up JT's Facebook page, scrolled through his available pictures till she came to a shot of an older version of the guy in the club pic, dressed in chef's whites, laughing with a large redhead. Took note of the name of the restaurant on the window behind them – a burger and steak joint in Huntingdon – and rattled it into Google.

'Need to give him a heads-up, let him know he could have an online lynch mob heading his way.'

'You could be warning the murderer we're on to him.'

'If I don't, he'll find out from somewhere else.'

'You're gonna message him?'

'Got his work number.' She loathed talking on the phone, but it was more immediate. Also, she couldn't discount the fact that if this did blow up, if it went full Forrest case, he wouldn't be talking to anyone. It wasn't like her to doubt herself – but she hesitated all the same. She grabbed her phone and clicked onto group chat.

MissingLinc#TeddyRyan

BobbieC, Rainbowbrite, Wicklowboy, You

@BobbieC @Rainbowbrite
Thinking about contacting John Tremain directly. Got evidence he couldn't have done it. Your thoughts? **6.07PM**

Rainbowbrite
OMG I don't know chris **6.07PM**

BobbieC
Guessing you want to touch base because of the flack he's going to get? **6.07PM**

Yup **6.08PM**

Rainbowbrite
It's on FB now chris **6.08PM**

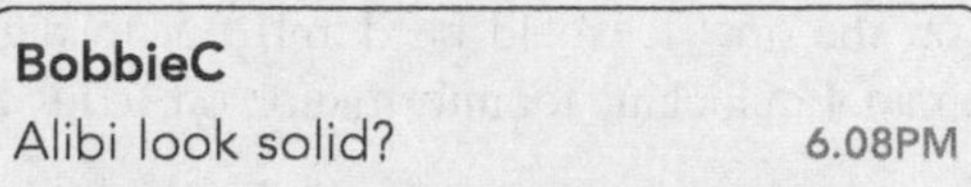
BobbieC
Alibi look solid? 6.08PM

Not sure 6.09PM

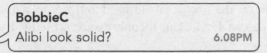

BobbieC
Your call. If you do get hold of him don't call him John, call him JT, see how he reacts to the nickname 6.09PM

'Smart.'

She tapped in the number before she could talk herself out of it, put it on speaker to free up her hands.

It was answered on the fifth ring. 'Dicky's Steak House how can I help you today.' The woman's voice was a flat monotone, punctuated by the crack of snapping gum.

'JT there?'

'He's busy. Who's asking?'

Scott was looking at her pointedly. She needed to turn on the charm. 'Sorry to call during work hours. I've got some information about a friend of his. Wouldn't ask if it wasn't urgent.'

A beat of silence, then: 'Hold on.'

Scott was leaning so far forward he was pushing the screen of his MacBook near horizontal.

She listened to a distant thunk, then came a man's muffled voice: 'Can't a guy smoke in peace?' and the monotone woman saying: 'Hey, don't blame me. Said it was urgent.'

A rustle as the phone was passed on then: 'Yeah?'

'Is this JT?'

'Yeah. Who's this?'

She should really alert JT to the possible incoming storm,

but now he was on the line, it would be dumb not to dig. 'My name's Chris Guzman. I'm looking for information on Teddy Ryan.'

'Who?'

'Teddy Ryan? Irish guy? He was in New York around '95?'

'Don't know anyone like that. Who told you to call me?'

'We've got a photograph of you and him together.'

A low hiss like air escaping from a tyre. 'Where you say you're from?'

'Missing-Linc. It's a missing persons' website.'

'He's gone missing?'

What to tell him? If he wasn't responsible, he should know that Teddy was dead; if he *was* involved in Teddy's death he knew it anyway. 'Not missing. He's dead. Murdered.' Scott flapped his hand, telling her to tone it down. 'Sorry to be the one—'

'Murdered?

'His body was discovered in '96. He's only recently been identified.'

'Murdered? Who killed him? He get in a fight or something?'

'That's what we're trying to find out.'

'You a cop?'

'Nope. He was found in Minnesota.'

'Minnesota? The hell was he doing in Minnesota?'

'Think he might have been on his way to see you.'

'Where you getting all this shit from?'

'Teddy mentioned in a letter that you might have some work for him.'

'Huh? Oh wait . . . Man, that's a long time ago you talking about. My uncle had a construction firm back then, might have mentioned that to him. He was looking for guys. Not in Minnesota.'

'Where exactly?'

'Colorado. Superior.'

'So Teddy could have been on his way there?'

'Wouldn't know. Never heard from him after I left New York. I enlisted soon after that.'

'You know what he was doing when you left? Where he was working?'

'Last I heard he got a lead on some work in Brooklyn.'

'What kind of work?'

'Think it was with one of those furniture removal companies? He was a small guy but he was strong.'

'We got some info that he might have been doing sex work.'

'No ways. Nuh-uh. He wasn't part of the scene. Wasn't into that.'

'Like I say, we've got photographs of both of you at a well-known club kid venue.'

'Went there a couple of times, so what? Doesn't mean anything. Look are we done playing twenty questions? I got work to do.'

'You weren't together?'

'I'm done here.'

'Wait – one more thing.' Now she was sounding like Columbo. She hadn't even begun to broach the subject of the impending mob. 'You said you were in the military.'

'Uh-huh. Four years. Got out, didn't re-enlist.'

'You ever train at Fort Drum? Black River?'

'What?'

'Were you ever at Fort Drum?'

'Why you asking that? No. I wasn't there.'

'Where were you in October '95?'

'Would've been in Dawson.'

'You got proof of that? You go on furlough during that time?'

'Hell, no. Weren't allowed off base till graduation. I know what you're saying, wasn't me who did it. Can't have my name near this thing. I've got kids. I've got *grand*kids.'

'Might not have a choice.'

'What do you mean?'

'You might want to light another smoke for this.' Chris gave him a crash course in what to expect over the next few days, and how to cover his back.

'They're going to say I'm a homo, aren't they?'

She considered lying. 'Yeah. They're going to say a lot of things. You have to be ready for that.'

Ratking1 [admin]: I have been in contact with John Tremain and he HAS A SOLID ALIBI. I'd appreciate it if our members could help spread the word. This is an innocent man. Also have new info RE Teddy Ryan. Will post an update soon.

Bobbiecowell: I'm on it.

MissingLinc#TeddyRyan

BobbieC, Rainbowbrite, Wicklowboy, You

@BobbieC Hey. Thanks for the back up 8.15PM

BobbieC
Sure. You buy his alibi? 8.15PM

Yup 8.15PM

BobbieC
Then that's good enough for me 8.16PM

Hope we stopped this thing in time. 8.16PM

BobbieC
You did what you could. Out of your hands now 8.17PM

Gonna get Mommydearest to look into Dotspot too, try and track down the user who posted the pic 8.17PM

BobbieC
Good thinking! Let me know if you need help with that 8.17PM

Thanks 8.18PM

Bobbiecowell

Lost in thought, he almost missed the Lakeview exit. He yanked the wheel and sliced across the lanes, ignoring the hoots screaming in his wake. He rarely drove into Seattle, had to rely on the snotty tones of the sat nav to direct him to a parking lot.

He squeezed the truck between a jerk-mobile sporting vanity plates and an Audi A4 and retrieved the phone.

What a damp squib. Where were the gonzo YouTubers chasing JT down the street demanding a confession? Where were the Antifa, Black Lives Matter and MAGA Twitter wars? Since when had Reddit turned down a witch-hunt? What happened to goddamned fake news? He'd handed the online mob the perfect stooge – a self-hating gay black guy with ties to Teddy, GI Doe and with a goddamned criminal record – but not even the racist nut-jobs who thrived on unsubstantiated accusations were running with it. The bomb was a dud. Helping diffuse it on Missing-Linc was a calculated decision – another stab at winning Ratking's trust – but he hadn't considered for a second that people would *actually* believe JT was innocent. His plan, to seed discord on the site, draw more attention on the case, and toy with Ratking and Rainbowbrite – who, let's not forget had form where unsubstantiated accusations were concerned – had backfired. All he'd done was make his position more tenuous. Mommydearest was no fool. Came across like an obsessional freak. He wouldn't be able to track down whoever had tweeted that pic because there *was* no tweeted pic, but the last thing he wanted was some techie autist digging into Dotspot's profile.

A message came in from Rainbowbrite: **<Chris says you were GREAT with the JT thing!!>**

Oh, did she. Whoopee-fucking-do.

Enough. Time to go shopping.

He wasn't the average Capitol Hill thrift store customer, but the hipsters behind the counter were too busy grooming each other to pay him any mind. He'd have more luck searching on eBay, but he could hardly get a prom dress delivered to the house, could he? How would he explain that one to Margie? He shouldn't be doing this at all, but like an addict who chain-smoked instead of shooting up, he had to do something to keep himself in check. Another outlet.

As he flipped through the racks of dead women's clothes, that phrase from the profile stuck in his mind like gum in a pre-schooler's hair: *'wanted to be the wearer of the dress.'*

Perhaps – just perhaps – there was a seed of truth to that, after all.

He picked out an acceptable facsimile, and took his prize up to the till, ready with a seemingly off-the-cuff excuse about a daughter's first school dance. It was needless – the hipsters didn't ask, so he didn't tell. Next, he treated himself to a latte with extra cream at a coffee chain – he'd work that off later – then headed back to the truck. He crammed the thrift store dress into the box containing the last of Teddy's belongings. It would be safe enough. Margie would no more drive the Dodge than she'd give up her Tuesday night gun habit. He piano-ed his fingers over the steering wheel, then fired off another Guzman email for the hell of it, seeding in a little Easter egg that Chris may or may not pick up on.

And screw it. It was time to drop bomb two – a grenade with Rainbowbrite's name on it.

Civil war breaks out on /r/gratefuldoe when user names and shames websleuths involved in innocent man's suicide attempt. Self.SubredditDrama

submitted 3 hours ago

76 comments / share / save / hide / give gold / report / crosspost

[-] Carpenter_Face –13 points 6 hours ago
'You either die a hero or you live long enough to see yourself become a member of Missing-Linc'

Seriously STAY AWAY from this site! I know it's getting a lot of hype thanks to the breakthrough with the Teddy Ryan/Boy in the Dress case but there are so many better sleuthing forums out there with WAY better communities. Missing-Linc is TOXIC and CLIQUEY. The Admin is a power-hungry control freak and runs the place like a dictatorship with the help of his minion moderators. It's also just completely unethical to support this site. Think I'm overreacting? They have ruined INNOCENT LIVES. Why do you think they stopped sleuthing cases out of nowhere? Because of guilt.

Don't believe me? Ever heard of the Forrest case? No? Don't like clicking links? Well then gather round, Kiddiewinks and I'll tell you a story. Once upon a time there was a fat little websleuth named RAINBOWBRITE. She wanted to be the greatest online detective in all the lands but sadly she was not as BRITE as her name would suggest. One day a sad old man asked Rainbowbrite and her small army of rabid armchair autists for help. His beautiful daughter had killed herself because of a nasty stalker man and the mean police weren't doing anything to punish him. "OMG!!!!!" said Rainbowbrite, joyfully. "We can totally help you ☺ ☺ ☺ we know more about this kind of thing than the silly police who have been doing this YEARS!!! I'm sorry for your loss BTW ☹ ☹".

Anyway, long story short the members of Missing-Linc decided this supposed stalker was 100% guilty DESPITE the fact that there was 0 evidence and basically doxxed him. It was all a lie made up by the crazy-ass parents but this dude's life was ruined. He ended up attempting suicide.

But by all means PLEASE keep telling me about how amazing Missing-Linc is and how they're a pillar of the community after identifying the Boy in the Dress.

Rainbowbrite

'I saw it. No one's paying much attention to it.'

'It's *everywhere*, Chris.'

'Dude, it's one thread and it's not even on the front page.'

Ellie refreshed the link. She couldn't bear to read the entirety of the replies and comments; just seeing her username there was enough to send her into the den, begging for a Skype call with Chris. She'd been bursting with it, needed to talk, almost blurted it all out to Noah, before she came to her senses. She couldn't do that, couldn't let on that the Forrest case still had the power to poison her. He may be turning a blind eye to the number of hours she was putting in – he wasn't a fool – but she couldn't admit that she was spinning out. *Fat little websleuth.* That was personal. That stung.

She scrolled through. Chris was right. The thread hadn't gained much traction, if anything it had attracted a fresh slew of down-votes.

'Trust me on this, it'll be buried in a couple of hours. Stop stressing. It's just some asshat ex-member who's bitter they left the site before the Teddy Ryan case blew up. That's not all they're doing.'

'What do you mean?'

'Just that someone's got it in for the site is all. It's not just you.'

'Cos of envy, you mean?'

A pause. 'Maybe.'

'Are you going to get Mommydearest to look into who's behind it? He was the one who sent me this link. He's really thorough.'

A longer pause. 'Maybe.'

The kids' footsteps thumped above her head. 'You really think it'll be okay?'

'It *is* okay. You made a mistake, and you paid the price for it. You did everything right after that. Wrote to that guy and apologised.'

'He never wrote back.'

'Do you blame him?'

'No.'

'And listen, JT could easily have gone the same way. People were already running with the accusations. Fact that it didn't is down to you and Bobbie. I should have deleted his name soon as it came up.'

'You did.'

'Yeah . . . I kinda didn't. And I was a real bitch to you when you messed up.'

'Well . . .'

'You can say it.'

'Okay. You were a real b-word to me.'

'Can't you even say the word?'

'I can, I just don't want to.' Ellie caught the low tones of a man's voice in the background. 'Who's that?'

Chris sighed. 'Aqualung. Scott. Your dress buddy.'

'You *know* him? Like in *real life*? Are you two *together*?'

'Ellie . . .'

'Are you?'

'We're just friends.'

'He never told me that he knew you. Can I say hi to him?'

'He's in the kitchen.'

'Can I tell you something, Chris?'

'Have you ever needed permission before?'

'I always thought maybe you were . . . you know. A lesbian.'

'I'm taking that as a compliment. Why did you think that?'

'Because whenever I asked you any personal questions you always dodged them. So, I thought maybe you were hiding something.'

'Yeah, well it isn't that.'

The door flew open. Sammy stood there, red faced, out of breath. 'Mom, Danny's trapped his finger in the door, there's *blood*.'

'That doesn't sound good,' Chris said.

Ellie slammed the laptop shut without saying goodbye, already thinking of ways to bribe the kids so that Sherry – and Noah – wouldn't find out.

Bobbiecowell: You okay? Saw that thing on Reddit. They shouldn't be allowed to dig up the past like that. Here if you need to talk

Rainbowbrite: That's so kind of you! Kinda relieved it's out in the open. I'm SO sorry I didn't tell you about it before

Bobbiecowell: You're really okay? Must have stung reading that ☹

Rainbowbrite: 100 percent okay!!! Thanks for caring ☺ ☺

Wicklowboy22

Some bastard had drawn a penis on the plastic sleeve shielding one of the 'missing' posters next to the estuary. He'd tried to wipe it off with his sleeve, but only succeeded in casting a smudged pall across Keith O'Neill's features. Shaun was even more aware of the flyers now; seemed to see the man's face all over the town.

Eager to return to the warmth of her basket, Daphne dragged him across the bridge, blissfully unaware that he was seriously considering abandoning her for two weeks. He'd found a kennels in Arklow that had a good rep, and he was planning to check it out at the weekend. He had to make a decision soon. Chris and Bobbie were pushing him to confirm dates and book his ticket, and Rainbowbrite had practically sent him a questionnaire to fill in about his dietary requirements. He didn't know how to tell her that he'd rather stay in a motel. Just the thought of sleeping in a stranger's house brought on a whisper of anxiety.

He'd been longer than the 'back in 5 mins' sign promised, and there was a customer waiting outside the shop. He called out, 'Sorry!' then did the kind of double take he'd always assumed was the sole province of slapstick movie characters.

It was no wonder he didn't recognise Johnny at first: the pompadour was no more. Without the hair to distract the eye like a magician's misdirection, the beating life had given the man was all the more apparent. The new short back and sides made his head look tiny – like a wrinkled potato that had been left too long on a window ledge.

'Why did you do that?'

'Felt like a change. Got sick of people taking the piss out of me. Quick drink?'

'Can't. I've just been out.' Johnny wasn't getting off that easily.

'Sorry about the other day, son. Sorry you had to see that.'

Shaun couldn't take his eyes off the man's head. Perhaps Johnny did it as a symbolic gesture – a low-rent Samson. Was this how Teddy used to behave? Lashing out at all and sundry, followed by a grandiose display of penitence?

'How's things going? Any leads?'

'You could check for yourself.'

'Told you, don't do any of that shite.'

Shaun gave in and told him about his plans to fly out to visit Teddy's grave.

'And they're paying for that, are they?'

'People on the internet are.'

'Strangers? Why would they do that?'

'Out of the kindness of their hearts. How would I know? Might not go anyway. Worried about leaving the dog.'

'I'll look after her. My mother would love that.'

'You'd do that?'

'Course.' Johnny picked up on Shaun's reticence. 'I know what you're thinking. I won't kick her to bits. I only went after Pat because he was abusing you.'

'Bit of an overreaction.'

'Mebbe. Got all . . . protective, you know.' His voice took on a gruffness Shaun hadn't heard before. 'If you need me to help with anything else, you let me know.'

'Why?'

'Why what?'

'Why . . .' Shaun wasn't sure what he was trying to say. 'Why are you helping me? You don't owe me anything.'

'That's a daft question. Teddy was a good mate. Felt like I let him down.'

'Fair enough.' Shaun let the silence stretch. 'Better get in.'

'Fair enough.'

He was halfway through the door and almost out of earshot when Johnny said: 'You ever think you might be helping me?'

'I'm getting out, Mam.' He knew he'd end up talking to her eventually. Maybe it was from guilt. He hadn't been to see her since he climbed aboard the Teddy rollercoaster. The family row was full up. There was no room for Teddy next to her, but in any case, there was nothing he could do about the remains while the case was still open. He'd bring him a cigarette, a Marlboro or whatever they smoked over there.

He jumped as his phone parped out the *Jaws* theme tune – the alert he'd selected for Auntie Janice. He'd rather ignore it, but she'd only add avoidance to his long list of crimes against the family.

'Hi, Auntie—'

'You've done it now, Shaun. I knew this would happen. The *shame* of it.' It took him a second to clock why her voice sounded so alien. She was crying.

Ratking 1

'Vinegar and salt. And a toothbrush.'

'And that'll work?'

'You're supposed to soak the metal in it, but it might.' Kelly crouched next to one of the leopard lizard sculptures, and using her sleeve, rubbed at the dust cataracting its Coke-bottle eyes. 'I can help you restore them if you want.' An anxious glance: 'I mean, only if you want me to.'

'I'd be glad of the help. Been meaning to do it for years.'

'They're so cool.' She moved along the path. 'Is this one a phoenix?'

'Yeah. My dad had a thing for mythology.' He had a thing for everything, a scattershot mind that he'd passed on to Jeanie. He'd taken his inspiration from everything: wildlife, books, his imagination, the bottom of a bottle. 'He was a mechanic, hated seeing anything going to waste. Guess you could say he was one of the early recyclers.' The largest of them, a crude rendition of a Gila monster, was partially constructed out of her old V6's inlet manifold, its back a pitted oil pan. The rest of the Chevy was in the shed, shrouded with an oil cloth.

Kelly bent to inspect a coyote – its body a cylinder head, its eyes rimmed with gasket seals.

The girl's enthusiasm was helping dispel the shadow of another of those messages about her mother. She'd gone back through the site, made a shortlist of members she'd banned or riled over the years. She even wondered if it might be Mack, then shelved that. He wasn't tech savvy, and apart from a couple of clearly booze-fuelled late-night texts, hadn't given her a hard time for ending their relationship. The fallout from the latest one had left an extra tinge of uneasiness. The message, accompanied by a link to a banned YouTube clip featuring a celebrity's autopsy, had contained a throwaway word that had brought her up short: 'Come up to the lab, & see what's on the slab . . . wouldn't it be coolio if u found her??' *Coolio*. There was only one person she knew who used that word regularly. And he knew her private Gmail account address, but then 'ChristinaGuzman123' wasn't exactly a jump, was it? Scores of people had it, and back in the day she'd used it on the site. Had to be a coincidence. Mommydearest had no reason to taunt her like this. They were friends, colleagues. Never been anything but. Only . . . People could harbour grudges; it was one of the reasons she'd started her own forum. The early websleuthing sites she'd joined had mostly dissolved due to partisanship and infighting. On Missing-Linc it was her way or the highway. Had this begun to burn him? Did he feel like she was taking him for granted?

No way. She turned her attention back to Kelly.

'What happened to your dad, Chris?' A wince. 'Sorry. I shouldn't have asked.'

'It's cool. You gotta stop apologising.'

'Sorry.'

Chris gave her a look, and Kelly smiled, shielding her mouth with a hand, mirroring her dad's habit. 'He had a bad heart.' In more ways than one. Her mother's disappearance had gnawed at him as greedily as it had her. 'Didn't look after himself. Drank, smoked. That's why so many of the sculptures are made out of Jim Beam bottles.'

'I'm sorry.'

'I'm going to let *that* apology go.'

Kelly looked at her shoes. 'Can I ask you a question?'

'You want to know how come I'm in the chair?'

'No! I'd *never* ask that.'

'Can if you want. So what do you want to know?'

'Are you my dad's girlfriend?'

'Nope. We're just friends.' True. He hadn't made another move on her, and something was holding her back from taking the jump. But there had to be a reason why she'd canned her sessions with Mack. 'He must have told you the same thing.' She was digging.

'He hasn't said anything. He likes you though. I can tell.'

'I like him too.'

'He used to get sad sometimes.'

'We all get sad.'

'I mean *sad* sad.'

'Because he split up with your mom?' She shouldn't pry; it wasn't her business. But Scott had crept up on her, and she needed to know what she was dealing with here.

'I don't think so. They were fighting a lot. But he seems better now. Only, now he's like, *obsessed* with dresses.'

'It's for the case we're working on.'

'I know. It's so cool what you do.'

'You think?'

'Totally.'

There was something endearing about the girl's odd mix of upbeat enthusiasm and low self-esteem. 'And you? You got a boyfriend?'

'No!'

'Girlfriend then?'

'No! Not that there's anything wrong with that . . . that's cool and everything. No one would want to be with me.'

'That's bullshit.'

'It's not.' Kelly made a show of picking flakes from the Gila monster's back.

'Yeah it is. One thing you should know about me is I don't bullshit people.' *Bullshit.*

A half-smile. 'Yeah. Dad told me that.'

'I bet he did. People giving you a hard time at school?' She looked the type the in-crowd would victimise.

'Not really. They think I'm weird.'

'Weird is cool.'

Kelly met Chris's eyes. 'I think so too.'

'Good. You gotta own it. Who wants to fit in? I didn't.' A beat, then she made the decision. 'Open the shed for me. There's a hook there.'

'Why?'

'Want to show you something.'

Kelly unhooked the latch, and the door swung open with a creak. Chris reached over and dragged off the cloth. There it was, the Chevy's frame, the black paintwork still pristine. And her number: 123. Back when she first started the site, that had formed part of her avatar: *Chris123*. She still used it occasionally. When had she last looked at it? Had to have been as long as a year.

'A race car?'

'A stock car.'

'Was it your dad's?'

'Nope. Mine.'

'Wow. You were a racer?'

'Low-level.' It was the truth, but she wasn't immune to Kelly's admiration – could easily do a Bobbiecowell and big herself up.

'Is that how you—'

Scott banged out of the trailer. 'Houston, we got a problem.'

PART THREE:

UNDOING

Bobbiecowell

Perched on the edge of the tub, left foot tap, tap, tapping on the tiles, he couldn't stop reading, couldn't stop scrolling; couldn't figure out how he should be feeling about this latest turn of events.

He could almost smell the panicked sweat rolling off Twitter, as celebs and their PR people backtracked and attempted to distance themselves. It had started small, little more than the seed of a rumour on an Irish blog, but overnight its roots had spread. And it wasn't just the alt-right that had whipped itself into an orgasmic frenzy; there was outrage coming from all quarters. The #JusticeForTeddyRyan Facebook groups were imploding left, right and centre. He clicked onto one of the more restrained op-eds, which was pretentiously – and stupidly – bylined with a Nietzsche quote:

When the Abyss Stares Back

"He who fights with monsters should look to it that he himself does not become a monster."

For weeks, thousands of amateur sleuths have been entranced by the tragic tale of Edward 'Teddy' Ryan, the Irish-born club kid who fled to the U.S. in the mid-nineties. After dropping out of the NYC party scene, Teddy disappeared, and no one thought to question why. It wasn't until a group of online sleuths started looking into a Minnesotan cold case, known as the 'Boy in the Dress', that Teddy's whereabouts were discovered. For over two decades, Teddy's bones languished in a Stenton County pauper's grave, his death little more than a footnote in the county's unsolved crime archives. Brutally murdered and dumped on the outskirts of a reserve in Millar Town, MN, Teddy's body was found dressed in an unusual outfit, a pink prom dress. Was Teddy the victim of a hate crime? Did he fall victim to a serial killer?

[See: MN cold case murder victim identified as missing Irish man]

After the websleuths positively identified the Boy in the Dress as the missing Irish man, the case went viral. Celebrities tweeted about it, and for many, Teddy Ryan's violent end became a symbol of a world rife with hatred and intolerance. What kind of monster was behind this horrible crime? Who could perpetrate such a horrific act? Only, what if while hunting a monster, the sleuths had uncovered one? What if Teddy Ryan was actually a monster himself?

A local Irish man, who had some startling information about why Teddy Ryan left for the States twenty-two years ago, recently approached a reporter documenting the case. According to the reporter's source, Teddy Ryan was allegedly accused of molesting a ten-year-old local boy and fled Ireland to avoid being prosecuted. Charges were never filed, but the source insists he has 'proof' of Teddy Ryan's guilt. This has sent shockwaves through—

'Pete.' Margie knocked on the door. 'Come *on.* We'll lose the slot.'

'Gimme a minute.' He couldn't stall her forever. It was gun

range night, and he was either going to have to come up with a good excuse to duck it or wait till he got home to catch up on developments. Bookmarking the latest glut of comments, he flushed, ran the tap, and joined Margie in the kitchen. She was leaning against the counter, twitching with impatience.

'Guts are playing up again. Plus, got a client wants a call. A big fish. You mind if I give tonight a miss?'

'Tell the client you'll call them tomorrow.'

'Yeah . . . kinda in the middle of it now. Like I say, it's a biggy.'

'Show me.'

'What?'

'Show me.' She held out her hand for the phone.

Keep it light. 'You don't trust me or something?'

'There's *something* you're not telling me. You've been distracted for days now. Disconnected.'

True. He'd overestimated the number of brownie points he'd earned by handing Ms Albright her ass. He could do a Gary and capitulate, or fire back. Giving in would keep the peace; she'd respect him more if he sniped back at her. 'Disconnected, huh? Does Tash think I'm disconnected? Was I disconnected when I was in that clinic, fighting my phobia and jerking off into a fucking jar?' He bit his lip – even to his ears that sounded unintentionally hilarious.

'You know what I mean. Your head's not in the game.'

'This is a *game* to you?'

She was too smart for such a lame misdirection. 'Don't be childish. You know what I mean.'

'I don't. I honestly don't. I've made an effort with Tash, I'm doing everything I can to build a life with you, and you accuse me of playing around.'

'Are you?'

'Of course I'm not. You think I got time for that? Why would I want to?' He shrugged. 'But hey, if that's what you think of me, then that's your call.'

She slung her bag over her shoulder. 'I'm going. You coming?'

He weighed it up. The new development needed to be

experienced in real-time, who knew what he'd miss out on while he was inhaling cordite in that shithole? He hadn't yet checked the group messages – that couldn't wait. 'Nope.'

'You're *actually* going to let me go by myself?'

'You want to do that, then fine.'

A moment as she looked him straight in the eye, trying to bend him to her will. He stared right back. '*Fine.*'

He waited for the SUV to start up before he returned to the bathroom. It was their first official fight. He'd patch it up later.

Missing-Linc was nothing but a slew of 'comment deleted by moderator'. He checked the time in Ireland: three a.m. – Shaun wouldn't be around for a while, but he carefully composed a message to the gang: **<Can't even imagine how you must be feeling about this news, Shaun. Just so you guys know, here for you. Day or night. And wanted to say we can't take this at face value. Where's the proof?>**

And just how was good ol' Rainbowbrite dealing with this? His canary in the mine hadn't notified him about the news – it had come up on one of his Google alerts. The Forrest debacle barb hadn't hit home, but she was a mom with two small boys, this had to be needling her. He sent her a direct message. **<Hey Ellie, have you seen the news??? Can't be true. Is Shaun okay? V worried about him. What a shock ☹>**

No response, although he could see she was online. He sent another: **<V worried about you too>**

This time he received a flaccid response: **<I can't deal>**

<Want to hash it out?>

Nada.

Next, he fired off a message to the Missing-Linc admin account: **<Hey, see that you guys are inundated. Abuse I'm guessing? Let me know if you need help modding>**

Chris sent back an uncharacteristically warm message: **<Appreciate that. Will let you know. Not sure what we're dealing with yet>**

The mods on the other sites weren't as circumspect as Ratking1 and her crew, and some of the comments were priceless:

<Maybe he was killed for revenge after he abused someones kid and you can't blame them for that becos if anyone touched my kid I would fukin kill them know what I'm saying?>

<Yeah I hear you! Someone comes near my kids they'd get their ass handed to them. Also check your spelling>

<Fuk spelling they send there perverts over here like the priests that they moved all over the place & this guy was just like that he was a monster>

Could it be true? It had been a while since he dared examine the Teddy Ryan showreel in any detail. Like the snapshot he'd used in the fertility clinic, it was dangerous territory. He'd learned over the years that it was safer to disassociate himself from it.

But Margie wouldn't be back for a while. Why *not* check it out?

He made himself comfortable, dug it out of its vault, dusted it off, and then, before he could reconsider, let it run:

There's Past Pete at the bar, that goddamned bar where Carl, his stepfather, used to take him during his 'make Pete a man' campaign. That dump, a haven for the alcoholic and the aimless.

The memory was so imprinted he could almost smell the beer and sweat-stained wood. What made him go there that night? He hadn't needed space; he had the house to himself. His mother and Carl were away in Eau Claire for a funeral. Or was it a wedding?

No matter. Onwards:

There's Past Pete, on his second beer of the night, trying to ignore the asshole next to him. Then, the door bangs open, letting in a guff of freezing air like a clumsy director's attempt at foreshadowing, and in he comes, the Boy in the Dress.

The boy's trembling from the cold, makes straight for the bar, shakes back his head and runs his fingers through his hair, smoothing damp, dirty blond strands. The boy looks around, grabs the bartender's attention. As he leans across the bar, jacket riding up, something inside Pete sparks to life, a flicker of excitement deep in his belly. Pete's neighbour starts droning on about the Million Man March, and he's forced to give the asshole some attention. He can't take his eyes from the boy, tries to be surreptitious about it, but it's a losing battle.

Had he known then what he was going to do? Yes. No. Maybe: *If he doesn't approach me, I'll leave him alone.*

Fastforward: *The bartender calls time, starts upending stools, mouthing along to 'Just Dropped In.' Pete's neighbour staggers to his feet, lurches out, and now Pete is directly in the boy's sightline. The boy looks over, catches Pete's eye, smirks at him. Makes as if to approach. Pete turns away, hangs back for a minute then heads out, keeping his eyes fixed to the door, ignoring the boy's gravitational pull.*

Out into the night, the wind sending snowflakes spiralling, pushing drifts against hubcaps and doorways. He pauses to zip up his jacket, pull on his gloves. Waits.

A tap on his shoulder, and he turns to see Teddy, one hand tucked under an armpit, the other holding a cigarette, leaving black spots in the slush wherever he tamps his ash. 'I saw you watching me.'

'I wasn't watching you.'

'Ah, I'm just messing.' The boy is shivering now. 'I'm looking for someone who lives around here.' He hands Pete a photograph: Teddy mugging into the camera, his arm around a good-looking black guy, their eyes red from over-exposure, a neon backdrop: 'John Tremain? JT?' He's upping the Irish lilt, talks very fast.

'Nope. Haven't seen him around. You don't got an address or number for him?'

'Did have, lost it, but. He said I should look him up if I was in the area. And I'm in the area. Said he'd have work for me.' The wind whips the snow into a mini twister, icing the tips of the boy's hair. 'He didn't mention it was right next to a fucking big lake, but. There a cheap place to stay around here?'

'How cheap?'

'Ten, twenty dollars?'

'Not that I know of. Might find somewhere in Duluth.'

'Where's that when it's at home?'

'Couple of miles across the bridge.'

The boy shivers again. 'Any chance of a lift? I'll freeze out here. Lost my bag. Left it on the bus.'

How could he say no? Into his mother's old Honda with its smell of damp and gas fumes, Teddy fiddling with the radio like it's his car. Pete saying: 'I've got a couch you can use.'

'Ah that's good of you.' No surprise. A sly grin. He knew the offer was coming.

The rush and hump of tyres over snow.

Pete surfaced. He'd gone so deep he was momentarily disorientated. What did they talk about on the drive? That was a blank, all he can remember is the air humming between them, knowing, sensing that something was going to happen. Then . . .

. . . Leading the boy into the basement. It's midway through its transformation into Carl's workshop, but the old PVC couch is still here, as is his coffee table, gaming console and CD rack. A poster of Pam Anderson on the wall – window dressing – the comforting grumble of the furnace in the background. Teddy flumping onto the couch, instantly at home – a talent Pete envies.

'Got something to drink?'

'Sure.' Eager – too eager – Pete runs up to the kitchen, digs through the cupboards, unearths half a bottle of Jim Beam and a bottle of the sweet wine that got his mom through his dad's abandonment.

He's never been with a man. Isn't sure if he wants that, even if it is on offer. The wine mixes with the beer, he hasn't eaten, and he's giddy with false bravado and confidence. On to the bourbon, Teddy dominating the conversation, witty, loud, sharp-tongued, full of himself, full of tales about the 'fuckwits' he met on the bus ride from New York, fights in Brooklyn streets, running from the cops. Past Pete matches him drink for drink; doesn't even try to match the stories.

There's only one thing he's ever done that comes close. And if I tell you that I'll have to kill you.

'Why did you leave Ireland?' Did he ask that? He must have asked that.

'Family troubles.' Pete's memory is paraphrasing now, but there wasn't a hint of anything to do with child abuse allegations. But then, Teddy would hardly reveal that to a stranger. *'But I've got to go back. For my sister. She's knocked up. I need money.'* Then, something like: *'You wouldn't believe the stuff I've done for cash.'*

'I can give you some money.' What made him say it? No matter.

'What for?' Shrewd, streetwise.

Smart self yelling stop it, stop it, stop it, Pete glides to the trunk he'd inherited from his grandparents, unlocks it, and removes the dress. He washed it after he'd dumped the rest of her things; he was lucky it hadn't shrunk.

'What the fuck's this?'

Numb now, can't stop. 'Can you put it on?'

Cold, calculating: 'How much will you give me?'

'Fifty.'

'Fuck off.'

'Hundred.'

'Two hundred.'

He doesn't have two hundred dollars. 'Okay.'

'But that's it, yeah? I'll put the dress on but that's all I'm fucking doing.'

He strips off his jacket, then his tee. Skin so white it's almost blue, says: 'This your sister's?'

'No.'

'Girlfriend's? That what you always wanted? Your girlfriend to be your boyfriend?'

'No.'

'Your mam's then.'

'No.'

Off with the jeans, taking his time, shedding them like a skin. Taunting him. Then on with the dress. The boy's smaller than she was, and it bags around him, the top part gaping like a mouth. 'How do I look?' Cocks a hip and goes to the bourbon without waiting for an answer.

Pete glides up to him, reaches out, strokes a hand down his back. The boy rounds on him, face a snarl, out of reach: 'I'm not going to fuck you. Told you. Look at yous.'

Pete paused the action: was there rage at the rejection? No. But there was something.

More. He wants more.

Pete floating to the ceiling, looking down at his other self who's casually grasping the wine bottle. A graceful half-turn, then he smashes it against the boy's head. Thonk. It doesn't break. Teddy staggers, loses his balance. It wasn't like it was with her. No fear in the eyes this time, just a blink of shock, then rage, a roar, and then the boy's running for him. Pete-on-the-ceiling watches dispassionately as his body acts on instinct, swipes blindly, whacks the boy's throat, a lucky shot. A 'gah', then Teddy falls over the coffee table, disoriented, eyes clouding, cocks his head, vomits. Now whole again, Pete gags – almost absent-mindedly, as if he's playing a part, reacting as he thinks he should.

The boy on the floor is twitching, hacking, air and sputum hissing in his gullet. Lets out small shallow breaths, like a glazed-eyed rabbit that needs dispatching. Numb, dream-like, Pete goes to the box of tools, takes out the wrench.

How many times? He couldn't recall.

A lot.

A pearl of blood spatter hits his mouth, and it's the sweet, iron tang that makes him heave, makes him stop. Lunges for the trash can, makes it in time. Then, up to the bathroom, the sink coming up to meet him, catches his weight at the last second. Dry swallowing aspirin, gagging on the chalky bitterness. Gargles with mouthwash, then dares to look at his reflection. Bares his teeth. The panic is a distant hum, like the onset of a migraine. Into the kitchen, knocking back cold coffee. Cup after cup of it.

Back into the basement, entering slowly, carefully, like a debutante in a horror flick, half-expecting Teddy to be gone, a figment of his imagination, or up and on his feet, waiting to pounce. Muddy-brained with the alcohol, thinking: hide the evidence, conceal the crime. Fingerprints ID victims. Back to Carl's tool box, out with the wire cutters. Hands slippery with blood. Clumsy. Snick. Snock. Like cutting chicken necks with scissors. Dragging the body, pure, dead weight into the garage, a plastic bag over the head to contain blood spillage. Knowing he should remove the dress and burn it, knowing he should throw the passport, wallet and the photograph in the furnace, not sure why he doesn't.

It hadn't occurred to him to dump Teddy elsewhere. Drove

all that way, despite the weather, despite the danger. Jennifer hadn't been found, he'd waited years for *that* knock on the door, expected her remains to be finally discovered when the snow melted around Teddy and the cops swept the scene. The dress. Leaving the dress on the body. Why? Did he *want* Teddy to be found? He couldn't take him all the way into the safer areas of the reserve, not then, not in '95, did he use that as an excuse to leave him in plain sight?

Enough.

He rolled his shoulders, yawned, as spent and oddly fulfilled as if he'd just finished working out.

Back to real life, back to the online world. On one of the Reddit threads, the highest-rated comment was short and to the point: **<whoever killed this guy should get a fucking medal>**

Wicklowboy22

'She doesn't want to see you, Shaun.'

Even for someone of Shaun's diminutive stature Keith was a hopeless barrier. Shaun ducked under his uncle's arm and ran to the kitchen. His aunt wasn't at her usual place next to the stove or the sink. A howl floated from the yard outside, followed by the scrabble of claws on the back door. He'd dumped Daphne unceremoniously behind the gate before he pushed his way in here, but he couldn't let her distress sidetrack him. Keith was now begging him, 'Leave it alone, Shaun, leave it,' but he ignored him and retraced his steps, the phrase *can't be true, can't, can't be true, can't* a constant, timpani beat in his head. He found Janice in the lounge, staring at the TV, clutching the remote like a weapon. She didn't look up when he entered, motionless for once – a grounded shark.

'Did Mam know?' he asked.

She flicked to another channel.

'Auntie Janice. Did Mam know?'

Keith hovered at the door, knotting his fingers together like an old woman in a fable. 'If you don't get out of here, Shaun, I'll call the boys to come over.'

Janice finally looked up, distress emphasising the marionette lines bracketing her mouth. 'Don't you bloody dare. I don't want them involved.' She threw the remote onto the sofa, stood, and with a sideswipe glance at Shaun said: 'Come on.' He followed her into the bedroom at the end of the hall. 'Shut the door.'

It was the last place he would have chosen for this conversation.

Janice had taken over his grandparents' house when they died, and she'd kept it much as it was back then, its Fleur de Lys wallpaper and blue carpet a shrine to outdated decor. It smelled of talcum powder and Keith. There was a pile of clean laundry on the bed, and she began to fold it automatically, leached of her usual energy.

'Why didn't you tell me?'

'Why do you think? Swore to Eileen I wouldn't.'

'So she *did* know about it.'

'Your grandparents told her everything when they found out she was planning on going to Galway. She didn't believe them at first. Well, who can blame her? She loved him. He was always her favourite. She made me and Donny promise that we'd never tell you. She knew you were sensitive and you looked so much like him.'

'Who was the boy? The one who accused him?'

'What does it matter now?'

'Who *was* it?'

She jumped as if he'd slapped her. 'Dylan Carey.'

'Pat Carey's cousin?'

'That's right.'

He couldn't bring Dylan Carey's face up with any clarity. All he remembered was a weedy fellow with jaundiced skin who used to hang out on the outskirts of Aidan Sullivan's gang. Dylan didn't join in with the taunts they threw at him, and he seemed to recall that Dylan was held back in school, which made him a couple of years older than Aidan and the other thugs. *Process, process*. 'And you just believed it? I ran into Pat, he had something against Teddy, he—'

'Of course we didn't just believe it.' A glare – a spectre of old Janice's bite. 'They had proof.'

'What proof?'

'Sit down. I can't talk to you while you're pacing like that.'

He didn't want to sit; a ball of nervous energy was building inside him. But he did as he was told, dug his fingers into the duvet's polyester skin.

'A week or so after your mam was sent off to Dublin, Teddy arrived home from London.'

'I know this—'

'Let me tell it in my own way.'

'Sorry.'

'Teddy was raging about Eileen, wanted to know where she was. Da wouldn't tell him, and that's when Teddy lost it, screamed at them, told them he was gay and that he was going to track your mam down and take her over to London. You've never heard so much fighting in your life. Da threw him out, and Teddy went round the town for the next couple of days asking after Eileen. We found out he was staying at the Careys. Him and Pat had a falling out before Teddy went to London, but Teddy had blagged his way into their house. Next thing we know, Teddy's hammering on the door. Late at night, this was, his face covered in blood, wouldn't say what had happened to him. Not long after that Iain, that's Pat Carey's da, came over. I've never seen a man so angry. That's when it all came out. Iain said that Teddy had been messing with Dylan, and the boy had told a priest about it. Iain was close with Da, they drank together on occasion, and Iain said Da deserved to know what had been going on before he went to the guards. Teddy was yelling and shouting, saying it was all lies, and that he'd never touched the boy. Iain said he had the proof. He said Dylan knew things about Teddy's . . . he knew he had a scar just . . .' she touched the top of her groin. 'How would he know that? He knew things about him. Personal things. Iain said he'd also found a photograph of the boy in Teddy's things. Filthy, it was. Perverted.'

Shaun couldn't speak.

'My mam didn't want to believe it. Her youngest daughter pregnant from that layabout, and her son caught fiddling with children. That's what made her sick, gave her cancer. Killed Da too. Iain and Da locked themselves away, and they came to an arrangement. They wouldn't go to the guards, and it would be buried as long as Teddy went away and never came back. London was too close to home – Iain had family there. Ted agreed to it, of course he did. Better than gaol, and he was always saying he wanted to go to New York. Da took a loan for the cash and he was gone the next day. Your ma would have gone after him, they were that close.'

Now he was grateful he was sitting down. 'It must have killed her when she found out.'

'It did. Refused to believe it, couldn't. She went over to talk to the Careys, and they confirmed it. She looked for Teddy of course. Harder back then without the internet, before everyone flashed their knickers all over twit-snap. She never forgave us for not telling her the truth. Most of all because she'd made Teddy out to be a hero to you. And him leaving like that? She saw that as an admission of guilt more than anything.'

'And you've all been hiding this for years.'

'We have. Can you imagine what I was thinking when you came over that day saying you were searching for him? And it's all out now. I won't be able to hold my head up. The boys know, and Cal with the new baby on the way. And now Donny says Carmel's gone to her mam's and she's taken the kids.'

'Why would she do that?'

'Donny didn't tell her about Teddy being . . . you know. She thought he was sent away because of your mam.'

There was relief that Carmel wasn't in on all the lies – ever since she gave him the photograph he'd thought of her as a co-conspirator – and it was somehow less lonely knowing that he wasn't the only one left out of the family's circle of trust. 'I was going to go out to America and see him. See where he was buried. How can I go now?' He'd been half-dreading the trip, but now that it was ripped away from him, the loss of it ached. 'I'm sorry. I should have come to you before I went to the guards.'

'You should, Shaun.' Fatigue weighted every word. 'I handled it badly. She made us swear we'd never tell you. You weren't to know. Your heart was in the right place. Makes me shiver thinking that he ended up that way. Whatever he did he was still my brother.' A sob as abrupt as a hiccup, and then the tears came.

Shaun went to touch her, but she shook her head. Keith, who

must have been listening at the door, came in, gestured for Shaun to leave and then took her in his arms.

'Bollocks he did that. Pat Carey got the boy to say it.' Johnny roamed the kitchen, smoking furiously.

'Why would he do that?'

'Cos he's a cunt. I'm going to fucking kill him.'

'They've got proof.'

'What fucking proof?'

'Dylan described things about Teddy he wouldn't know unless he was . . . you know, involved with him.'

'It's bollocks.' Johnny dumped the butt into the sink and screwed a fresh rollie into his mouth. The man was red in the face, and after witnessing first-hand how unpredictable he could be, Shaun instinctively kept close to the door.

'Janice says there was also a photograph in Teddy's things. A photo of Dylan. A bad one. Compromising.'

That brought him up short. 'Anyone could have taken it. Do you believe it?'

'I don't know.' It explained why Donny wanted to keep it under wraps. Explained why his mother stopped talking about Teddy so abruptly. Explained why Teddy agreed to leave for New York. Then again . . . 'In the letter he told Eileen not to believe what they're saying about him.'

'There you go then. It's bollocks.'

'But he would say that, wouldn't he?'

'I don't need to hear this. You're his fucking family, Shaun. You can't turn on him too.'

'He's *dead*. He's long past that.'

'So you're giving up, are you?'

'What else is there to do?'

Johnny's face shut down. 'Get out.'

'What?'

'You heard me. Get out.' There was no implied threat to this; his voice was thick with defeat and disappointment, which was somehow worse. Johnny turned to the sink. Shaun considered reasoning with him, then decided it was safer to leave. In any case, after his dealings with Janice he was emotionally exhausted, doubted he had the energy to walk home. He collected the dog from Bridie's lap and hurried out into the street.

His phone trembled. A message from Bobbiecowell. Chris and Rainbowbrite hadn't posted anything for hours: **<just to let you know I'm here for you Shaun if you want to talk. This changes nothing for me>**

This unexpected kindness almost brought him to tears, pushed him over the edge. It might not change things for Bobbie, but it changed things for him. He couldn't shake the sense that he'd been betrayed. Not by Janice, his mother or even Donny, but by Teddy. As if all this time his uncle had been waiting in the wings, watching Shaun going into bat for him, fighting for him, only to have a good laugh at his expense.

Rainbowbrite

For the last three days she'd been hiding out in the bedroom, watching trash TV, pretending to Noah that she'd come down with something. The bruise wasn't fading and she couldn't stop prodding at it. It was the unfairness of it more than anything, the *waste*. She'd neglected the boys and put her marriage in jeopardy for nothing. Worse than nothing: the Boy in the Dress wasn't some innocent victim who the world had forgotten; he was a goddamned monster.

It was poisoning everything. She didn't want to let the boys out of her sight, as if one of those perverts they were warned about in school was hiding around every corner. Nor could she bear to go on the site or check the WhatsApp group. She'd changed her privacy settings so that no one could tell when she was online – something she'd never done before. Her inbox was full of messages from Bobbie that she'd been ignoring, as well as missives from Chris asking her what they should do about the GoFundMe, seeing as people were howling for refunds or for the money to be donated to a child protection charity.

Then there was Shaun, who she'd invited into her home. At least now she wouldn't have to broach that subject with Noah. Remembered gossiping with Chris about Shaun's family, thinking how cruel they were to have disowned Teddy. Now she didn't blame them at all.

She clicked onto *Pretty Little Liars*, made a nest with the duvet, and let it run without following any of it. *Forensic Files*, her usual Netflix fix, was too close to home. There was something she was supposed to do today, but she couldn't put her finger on what.

Noah poked his head around the door. 'Gotta go in to work.'

'It's Saturday.'

'Couple of guys have called in sick.'

'Okay.'

'The boys are in the den.'

'Okay.'

'How long is this going to go on for? This moping around, feeling sorry for yourself?'

'I'm not moping. I'm sick.'

'You're not sick.'

'I *am*.'

He shut the door. 'You fallen out with Chris again?'

'No.'

'Then tell me what's up.'

'You don't know? Eric hasn't told you? You haven't been spying on me again?' What was she doing? Did she *want* to pick another fight?

'Might've escaped your notice but I've been pulling doubles.'

She turned up the TV's volume, goading him. He didn't rise to it.

'Tell me.'

'You were right, okay? You were right. I shouldn't have got involved with this stuff again. Happy now?'

Again, he waited. It was infuriating. She knew that diffusing confrontation was a big part of his work, but Lord alive for once she wished he'd just blow up. But she may as well come clean now that it was all over. She rattled it all out: being late for the boys, seeing Mrs Jensen, buying the dress from eBay, the interviews, the GoFundMe, inviting Shaun to stay without running it past him first.

'How do you know I wouldn't have let him stay? We got the pull-out, don't we?'

Shame came then – and guilt. She could have told him everything. Could have asked him. But maybe, just maybe, she'd enjoyed the sneaking around. Doing more than she'd let on. Being the centre of it. Playing a game, seeing how far she could push it. Like those people who had affairs.

'Go on. That's not all of it, is it?'

'No.'

Noah let her tell it in her own way, then said: 'They got proof about these allegations?'

'Someone came forward.'

'Yeah? Easy to sling things like that around. The CCTV we got up at work isn't just to protect the inmates. Accusations like that will ruin someone's life.'

'If they're guilty then they deserve to have their life ruined.' She sounded peevish, childish, bitter. She *was* bitter.

'So let me get this straight. You put in all this work, found a way to do that and take care of the house and the boys, and now you're just going to dump it? I mean I knew you were doing more than you said you were, but you seemed happier than you've been for a long time.' He was right. She had been happier. 'Doesn't seem right to just quit like that.'

'What else can I do? I have to quit.'

'Then you're not the Ellie I know.' And with that patronising grenade, he left, closing the door softly behind him. She wanted to throw the water glass at the door, went so far as to reach for it, screamed into the pillow instead. It wasn't fair of him to hit her with that.

She considered having a bath, catching up on all the body maintenance stuff she'd been neglecting for weeks, but instead flipped back to Netflix.

She was dozing when the boys hurricaned into the room. 'Mom. The party.'

'Huh?'

'Danny's party. We're going to be *late*.'

Despite a panicked dart into Walmart for a gift, followed by frenziedly wrapping the present in the car, they were still thirty minutes late. And when Sherry opened up, her body language was enough to send blood whooshing to Ellie's cheeks, already burning from panic and exertion.

'Go on in, boys,' Sherry said, 'we've got a clown coming.' The boys whipped inside. Sherry looked down at Ellie's feet and frowned.

'What?' Ellie followed her gaze, stomach plummeting as she realised that she was wearing mismatching Sorel boots – one new, one old. 'Oh.' And there was a coffee stain on her jeans, along with a shameful crust of what she suspected was a glob of salted caramel ice cream. A sob parped out, taking them both off guard.

'Come inside, Ellie.'

'I . . .' And then came another, followed by what could only be described as blubbering.

'Come on in. You can't stand out here in this state.'

Wiping a sleeve over her face, which did little more than slime the mess from one place to another, Ellie followed Sherry through a blur of children, laughter and the *rat-a-tat* of video game gunfire, and into the kitchen. There was a fresh wave of mortification at the sight of Lisa, a core member of the Mom Brigade, perched on a stool and looking, as usual, like she'd fallen out of *The Real Housewives*.

Ellie automatically went to smooth her hair, then gave up.

'Get the wine,' Sherry said to Lisa, who immediately collected a bottle of rosé from the fridge as if she was following military orders. With only silent communication, Sherry took a trio of glasses from the cabinet, and Lisa filled them halfway. So this was what they got up to while Ellie was digging into coroners' reports and going through prom dress photographs.

The tears dried up, leaving her hollow and embarrassed. Sherry handed her a glass, its bulb the size of a newborn's head. 'I don't drink.' She took a sip anyway.

'There's no shame in admitting you need help,' Sherry said. 'You don't have to deal with this alone.'

Lisa stroked her arm. 'Is he violent? There are things you can do.'

'Huh?' Then it dawned on her. 'Oh. It's not . . . it's not . . . me and Noah you mean?'

'Danny said you were sleeping on the couch when you had him over for the sleepover. And you've been sketchy lately. I just put two and two together.'

She was working late on the case that night, the night of Danny's busted finger, but Sherry – thank God – didn't bring that up. She hadn't wanted to disturb Noah or the kids. 'Oh it's not that. We're fine. Better than fine.' They weren't fine, not even close. Could she patch it up? Maybe. She *had* enjoyed sneaking around, but at the same time, now it was all out in the open she felt lighter deep inside.

'What is it then?'

'The Boy in the Dress.'

'Oh yeah,' Lisa said. 'You're always putting that up on Facebook.' It struck her then that Lisa had been the one who'd told her about the Boy in the first place. It had come full circle. 'I shared it around. All of us did.'

'You did?'

'You didn't notice?'

She hadn't. She should have thanked them, only she'd been too stuck in her own bubble to notice. 'I'm sorry.'

'I donated to that fund you had going,' Sherry said. 'To support the dead boy's family?'

'They're thinking about refunding that now. On account of the dead boy being one of those perverts.'

'I heard about that.'

'And I keep . . . I can't keep investigating the case if the victim deserved it, can I? And I feel so bad because I've been neglecting the boys, you know that, Sherry, you've been picking up the slack.'

'I'd be doing that anyway.'

'It was all for nothing.' The wine was going to her head.

'I get why you stopped,' Lisa said. 'I'd kill anyone who came near my boy.'

Sherry scrunched her nose. 'I kinda agree with you that someone who does that to kids should be locked away for life, but it doesn't change the fact that whoever killed this guy is out there. And he put the body so close to where we live. In our town.'

'You think I should carry on?' She allowed Lisa to top up her glass. At this rate she wouldn't be able to drive.

'Up to you. Way I see it, if the murderer didn't know this dead boy was a paedophile, he could be out there somewhere thinking he got away with it. He could be killing more boys for all we know.'

Sense from the last place she expected.

'You know, I kind of admire you for doing all that websleuthing stuff,' Lisa said.

'Really?'

'Sure. It's cool. Like you're a PI or something. We were saying that just the other day, weren't we, Sherry?'

The doorbell buzzed. 'That'll be the clown,' Sherry said, downing her wine. 'Left it too late to get the guy with the pony. I *hate* goddamned clowns.'

Malcolmucka: HOWS IT FEEL HAVING A KIDDIEFIDDLER FOR A MASCOT????

OGKaplan: This place is like a damn shrine to the scum of the earth. You should be ashamed of yourselves.

Hiroko2: Let's all give a round of applause to the guy who killed this mofo.

Satana69: And this is why gay lives DON'T matter.

NerfJunkratpls: Hear that? Me neither. Where the fuck did all the social justice warriors who LOVED this sicko disappear to?

Jaywalker: [comment deleted by moderator]

Clownface7: [comment deleted by moderator]

Pedohunter88: [comment deleted by moderator]

MyWifeNow: [comment deleted by moderator]

PegLegged: [comment deleted by moderator]

RedRum76: [comment deleted by moderator]

SharkCHairawr: [comment deleted by moderator]

BonnieBlack: [comment deleted by moderator]

Mommydearest: Still can't track down that pic of Teddy

Ratking1: Losing your touch?

Mommydearest: Whoever did it must have deleted the account. Can't get access to that without Twitter's authorisation

Ratking1: That's not going to happen

Mommydearest: Think we should close comments for a while

Ratking1: And let the abusers win?

Mommydearest: Can't keep up with them there are too many

Ratking1: It's my site, my call

Mommydearest: I know

Ratking1: You resent the way I'm running things?

Mommydearest: No. Why would you ask that?

Ratking1: Maybe you should take a break

Mommydearest: Don't need to

Mommydearest: Are you pissed at me Chris?

Ratking1: Should I be?

Mommydearest: I don't know what you're trying to say

Ratking1: Not accusing you of anything, but have you been sending messages to me regarding my mom?

Mommydearest: No what kind of messages?

Ratking1: They're sick. Troll-style

Mommydearest: Why would you think I would do that? I would never do that

Ratking1: Had to ask

Mommydearest: You didn't. I WOULD NEVER DO THAT

Ratking1: Like I said, had to ask

Message not delivered

Ratking1: You blocked me?

Message not delivered

Ratking1

One by one, the rats were deserting the sinking ship, but she'd chucked Mommydearest overboard. *Coolio.* That word had nibbled at her, fed the paranoia and distrust. Didn't help that she was muddy-brained from lack of sleep, but she couldn't blame exhaustion for that appalling lack of judgement. Thinking about it, whoever sent those emails had bunged the word into the message randomly, where it made no sense. Mommydearest wasn't one to show his emotions, but she knew she'd hurt him. It didn't help knowing that he'd move to a site that wasn't run by a control freak. Somewhere where he'd be appreciated.

Bobbiecowell and a few hangers-on were the only ones left. Shaun had been reading her messages, but hadn't responded to any of them. He must be broken, and she didn't have a clue what to say to crowbar him out of his funk. What *could* she say? It was all going to shit. The site was a seething mass of abuse, and adding to the general misery there was something up with Scott. He'd run through his usual ritual – glasses on, laptop at the ready – but he was unusually subdued, hadn't met her eyes as he handed over tonight's sandwich. It could be the abuse accusation. It had to burn more if you were a parent. It was certainly burning Ellie. She'd left the WhatsApp group, and was blanking Chris's messages.

'You heard from Rainbowbrite?' she asked Scott, who was hunched over the MacBook, picking at his chicken and mayo sub.

'Nothing for a week.'

'Thinking about closing comments for a while. We're getting too much abuse.'

'Thought you'd done that already?'

'Just on the Boy on the Dress page. I'm talking about the whole site. The haters are posting all over.' GI Doe had never had so much attention.

'How's Shaun doing?'

'He must be feeling the strain.'

'You know any more?'

'Nope. It's not as if there's a Hallmark card for "sorry to hear you're related to a dead sex offender".' He didn't react to this. 'Been trying to pep him up, but that's not really my forte.'

'Yeah.'

'Thanks.'

'So what now?'

'Nothing's changed as far as I'm concerned. Someone out there killed him.'

'Yeah.'

'We've done all this work.'

'Yeah.'

'You're talkative. Kelly okay?'

'Yeah. She's good.'

'Okay. What's up with you? Is it the Teddy Ryan paedo thing?'

'No.'

'What then?'

'Have you taken a look at yourself lately, Chris?'

'Scuse me?'

'You could do with taking a break. When did you last eat properly?'

She held up the sandwich. 'I'm eating now.'

'Or shower?'

'You saying I stink?' She should stink. She'd been wearing the same sweatpants for three days now. Hadn't found the time to go up to the house and do the laundry.

'No. Just that you're not looking after yourself.'

'I'm doing fine.'

'Jeanie's worried.'

'Whatever.'

He removed his glasses, sat back in his chair. 'Why didn't you tell me about your mom?'

'Where the hell is this coming from?' Had he been reading her mind? Ellie must have told him. Goddamned Ellie. 'So you and Rainbowbrite *have* been gossiping about me.'

'Nope. Jeanie told me.' *Goddamned Jeanie.* 'Like I say, she's worried about you. Asked if the way you are . . . asked if the stress was to do with that. She said your mom's up on the site.'

'She is.'

'Why didn't you tell me?'

'Haven't told hardly anyone.'

'Why not?'

Good question. 'Lots of reasons.'

'Go on.'

How could she tell him the truth without sounding like an asshole? That when she first started sleuthing – back when it was still a niche activity – a connection to a real-life misper was seen as a badge of honour, and she'd come too close to exploiting her mom's disappearance. And then there were the emails, and how vulnerable receiving them made her feel. It was too much. 'I don't need to explain myself to you.' *Not fair.*

'You're right. You don't. I get that. But we're friends, Chris. Wish you'd said something. You have any leads on her?'

'Nope.' Not lately. Not for years. She still checked NamUs every morning, part of the ritual.

'Jeanie said she probably ran off with some guy.'

'I know what Jeanie says.'

'You don't think she did?'

'Nope.'

'Jeanie says that she had a history of—'

'I know what Jeanie says. It's not your business, Scott.'

'Right. We going to do this again?'

'Do what?'

'We touch on anything personal and you lay into me. I can help you with this.'

'I don't need your help.'

'Okay. That's it.' He snapped the laptop shut, gathered his car keys, kicked back the chair.

'Where are you going?'

'It's the second time you've taken your shit out on me, Chris.'

'I'm not taking my shit out on you.' But she was – knew she was.

'Yeah, you are. You think you can talk to me like that and I'm just going to take it? I'm not your whipping boy.'

'You had no right to talk about me behind my back.'

'You see, that's unfair. I wasn't talking about you. Jeanie told me. I wasn't prying. You need to get over yourself, lady.'

'I'm not the only one.'

'Nice. I'm out of here.'

Sick inside: *Apologise.* 'Knew you'd leave eventually. Knew this whole deal would be too much for you.'

He stopped at the door but didn't turn to look at her. 'It's not all about you, Chris.'

MissingLinc#TeddyRyan

BobbieC, Wicklowboy, You

FYI decided to refund the GoFundMe 11.38AM

BobbieC
Got to be an admin nightmare. Can I help? 11.38AM

I'm on it. Got time now that the comments are disabled BTW you heard from Rainbowbrite?
11.38AM

BobbieC
Nope. She okay? 11.39AM

Wicklowboy
@BobbieC @Ratking Sorry 11.39AM

You got nothing to be sorry about Shaun. Relieved to hear from you. Saw you were reading the msgs but been worried. You holding up? 11.40AM

BobbieC
@Wicklowboy sorry it's come to this
11.40AM

Wicklowboy
Kept quiet because I didn't know what to say. It's the shame of it. If I hadn't looked into Teddy's past this would never have come out
11.41AM

You don't mean that
11.41AM

Wicklowboy
I do. Feel bad for you too. You did all this work and now all you're getting is abuse
11.42AM

It will die down. Haters will move on to another target
11.42AM

BobbieC
You getting flack personally, Shaun? Not just online I mean
11.42AM

Wicklowboy
A note under the shop's door saying Teddy deserved to be in hell. Bad looks from people. I've had worse
11.43AM

BobbieC
You got support there? 11.43AM

Wicklowboy
I've got the dog. Thanks for your msgs BTW 11.43AM

BobbieC
Welcome. Don't beat yourself up.Double checking, no charges were brought, right? 11.44AM

Wicklowboy
No charges. Enough proof to convince the family though 11.44AM

BobbieC
Do you believe it? 11.44AM

Wicklowboy
They say they have proof 11.45AM

BobbieC
You know who made the accusation?
11.45AM

@BobbieC Dodgy ground here
11.45AM

BobbieC
Not saying you should confront them. Saying it won't hurt to dig a little deeper
11.46AM

Wicklowboy
Maybe
11.46AM

Bobbiecowell

Heading down Aurora Avenue was the obvious choice, but the motel in Belltown was the smarter option. A room paid for in cash, a clerk who'd seen it all, a number harvested from an ad on Backpage. He'd parked the truck in an area less likely to be blanketed with CCTV, and smeared mud on the licence plates just in case. It was still a risk, but hey. Risk seemed to be how he rolled these days.

And he had to do *something* to release the steam. 'Supporting' Shaun online and acting the puppeteer by pressing him to dig into Teddy's possible perversions weren't enough to curb Past Pete's growing greed for involvement. There had been a moment – well, more than a moment – when he'd almost bought into the Bobbiecowell persona he was playing: Ratking's right-hand man; Shaun's cheer-leader; Teddy's champion, one of the few who wasn't getting off on thinking the worst about the man. A moment when he'd seen himself as an integral part of the team, a warrior for justice, before he'd come to his senses. Mommydearest hadn't been on Missing-Linc for a couple of days, so that long shot seemed to have paid off, but again, this wasn't enough to sate him. The site was on lockdown, Rainbowbrite was absent from life and social media, and the GoFundMe cash was up in smoke. He almost laughed: *Looks like the Websleuth Massacre is on hold.* It was only ever the seed of a fantasy. Never would have happened. Simply a manifestation of Past Pete, who longed to become the fantasy Bobbiecowell was spewing online: a ruthless killer who trawled the highways picking off victims like a mobile Jeffrey Dahmer. *You're not a serial killer if you've only killed two people.*

The bag containing the dress he'd bought from the hipster store placed next to his thigh, he sat on the bed and waited for the knock on the door. Judging by its lumpen feel, the mattress, like the clerk, had seen it all. There was a stain on the carpet – could be blood, could be wine – a print from the eighties on the wall that reminded him of the paint-by-numbers stag at the infertility office, a bathroom that was an ode to linoleum and Clorox.

The tap of nails on wood: she was on time. He opened up, and she smiled in at him. 'Hey there, honey. I'm Komi.' She was slender, several inches taller than his five-eight, a shaggy blond wig. And Asian: not what he was expecting. Not what he'd ordered. High black boots, a belted red wool coat that looked expensive.

'Ad said you were blond.'

Komi shook out the wig. 'I *am* blond, honey.' She slid her eyes up and down his body. 'You a cop?'

'I look like a cop?'

'Kinda.'

'I'm not a cop.'

'Okay then, what shall I call you?'

'Bobbie.'

'Well now, Bobbie, you got something to drink?'

'Nope. Place doesn't have a mini-bar.'

'Hmmm.' She walked around, inspecting the room. 'You an outta-towner, Bobbie?'

'Yeah.'

'Business or pleasure?'

'Both.' She came closer, narrow-hipped, silicon-lipped. He took in the make-up pooled in her pores, the spidery eyelashes, looked down at her hands – now he wasn't certain Komi was strictly female. Would that matter? He didn't think so. She – or he – or they, he couldn't keep up with the terminology, Tasha would know – patted the bed. 'Shall we get to know one another?'

'Where are you from, Komi?'

'Where do you want me to be from?'

Pete thought about it. *Where indeed.* 'Wisconsin.'

'How do they talk in Wisconsin, honey?' Komi didn't have the feral look of someone who did this work to feed a habit. He couldn't decide if that was a plus or a minus. His heart rate was picking up; he was beginning to sweat.

'Forget it.'

'Okay. You're the boss. So. Clock is ticking. What can I do for you today?'

He removed the dress from its bag, passed it to her and she shook it out. The threads would get everywhere, scatter the carpet like veins. It stank of must and dead people's sweat. *Should've washed it.*

'You want me to wear this?' No surprise, no shock. All in a day's work for Komi.

'Yes.'

'Four hundred.'

He handed over the cash. 'You can get changed in the bathroom.'

'You don't want to watch?'

'Nope.'

'Back in a minute.'

He could, at any time, cancel the transaction. His pulse was throbbing, but that was the only part of him that was. There was little sense of arousal, more a distancing, as if he was just going through the motions.

She returned, holding the straps to keep the dress in place over her breasts. It hung off her. It was nothing like the original, after all. 'How do I look?'

Nothing like her. 'Lie on the bed.'

Komi did as he asked, inching the skirt up her thighs.

'No. Just lie there.' He handed her a pillow. 'Put this over your face.'

Komi's expression changed from flirtatious to brittle. 'No. No fucking way.'

'I'm not going to hurt you.'

'Yeah? Honey, you should know, I used to be in the military, you mess with me, I know how to handle myself. I got protection.'

'A gun?'

Without taking her eyes off him, she unzipped her bag, held it open, showed him the contents. In a separate pouch above a chaos of make-up, KY and tissues, he could see the handle of what looked to be a semi-automatic – one of Margie's weapons of choice. A stand-off. This wasn't going to plan. He wasn't in control. He gestured to the far corner of the room. 'How about if I stand over there while you do it?'

'You don't want to touch me? You don't want to—'

'It's part of my thing.'

Still wary, and without taking her eyes off him, she dug in her bag and took out a phone. 'Okay. Here's the deal. I'm gonna to take a picture of you. You try anything, it'll take me less than a second to fire this off to one of my girls. You behave yourself, I'll delete it. Deal?'

Don't do it. Don't do it. But now he was beginning to feel something, a warmth deep inside. 'Deal.'

He'd planned to dump the thrift store dress en route, but couldn't quite bring himself to do so. Instead he crammed it into the box with the photograph of JT and Teddy's passport, locked it, and slid that beneath his portable workbench in the truck.

Margie's car was in the driveway, but the house felt emptier than it should, quieter, as if it was holding its breath. 'Anyone home?'

'In here.'

Margie was sitting, straight-backed on the couch in the darkened lounge area.

'Hey, hon. What you doing in the dark?'

'Waiting for you.' Her voice was flat.

A chill as paranoia's old stain reappeared. *This is it.* She knew. She'd found out about him. How though? Impossible. All the same, he automatically swept his pockets for his phone, itching to double-check that the sync functions were disabled. *Don't panic, ride it out.* 'Where's Tasha?'

'With Gary. We need to talk.'

'Are you okay? Is Tasha okay?'

'I'm fine. She's fine.'

'What is it, then?'

'Here.' She handed him a small blue box. Inside it, nestled on a bed of cotton buds, sat a pregnancy test: a double blue line. 'We did it.'

Relief that he was in the clear; shock as it hit. He looked at Margie, at the plastic stick that held his future, at the portrait of Margie and Tasha on the wall. He composed himself, aware that whatever he said next would colour their relationship forever. He lowered his voice to a husky, emotion-filled whisper. 'Oh *honey*.'

Rainbowbrite

Ellie's stomach was on full spin-cycle again as she turned into Mrs Jensen's street. As much as she loathed the idea of going after justice for Teddy, maybe Noah was right, maybe Sherry was right. She had to see this through to the end.

Which was why, after she'd taken the boys to a movie, instead of returning home she found herself driving here. Despite the amount of sugar they'd inhaled (she'd let them have free rein at the concession stand), Philip and Sammy were sitting quietly in the back of the car, no fighting, no pinching, no questioning where the heck their mom thought she was taking them. They'd picked up on the hugeness of this. The lights were now visible, a twinkling oasis amidst the lumps of dirty ploughed snow.

'Oh cool,' Sammy whispered. 'Christmas.'

Jared was on the front lawn, untangling a mass of lights and draping them across the reindeers' bones. There was a new addition, too: a Mrs Claus plastic mould figurine. She was Ellie's height and wore a muff and a red plastic dress. Her face was an indistinct blur, the only feature a pair of glasses, which made Ellie think of Dr Bunsen Honeydew from *The Muppet Show* – a character that used to give her night terrors.

'Hellooooooo!' Jared called as Ellie and the boys climbed out of the car. 'Look – look, we got one, we got one.' He lumbered up and took her hand in a gloved mitten. 'We got a Mrs Claus. Whatcha think?'

'She's just super, honey,' Ellie said. It was difficult to remain depressed when faced with such enthusiasm. 'Boys, say hello to Jared.'

'You got elves,' Philip said. 'And a Rudolph.'

'Got to have elves,' Jared said. 'Did you know that elves can be both male and female and German people used to believe that if you were good they would be good to you but if you were bad they'd come at night and play tricks on you?'

'What kind of tricks?' Sammy asked.

'*All* of them.'

'Like hiding your socks in the morning so that you'll be late for school? Or like covering your pillow in jelly?'

Mrs Jensen emerged, wrapping herself in her overcoat. She took in the scene, then shuffled over to Ellie. Gone was the garish make-up, and grey strands wisped from beneath her hat. Ellie had been right to suspect the red hair was a wig. 'You're back.'

'I am.'

'Why? I told you everything I knew.'

'I don't think you did.'

'That so?' One of those shrewd glances, then a nod. 'These your boys?'

'Yes. Sammy and Philip.'

'I like your house,' Sammy said.

'Good of you to say. Why don't you help Jared with the lights? You can be Santa's helpers.'

'Like the elves,' Philip said to his snow boots.

'Can we help, Mom?' Sammy says. 'Please?'

'Sure you can.'

Mrs Jensen cracked a smile. 'There'll be hot chocolate for you afterwards.'

'With marshmallows, Momma?' Jared added.

'Can't have hot chocolate without marshmallows.'

The twins whooped. Jared, calmer than the first time Ellie saw him, handed them both a string of knotted lights.

Mrs Jensen eyed her again. 'What made you come back here?'

'Just a feeling.'

'Sharp little thing, aren't you?'

Ellie laughed. 'First time I've ever been called little.'

'Say I did have something, what would you do with it?'

'I don't know. It would depend what it is.'

'Woman cop came over a week or so back. Asked me to look around, see if Sandy kept anything back from the case. You tell her to do that?'

'No.'

Another searing assessment.

'What did you tell her?' Ellie asked.

'I said no.' Mrs Jensen sighed. 'I lied. Come on inside.'

'Will the boys be okay?'

'With Jared, you mean?'

Ellie coloured. 'I don't mean to suggest that he's dangerous. I'm . . . Oh *shoot*.'

'They'll be fine. He gets excitable sometimes, but he's not dangerous.'

With a last glance at the boys, and fully aware that Mrs Jensen was testing her, Ellie followed the woman inside, the hallway less of an obstacle course now that the boxes had been removed. Past the kitchen, a living room that could double as a mausoleum for Hummel figurines and crocheted chair-covers, and on to a basement door.

Mrs Jensen took the stairs slowly, gripping the bannister. 'Careful here.' Ellie picked through a labyrinth of broken furniture and synthetic Christmas trees with crumpled spines. 'Haven't been able to bring myself to clear it out.'

Through the basement window, a sliver of dusty glass, the boys' feet danced around the lights.

'Sandy wasn't perfect. I waited to see what they'd do with the case. Nothing. They've got a bad history. No accountability. Internal politics. It used to burn at him. I told him to move to the state department, but he stuck in there, thought he could change it from the inside. Wore him down.'

'Is that what made him sick? The stress, I mean.'

'I'm not getting you. Sick?'

'Eric said he died of cancer.'

'Cancer? He didn't die of cancer. He ate his gun. Did it right, too.'

'Oh.' Saying sorry seemed inadequate. Eric hadn't actually specified how Sandy had died. *She'd* made that jump.

Mrs Jensen bent, knees making a gunshot crack, and plucked a cardboard box from a lower shelf. Judging by its label, it had once held cans of tomato soup. 'Here.'

It was lighter than Ellie was expecting. Inside it sat a paper bag, like the type they used at the Stop & Shop, the top scrunched over.

'I'm going to trust you with this. Can't have this blowing back on me or Jared. Can I trust you to keep me out of it?'

'You can.'

'Good. Now let's get some hot chocolate into those boys' stomachs. Cold out there.'

Ellie ushered the boys into the house, and carrying the box as if it was made of crystal, joined Noah in the kitchen.

'What you got there?'

Before she could answer, Sammy tumbled in. 'We went to see Christmas.'

Noah raised an eyebrow.

'I went to see Sandy's widow again.'

'And that?'

'It's the dress.'

He broke into a smile. 'Good. Chris called. Never thought I'd say this after all that went on between you, but reckon you should call her back. Says she's worried about you. Says she's got some news.'

'What news?'

'Didn't say. Didn't ask. Call her back, hear it for yourself.' A pointed glance at the box. 'Go on. I'll get supper.'

'Oh Noah, thank you.'

She didn't pause to wallow in the relief that they were back on an even keel; didn't reach for the handset to call Chris back. All of that had to be ring-fenced. This was more important. She ran upstairs, took a pair of plastic gloves from the bathroom cabinet, and laid a white sheet across the bed. She'd watched enough episodes of *Forensic Files* to know that what she was about to do was foolhardy, but she was damned if she was going to stop. She lifted the dress out of the bag, and placed it on the sheet, the underskirt unfurling as if relieved to be free. Faded pink, and a tinge of yellow. It was nothing like the dress she and Aqualung had picked out on eBay; the colour was all wrong for a start, and she was way off base about the size. It was at least a twelve, but there were no labels inside it – definitely hand-sewn. She turned it over. The back of the bodice was peppered with light brown stains. *Blood.* So he was wearing it when he died. She shivered. Focused instead on the pinpricks where a corsage may have been placed, and examined the skirt once more, the netting beneath the stiff satin giving off a whiff of must. It had been turned up at some stage, and the stitches were coming loose, disintegrating with age. She unpicked them, telling herself that she just wanted to see the true colour of the dress, that she wasn't doing any harm.

She did it quickly, guiltily, half-expecting Stillson or Eric or someone who knew better to burst in on her. Then: 'Holy *crap*.' How could they have missed *this*?

MissingLinc#TeddyRyan

BobbieC, Wicklowboy, You

Major heads up. Incarcerated guy has confessed to killing Teddy. About to put all the deets on the site 2.17PM

BobbieC
Holy shit 2.17PM

Yeah 2.17PM

BobbieC
You believe it? 2.18PM

Not sure. Yet. If it is true, looks like your theory was right after all 2.18PM

Bobbiecowell

It should have been what his mother used to call a 'red letter day'. He should be giving himself fist-bumps, doing pirouettes. A *father*. Breeding was the ultimate act of creation and destruction. And now there was a confession, he could be free, in the clear.

It wasn't official, wouldn't be for a while – Warren K. Delaney had only spewed his guts to a reporter so far, and the county wasn't yet proclaiming him as a 'person of interest'. It was the twist to end all ironic twists. As Chris had pointed out, now a serial killer was owning up to the crime, it seemed that ol' Bobbiecowell was right after all. Delaney was on the 'List of serial killers in the United States' wiki page, under the 'killers with fewer than five proven victims' sub-heading. Went on a spree in the nineties, only three known victims – all female – but said it was more. He was caught dumping the body of a young, female sex worker he'd picked up at a truck stop in Detroit on the side of the I-94 in '98. *Lazy.*

Pete scanned the 'exclusive' splashed across the screen, illustrated by Delaney's mugshot. *In the clear.* Only . . . it wasn't right that this small-eyed, wholly unremarkable man with rat-tailed hair and a limp moustache was taking credit for Past Pete's work.

Whoever killed him deserves to get a fucking medal.

Margie emerged from the bathroom and leaned into the mirror to check her make-up. 'What you reading?'

He swiped the screen, showed her the front page of the *Washington Post*. 'Seeing how screwed up the world is this morning.'

'Uh-huh. How screwed are we?'

'Six out of ten.'

'And we're going to bring another person into this six out of ten world.'

Counting back, it would have happened almost to the day that Rainbowbrite contacted him about the ID. 'When are you going to tell the board?'

'After the amnio.' Margie never left anything to chance.

'And Tasha?'

'Still reckon we should wait.'

'And you're feeling okay?'

'Why wouldn't I be feeling okay?'

'About everything.'

'I've been thinking. Don't take that job in Seattle.'

A moment where he almost said, 'What job?' then caught himself. 'I've got to bring something in.'

'You do enough. I've transferred some cash into your account.'

'That makes me feel inadequate.' It didn't. He couldn't care less.

'It's only money.'

'You're the best, Margie, you know that, right? I don't deserve you.'

She bent to kiss him. 'Damn right you don't. Just for saying that, I'll go put the coffee on.'

He watched her leave, then flipped back to Delaney's bullshit.

'Pete?'

It had been a while since Tasha's 'kid from *The Shining*' shtick made him jump. 'Yeah?'

'Can you pick me up from school today?'

'Sure. Why?'

'I want to go somewhere.'

Pete didn't ask where.

He pulled up directly opposite, and leaned back in his seat so that Tasha could get a good view of the house. He was surprised she hadn't asked to come here before.

'It's so *small*,' she said. 'Way smaller than our house.'

'What did you expect?' Other than the colour – a defiantly cheerful blue – its compact shape, clapboard cladding and well-kept lawn were wholly unremarkable.

He knew Bundy had grown up in the city, but had only learned the man's childhood home was within walking distance of Margie's pad when a client mentioned it. By then, he'd been using his Bobbiecowell username for months. A happy coincidence. *Maybe.*

'I don't know what I expected.' She turned away. 'On Wiki it says that they think he killed a girl who lived around here, but they couldn't prove it.'

'You remember her name?'

'No.' Not even Tash had stored that information. *You never remember the names of the victims, only the perpetrators.* 'He got away with it for years, didn't he?'

'Yeah.' Only at the end, Bundy must have felt them breathing down his neck. Maybe he enjoyed that. His Past Pete self had enjoyed it too. Was he enjoying it now? Did he miss it? Was that the crux of it?

'Ted Bundy is the smartest one of all.'

The smartest ones don't get caught. 'Seen enough?'

A nod. 'I read that a man said he killed the Boy in the Dress. Why didn't you tell me?'

'Only just found out about it.'

'Is he a serial killer?'

'A minor one.'

'You were wrong about that. It was a serial killer after all. Do you feel dumb?'

'I wasn't wrong.' *Oops.*

'Yes you were, you said it was someone who knew the boy in New York.'

'My mistake. You shouldn't get so stuck on this stuff, Tash. You don't want your teacher giving you a hard time again.'

'I'm careful. I won't.'

'I believe you.'

Back at home, he parked, switched off the engine and waited for her to climb out and dart for the front door. She hesitated, hand on the lever, then turned to face him. 'If you want to marry Mom that's okay.'

'Really?'

'Yeah.'

And there it was: the perfect life for the taking.

MissingLinc#TeddyRyan

BobbieC, Ratking, You

If I wanted to find someone online, how would I go about it?
9.07PM

Ratking
You talking about Teddy's accuser? The confession brought this on? Don't get your hopes up on that. Could be bullshit
9.08PM

It's that & something you said. Uncertainty is a bitch. It's time to be sure. Need to hear it for myself. Either way need to face it
9.09PM

Ratking
Okay. Careful here though Shaun
9.09PM

I will be
9.09PM

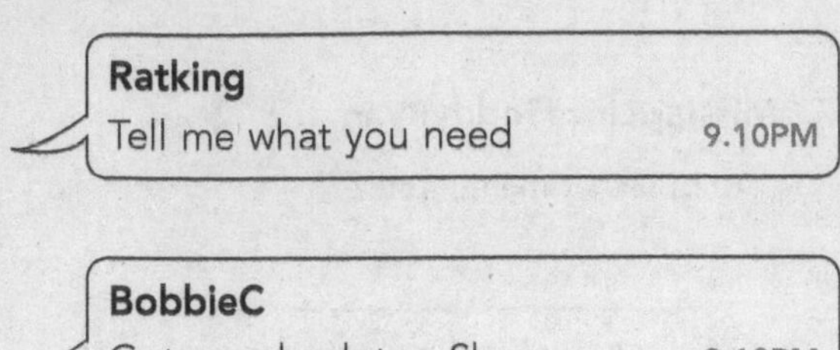
Ratking
Tell me what you need 9.10PM
BobbieC
Got your back too Shaun 9.10PM

Wicklowboy22: Hi Brendan can you ask Aidan Sullivan if he knows where Dylan Carey is these days?

Wicklowboy22: I'd ask him myself only Cal will find out & Janice hates me enough already

BrendanT: Why? U okay???

Wicklowboy22: Can you do it or not?

BrendanT: He's in Dublin but this can't get back to me don't want to be linked to all this

Wicklowboy22: Where in Dublin?

BrendanT: No clue that's all Aidan knows except for he got into the drugs and I had to lie about why I was asking and said I was looking to buy some weed

BrendanT: I miss u. Also FML

Wicklowboy22

In films and TV shows whenever a PI tracked someone down they were always at home. But he'd been sitting on a broken wall outside the tenement for an hour now, smoking himself half to death, a pile of cigarette ends at his feet, Daphne worn out from barking at passing men and dogs.

It had been a slog to get this far, but there was also a sense of achievement to it. It had taken a combination of Chris's advice to scour Dylan's family's social media accounts and calling in favours from Brendan to get here. He was growing up, toughening the fuck up. Facing this alone. He could have asked Johnny to come along – the man hadn't been back to see him, but Shaun knew he'd approve of this mission. Had it been the confession that had brought him to this point? No. Throughout the ups and downs, Teddy's murderer had never truly taken centre stage in Shaun's thoughts. When he did attempt to picture him, what popped up was a man with dirty nails and coals for eyes, a little like the fellow who used to hang around the skate park. Nothing like the confessor's mugshot, with its stringy hair and smirk. That part of the story wasn't yet real to him. *This* was real. Waiting outside a shitty tenement in Summerhill, stomach knotted, mouth tasting foul from too many cigarettes.

And he had to do something. The content of that letter still stung. It had been pushed under the shop's door in the night, waiting for him to find it. 'Teddy Ryan will ROT in Hell and so will YOU'. Unsigned, the coward's way, like the haters on the internet who hid behind anonymity. It could be worse, they could be throwing bricks through the shop window or forming a pitchfork-wielding mob, like the illiterate vigilantes he'd read about who had targeted a paediatrician in the UK. *Paedogeddon.* Part of him still couldn't believe it had come to this. He hadn't yet resorted to the booze. He'd moved Daphne's basket into the shop (keeping her closer helped) and he'd hidden the photograph of Teddy in the drawer. Thought about burning it, but he was done with the histrionics. One day at a time.

A pair of sulky teens minced past. Behind them came a skeletal fellow in a hoody and long-expired jeans, a plastic bag screwed around a wrist. Shaun caught a glimpse of the Carey cheekbones, the same bow-legged gait as Pat's. The man dug through his pockets, dropped his keys, his centre of gravity all over the place as he bent to retrieve them.

'Dylan?'

Naturally, Daphne chose this moment to regain her energy and lunged at Dylan's trainers. Dylan showed no surprise at being victimised. Shaun tightened his grip on the lead, yanked her too sharply back to him. Something sparked in Dylan's muddy irises: 'I know you.' He sagged. 'Is this about Teddy?'

'Yes. Can we talk?'

Dylan seemed to curl even further in on himself. 'Knew someone would show up. You'd better come in. Not the dog though.'

'We can't talk out here?'

'No.' Dylan shivered. 'I'm fucking freezing.'

Shaun thought for a second, then slung the lead around a rotten gatepost. 'Stay,' he said to the dog. He doubted anyone would try and nick her, and much as he'd rather not go in alone, Dylan wasn't much of a threat. With his raw, red fingers, sharp bones and brown teeth, life hadn't just given him a beating, it had locked him in a basement and used him as a punching bag.

Ignoring the dog's whines, Shaun followed Dylan into a hallway with blistered paintwork, up a flight of vertiginous stairs and into a one-room flat, which, if anything, was in a worse state than its occupier. There were sooty cracks where floorboards should be, a lone recliner that was struggling to stay upright and a mattress leaking foam and topped with a faded Powerpuff Girls duvet. The kitchen was similarly depressed: a stained fridge and a hole spewing dangerous looking wires where a stove should sit. 'You want a cup of tea or something?'

'No thanks.' There was no visible sign of a kettle, tea or mugs.

Dylan dumped the bag on the counter, took out two cans of corner shop lager, and cracked one. Froth spilled over his fingers and he sucked it up, losing his balance in the process. 'Have you got a smoke for me?' Shaun handed him the packet of Vogues. He took two, put one behind an ear and lit up the other. 'Thing is Shaun, I'm not doing well. Things are a bit tight at the moment. You couldn't do the decent thing and help me out? I'd pay you back.'

'I don't have much.'

'Anything would help.'

Shaun handed him a twenty euro note. 'Here. All I've got.'

Dylan tucked it into his waistband, wobbled again. He propped himself against the counter. 'I remember you. They gave you a hard time. The boys on the estate, I mean.'

'Some of them did. You didn't.'

'I was older than them. Didn't have anything against you.'

Shaun wanted to blurt: *why* didn't you? Everyone was always saying he was the spit of his uncle. Surely seeing a carbon copy of his so-called abuser around the estate would be enough to send Dylan mad. It was this fact, more than anything, that had fed the hope that Johnny was right about Teddy's innocence.

'I know why you're here. It wasn't me who told the reporters all that. It was Pat, he was the one who went to them, not me. Made him angry to see all those people thinking Teddy was some kind of hero.'

From what Shaun had seen of Pat, the man hadn't looked as if he had the nous to run to the press, but really, how much guile would that have taken? A ten-second Google search would have kicked up a slew of possible news outlets or blogs. And he wouldn't have been short of takers. It was a juicy story, guaranteed click-bait. The ones he'd read had been carefully annotated with 'allegedly', but they would have known that this meant less than nothing when the rumour mill started to grind.

'Did he do that to you?' Shaun asked.

'Did who do what?'

'Teddy. Did Teddy hurt you? I'm not judging you, Dylan. I just want the truth. Either way, I have to know. You get that, right?'

Dylan took a drink. Eyed Shaun. Smoked.

'Please.'

'He didn't hurt me. Pat made me say all those things about him.'

'Why would he do that?' Was Dylan telling him what he wanted to hear? He wasn't avoiding Shaun's gaze, but that could be because he was off his gourd.

'Because of what Teddy was going to say about him. About him being queer as well. That they had been together.'

Pat and Teddy together – that broken man and his uncle. Shaun was a past master at rolling with the punches now. 'Go on.'

'After Teddy came back from London he was staying with us. I was sleeping over, heard them fighting. Teddy was saying to Pat that he should come clean, be honest about who he was. That maybe if he was they could be together like they were before Teddy went to London. Took me years to figure out that Teddy meant that him and Pat were together. Didn't understand what I was hearing back then. Anyway, Pat said he'd never do that, there was no fucking way he was going to admit to that as he had a girlfriend and she was after him to get married.' The words tumbled over each other, and Dylan drew breath. 'And then Pat said I had to say Teddy messed with me and I did but I didn't know what I was doing. I was only a kid and I was scared of Pat.'

'But you knew all those details about him. Teddy had a picture of you.'

'Pat did that with my dad's Polaroid. Took it and put it in his bag and he knew all those things about the scar on his cock, like, and told me to say that.'

'Is that the truth?'

'Swear on the baby Jesus. I'm sorry I said it, Shaun, I'm sorry, I didn't mean for this to happen. I didn't know Teddy would be sent away and he'd end up murdered, I thought he'd gone away to New York where he'd have a good life.'

'You have to clear his name.'

'Wha'?'

'Go to one of the reporters and tell them the truth.'

'No. No way. *No.* I'm not going to do that. Pat will kill me. *Kill* me. Look at me. You think I can stand up to him? You can do what you like about it. I'm not saying anything.'

'The whole world thinks he did it.'

'I can't help that. Please, Shaun, I *can't*.'

'I'll pay you.' *With what?*

'No.'

'Why tell me then?'

'I had to. I felt bad, for years I felt bad. But I can't say anything Shaun, and if anyone asks I'll say you were lying.'

Shaun checked himself. There was no anger at this. No rage. There was nothing he could do to Dylan that was worse than what he was doing to himself. And so he did the only thing he could do – he left.

Outside, Daphne had almost gnawed through her lead – he'd made it just in time. He walked away, then ducked into an alleyway between a Chinese takeaway and the boarded-up shell of a butcher's shop. There was someone who deserved to know what he'd learned. He took out his phone.

Shaun didn't bother greeting Johnny, got straight into it. 'Dylan said it was a lie. Pat made him do it.'

'I fucking *knew* it.' In the background, Bridie called for something.

Shaun opened his mouth to spill the rest, reveal that once upon a time Teddy and Pat had been lovers of sorts, then decided against it.

'Will he go to the papers now?'

'He says no. I asked him but he says he'll deny it if anyone else asks.'

'I'll make him do it.'

'*No.*'

'You can't just let it lie, Shaun.'

'He won't do it. Anyway, there's no need. I recorded it on my phone.'

'You little beauty.' That tip had come from Bobbie: *try and get proof, either way*. 'You can send that to the papers.'

He could, but he'd need to work through the implications of that first. It might help extinguish the rumours about Teddy, but if he put it out there, he'd expose decades of lies and shame. Teddy was dead. While Shaun loathed Pat for what he'd done, the man had clearly felt like he was backed into a corner. Poisoned by prejudice, the fear of being outed had run so deep that there were still lads like Brendan who were as deep in the closet two decades after Pat had ruined Teddy's life.

At least now he knew the truth, and he could let Donny and Janice know. Would that be enough?

Ratking1

The majority of the other sleuthing sites were running with the Delaney narrative, but she was still reluctant to give him too much oxygen. Delaney was elaborating now, saying that he picked up Teddy on the outskirts of Michigan, mistook him for a girl. Said Teddy was wearing the pink dress when he encountered him. Said he couldn't remember much after that, except 'God told him to do it'. There was no explanation for why he chose the outskirts of a reserve in Millar Town as a dumpsite. All of these details could have been extrapolated from any number of #JusticeForTeddyRyan threads. It wasn't proof of anything other than a desire for attention.

But then there was no concrete evidence backing up her latest Boy in the Dress update – a transcript of the audio clip Shaun had sent through, the names redacted. Going against her better instincts, she'd enabled the comment function and it was already being picked to pieces and questioned:

Marlborowoman: You call this proof? What's going on? This site used to be TRUSTWORTHY

Vladtheromantic: Nice. So Missing-Linc is into victim blaming now?

Bobbiecowell: You think it's false? Fair enough. But remember that it works both ways. There's no concrete proof Teddy Ryan IS guilty of abuse either. No other victims have come forward.

Good old Bobbiecowell. He'd been a rock. Vlad and Marlborowoman's comments didn't strictly flaunt the guidelines, but she removed them anyway. *So sue me.* Scott's chair sat empty in silent accusation. He hadn't been back. Kelly had been messaging her, but hadn't mentioned anything about their bust up. She missed him; missed Mommydearest.

Delete, delete, delete.

A pop, and the left-hand monitor screen gave up the ghost. She smacked it hard enough to make it wobble, bruising her palm, stared at herself reflected in its lifeless face. The darkness waved a tentacle in her direction, she could easily flump on the desk and howl. Couldn't – *wouldn't.* She should get out of here; hadn't seen the sky for days now. And how long had it been since she'd exercised? She'd do both now – run through her pressure relief, then continue the work Kelly began restoring the sculptures. She went so far as to pick up the long-neglected tension bands she was supposed to use every day to stretch her tendons, before straying back to the inbox flashing on the remaining screen. With perfect timing, as if in punishment for ignoring her resolve, her nemesis arrived with one of its 'RE: Eliza Guzman' grenades. The message was brief: 'dead women tell no tales LOL'. There was another attachment.

The Skype tone slapped her out of it. There was only one person who contacted her via Skype. *Saved by the bell.*

'*Finally.* Where the hell have you been, Ellie?'

'I'm so sorry I've been gone for so long. It was the shock of it. I just . . . I just couldn't deal. Not when I've got boys, not when . . . But listen, I've got so much to tell you.'

'Well don't keep me in suspense.'

'I've found the dress.'

'*What?*'

'I went to see Sandy's widow. She gave it to me.'

'Holy. Fuck.' For once Ellie didn't upbraid her for cursing.

'I went there before only I didn't tell you because I knew you thought it was a bad idea and in any case she said she didn't have anything and then I went back and she gave it to me.'

'Did you give it to the cops?'

'Not yet. I promised Mrs Jensen I'd keep her out of it. I've been . . . I've been sitting on it, I guess you'd say. Trying to decide what to do, only now we know that Teddy wasn't a . . . you know, a pervert, well, that's why I'm calling you.'

'The cops need it, Ellie. They can test for DNA. See if Delaney's story holds water.'

'It doesn't hold water. The dress is stained with all kinds of things but I unpicked the hem and there was a line of red right in the crease. That ever happened to you when you washed stuff?'

'No.' Then she got the implication. 'You're saying it was originally red? You sure about this?'

'I'm not sure. It's not definite. The cops never mentioned it was red, and nor did Eric. If Sandy knew that I'm sure Eric would have told me. Delaney said the dress the boy was wearing was pink, didn't he?'

Chris flipped to one of the bookmarked articles. 'He did.'

'Then it can't be him. It has to be a false confession. And everyone we've spoken to, JT, Teddy's friends, the people we can actually verify who knew him said that he wasn't into drag. Why would he be hitching through Michigan wearing a dress? I mean, it was winter.'

'Good point.'

'All this time we've been looking for a pink dress. This could change everything.'

'Have you told Aqualung or Bobbie?'

'Only person who knows is Noah.'

'Thought you and Aqualung were working on this together?'

'We were. I couldn't . . . I swore to Sandy's widow I wouldn't get her involved.'

'Have you heard from him though?'

'I thought you and him were friends?'

'Yeah. Chased him away.'

'Why?'

'Because I'm a bitch that's why.'

'Have you apologised to him?'

'No.'

'You should do that.'

'Thanks, Mom.'

'Welcome.'

Her eye strayed back to the attachment. *Not today, Satan*. She deleted it without opening it.

'Chris? You still there?'

'Yeah. Just . . .'

'What?'

'Someone's been sending borderline abusive messages about my mom to the site. You told anyone about her being on there?'

'Oh . . . oh that's just awful. You asked me not to say anything. I haven't even told Noah. Or Aqualung, or Bobbie. Who do you think it is?'

'Someone I kicked off the site. I accused Mommydearest of doing it.'

'*Mommydearest?* Seriously?'

'Yeah. Something that was said in the messages rang a bell. I was wrong. Poor guy. He must hate me.'

'You apologised to him too?'

'He's blocked me.'

'Do you want me to talk to him? Say that you were stressed out?'

'No. It's on me. I'll deal with it.'

And she would. Talking about the messages was taking the power out of them. What was wrong with her that she'd let this fester for so long?

'Is there anything I can do?'

'It's fine. I can handle it. Okay. So you need to take this to the cops. You can do it anonymously.'

'How? They've got CCTV. They'll know it was me. I *promised*, Chris.'

'Post it?'

'Can they trace that too?'

'Yeah, maybe. Can you ask that guy Eric to do it? See if he can find a way to keep Mrs Jensen out of it?'

A pause. 'I'll talk to him.'

'Okay. Then you got to let them handle it.'

'I will.'

'And maybe keep this to yourself for now?'

'Of course. You don't have to tell me *that*.'

'And Ellie?'

'What?'

'You're fucking amazing, you know that, right?'

Rainbowbrite: Hi sorry I've been so quiet. I have some news

Bobbiecowell: Hey! I've been real worried about you. We got a LOT to catch up on!! What are your thoughts on the confession???????

Rainbowbrite: He's lying

Bobbiecowell: How do you know?

Rainbowbrite: Because the dress isn't pink, it's red

Wicklowboy22

Head down, avoiding eye contact, Jack Devilly shuffled in, placed the stolen copy of *The Spinning Heart* on the counter, then turned and scuttled out. Shaun watched him go, then flicked through it. The spine was bent, the pages swollen as if it had fallen in water, and there were notes in the margins, written in red pen: 'THAT IS RITE. PAIN'. On another, the words, 'SHE NEVER LOVED ME DID SHE?????' were imprinted with such force the pen had torn through the text. It was a reminder that there were other people in the world with more severe problems than his, but that was cold comfort right now.

He'd sent audio files of Dylan's confession to Janice and his cousins, asking them to pass them on to Donny, and Chris and Bobbiecowell were doing their best to spread the word, but no one cared that Teddy wasn't the monster he was made out to be. *Mud sticks*. The only recent bright spark was a long, heartfelt email from Rainbowbrite, in which she'd apologised for 'going dark' and cutting herself off from the case.

The bell jangled, and Shaun looked up from his phone expecting to see Jack again. Donny, sinister as always in one of his all-black ensembles, pushed through the door. Shaun wasn't surprised, knew it was coming. In her basket next to him, Daphne let out a baseline grumble, and Shaun grabbed for her collar. Donny may have shaken the dog, but he hadn't broken her spirit. Shaun took his courage from her. 'What do you want?'

Donny ignored the dog's efforts to get to him, kept his eyes fixed on Shaun. 'I'll see you outside.' He exited the shop without waiting for Shaun to agree.

'Good girl.' Shaun gave Daphne a couple of chews to keep her busy, then reached for his coat slung on the back of the chair. There was nothing more Donny could do to him now, but the nerves were biting all the same.

His uncle was waiting for him directly outside the entrance, hands clasped behind his back, mask in place. Making an effort to stop his hands from shaking, Shaun lit up a Vogue and waited for him to begin.

'Listened to that fucker admitting he lied about Teddy. Made me sick. He swore to us he was telling the truth back then.' A twitch of the lips, a crack in the veneer.

Shaun shrugged. And just like that, the nerves dribbled away, leaving him remarkably calm. So much so he was tempted to blow smoke right in Donny's face.

'The Careys are going to pay for what they did.'

'What's the point? Pat Carey's a broken man, so's Dylan.' A steady voice; a steady hand. Johnny would be proud. 'What do you want, Donny?'

'There's some bastard saying he killed Teddy.'

'Have the guards given you more information? Did they confirm it?'

'They need to back it up, the lazy fucks. Heard you were planning on going over to the US.'

'Who told you that? Janice?'

'Yeah. And Carmel said there was some funding thing that went tits up.'

'Janice said Carmel left.'

'She's back. Never stays away for long. Were you going over there to see where they'd laid him to rest?'

'That's right.'

'There are pictures of where they put him on that fucking website.'

'There are.' A stilted conversation, but Shaun somehow felt he had the upper hand. He killed the cigarette, then tucked the butt back into the packet. It was the kind of prissy gesture he suspected would irritate Donny. If it did, he didn't show it.

'Family let him down.'

'You believed what you wanted to believe.'

A sneer – finally. 'You think I wanted to believe my fucking brother was a nonce?'

'You were ashamed of him.'

'That a question or a statement?'

'Statement.'

'You've grown some balls lately, haven't you?'

'What do you want?'

Donny took an envelope from the inside of his jacket and handed it to him.

'What's this?'

'Open it.'

He ripped the seal, stared down at a thick blue wodge of euro notes.

Donny came very close. 'You're going to America, Shaun. Someone from the family's got to go over there. You fought in Ted's corner, you should be the one to go. You're going to America to bring Teddy the fuck home.'

PART FOUR:

OMG

Bobbiecowell

<He talks so fast!! Have to keep asking him to repeat himself LOL. His accent is so so cute>; <OMG he smokes ☹>

Rainbowbrite had been sending him increasingly banal updates ever since Shaun landed that morning. While he was relieved that her house guest was distracting her from other, more potentially dangerous endeavours, there were things he needed to know. **<Hope you said "hi" from me!! Will whatsapp later! ☺ BTW, cops got the dress yet?>**

<OMG I didn't tell you!! Eric gave it to Cmdr Stillson yesterday & asked her to keep Mrs Jensen out of it if poss. He says she agreed to do that for now & was decent about it. She was a real b-word to me though ☹>

<They discuss the fact it might be red?>

<She wouldn't tell Eric anything about the case or if they think it will prove Delaney is lying but I can ask her that when she comes to meet Shaun>

Okay. **<When's that happening?>**

<Next week. Shaun says hi back!!>

<Hey Shaun!! Hope the cold weather isn't getting to you!! ☺>

Pete pocketed the phone and headed out onto the deck, running his boot over the head of the tack. It was only a matter of time before a sharp-eyed cop, an army on the internet, or maybe ol' Rainbowbrite herself made the connection. *That goddamned dress.* If Past Pete hadn't washed it, leaching it of colour, if Sandy Eversham hadn't been such a wildcard and squirrelled away evidence, the link would have been made when the case first surfaced on Missing-Linc. And even if they did put the pieces together, all he had to do to remain in the safe zone was erase Bobbiecowell, and pootle on with his life. The thrift store dress was still in the lock box in the truck, but so what? What did that prove? Nada. He'd dumped Teddy's passport, wallet and the JT photograph in a trash can outside a McDonald's drive-thru twenty minutes after Rainbowbrite dropped her red dress revelation. He was regretting that now – regretted it as soon as he drove away.

Here he was at a crossroads. He could go either way. The Margie groundwork he'd laid during his GoFundMe massacre fantasy was still there just in case: a boys-only trip with his old pal Millet who needed some man-time on account of his wife was cheating on him again, coupled with a tug-on-the-heartstrings visit to where his mother and Carl were buried. It was a two-day drive to Stenton County, which meant he'd be away for a week at least. He'd asked Margie to come along, comfortably aware that the notice was too short.

He poked at the tack, fighting the compulsion to take off his boots and dig in. *You're not a serial killer if you've only killed two people.* He wasn't a monster; he wasn't like those lame fucks who shot up schools or clubs for notoriety. *Was* he? Years ago, just after he made the decision to bury Past Pete, he'd read an article about a man who'd accidentally killed a jaywalker when the guy stepped out in front of his car. The driver wasn't blamed for it, but it destroyed him, couldn't live with the guilt, it coloured every aspect of his life. And this was the crux of it – where was *his* goddamned guilt? Until the case had re-emerged on the site, he could go for as long as a year without thinking about it. *By putting on the dress the killer was unconsciously 'undoing' the crime . . .*

He was nothing like the loser he once was. He was admired. Things couldn't be better with Margie, and Tasha, once the thorn in his side, was now – ironically – his greatest ally. Risk it all, and for what? For the legacy of becoming a Wikipedia footnote?

More than a footnote. *It'd be a story that no one would forget.* He'd be all over the site, the extent of his machinations there for all to see. He'd be the subject of PhDs, criminology lectures, op-eds, social media storms. But that route could only end with incarceration – or worse. Death row, even – depending on which state he was apprehended in. Madness.

There was the other direction, which didn't entail him leaving the house at all; didn't entail him risking a hair on his head. He could stay as he was: Pete the stepdad, Pete the *father*, Pete who lived in his high-end house with his high-end wife. Pete who was part of the Missing-Linc team, fighting injustice on the internet. *Ha de fucking ha.*

Rainbowbrite

'What do you think of him, Noah?'

They were in the kitchen, talking in whispers. 'What's not to like?'

'I keep having to ask him to repeat himself.'

'Don't sweat it.'

'He's just . . .'

'Not what you expected?'

She thought about it. Shaun was exactly what she'd expected. Quiet, eccentric, bookish, small – so tiny she felt like she could fit him in her handbag. 'He smokes.'

'There a law against that now? I used to smoke. Where you going with this? You having second thoughts?'

'No. Not at all.' She knew what was bothering her. The shadow of the child abuse allegation hadn't gone away entirely, and he looked so much like his uncle it was spooky.

'You're just being a drama queen, whipped yourself up over nothing. He's only been here a few hours.'

'Do you always have to be the voice of reason?' But he was right. She was just being dramatic. She'd been looking forward to this for days now. Cleaned the house from top to bottom, agonised over whether he'd be comfortable enough on the pull-out in the den, planned meals, swapped recipes with Sherry, and now he was here. And Noah had made a real effort to be friendly. 'Thanks for doing this.'

'Doing what?'

'Being supportive.'

Laughter came from down the hall.

Noah grinned. 'Boys seem to like him.'

'I better get them to bed.'

She went through to the TV room. Unseen, she hung back by the door to eavesdrop. Shaun was sitting on the couch, a twin on either side, *The Batman Lego Movie* playing in the background.

Sammy: 'Do you have a girlfriend?'

'I don't.'

'I don't either.'

Philip: 'Do you have a wife?'

'I don't.'

Sammy: 'I like how you speak.'

'Thanks. I like how you speak too.'

'But we speak like regular people.'

Shaun laughed, and some of the tension leaked out of Ellie's shoulders.

'What's your house like?'

'It's tiny, smaller than this room. I live above a bookshop with my dog.'

'What's his name?'

'Daphne. He's a she.'

Philip giggled. 'Daphne!'

Sammy: 'I want a dog, but Dad says we can't until we learn how to do our chores. If I had a dog I'd call it Batman.'

'Or Groot.'

'I . . . am . . . Groot.'

Ellie cleared her throat. 'Time for bed. Shaun needs his sleep.'

Sammy sighed. '*Mom.*'

'Go on up and brush your teeth. I'll be up in five minutes. Shaun will still be here in the morning.'

The twins shared a look, Philip shrugged and Sammy said, 'Okaaaay. Good night, Shaun.'

They raced out, feet thundering up the stairs.

Shaun looked over. 'You're a good mam.'

Whoosh, the unexpected compliment stole her breath. 'I'm really not. They run rings around me.' And she let them. She still hadn't learned how to parent without bribery – or blackmail.

'You should meet my cousins. You'd think they were straight out of *The Omen*.'

She sat next to him. 'How's the jetlag?'

'It's fine.'

'Shall I get you some hot milk? It might help you sleep. Tomorrow . . . well, tomorrow will be a busy day. Eric says he'll meet us at the reserve, and show you exactly where Teddy . . .' She couldn't say it. Not now Shaun was within touching distance. Instead she blurted: 'I need to tell you something. I feel so terrible that I believed the rumours about him.'

'Don't. I believed it too. Even my mother believed it was true. The only person who didn't was Johnny.'

'Who's that?'

'A friend of Teddy's. His best friend.'

Without being asked, Shaun took a photograph out of his pocket. It was the original of the first image she'd seen of Teddy, sitting on a couch with two girls with wild springy hair and a good-looking boy who glowered at the camera. They all had the same asymmetrical features. 'That's my mam, my aunt Janice, Teddy's older brother Donny and Teddy of course.'

'You look so much like him.' But now she realised that wasn't entirely true. Up close he did resemble Teddy, but under the skin he was . . . softer somehow. Even in a photograph, Teddy dominated the space around him. 'Your mom was very pretty.'

'She died when I was at school one day. Suddenly. No one expected it.'

Chris had told her that. 'I'm so sorry. And now you have to deal with this. With your uncle being . . . I can't even imagine what that must be like.'

'My uncle Donny says I'm to bring him home. I don't even know if he'd want to come home. Why would he when his family all turned on him?'

'You didn't. Not when it counted.'

And then he smiled at her for the first time. 'Nor did you.'

Wicklowboy22

The outdoor wear store was a bewildering mish-mash of clothing, tools and hunting gear, a world away from the charity shops where he usually bought his clothes. In the end he let Ellie choose a jacket for him – a squishy, tangerine puffer with a hood, the last thing he would have picked out. He hadn't yet dared to glance in the mirror.

Ellie narrowed her eyes and yanked down the edge. 'Move your arms back and forth. You got enough give?'

'I think so.'

'Are those boots working out? Stamp your feet.'

The faux fur-lined clod-hoppers with gaudy laces were heavier than he was used to. His feet felt like they'd been wrapped in a duvet and then dipped in cement. 'I think so.'

'And you'll need a hat. And gloves. I'll just be a minute.'

Calling after the boys, who were whooping and hollering through the racks, she waddled away.

Ellie was right, his tweed ensemble wasn't up to the job. The cold had been the biggest shock of all; blasting straight into his ears and making his teeth ache whenever he snuck outside for a cigarette. He still felt unsteady from the flight, the store's shiny floor undulated beneath his feet. Jetlag, or culture shock. Maybe both. He knew it was a cliché, but everything did appear bigger to him – the houses, roads, the sky. Even Noah was like a giant, Ellie a larger-than-life version of Máirín, smothering him with non-stop talk and bustle, mothering him half to death. She was only a decade older than he, but seemed to have leaped straight into middle age. He was expecting days of mortification and stagnant small-talk, but after the first few hours, and mostly thanks to the boys, any awkwardness had drifted away.

'Look at us Shaun.' Sammy, the noisy one, was leopard-crawling through a rack of snow gear, a balaclava pulled over his head. Philip hung back, laughing at his brother. They were non-identical, and their genetic make-up seemed to have been parcelled out neatly between them. Sammy had his mother's florid skin and talent for chatter; Philip was a kid of few words like his dad, and had inherited Noah's broad face and carroty hair.

Ellie returned with a hat lined with fake fur and ear flaps. She put it on his head, adjusting it like he'd seen her do with the boys. 'You look so cute.'

The tweed skin of his old self discarded on the floor, he dared to look in the mirror. *If only Brendan could see me now.* 'I don't feel like myself.' He hadn't meant to say it out loud.

'Is that a bad thing?'

Was it? 'I don't know.'

She rubbed his arm. 'You ready?'

Was he? 'I'm ready.'

A picnic area. A snow-sodden bench. Trees garlanded with snow. The sky a muddy blue. It wasn't as bereft as it had looked in the photographs.

The twins danced along ahead of them, kicking snow, and Shaun hung back behind Eric and Ellie. Ellie had warned him that Eric was a man of few words, but that was an understatement. He was a Noah clone, a big, stolid, unflappable man, only without Noah's dry sense of humour. Last night, when Shaun slipped out for a cigarette, Noah had joined him, took a sneaky drag, tipped him a wink and then popped a mint.

Ellie turned to give him one of her concerned glances. He smiled back at her, although the cold was making his teeth twinge again. They were the only people here. Shaun's boots crunched through the snow, and cocooned in his new coat and the ridiculous hat, the tip of his nose was the only extremity that was being scoured by the air. It was so quiet he could hear his breath and pulse.

'It was here,' Eric said, stopping abruptly and gesturing to a flat patch peppered with tree stumps. Not knowing what else to do, Shaun went over to inspect it. They'd already been to the grave – the first stop on what he was beginning to think of as the 'whistle stop death tour' – which was also something of an anti-climax. The Rathnew cemetery, with its elaborate stones and portraits of the dead, put the pauper's graveyard where Teddy lay to shame. He hadn't been sure what to say or how to react as he'd looked down at the simple numbered cross above Teddy's resting place. Feeling faintly ridiculous, he'd lit a Marlboro and funnelled the smoke onto the ground, just like he'd promised to do.

'How are you feeling?' Ellie asked.

'You're always asking me that.'

'I know.'

He pictured Teddy lying under the snow for all those months. Tried to feel *something*. Anything. If Teddy hadn't died – been *murdered* – if he'd fulfilled his plan to help Eileen move over here, what would Shaun's life have been like? He'd be American. He'd be a completely different person, not a 'fucking weirdo' who made minimum wage in a book store. And when his mother died, when the time bomb in her head exploded, Teddy would have been there for him.

Bollocks, Johnny's voice said in his head. And, as he turned away, Shaun had to admit the man was right.

Ratking1

The bristles barely made a dent on the phoenix's rusty skin. Her fingers were numb and stung from the vinegar, but she didn't stop. It was better than being inside, staring at the surviving screen. Now that Shaun was in Minnesota with Ellie, she couldn't settle, felt like she was on the outside of the action. She could've easily invited him to spend some time in Nevada, given him a day in Vegas, and that was on her. Then there was Scott's empty chair, a constant reminder that she'd chased him away with her usual bullshit. Mommydearest hadn't responded to the apology she'd sent him on Facebook, and she didn't blame him for that. She'd even considered messaging Mack, inviting him over for old time's sake, but mindless sex wasn't the cure for this.

'Chris.' Jeanie came trip-trapping along the path towards her, a beer in her hand as usual, an old serape blanket draped over her shoulders. 'What you doing out here in the dark?'

'What's it look like?'

'Come inside. It's freezing out here.'

'Can't.'

Jeanie squatted next to her, and handed her the bottle of Coors. 'You don't think we should let them go?'

'Maybe.' The lip of the bottle tasted of Jeanie's lipstick.

'C'mon. Let's get inside. You're gonna get hypochondria.'

'Hypothermia.'

'That too. C'mon.'

'I'm not in the mood for people.'

'You never are. Devin says Scott's still cut up. He was into you.'

'Yeah.'

'You still mad that I told him about Mom?'

'Yeah.'

'It's not a secret.'

'You told him she was on the site.'

'So? She is on the site. Why did you put her on there if you didn't want people knowing about it?'

'Can't run a site for missing people without including my goddamned missing mom, can I?'

'You got to let this go. She'd be . . . eighty by now. She's probably in a retirement home in Florida, driving all the other seniors crazy.'

'That's just bullshit.'

Jeanie cackled. 'Yeah, it is. Come for one drink, then I'll leave you in peace. Scout's honour.'

Jeanie hung back with her as they made their way to the house, bouncing the beer back and forth.

It was too cold to hang out on the porch and Devin, Paula and Michael were crammed on Jeanie's couch, Mack perched on an arm. She must've been distracted if she hadn't noticed his bike out there. They all fell silent when she and Jeanie entered the room. Devin handed her a beer from the six-pack on the floor.

'What's this? An intervention?'

'Jeanie's worried about you,' Paula said.

'I'm okay.'

'Yeah, you're totally not okay. Is it because of Scott?'

Chris glanced at Mack. He gave her a 'fine by me' shrug. A jab of self-pity – it hadn't taken him long to get over her. 'Nope. This case I was working has got to me, is all.'

'The website stuff?'

'Yeah.'

'What about it? You may as well tell us. Got nothing else to do.'

Devin handed Chris a joint. She passed it on without taking a drag. 'Okay.' She ran through it, Jeanie interrupting every so often to ask for clarification. It was easy to forget how embedded she was in the case; easy to forget that just because she'd thought of little else for the last six weeks, a lot of this information was new to her audience. The thing that got them the most was the child abuse allegation – that got *everyone* the most. Mack handed her another beer as she went through Rainbowbrite's red dress revelation and Warren K. Delaney's confession.

'And you're thinking they got the wrong guy?' Jeanie asked.

'He confessed, but the facts don't add up. Cops are looking for corroborating evidence, but if you ask me I reckon they just want this off their slate.'

'So Teddy was headed for Colorado?' Michael said out of the blue. She wasn't aware he'd been listening.

'Yeah. Least, that's what we're thinking. Friend of his had given him a lead on some construction work out there.'

'And he ended up in Minnesota.'

'Yeah. Place called Millar Town.'

Michael took out his smartphone, tapped something into it. He was adept with it – another surprise. Paula and Jeanie were stuck firmly in the eighties and could barely send a text without making a song and dance about it. 'Millar Town's a helluva distance from where he was headed.'

'The smart killers dump their victims across state lines, don't they?' This from Devin.

Michael was on a roll: 'Lot of trucking routes run from NYC through there. Hubs around Chicago and Michigan 'specially. You said he was a faggot who used to sell sex?'

Chris should pull him up on the F-word – decided to let it go. For now. He probably didn't know or care that it was pejorative. 'Info's sketchy on that.'

'If Teddy had a history of doing that kinda thing, he might've been a lot lizard.'

'A what?'

'A whore who works the truck stops. That's what they're called. Female ones anyway.'

'Way to keep it classy, Mike,' Paula said.

'I used to be a trucker. Some of those stops, they were crawling with whores. If you were into killing and shit you could pick one up easy. Just sayin'.'

Paula gave him a look. '*Okay.*'

'Hey, I'm not a saint, but I'm not a violent son of a bitch. You know that.' He turned back to Chris. 'Where in Colorado?'

'Township called Superior.'

'Uh-huh.'

Jeanie lit up a Merit, adding to the haze in the room. 'The guy who confessed, did he say why he—'

'This might be nothing,' Michael interrupted. 'But if someone told me they were from Superior, first place I'd think they meant was Wisconsin. Could Teddy have got it wrong? Mixed it up? Like, everyone knows Superior, Wisconsin, right? That's just across from Minnesota.'

Chris stared at him. 'That's a good point.'

'Yeah, it's kinda obvious.' It was oddly reassuring that his snark hadn't disappeared entirely. 'You said one of the theories is that the killer had local knowledge. Superior is only a three-hour drive max from where they found the body. That any good to you?'

'Maybe.' That caffeine thrill was back, she handed Jeanie her beer and spun the chair. Jeanie didn't try and stop her.

'Hey!' Michael called as she reached the door. 'How did you really end up in that thing?'

She looked over her shoulder. 'C'mon, Paula must have told you by now.'

Paula gave her a wicked grin. 'Nope. That'd spoil my fun.'

'Heard you used to race. That how you got hurt?'

'That would make a good story, right? Heroic stock car driver, battling a long-term rival, takes it too far, crashes.' *Locks herself in a trailer, runs a website for the dead.*

'That what happened?'

'Nope. You really want to hear?'

'Yeah.'

'Used to drive a limo in the city. I was heading home after dropping this high roller off at McCarran, got T-boned by a bunch of stoner kids in a pick-up. Woke up in ICU.'

'That the truth?'

'Yeah.'

'That sucks.'

'Tell me about it.'

'Those kids get hurt too?'

'Nope. They all walked away from the scene.'

Ratking1: Hey Scott gonna say it again. I'm sorry. You're right. I'm confrontational, a hard ass, a total bitch

Ratking1: Always been like it

Ratking1: Hope Kelly is okay

Ratking1: Have new info that Teddy might have been headed for Superior Wisconsin. Now we know the dress was red, it might narrow the search field? Long shot, but hey

Ratking1: Haven't told Rainbowbrite yet. Think she goes to bed at like, 9pm

Ratking1: That's why I'm telling you. Not just that. Also wanted to apologise

Ratking1: Get that you don't want to be involved in this anymore & don't blame you. But wanted you to know

Ratking1: Okay. I've started looking. Nothing yet

Ratking1: Don't blame you for the silence. I'd cut me out of my life too

Aqualung: www.facebook.com/helpfindJenni

Rainbowbrite

She was up and reaching for the receiver before the phone had rung out twice. Noah groaned and put a pillow over his head. Five a.m. – still dark outside. She knew who was calling before Chris even said hello.

As usual, Chris got straight into it: 'Get online.'

'Why?'

'Do it.'

Ellie didn't bother with a robe or slippers, padded down into the kitchen and fired up her laptop in nothing but her sleeping shorts and tee. It seemed to take forever to shimmy into life. 'Shall I wake Shaun?'

'Have a look at what I've sent you first. How's he doing?'

She opened her email. 'Good, I think. Yesterday we went to . . .' She clicked on the link, a website for a missing girl from Superior, Wisconsin. 'Jennifer Alice Kastriber, missing since October 1994. Help Bring Jenni Home'. A photograph of a girl with straight blonde hair, a wide mouth and small white teeth. A tug of recognition – she'd seen this page before; must've floated into one of her Facebook feeds at some stage. 'What's this?'

'Scroll down.'

Midway down the page was another photograph: Jennifer in a red dress, next to a spotty guy in a tux mugging at the camera. 'Our Beloved Prom Queen & Lady in Red.' Her heart stuttered.

'Well? Is it the dress?'

Ellie zoomed in. The shape was the same – that boned bodice and full skirt was branded on her brain. The corsage was pinned at the exact place where she discovered the pinprick holes. There was no doubt. 'It's the dress.'

'How sure are you?'

'Hundred percent.'

'Good.'

'How did you find it?'

'I didn't. Scott – Aqualung did. Got a tip that Teddy may have been headed for Superior, Wisconsin, and coupled with the new info that the dress was red, it gave us a narrower field to search. Said he kept putting it into Google images till he hit on it.'

'I checked that area so many *times*.' She didn't admit that she'd seen the page before. Didn't make the connection, didn't recall looking at all of the photos and if she had, at that stage she was fixated on the dress being pink.

'It's a win for you guys. Team Dress hit it out of the park.'

'Have you told the county?'

Five seconds of dead air. Did Chris even *breathe*? 'No.'

'Why?'

'We should work it first.'

'*Really?*'

'Yeah. Check it out before we pass it on.'

Ellie wasn't about to argue. 'Could this . . . do you think this proves Delaney is lying? We know he lied about the dress.'

'Not necessarily. Could be that he picked Jennifer up, killed her, kept the dress as a trophy, staged Teddy's scene with it. We don't know for sure.'

'Except he said Teddy was wearing the dress when he picked him up.'

'Yeah. That doesn't add up, unless Teddy got it from Jennifer, or she got rid of it and he bought it from a thrift store or something. Says on the page they don't know where she was headed when she left. Could've gone to NYC for all we know. The cops didn't look into it, treated her as a runaway.'

'Did she take the dress with her when she left?'

'It doesn't say.'

'But in any case JT and Teddy's friends were adamant he wasn't into drag or cross-dressing.'

'Exactly. That's why I'm saying we should work it. Whoever killed Teddy might have a connection to Jennifer.'

She couldn't keep still. 'Like a family member or friend or something?'

'Long shot, but yeah. So I've looked on the voter registry. The girl's mother, Linda Kastriber, is registered at an address in Superior. That's not too far from you, right?'

'Right.'

'What vehicle you got?'

'Huh?'

'What car you got?'

'A people carrier. Why?'

Ratking1: Hey Scott. Want to go to Wisconsin?

MissingLinc#TeddyRyan

Rainbowbrite, Ratking, Wicklowboy, You

Rainbowbrite:
OMG bobbie We've found the dress!!!! Or we think we have. It looks like a match to me & Aqualung & it belongs to a girl who went missing from Superior WN. 9.11AM

You sure it's the dress?????? 9.11AM

Rainbowbrite:
I've sent you the link. I'd know that dress ANYWHERE!!! So if Warren K Delaney is lying then the killer could be linked to this girl 9.11AM

You told the cops? 9.11AM

Rainbowbrite:
Not yet. Going to follow it up first. And listen to this!! Chris & Aqualung are flying to Duluth to meet us on Fri & we're going to see Mrs Kastriber the next day & talk to her!!! 9.12AM

WOW. You're getting the team together in person, huh? 9.12AM

Rainbowbrite
LOL yes!! WISH you could be with us
9.12AM

Me too ☹ @Ratking RE the cops, you okay not giving them a heads up Chris? 9.12AM

Ratking
My idea. You reckon that could backfire on us? 9.13AM

My cop hat says you should let them know. But can't see the harm in it if you're careful. Go for it! 9.13AM

Rainbowbrite
Knew you'd agree!! You sure you can't fly down? Won't be the same without you 9.14AM

Will be there in spirit 9.14AM

Bobbiecowell

'You sure you don't want me to take you to the airport?' Margie, business-suited and booted, leaned against the bedroom door, watching as he zipped up his bag.

'I'm sure. Got a good deal on long-term parking. You've got to get to work.'

'Well, call me when you land.'

'I will. You gotta meet Millet one day. Hey, how about I invite him for the wedding?'

'We're having a wedding now?'

'If you want one.'

'Is this a proposal?'

Why not? 'If it was, what would you say?'

'I'd say let's discuss it when you get home.'

'That isn't a "no", right?'

'That isn't a no.'

'I'm going to miss you, hon.' The catch in his voice sounded genuine. Maybe it was. 'Better say bye to Tash.'

She took his hand as he passed, squeezed it, whispered, 'Love you.'

He knocked on Tasha's door, opened it to find her perched on the bed in her usual prissy fashion, waiting for him. He sat next to her. 'Want anything from Wisconsin?'

A hug would be too much to expect, but she gave him a smile, leaned in close and whispered, 'Bye, Bobbiecowell.'

She'd done it again, given him the mental equivalent of slipping on ice. He wasn't sharp enough to fake a denial.

'It *is* you. I *knew* it.'

'How?'

'It was *easy*. So like I knew you were messaging with someone called Ellen and there was an article about Missing–Linc and she was in it and said she used the name Rainbowbrite, which I still think is lame. And Cowell is Ted Bundy's first surname and his grandfather who was like, really evil was called Robert Samuel and Bobbie is short for Robert. Is that where you got it?'

'You're too smart, Tasha.'

'You say you're a cop on the site.'

'Yeah. I know. My bad.'

'Why? That's lying.'

Pointless to deny it. 'It is.'

'And Bobbiecowell said it was a serial killer all along. You were right. You *lied* to me.'

'Not cool. But hey, if I said I thought it was a serial killer, you'd have bust me straight away. Figured it out.'

'So?'

'So where's the fun in that? You got there in the end.'

She smiled. 'It *was* fun.'

'We'll hang out when I get back, okay?'

'Okay.'

'And you have any problems, you call me anytime.'

'I don't have any problems.'

'If you just want to talk then.'

'Kay. Bye.'

Dismissed.

A final kiss from Margie and then he was on his way, the Glock in the glove box, the dress in the back.

Ratking 1

She hadn't flown since the accident, expected it to be a nightmare. It wasn't, even taking into account an hour's layover in Minneapolis and a delay while she was transferred from the aisle chair to her own. Despite the short notice she'd secured the wide aisle seat; seemed like no one felt like heading to Duluth in early December. She'd shelved the attitude and buttered up the pre-board staff to ensure she wasn't stranded on board waiting for her chair to arrive, and it helped that she was accompanied by a guy who looked like he headed up an outlaw motorcycle gang. Scott was still being borderline monosyllabic. She'd apologised as soon as he arrived to collect her for the drive to McCarran, but he refused to be drawn into anything personal: wouldn't talk to her about anything other than the case. The distance between them was growing; they might as well be two businesspeople off on a work junket.

A bathroom break – she'd been holding it in for hours, hadn't dared drink or eat anything on the plane – and then she and Scott headed through to arrivals. She scanned the crowd, spotted Ellie straightaway, next to a skinny guy in an orange puffer. Shaun. There was a ghost of a resemblance to his uncle, but that was it. Ellie's eyes skated over them, but Shaun ducked under the barrier and came straight up to her. 'Chris?'

Chris grinned: 'You got it.' How in the hell had he known it was her? Wasn't as if she was wearing a name badge, and she was careful not to plaster pictures all over social media. Before she could grill him, Scott introduced himself, and Ellie approached, pink-cheeked, wide-eyed.

'Chris? You're . . . Why didn't you *tell* me?'

Chris had never actually seen anyone goggle before. 'Tell you what?'

Ellie flapped at the chair. 'That you were . . .'

'Never came up.'

'That's why you asked what kind of car I've got?'

'Chair's lightweight, we can manage. Aren't you going to say hi to your dress buddy?'

'Oh! Of course.' She gazed up at Scott. 'You found the dress! I'd seen that page before, but it didn't sink in, you were so right about not being hung up on the colour.'

'Wouldn't have known what to look for if it weren't for all your research.'

'Oh bless you for saying that. I found a motel and I hope you like it and I booked for two nights like you asked, Chris. I got a family room and I packed some food for tonight, it's nothing fancy but we should be okay and—'

'Ellie? Chill.' Chris turned to Shaun who was hanging back, hugging himself. 'She always like this?'

'I don't mind it, she's grand.'

Ellie shook her head. 'I talk too much when I'm nervous.'

They were clogging up the walkway. A couple of passing seniors tutted and shot Scott vicious glances. 'There's nothing to be nervous about. Shall we get this show on the road?'

Wicklowboy22

Ellie hadn't stopped talking and fussing since they'd arrived in their 'family suite'. It wasn't much to look at – a small kitchenette with a fridge that let out a gasp every so often, two double beds in one room, a pair of bunk beds in the other. '. . . Chris you'll have to have one of the doubles. There is enough room in here, isn't there? Shaun and I can share or we could do girls in one room, boys in another.' It was clear she was digging for details about Chris and Scott's relationship. There was something there, Shaun was certain of that, but they rarely shared eye contact.

'Fine by me either way,' Scott said.

'But we have to decide. I don't know where to put my bag. Shall we vote on it?'

'Oh Christ no,' Chris said. 'Boys in one room, girls in another.'

Shaun hadn't slept in the same room as someone else since he was a child. Brendan didn't count – what they got up to in his small room above the shop couldn't be termed 'sleeping'. He should be twitchier about it. Scott – Aqualung – looked like he could eat Johnny for breakfast.

'Dibs on top bunk,' Scott said, deadpan.

Before Ellie could let loose with another stream of nonsense, Chris said: 'We got to have a game plan for tomorrow. Think about what to say to Mrs Kastriber.'

'We're not going to tell her the truth?'

'As it stands, all Jennifer's mother knows is that we want to help track down her daughter. Haven't mentioned the connection to Teddy yet.'

'Shouldn't we? Won't she think it's weird if she's seen the site?'

'That's the thing, picture of the dress is buried deep. We haven't put out that we think it's red. You got to remember, she thinks her daughter is missing. Linking her to Teddy,' a glance at Shaun, 'who we know is deceased, could be hard to hear. What do you think, Shaun?'

He blinked, taken off guard to be asked. He was quieter than the others; they were all people with their volumes turned high, and he'd assumed he would fade into the background. 'She'll find out eventually, but I think you're right. It's kinder not to say that until we know for sure.'

Scott was watching him. 'Man. I could listen to you talk all goddamned day.'

'Oh I *know*,' Ellie said. 'I could too. I'm always saying that to Noah.'

Chris caught Shaun's eye, rolled her own. 'Okay. Back to business. If Teddy's killer is someone connected to her daughter, we know they had local knowledge. We should cross-check to see if any of her friends or family are connected to the area where Teddy was found.'

Scott nodded. 'Yup. Get a list of her friends, classmates, exes; go from there. A yearbook would be a good plan.'

Antsy from the intensity in the room, he eyed the door. Ellie, attuned to him, mouthed to the others: 'He wants to have a cigarette.'

'It's not a crime, Ellie,' Chris said.

'I'll only be a minute.' He was already zipping up the mad, tangerine jacket.

'Make sure you wear your scarf,' Ellie said. 'And tuck it in.'

The air greeted him with its usual slap in the face. The door opened out onto a walkway, which ran parallel to a parking lot. Beyond it was a foggy tree-lined smear that supposedly led down to the edge of the lake. It was hard to tell. The light was dimming now, fat snowflakes falling lazily onto the cars directly in front of him. An L-shaped diner was carbuncled onto the motel, its windows misty with steam, customers ghosting back and forth within. He lit up, shook out his hands. Breathed in.

'Give me a drag.'

He turned to see Chris emerging through the door, which was only marginally wide enough for the chair. He'd wanted some alone time to digest the situation, but curiously, his heart didn't sink at the sight of her. He handed her the cigarette.

'Don't tell Ellie. Can't have her giving both of us lectures about cancer.'

'She's okay.'

'She is.' She shivered, took a drag, expelled the smoke out of her nose like Johnny was wont to do. 'Always think these things are going to warm you up, but they never do.'

She handed it back, assessed him. 'How did you know it was me at the airport? You found a pic of me online or something?'

Shaun considered the question, relieved that he hadn't inherited the Ryan propensity to show every emotion on his skin. The truth was, he didn't know. Something about how her online voice reflected in her eyes maybe. 'I don't know. I just did. Is that mad?'

'Totally.'

She wasn't a talker like Ellie, but he didn't feel the need to search around for something to say. Comfortable. Even Scott reminded him of Neil from the guards, unflappable, phlegmatic, a kindness to him beneath the bulk and the leathers. Natural inclination to distance himself aside, the whole thing was *too* comfortable.

'See you still haven't joined the site.'

'No.' It had been a while since she'd encouraged him to do so.

'You weren't lying about not being a team player.'

'No.'

'I'm not much of one either. I'm a borderline shut-in. A hoarder, without, you know, all the shit.'

He laughed. 'This is easier than I thought it would be. With all of you I mean. I'm not usually great with strangers.'

'We're not really strangers though, are we?'

Then he got it, the reason why he was so at ease around them. 'You're all like you are online. In real life I mean.'

Chris blinked, cocked her head. 'Yeah. You know what? You're right.' She waved for the cigarette. 'One more drag then I'm done.'

Bobbiecowell

The call came in as he was pulling into a rest stop, the phone dancing on the passenger seat, the ID flashing 'Margie'. He was due a break. The jittery, artificial buzz from the Waklert tablets was wearing off, and he was close to crashing. If he didn't pace himself, take a power-nap, he was liable to run the truck off the road. With no snow tyres, and the weather turning, he'd need his wits about him.

Taking a sip of Coke to blast the fog out of his voice, he made himself smile. 'Hey. I was just about to call you.'

'Tasha knows.'

'Knows what?'

'About the pregnancy. Gary told her.'

This news slapped him fully alert. 'You told Gary about it?'

'I know we were planning on waiting until the second trimester, but he was being his usual asshole self and it just came out.'

'She okay? How did she take it?'

'She was better than okay. Says she can't wait to tell her friends she's going to have a baby brother or sister.' That didn't sound like the Tash he knew. 'How about we fly down and meet you? We can spend Sunday together.'

'I'd love that, hon, but Millet's not in a good place. Fact that I've got my life on track is kinda bringing it home to him that his is a total mess. Tell you what, how about I cut short the trip? We can have a celebration when I get back.'

'You sure?'

'Course. Millet will understand. Hey, can I talk to Tash?'

'She's with her dad. Where are you?'

'Huh?'

'I can hear traffic.'

'Me and Millet are thinking of heading up to Silver Lake. I'm en route to pick him up. If you can't get hold of me it's cos I'm on the slopes.'

'Oh that sounds like fun. We'll have to go skiing one day.'

'We will.' He pictured himself picking out a snowboard with Tasha, lounging in a high-end chalet, sipping hot chocolate and playing board games. The baby – *his* baby – wasn't included in this little scene of privileged family bliss. When he thought about it at all, all that came up was a nebulous, sexless blob. Keeping it at a distance, not letting it become real to him, was a calculated defence mechanism.

There was nothing stopping him turning around. Now Rainbowbrite and the gang were on the Kastriber trail, his options were narrowing, but it wasn't too late. *Push-pull, push-pull.*

Rainbowbrite

'You think this will be enough?' Ellie stood back and evaluated the spoils she and Shaun had bought from Costco en route to the airport: tubs of slaw, a cooked chicken, cranberry juice, three types of pie and an assortment of chips. 'I wasn't sure what to get, or if you or Scott were vegetarians or whatever.'

'It's more than enough,' Chris said. 'Don't let anyone tell you you can't organise an outing.'

Ellie had to keep reminding herself not to stare – Chris had one of those faces that swung from stunning to plain in a heartbeat, and she envied her relaxed attitude to her appearance. No make-up, her hair couldn't have seen a pair of scissors for years, and her clothes could have fallen out of the eighties – although her sweat pants and leather jacket wouldn't keep out the cold.

'Ask them,' Chris said.

'Ask what?'

'All the questions. I can see you want to.'

She was right. *How did you end up in the chair? Are you and Scott together? How long have you been disabled?* She settled on the most pressing: 'Why *didn't* you tell me? I mean, not that you should have to, it doesn't matter, of course it doesn't matter, it's just that we were friends, I mean we are friends.'

'Didn't tell you because it didn't come up. Next?'

'You and Scott. Are you . . .'

'Together? Nope.'

'He's such a big man, isn't he?'

'You wondering if I can have sex?'

'*No*. Of course not.' But she was. Cue a flush of blood to her cheeks.

'I can. And I do.' Chris smiled. 'You done?'

'Yes.'

'Good. My turn. You still think we're doing the right thing? Coming here, going to talk to Mrs Kastriber? Not going straight to the cops?'

'Definitely.' She *was* sure. Commander Stillson's 'Doe Nuts' swipe still stung. 'And Bobbie agreed, didn't he?'

'Okay. Hold that thought. Need a bathroom break. Too much coffee.'

Ellie bit back the instinctive (and patronising): 'Do you need any help?'

She sent Noah a message letting him know they were here safe, then gave Sherry a quick call to check on the boys. She was hanging up when a Facebook friend request and DM from someone called 'Tasha W' pinged in: **<Hi ellen caine can I talk to you about something? It says in your profile you're Rainbowbrite from Missing-Linc>**

Ellie checked out Tasha's wall. There wasn't much there, other than a link to a GoFundMe, pictures of kittens and a series of screenshots from *Teen Titans Go!*, one of the boys' favourite shows. A child? **<How old are you honey?>**

<9>

<Does your mom know you're messaging me?>

<No but she won't care. Are you the ellen who was talking to my mom's boyfriend he uses the name bobbiecowell>

Bobbiecowell had a *girlfriend*? He'd never mentioned that. He said he barely left the house. It couldn't be him. **<We talking about the same Bobbie Cowell? Real name Mark Starmer?>**

<his name is pete kazinski not mark>

Pete? The girl couldn't have it right. **<ARE YOU SURE HES BOBBIE COWELL?>** She pressed send before she realised she'd accidentally put caps lock on. **<sorry, didn't mean to shout ☹>**

<I'm sure I've been trying to figure out who he is for ages and I know because of Ted bundy we went to his house and ted bundy

used to live near us in Tacoma and like ted bundy's granddad's real name is robert Sammy cowell and I figured it out & he admitted it and you should know that he's lying he's not a cop like he says he's like a handyman or something & he's always saying that your username is lame>

Ellie paced to the window, looked outside to where Scott and Shaun were walking across the parking lot, returning from a coffee run at the diner. They paused for Shaun to light a cigarette. Ellie had never smoked in her life, but she could use something to calm herself down right now. She'd need to check out Tasha's story, look deeper into Mark Starmer's life, but she already knew what she'd find. Tasha's messages had the ring of truth to them.

<Why are you telling me this honey?>

<because he & my mom lied & they're having a baby & didn't tell me & I hate them so much & you should know. He admitted it to me also & said he lied & that he pretended to be a cop because it was fun>

Lord alive. Be a responsible adult. **<Have you spoken to your mom about this?>**

<no I'm at my dad's house. Are you going to punish pete for lying?>

'What's up?' Chris had returned.

'Nothing.'

'Bullshit. You look like you've seen a ghost.'

'Bobbiecowell isn't Bobbiecowell.'

'O*kay*. You want to elaborate on that?'

No. But she did, for once keeping the babbling and prevarication to a minimum.

'You sure this kid isn't bullshitting you?'

'Why would she do that?'

'People are weird.'

She could scour social media later to confirm it. 'I feel so dumb.' Worse than that. Betrayed and bone-deep embarrassed. 'I trusted him. He said he was shot in the line of duty. He showed me an article about it – I told you about it, remember? He even showed me the scar from where he was shot.'

'You looked this Pete . . . what's the name again?'

'Kazinski. Peter Kazinski.'

'You looked for him on Facebook?'

'Not yet. He said he wasn't on social media, but that could be a lie too. I checked him *out*, Chris.' A whoop as a text came in. Speak of the devil. **<You there yet? ☺>** 'He's just sent me a message. Should I tell him we know he's a faker?'

'No. Let him sweat.'

'Are you going to block him from the site?'

'We've got more important things to think about. Look, don't beat yourself up, he took me in too. After the JT thing I practically thought he was Jesus. Shaun did too.'

'Should we tell Shaun and Scott?'

'Better confirm it first. Also, do we really want to distract them from what we're doing here? One thing at a time.'

Chris was right. 'You suspected he was catfishing us weeks and weeks ago and you only let that go because I told you I'd checked him out.'

'It's not that big of a deal, Ellie. So he hoodwinked you. All of us. So what? That's basically the internet for you. Long as you didn't give him your bank details and he's not trying to steal your identity, what you're dealing with here is some sad fu— some sad asshole who wants to make himself look good on a forum. You tell him things about yourself you shouldn't?'

'There are no things.'

'Like I said, don't sweat it. It's happened to all of us. Most users on the site think I'm a man – Mommydearest still does for all I know. We got to prioritise. We can deal with him after this.'

'But he knows what we're doing. He could go to another site, give them our info. He could tell the cops that we're looking into this ourselves.'

'Why would he? He's played along this far. Gets off on us all thinking he's some big NYPD hero and we value his opinion.'

'Maybe.'

'Okay then, string him along. Don't let on that we know he's bullshitting. That way he's got no reason to screw us, right?'

'Right. Unless Tasha tells him she's told us.'

'Ask her to keep it to herself until we're done here.'

'She's a child. I can't ask her to lie.'

'It's just until tomorrow, Ellie.'

It didn't sit right with her, but she did it anyway: **<Can you keep this to yourself for now honey? Just till we figure out what to do?>**

<Okay. You mean don't tell pete?>

<Unless it makes you feel uncomfortable and then you must tell an adult. I don't want you to do anything that makes you feel bad. Okay?>

<Okay. I don't feel bad>

The late-night chats, the thrill she'd felt in the early days whenever he sent her a message. It made her feel sick to her stomach. Fingers trembling with anger, she wrote back to Bobbie: **<All good! Tired having an early night>**

Bobbiecowell

He'd parked between a pair of snow-shrouded SUVs twenty yards down from Jennifer's lot, run the engine every so often to keep the truck's temperature above freezing. Jennifer's mother hadn't moved on; still lived four lots down from the house where Teddy Ryan bled out into the basement. His stepfather's old place had been reshingled, revamped, remodelled. In contrast, the Kastriber house was running to seed. Its yard was the only one that hadn't been cleared of snow, and the peeling paint added to the pall of depression hanging over it. It was almost as if it were stuck in time, waiting for something to happen. *Well, here it comes. The wait's over.*

If someone asked him what the hell he thought he was doing, sitting in a van out in these temperatures, he wasn't sure what he'd say: *'Don't panic, ma'am. I'm a cop on a stakeout.'* The buzz from the pills had made way for a zen-like state where anything felt possible. *Past Pete. New Pete.* The two were converging, and he'd given up attempting to stop it.

Five a.m. His personal witching hour. It was around this time that he'd delivered the fatal blow to Teddy; it was near enough this time when he'd dragged Jennifer to her forever home. *A covert killing.* Keeping the victim at a distance. Not overt, like Teddy's had been. Jennifer Kastriber, aka The Girl in the Dress. Like Teddy, she had a grace about her, a fluidity and confidence that infested every movement. You couldn't fake that – only he'd tried, hadn't he? Tried for years. He knew she knew he watched her sometimes.

The last time he'd thought about her – *really* thought about her – was in that sterile clinical room. He had hours to kill, a quick reminisce wouldn't hurt – would it? Back he went, circling the memories like a shark, not quite sure where to start. Flashed on that night, senior prom, when it had begun:

. . . warm inside from the bourbon Jason Pickett's smuggled in, he watches as she and Kevin pose for their 'King and Queen' couple's shot, Kevin making devil horn hands, Jennifer pouting. A red Audrey Hepburn dress, a bright pink corsage, that smile. Watching again, later, as their body language changes, Kevin dragging her into a corner, the silent film of a fight playing out. Jennifer whirling away, giving Kevin the finger, running outside, infected with the drama of it, enjoying it.

Following her outside, the glint of her cigarette, heart in his mouth, saying: 'You okay?'

Eyes glazed with alcohol, stumbling on her heels. 'What's it to you?'

'Hey, I'm just checking to see if you're okay.'

'Were you spying on me?'

'No.'

'Yeah you were. You're such a freak, Pete. You know that? You're a loser. You'll always be a loser. Everyone says you're a fucking fag.' A triumphant grin, then: 'Why don't you just fucking die?'

Up he came, shuddered, cranked up the heat. Even now, now that she was gone, now that he was New Pete, middle-aged, all grown up, he could still feel the hole she'd punched in his gut that evening. She'd meant it. She was drunk, but she meant it. It had poisoned him. No amount of *just words, they're just words* could wash that away. Then, three months later, fate intervened:

. . . that middle-of-the-night hush, snow freezing into diamonds, that hush where you believe everything is possible, like it's a do-over. All the smog and the sorrow gone. Pulling over to swill mouthwash and erase the scent of smoke and booze, back from an all-nighter, a party he'd crashed with Jason, playing Russian roulette with a DUI.

Coming towards him, dragging a suitcase behind her in the snow, stopping every couple of steps. She doesn't see him at first, jumps when he cranks the window.

'Hey.'

'Oh. It's you, Pete.'

'You going somewhere?' trying to sound cool, nonchalant.

'Anywhere but here.'

'Why are you leaving?'

'Asshole my mom's hooked up with. Giving me a hard time.'

'Got the same problem.' He hasn't.

'Just need to get away, you know? Twin Cities maybe. California.'

'You need a ride? I can take you.'

'To California?'

'Whatever you need.' Desperate, too desperate, she's unsure now. 'Hey. We're friends, aren't we?'

Indecision, then she nods. The snow dampening the creak of their footsteps, the crank of the trunk opening. Taking the case from her, heavier than he thought, dropping it, the catch coming open and spilling clothes on the ground, a splash of red fabric like blood in the snow.

'What the fuck, Pete?' Jennifer looking at him as if he's nothing, less than nothing. 'What's wrong with you? You're a loser, a total—'

Lashing out, never thrown a punch before – Christ it hurts – doesn't care, she reels back, disbelieving, clutching her face, eyes wide with fear. He sees it then, the tire iron in the back, chucked it in there after he changed to winter treads, doesn't stop to think, wants her to shut up, shut up, shut up, stop . . .

And then she's on the ground. There's no blood, he only hit her once, it didn't split the skin. Drops the weapon, kneels, snow soaking his jeans.

'Jenni?' Tries to feel for a pulse, fumbles to push up the sleeves of her coat. Can't feel anything. Lifts an eyelid, like he's seen some doctor do on TV. Her face is slack, but she's still alive. She's still breathing.

Now what? They're out in the open, anyone could see, anyone could call the cops, call, 'Hey! What's going on out there?' Just him and Jenni in the snow.

He's calm, calmer than he should be. The cushion on the back seat. The one his mom uses when she drives. He collects it, returns, places it over her face, pressing down. Straddling her chest, breasts squashed against his thighs . . .

A car door slammed, slapping him awake. The thrill of revisiting Jennifer's last moments had been snuffed out by exhaustion. He'd slept – but for how long? Stiff-necked, disorientated, he looked up.

And then he saw them: Rainbowbrite, as puffy and colourful as her pics on Facebook, climbing out of her Mom-mobile. Then came a smaller figure who had to be Shaun, little Shaun, dwarfed in an orange puffer jacket, face hidden by a trapper hat and scarf. No sign of Ratking, other than a bob of grey hair on the back seat. He hadn't counted on the giant, some Neanderthal throwback in leathers and boots, a long ZZ Top beard rounding out the biker cliché. *Aqualung.*

They were in the middle of a conflab of some sort. He couldn't make out what they were saying – wouldn't be able to, not unless he wanted to wind down the window, risk drawing attention to himself. The big guy leaned into the car, said something, then climbed back into the front seat.

Pete reached for the phone, typed in: **<Hey! How's it going? Have you spoken to Jennifer's family yet? Thinking I might come and meet you guys after all!!!!>** Rainbowbrite had been lax on the updates, and he'd been too busy driving to nudge her. He watched as she checked her phone, frowned, then tucked it back into her pocket. That wasn't like her, but then she did have her hands full ferrying her motley crew of misfits around. He sank back in his seat and watched as Rainbowbrite and Shaun headed up the stairs and into the house. Maybe he'd have more luck with Chris.

MissingLinc#TeddyRyan

Rainbowbrite, Ratking, Wicklowboy, You

Know you guys must be busy but let me know if I can help. Could even be on skype while you talk to Mrs Kastriber if you like?
8.30AM

Ratking
Got it under control thanks 08.31AM

Bet it's cold there for you Chris after Nevada!! 08.31AM

Ratking
Yeah 08.31AM

Okay well let me know if you need me 08.32AM

Wicklowboy22

The wall was a shrine to the missing girl, an age progression that stopped with an airbrushed, gold-framed portrait of Jennifer in her prom dress. Ellie hadn't taken her eyes off it since they'd arrived, and was far more subdued and circumspect than he'd seen her before. Perhaps she was stymied by Mrs Kastriber's grief, which hummed out of the woman's skin like radiation.

'She didn't tell any of her friends where she was going. When she didn't come home, I asked and asked them.' A tissue kept clamped in a fist at all times, Mrs Kastriber's voice and eyes had a tranquilised flatness to them; the story of her daughter's disappearance had the ring of being told too many times, as if it was a piece of clothing worn out from too many washes. '. . . the cops didn't do nothing on account of the note she left. They said she was a runaway. You want to see it?'

When Ellie didn't answer, Shaun said: 'That would be helpful. Thank you.'

The woman struggled up from the chair and left the room, taking some of the pain with her. Ellie seemed to visibly relax. 'I feel so bad for her.'

Shaun was feeling worse than that. If anything, he was getting imposter syndrome. His loss was nothing compared to this woman's. There was no shrine to Teddy back in Ireland, Eileen only had the one photograph; Donny had locked his away in a safe.

Mrs Kastriber returned. 'I didn't ask if you wanted coffee.'

'We're grand thank you.'

'Ireland . . .' She looked into the distance. 'I forgot. Did you say you live here now?'

'Just visiting.'

She looked to Ellie. 'And you're the one who wrote to me?'

Ellie cleared her throat. 'That was Chris. The one who runs the site? She wanted to come today but she's . . . she's in a wheelchair and with the steps up to the house, we didn't, she couldn't . . . she's in the car.'

It wasn't clear if Mrs Kastriber was taking this in. 'Here.' She placed the note on the coffee table in front of them, arranging it carefully as if it was a priceless artefact. To her, it was. The paper was soft, folded many times. There was a scrawled shopping list at the top – 'milk, soda, eggs, cat litter' – and below it: 'Hi mom, I got to get away from here. It isn't cos of you. I'm sorry and you mustn't worry about me. I love you don't be mad will call soon xxx'.

'She didn't say where she was going. That's all she left. Took some money out of my housekeeping and off she went. I looked for her so *hard*. I asked all her friends if they knew where she might have gone. Everyone I could think of. No one could help me.'

Mrs Kastriber was running out of steam. It would be cruel to stay much longer. Shaun needed to step up. 'On the website, there was a boy in the prom photo.'

'Oh. That's Kevin. They were so cute together. They dated all through high school, broke up just after prom night.'

'Does he live locally?'

'Married now. Two kids. I can't even pass them by without . . .' her hand tightened around the tissue. 'That was the last photo we have of her.'

Ellie came to life. 'Did she take it with her? The dress I mean. It's so pretty and I wondered if maybe she took it.'

Shaun waited for Mrs Kastriber to question this subject jump. She didn't. There was no easy way to say: *my murdered uncle was found wearing your missing daughter's prom dress*. Saving her from learning about the link was the right decision.

'She did. It was her favourite. She bought it from a thrift store, and we fixed it up together. She looked so beautiful that night. She took all of her favourite things.'

Seconds passed while they all stared up at Jennifer. 'It would be helpful if we could talk to her friends,' Ellie said at last.

'Most have moved away. You want a list?'

'Thank you.'

'Do you have a yearbook we could borrow?'

'I'll need it back.'

'I'll bring it back tomorrow before we leave, I promise.'

'You think you can find her? She's been on lots of websites, we had lots of sightings at first. Then nothing. No one cares any more.'

'We'll do our very best for you. We've found people before. Shaun's uncle went missing and we . . .' Ellie's voice trailed off as it hit home where this could lead.

Mrs Kastriber turned her numb gaze to Shaun. 'Did you find him?'

'Yes.' What else was there to say?

Ratking1

<Gotta go>

She swiped the phone to silent, and chucked it onto the seat next to her. Bobbiecowell. Catfishing asswipe. She should have looked into him herself, but then again, she'd had no reason to. It was he who'd suggested the GoFundMe, and he'd backed her up during the shaky JT business. So he'd lied about being a cop – big deal. She'd lied about a lot of stuff – well, not lied exactly; omitted things.

She shivered. Nothing she'd brought with her was up to the job of coping with sub-zero temperatures, and Ellie had insisted Chris borrow one of her gaudy jackets. It smelled of lavender body spray and was embellished with embroidered flowers. Everything Ellie wore was decorated with beads or crystals or something: *Rainbowbrite*. Shaun was right on the money there; they all wore their alter egos on their sleeves. Except for Bobbiecowell – probably.

Scott's only concession to the climate was a leather jacket that creaked when he moved. They hadn't spoken since Ellie and Shaun disappeared into the house. He'd been generous about hiding his reticence; the others hadn't picked up on it, and she hadn't given up hope that she could heal the rift. Last night, as they sat around making game plans and working their way through the mountain of snack foods Ellie had brought along, he seemed to thaw a little towards her. And now they were alone; she should take advantage of this.

'You didn't need to stay here with me,' she said to the back of his head.

'It's cool. We could've helped you up there.'

'Yeah. You really couldn't.' Her heart had sunk when she'd taken in the narrow steps leading up to the door, glinting with a skin of ice, but it was probably for the best that Shaun and Ellie had gone alone. She'd only caught a glimpse of Mrs Kastriber as the woman opened the door, but it was enough to see that she was fragile, leaking pain, and Chris knew herself well enough to admit she wasn't the best candidate for dealing with emotion. It wasn't a bad thing that Scott had stayed behind either. It was only when you got to know him that his intimidating Hells Angels facade melted to reveal the softy beneath. 'Heard from Kelly?'

'Yeah.'

Silence descended. Ellie and Shaun had been gone for upwards of twenty minutes. 'Are we going to talk about what happened or just dance around it?'

'Nothing to talk about.'

'I'm sorry for what I said.'

'You've already apologised.'

'I'm such an asshole.'

'You're not an asshole. You're annoying and self-obsessed, but you're not . . . No, you're right, you are an asshole.'

She laughed. 'Told you. I'm always right.'

He shifted in the seat and turned to face her. 'The way you are, does it have to do with your mom?'

'A psychologist would say so. Don't want to get too close to anyone for fear of being hurt. Fear of being abandoned.' She'd meant it to sound facetious, but it came out with a ring of truth to it.

'We all got that.'

'Kelly said you used to get sad.'

'Did she?'

'You get depressed?'

'Sometimes. Who doesn't? Went through a bad patch, life wasn't turning out how I hoped it would.'

Despite her lavender layer, the cold was beginning to worm into her marrow. Poor circulation. She shivered again.

'Want me to crank the engine, give us some heat?'

'Can't. Ellie took the keys.'

'Shit. You want my jacket?'

'What's this, chivalry hour?'

'You can if you want. I run hot.' A beat of silence, then he opened the door, and padded around to her side. He climbed in next to her, shrugged along the seat until his thigh met hers and without a word, wrapped his arms around her. She let him.

Bobbiecowell

He'd followed them to the diner, a sad sack of a place tacked onto a motel that promised lake views and didn't deliver. He couldn't resist sitting close enough to eavesdrop, chose a booth one down from theirs and across the aisle.

He couldn't see much of Shaun – he was sitting next to the giant, his back to Pete, and much as he'd wanted to scour the boy's features for that Teddy spark, that would have drawn too much attention. Besides, it was Ratking who'd been the shocker of the day. Chris, the witchy woman in a wheelchair. Rainbowbrite hadn't mentioned *that* interesting nugget. He'd watched her slide into the chair in the parking lot, waving away any offers of help from the others as she humped it over the curb and into the diner.

They were midway through the Mrs Kastriber post-mortem, Shaun's lilting accent rising and falling, humming in with the gruff tones of the fat biker and Rainbowbrite's Minnesota Nice. Shaun, little Shaun, said the least, but whenever he did say something everyone listened, so maybe he did have a seed of Teddy's confidence. Pete doubted it – couldn't imagine the Teddy he'd met hanging out with this bunch of losers. Still, there was a camaraderie between them that he almost envied. He'd never had that. Imagined sliding into the booth, shucking up next to Shaun, saying: 'Hey guys, surprise! It's me, Bobbiecowell, how you all doing?' leaning across the table, sipping crappy coffee and bouncing theories. He checked his phone. Why the hell weren't they filling him in? He was part of the sacred circle of trust, wasn't he? He swiped left, Rainbowbrite had read his latest missives, so had Chris.

He fired off another one. Neither Chris nor Shaun reacted, but Rainbowbrite's pink-cased iPhone trembled on the table, knocking against the yearbook and the ticking time bomb inside it. She reached out a hand to take it, then pulled it back.

'So yeah, let's start with this Kevin guy,' Ratking said in her deep, raspy voice, that despite himself, Pete found pleasing to listen to. 'Then work through her close circle.' Without warning, she looked across at him, catching him staring. For a second, just a second, he was tempted to give her a salute, call: 'Found your mommy yet?' He dropped his eyes, fiddled with his phone.

'The ex is the most likely suspect, I reckon,' the giant rumbled.

'Could be.'

'Or they're not connected at all and it's someone she met along the way,' Rainbowbrite fluttered in, spouting the obvious. 'I wish we knew where she was going. Either someone she knew made her disappear and kept the dress, or she left the area, sold the dress on and someone found or bought it, or they stole it from her, murdered her and kept it as a trophy. So when he ran into Shaun at a later stage—'

'Teddy,' Ratking barked. 'Ran into *Teddy*.'

'Oh my gosh. Sorry, Shaun.'

'It's okay.'

'It's not okay.'

'It is.'

Pete smirked into his mug.

'Let's go back to the room.' This from Ratking. 'Make a game plan. Reckon we should see whoever we can this afternoon. We only got two days.'

It took them a while to get their act together, Shaun and the giant heading out first, and once again depriving Pete of a clear glimpse of the boy's face.

'He's taking the strain,' Ratking said the second Shaun exited.

'I can't believe I called him Teddy.'

'Don't sweat it. It isn't that. He's been down since you spoke to Mrs Kastriber. Plus, he's an introvert. We must be sucking the life out of him.'

'You think?'

'Yeah. We're hardly what you'd call quiet.'

Pete was signalling for the check when Ratking said: 'You still bummed about Bobbiecowell?'

'I couldn't sleep last night, Chris. I still can't believe how he took me in.'

'Shame Mommydearest is out of the loop. He'd unmask him in no time. Asshole wouldn't know what had hit him.'

'He keeps sending us messages.'

'Yeah. Ignore them.'

Guts in his boots, stunned to the point of disorientation, he strained to catch the rest. '. . . I really should talk to Tasha's mom. She shouldn't be contacting strangers on the internet.'

Tasha. The place seemed to shrink; his ears rang.

And there it was: the end of the road.

Rainbowbrite

Chris had commandeered the room's only desk and Ellie's laptop. 'What's the password, Ellie?'

Ellie squirmed. '"FriendshipisMagic".'

Chris was too involved to scoff at this, thank goodness – there was only so much mortification Ellie could deal with for one day. She was still smarting from Bobbiecowell's latest message: **<Hey! Any updates? You spoken to Mrs K? Haven't heard from you for aaaaages ☺>** Just the thought of his deceit brought on another flush of shame at being so goddamned gullible.

'Far as Jennifer's inner circle goes, we got one in Bemidji, two in Duluth and one in St Clair. Scott? Can you and Ellie go through the yearbook, make a list of names from the class of '94?'

'Sure.'

'When you've done that we can start calling round, see if we can set up something this afternoon. Shaun, you okay to help with that?'

Shaun waved his cigarette box. 'Okay to go for a quick ciggy first?'

Ellie didn't bother chiding him. She couldn't be everyone's mom, and Chris was right – Shaun had been quieter, more insular after their meeting with Mrs Kastriber. He needed some alone time. 'Take your time,' Chris said. 'See if you can find the elusive lake if you like. We got this.'

Shaun was still wearing his coat and scarf. 'I won't be long.'

'Want some company?' Scott asked.

'No, you're alright.'

Ellie dragged a chair closer to where Scott was perched on the bed, and together they flipped through pages stuck in time, shivering when she read that Jennifer was listed as 'most likely to make a mark on the world'. She turned to the 'class of '94' and scanned the faces. On the bottom row, beneath a sallow-faced teen with the shadow of a moustache, a name snagged her attention. 'Oh . . . oh.'

Scott looked up. 'What?'

'Peter Kazinski. One of them is called Peter Kazinski.'

Bobbiecowell

He'd parked behind Rainbowbrite's people carrier with its snow tyres and 'My Family' stick person decal on the back window. He'd always hated those things. Why advertise?

He kept the radio on, the volume down low. A distraction, something to ground him, stop him spinning out. He should have seen it coming. Hubris – it was how they all got caught in the end, Tasha's buddy Bundy included. He had to admire the kid for that move. *Well played. Check mate.* He'd known in his gut that her reaction to the pregnancy news was way too sanguine. Holding that back from her had been a mistake. He considered calling her, or Margie – it was only a matter of time before she told her mom about his secret online life. *It's still not too late.* He could manipulate his way out of the situation if he had to. Unless . . . would Tasha have told Rainbowbrite his real name? Maybe, maybe not. His fingers strayed to the ignition, then back to his lap. *Push-pull, push-pull.* Deep down, had he ever *truly* believed it would come to this point?

He could drive away. Disappear. Take whatever he could get out of Margie's account and flee. Or . . .

A door on the ground floor opened, and out he came, ducking his head into his collar to light a smoke. Call it fate. Or chance. Like before. Like before with his uncle and good ol' Jenni from the block. Snuggled in his hat, Shaun hesitated, then started walking towards the scrubby trees that fringed the parking lot, cupping his free hand under an armpit, just like Teddy had done way back when. He walked directly past the truck, close enough that Pete could have reached through the window and snagged his jacket.

What's it gonna be, Pete?

Softly, softly, catchee monkey.

Pete took out the box of Marlboro he'd bought at a 7-Eleven en route just in case, climbed out of the truck, and followed, keeping back, placing his feet into the boy's footprints. Waited until he was ten yards from him, then called: 'Hey! You got a light?'

If he doesn't approach me I'll leave him alone.

Ratking 1

Chris had never truly believed that time slowed down in life-changing moments. When the kids' truck T-boned the limo, her life hadn't flashed before her eyes; she hadn't experienced it in slow-motion clarity. It had been instantaneous, a millisecond of confusion, then nothing. It had changed her life, but like most life-changing moments, it wasn't the stuff of movies: a stock car crash, a plane plummeting from the sky. It was an exercise in how the mundane could fuck you up. But now she was aware of every detail: Ellie's eyes glassy with shock, cheek muscles slackening; the nylon swish of Scott's jeans on the duvet; the dust motes dancing in the light spiking through the window.

She found her voice first. 'We got to get hold of that kid asap. Call her.'

'I don't have the number.'

'Send the kid another message then.'

'Saying what?'

Scott was watching her. Good, steady Scott. 'You want to tell me what's going on?' he asked.

'Bobbiecowell's been catfishing us. His real name is Peter Kazinski.'

'*Shit.* Seriously? Bobbie Cowell from the site?'

'Yeah. It can't be a coincidence.' She turned back to Ellie: 'Ask if Pete Kazinski is originally from Wisconsin. Or Duluth. I dunno, if he comes from this fucking area.'

Ellie's complexion, usually as pink as her jacket, was now white. 'I'll also ask to speak to the girl's mother.'

'Do it.'

Ellie double-thumbed at her iPhone. Seconds later, the whoop of a responding message came in, and Chris released a breath she didn't know she was holding.

'She's asking why.'

'Tell her we think Peter Kazinski might be a dangerous fucker.'

'I can't do that.'

'Okay. Say it's an emergency. No. Ask if he's there and if we can talk to him.'

'Really?'

'Do it.'

Tap, tap, tap. Chris fought the urge to snatch the phone out of her hand, do it herself.

Ellie looked up. 'Oh . . . oh. He's visiting friends in Wisconsin.'

'Did you tell Bobbiecowell where we were staying?'

'No . . . no, but he knew we were seeing Jennifer's mother.'

It was Scott who said it: '*Shaun.*'

Wicklowboy22

The trees, which had seemed sparse from the motel, were thicker than they looked and provided a fair amount of cover from the wind. It was snowing again, and the sound of traffic from the I-35 faded away. Shaun paused to light a Vogue from the stub of the last. After this, he'd be out. He could quit now or run the gauntlet of disapproval and convince Ellie to ferry him to a shop to buy more. It'd probably be easier to quit.

'Hey! You got a light?'

Jolted out of his reverie, Shaun turned to see a man standing in the trees behind him, and he took an involuntary step back. He hadn't gone far – he was only midway between the hulk of the motel and the grey sliver of the water – but there was still a sense of isolation here. The atmosphere reminded him of the underpass near to the estuary, an odd pocket of peace in the centre of hustle and bustle.

The man stayed where he was and held up his hands. 'Sorry to bother you. Saw you were smoking, and my Zippo's given up the ghost.'

After a hesitation, Shaun approached. He handed over the lighter.

'Appreciate it.' The man slid a Marlboro into his mouth and cupped his hand around to light it. It took several tries before it fired up. 'Thanks. You staying in the motel there?'

'Yeah.'

'I tell ya,' the man said, inspecting the end of his cigarette, 'these things are going to kill me.' He stamped his feet. 'Cold out here.'

Shaun wasn't in the mood for chit-chat with strangers – well, when was he ever? Shaun took a deep drag, aping Johnny's smoking style. 'It is.'

'You got an accent. Irish?'

'Yes.'

'On vacation?'

'Sort of.'

The man didn't smoke like a smoker – he wasn't inhaling. Shaun's radar twitched, echoing the gut response he'd had when he first encountered Johnny. Only he'd been wrong about Johnny, hadn't he? Otherwise there was nothing overtly off about the fellow, nothing Shaun could put his finger on. He was blandly good-looking in the style of Brendan – stocky, conventional haircut, not someone you'd pick out in a crowd. His clothes were similarly nondescript: a grey hooded puffer, jeans and the type of clumpy boots Noah favoured. Greyish stubble, dark, small eyes.

'I knew an Irish guy once. Maybe you know him?' The guy chuckled. Another false note. 'Sorry, sorry. That sounds patronising, like I expect you to know everyone in Ireland. Hey . . . didn't I see you in the diner with your buddies?'

'Maybe.' Shaun hadn't noticed him. He hadn't noticed much of anything. He was still digesting the meeting with Mrs Kastriber. Was the guy coming onto him? There was a nervousness to him now. Shaun doused the Vogue in the snow and pocketed the butt. 'I'd better get back.'

'Yeah.' The twitchiness vanished. A stillness came over the stranger. He threw his own butt into the snow, slid a hand into his pocket. Then, softly: 'You're nothing like him, you know that?'

Rainbowbrite

Not Shaun. Not Shaun. She didn't pause to put on her snow boots, didn't stop to think. Hurtled outside, scouring for the slash of his orange coat against the snow, panic blurring her vision, vantage point blocked as a truck pulled in front of her.

The window hummed down, a slo-mo crawl of empty time as the driver's eyes locked with hers. Then the man – *Bobbiecowell, it's Bobbiecowell* – mouthed 'OMG', and gunned the engine.

Bobbiecowell

He'd ditched the Dodge outside a mall in Rapid City, amazed to have made it that far without the licence plate pinging, and using cash, bought four Greyhound tickets to different destinations and a couple of Amtrak tickets for good measure. It had taken him three days to get here via bus – he wasn't dumb enough to take a direct route – and he could still taste the acrid burn of three a.m. dispenser coffee at the back of his throat. He stank of adrenaline sweat, the kind you couldn't get out of your clothes however many times you washed them, and couldn't recall if he'd slept or not. He should really have dumped his ol' faithful phone in the trash and used a burner for the next stage, but they'd been through too much together and he didn't have the heart to do it. Instead, he'd taken the chance that dismantling it would be enough to stop them tracing him. He re-inserted the phone's battery and sim, made the call, and got to work on the final play, fingers clumsy from sleep deprivation.

You're nothing like him.

Nor was Pete. He was nothing like Teddy, nothing like Jennifer, never would be, and really, who gave a rat's ass? No one. No one except Past Pete, and look where that got him.

Business concluded, he sat on the bed, Margie's Glock warm in his hand, and waited for the knock on the door.

She was right on time, like before.

Missing-Linc.com

Matching Unidentified Bodies (UIDs)
With Missing People

How to join | FAQs | Current UIDs | Success stories | Rules

Thread dated: December 17/2017

Bobbiecowell: My name is Peter Raymond Kazinski and this is my confession. I killed Jennifer Kastriber in 1994 by stunning her with a blow from a tire iron and smothering her with the cushion my mother used on the front seat when she drove. She died easy (a covert killing they call that, don't they?). I killed Teddy Ryan by hitting him once with a bottle of alcohol and then with an 18inch wrench. I left Jennifer's remains 500 yards due north of where I dumped Teddy in North Park. Used to go there when I was a kid, so I guess that's score one for the profilers and their 'emotional resonance' dumpsite shit. Don't know the co-ords. There will be DNA in the basement of 14 Kendall Rise, where Teddy Ryan lost his life. He bled a LOT.

So far I have only killed two people.

So far.

What you all want to know is why I did it. What's my motivation? Where's my manifesto? Why didn't I kill Shaun Ryan and the team when I had the chance? You figure it out. You're the fucking websleuths.

Wicklowboy22

He'd be home tomorrow. *Home.* Wicklow Boy would be back in Wicklow Town, back with Daphne, back at the shop. Brendan had been bombarding him with messages, desperate for the details; Carmel had written asking how he was coping and he'd even received a clumsy email from Janice. He wasn't sure what to tell them. He kept waiting for the trauma to hit, but despite an hour of constant yawning directly after Peter Kazinski walked away, which Google said was a sign of the brain attempting to cool itself down, he was remarkably unaffected. If anything, he'd been more shaken after witnessing Johnny's attack on Pat.

He lit another cigarette from the stub of the last, unsure if he was huffing out smoke or if his breath was clouding in the freezing air. So much for quitting. Without being asked, yesterday Noah had bought him a carton, refusing to allow Shaun to pay him back. *The kindness of strangers.* Only, they were no longer strangers. From his vantage point in the front yard, he had a perfect view of the silent pantomime playing out in the kitchen. The kids darting in and out, Chris on Ellie's laptop, hammering at the keys, Scott and Noah leaning against the counter, talking, and Ellie fussing around, still mortified by Bobbiecowell's betrayal. Would he miss them? *Yes.* There was a hollow ache at the thought of no longer being part of this. For the last three days they'd been crammed into Ellie's house like a dysfunctional family – Chris and Scott had rescheduled their flights, and Ellie refused to allow them to book into a motel – the dynamics changing daily as they all adjusted and readjusted, the furniture moved aside to make it easier for Chris to get around. The tide of police and agents, including Commander Stillson, a motherly woman who could have been Ellie's sister, had slowed to a trickle. They'd all asked the same question – 'What was his intent?' – but Shaun couldn't answer that. He'd come face to face with Teddy's killer, looked into his eyes, and instead of the soulless holes of his imagination, saw doubt and false bravado, and an internal struggle Shaun recognised.

You're nothing like him. There had been an undercurrent of something in the man's voice: disappointment? Relief?

The man had made his radar jangle, but not enough to spook him. Shaun hadn't felt like he was staring death in the face. *Bobbiecowell.* The killer's alter ego had helped keep him going after he'd found out about the abuse accusation. Despite everything, and painfully aware of the deep, twisted irony of this, he was still grateful to Bobbie for this. If it weren't for him, he might never have gone to see Dylan, found out the truth. But he couldn't forget that the GoFundMe had been Bobbie's idea. If he'd been planning to target Shaun the whole time, why hadn't he done so? Why had he murdered Teddy and not Shaun?

You're nothing like him.

But he already knew *that.*

He mashed the black of the ash into the snow with his boot.

Ellie looked through the window. Like Brendan, she was an open book, and he could see on her face that it was over. Noah hustled the kids out of the room, Chris barked something at Scott, and Scott moved to the back door. Shaun knew what he was going to say before he opened his mouth:

'They got him.'

Rainbowbrite

'. . . it's alleged that Peter Kazinski, who sources say could be responsible for at least two murders, attacked the sex worker at around eight p.m. last night. Known as 'Komi', she shot the assailant twice in an alleged act of self-defence . . .'

Ellie had been watching the clips on a loop since she dropped Shaun and the others at the airport. Breathless reporters stood in front of the seedy motel, white-suited forensic technicians weaving in and out behind them. The networks and news sites were warring with each other to put the most salacious spin on the story, most running with the 'suicide by sex worker' angle, a couple treading into non-PC waters by pushing the irony of the killer of the Boy in the Dress being killed by an alleged 'boy in a dress'.

Over on Fox, there was new, aerial footage of Bobbiecowell's residence, a split-level Tacoma mansion on the edge of the Sound. Hesitantly, not sure she was doing the right thing, she sent Tasha a message: **<You okay honey?>**

Tasha and her mother wouldn't be okay. How could they be okay? If *she* was fractured by this, then they must be destroyed.

Five minutes later, came: **<can I keep talking to you rainbowbrite?>**

<Of course honey. Long as it's okay with your mom. Here anytime>

<Thanx>

<How's your mom?>

<She says she's okay but I know she's not>

<You let me know if there's anything I can do>

<thanx. Anyway he's not a real serial killer because he only killed 2 people is he?>

She was still trying to figure out how to respond to that when Noah poked his head around the den's door. 'You still watching that stuff?'

'Yeah.'

'You have to let it go.'

'I have. I'm done, Noah. Done with all of it.'

'No you're not.'

'I am.'

Noah sighed. 'Okay.'

The spectre of a fight; the darkening of the edges. She couldn't let that happen. Not now. 'Call the boys.'

'Why?'

'We're going out.'

'Where to?'

'It's coming up to Christmas. Let's go check out the lights.'

Ratking 1

Scott slept like the dead, one arm crooked behind his head, barely breathing. Chris watched him for a while, then went through to the office. Three a.m. She knew she wouldn't sleep; didn't bother trying.

The inbox and social media feeds were a seething mass of pending memberships, abuse, and interview requests from podcasters and docudrama producers. The story wasn't dying. The last time she'd looked elsewhere online, there were countless threads dedicated to discussions about Peter Kazinski's psychopathy, most along the lines of: **<he was FED by the internet. He got off on all the attention. That's what sparked him off again>** Obvious crap. Links to his confession had been embedded into articles and diatribes everywhere from 4chan to the *Washington Post*, and the site's traffic was off the scale. It was the gift that kept on giving. The manipulative asshole would've known that when he posted his final comment, and she'd been back and forth on whether or not to delete him and it from the site. Much as she hated the thought that Missing-Linc was benefiting from this, she wasn't an idiot. It could've been Kazinski sending her those messages about her mom; could've been him who'd fanned the flames about JT. Time would tell; the cops' tech people were no doubt still wading through his history. She'd also considered removing her mother's page from the site. Knew she wouldn't. She'd keep looking. *Lonely*.

'Coffee?'

Scott's shadowy shape loomed over her. She hadn't heard him rising. 'Yeah. Thanks.'

'You got it.'

It might work out with him; it might not. But for now, she'd take what she could get.

Wicklowboy22

'It's a miracle.'

'You believe in miracles?'

Johnny shrugged. 'Why not? Didn't think Mammy would talk again, but here she is, chattering away all hours of the day. Aren't you, Mammy?'

Bridie nodded. '. . . ar.'

Shaun wasn't convinced Bridie had improved at all, but he wasn't about to point that out. He was more concerned about the dog. Daphne had flown at him when he'd arrived, whining with joy, but she was now back on Bridie's lap, nudging her hand for a stroke. Shaun might as well not exist.

Johnny waved him into the armchair. 'Get you a drink?'

'No, you're alright, thanks.'

Shaun had given Johnny the potted version of his encounter with Teddy's killer outside so as not to alarm Bridie, and there would be time in the coming days to go over it in detail in the gulag – if Johnny wanted to. Shaun had half-expected him to rage at him for not attacking Teddy's murderer when he was in striking distance of him, but Johnny merely mumbled something about 'the bastard getting what was coming to him,' and a tepid, 'glad you're safe, son.' They both knew that while Shaun may have toughened the fuck up, he was never going to possess Johnny's hard edge or Teddy's street smarts – not that those attributes did either of them any good. In any case, now they were saying that Peter Kazinski *wanted* to die. The gun he'd used to threaten the sex worker was empty of bullets. Shaun was no longer able to bring up an image of the man's face in any detail.

'I'd better get home.' The pattern in the carpet was smudging out of focus, the first sign of the jetlag to follow, and his clothes reeked of stale plane air. He hadn't yet been back to his room: Donny and Janice had insisted on collecting him from the airport and dropped him off here. He'd much rather have taken the bus – you couldn't erase years of awkwardness and lies with an hour-long car ride – and they'd spent the majority of the journey sniping at each other.

'I'll get the dog's things,' Johnny said.

'You can keep her if you want.'

Johnny started. Bridie gave him one of her bright grins and nodded and nodded.

'You're leaving her here?'

'If you want her.'

'She's doing Mam the world of good. Are you sure?'

'I'm sure.' He wasn't. But it was the right thing to do. Seeing her snuggled up like that, mirroring the way she used to glue herself to his mother, he didn't have the heart to take her away. 'Stay, Daphne.' For once the dog obeyed as Johnny saw him to the door.

'I don't know what to say, son.'

'That's not like you.'

Johnny's jowls trembled. He looked away, clapped Shaun on the shoulder, said, 'Fuck it,' and pulled him into a hug. Johnny smelled of smoke, soap and booze. After three excruciating seconds, Shaun extricated himself.

Johnny sniffed. 'Don't take that the wrong way now.'

'As if.'

'Drink tomorrow? Molly will want to see you.'

'It'll have to be after work.'

'Suits me. Will you not be taking a few days off?'

'Why would I?'

It was the countdown to the Christmas rush – the shop's busiest time of the year. Part of him was looking forward to it. And Máirín would be back the following week and couldn't wait to hear the whole tale. Part of him was looking forward to that, too.

His wheelie bag hissing in his wake, he took his time walking home from Rathnew, pausing outside the cemetery gates. He hadn't intended on going in, but he'd run the gamut of everyone else and it seemed unfair not to drop in on Eileen. For now, Teddy would be fine where he was. Ellie promised to visit him, and once everything was made official the family could always choose to have him exhumed and brought over. He lit a Vogue for Eileen, automatically looking over at his grandparents' plot for the dog. He shook off the stab of loss. He'd have to get used to that.

Snug in his Minnesota coat, he picked up the pace. Compared to the snowy expanse and spacious architecture of the last two weeks, Wicklow resembled an old-fashioned toy town, all worn brown stone and soot-stained brick. He felt like a time traveller who'd been away for a hundred years. A bus slipped past, hissing through puddles, the dampness soothing in its softness after the icy slice of the Minnesotan air. On through the town, deserted but for a gaggle of kids messing about in the fish and chip shop's door, and in came the scent of his childhood – greasy food mingled with diesel fumes and salt from the estuary. There was a new 'Missing' poster tacked up above a bin outside Toolan's, Keith O'Neill's blurry photograph grinning into the drizzle. There was more information on this one: 'Last seen in the Arklow area on 3/3/16'. Shaun hesitated, then took out his phone and snapped a pic. He'd forgotten to turn it on after he landed, and a flurry of texts shuddered in. He flipped through them as he walked. Two from Ellie, asking if he'd landed safely, three from Brendan: **<call me when u get back>; <don't care how late it is>; <u should know I told her. Hope you're okay x>**

Deciding what to do about Brendan would have to be tomorrow's problem.

He let himself in through the shop's entrance, and breathed in the scent of wood and paper. Up the familiar stairs with their individual creaks and cracks, and into the room. It wasn't as musty as he feared, but he opened the window anyway, trying not to look at where Daphne's basket used to sit. He should get over himself. It wasn't as if she were dead, he could visit her whenever he wanted to, and without her needs punctuating his day, he could go anywhere. His ties were cut. Unfinished business sorted out. He had the cash, too. Donny had refused to take back the remainder of the money, and he had enough to leave if he wanted to. Enough for a ticket to London; enough for another adventure if he wanted one. *If* he wanted one.

He unpacked, kicked off his boots, hung up his new coat and lay on the bed. He closed his eyes, but he'd slid past exhaustion and come out the other side. Back to the phone. He clicked on Missing-Linc's 'How to join' button and signed up to the site. The 'verification pending' email was trailed by an immediate 'FINALLY' from Chris.

He thought for a minute, then forwarded the picture of Keith O'Neill's poster. **<Can we put this up on the site?>**

<You got it. The family local to you?>

<Yes>

<Can you get in contact with them? Get more info?>

Could he? Did he want to? **<Yes>**

<Do it>

He made a mug of black tea with extra sugar, then got to work.

'Day Four is smart, incisive and raises real questions about the world in which we live.... But the real praise is that I had to leave the light on in the bedroom after finishing it'
Scotland on Sunday

Day Four

By
Sarah Lotz

Three days in heaven. The fourth is going to be hell . . .

Four days into a five day singles cruise on the Gulf of Mexico, the ageing ship Beautiful Dreamer stops dead in the water. With no electricity and no cellular signals, the passengers and crew have no way to call for help. But everyone is certain that rescue teams will come looking for them soon. All they have to do is wait.

That is, until the toilets stop working and the food begins to run out. When the body of a woman is discovered in her cabin the passengers start to panic. There's a murderer on board the Beautiful Dreamer . . . and maybe something worse.

Available now in paperback and ebook.